# The Refuge

## HEIDI MARTIN

*The Refuge,* Published July, 2016

Interior Layout and Cover Design: Howard Johnson, Howard Communigrafix, Inc.
Editorial and Proofreading: Kellyann Zuzulo, Shannon Miller, Karen Grennan
Photo Credits: Front cover image: Sally McCarthy, Mosaic Studios.
Song Lyrics: Lyrics to the song "Love, Serve and Remember" by permission from
the author/composer, John Astin (www.johnastin.com)

 **SDP Publishing**

Published by SDP Publishing, an imprint of SDP Publishing Solutions, LLC.

SDP Publishing
Permissions Department
PO Box 26, East Bridgewater, MA 02333
or email your request to info@SDPPublishing.com.

ISBN-13 (print): 978-0-9972853-6-9
ISBN-13 (ebook): 978-0-9972853-7-6

Library of Congress Control Number: 2016943981

Printed in the United States of America

To Matthew, my rock.
Your unwavering support
made this dream possible.

# Acknowledgments

I have to start by thanking my wonderful husband, Matthew. Your love and support during the writing of this book has meant so much. You always encouraged me to keep believing in my dream no matter what. Thanks for all the sacrifices you made along the way. You're an amazing man, and I thank you from the bottom of my heart. It has been a wild ride these past twenty years and, the truth is, I wouldn't change any of it!

My children, Adeline and Malachi. You bring such joy to me every day. I love your boundless energy and love of life. And yes, the book is finally finished. ☺

Aunt Sue, you were there when this journey began. We have seen many things together, including the beautiful city of Charleston. Without your constant support and encouragement, this book may never have happened. Thank you!

Laura J. Swan, for introducing me to circling. My early experiences with you helped me reconnect with myself in entirely new ways. Thank you for allowing me to use the passages you wrote that call together "the four corners of the earth and all the elements of nature" in this book. Chapter 20 was inspired by one of your circles as it truly helped me discover my own passion for writing. These very circles continue to help and empower so many women around the world. Thank you for your kindness and for your unconditional love.

Shannon Miller and Kellyann Zuzulo, my editors at SDP Publishing Solutions. Your detailed edits and dedication truly helped this book be the best that it could be. You are brilliant editors, and I thank you for your patience and encouragement along this amazing journey.

Lisa Akoury-Ross, for your guidance and support during this entire process. You were always there to offer a helping hand if I needed anything. I'm so pleased that I have had the privilege of working with you! Sally McCarthy of Mosaic Studios, for the beautiful artwork you created. I love the cover! Howard Johnson, for your incredible book design talent. Your hard work and dedication helped pull all the pieces into a beautiful whole! And last, but certainly not least, Karen Grennan, for your keen proofreading skills catching those little things that can escape us during the production process. I thank you all for helping to bring my manuscript to life!

# 1

The crowded streets near Boston's Faneuil Hall smelled of fresh bagels and buttered lobster as Anna rushed down the cobblestone sidewalk. She stumbled slightly in her heels, reading her latest e-mail message. A light drizzle had begun to fall, its mist creating a haze across the harbor that disguised the steel structures dominating the landscape. Anna sighed, relieved that the meeting with her clients that morning had gone so well. She knew it was only a matter of time before the acquisition was complete.

Rounding the corner, she bumped into a street vendor, nearly knocking the phone out of her hands. "Sorry, sorry," she muttered, shoving it back into her purse.

The man's dark brown eyes flashed with amusement. She had the strange sense that he pitied her. She pulled her spine straighter, feeling slightly offended. And when she looked ahead, she froze. There stood the quaint little boutique she had found herself in eight months earlier. It looked exactly as she remembered it: pretty pastel outfits and velvety baby blankets elegantly displayed in the front window. A fuzzy brown teddy bear still sat in the antique rocking chair next to an oversized pillow. Resting on the top of a wooden table was the collection of children's jewelry.

As Anna scanned the assortment of trinkets, she gasped. A silver charm bracelet, exactly like the one she had bought for Claire, glinted in the light. When she purchased it, she had hoped to collect charms that would help preserve her daughter's memories, just as her mother had done for her. She planned to give the bracelet to Claire as a gift when she was older. But that was not to be. Instinctively, Anna reached toward it. Even as her fingers touched the cold glass of the window, she took a step back, her stomach churning. A tear streamed down her cheek. She turned abruptly and darted across the street. As car horns honked, a taxi slammed on its brakes.

"Hey, lady! Watch where you're going!" the cabbie shouted.

Anna quickly stepped onto the sidewalk, head down. The bracelet didn't mean anything anymore, and Frederick was wrong to always want to discuss it. Claire never seemed to be far from his mind. In fact, he had brought her up at breakfast that very morning.

Anna was leaving for work when she had glanced into the dining room and saw Frederick sitting at the large mahogany table poring over the market pages, as he often did. His bowl of fresh fruit and cup of coffee sat untouched.

"I'm going to be working late again tonight," she said.

"I figured as much," he said, without looking up. "There hasn't been a night in the last few months when you haven't worked well past dinnertime."

Anna crossed her arms. "Achieving partner three years ago wasn't easy for me, especially since I'm only thirty-five *and* a woman. They're counting on me. I can't disappoint them."

"No, I don't suppose you can," he said, folding up the paper neatly and setting it beside his bowl.

"You don't need to make me feel guilty about it. I don't complain when you work late."

"I don't think you really notice," he muttered.

"Let's not do this today, okay?"

Frederick straightened his tie and glanced up at her, his normally piercing blue eyes looking pained. "Okay, but you can't keep using work as an excuse. We need to go through all those gifts that are still sitting in Claire's closet. We can't just leave them there. I know it won't be easy, but we have to face reality. I was just hoping we could face it together."

"I can't," Anna said, her heart accelerating in dread. "Not tonight. I promised Tom I would finish up something."

Frederick slowly stood and walked toward her, reaching for her hand. "We have to do this at some point. We have to talk about what happened to Claire."

"I told you," Anna insisted. "Not tonight." She straightened her suit jacket and pulled away from his touch. "It'll have to wait."

"It always does," he said, turning his back to her.

Anna paused, wondering if she should reach out to him, but she held back. She wasn't ready to face the pain that she felt. Not yet. If she talked to Frederick, it would only make her fall apart. That was something she could never let happen. People perceived her as a resilient person, and she wouldn't let them down. She had to be strong. She had to fight her feelings because if she let herself fall apart, she might never be able to pull herself back together again.

❦

A car horn honked as Anna strode along the sidewalk outside Amalia's, the Italian restaurant she and her sister had agreed upon. Dabbing her eyes with a tissue, she took a deep breath. This was no time to be emotional. She needed to focus. Julia clearly had something on her mind when she had texted her that morning. Her sister never did anything on short notice, unless it was important.

Anna checked in with the maître d', relieved to be in the air conditioning. He directed her to a cozy round table in the back corner of the room where Julia was already seated. Stunning pictures of the canals of Venice lined the walls and reminded Anna of the majestic gondola ride she had taken ten years ago with Frederick, when he proposed. Italy had mesmerized them both. Now, as the fresh smell of basil and garlic permeated the air, she remembered those simpler times.

They both had been in their mid-twenties and filled with hope for the future. Frederick had surprised Anna with a trip to Italy as a law school graduation gift. They spent several days in Venice and, on that particularly warm afternoon, they had wandered through the square near Saint Mark's Basilica and sipped tea on the terrace of a nearby café. Afterwards, they walked along the narrow streets hand in hand, and Frederick led her to a canal where a gondola was waiting for them.

Wrapped in each other's arms, they glided past the beautiful baroque and Renaissance architecture that gave the city much of its romantic atmosphere. Frederick had pulled a bottle of Chianti from his bag and poured them each a glass. Anna joked at his ingenuity to bring wine along for the ride. As their laughter filled the air, Frederick's smile captivated her. He kissed her then beneath a brilliant sunset. She was shocked when Frederick pulled away to maneuver onto one knee in the rocking boat. He slipped a diamond ring on her finger and asked if she would make him the happiest man in the world by becoming his wife.

Approaching the table where Julia waited, Anna

sighed. She had believed that their love would always endure. "Sorry I'm late," she said. "The walk over here took longer than I thought it would."

"I've only been here a few minutes," Julia said. Her blond curls were pulled back in a ponytail and she wore no makeup, other than a light shade of lip gloss. Her tanned skin had a radiant glow from the endless hours she spent outdoors landscaping. Unlike Anna, Julia didn't worry about appearances. She was naturally beautiful and her warm smile had a way of drawing people in. Julia's husband, Ben, often said that was something he loved about her. However, if there was one thing that irritated Julia, it was tardiness. Her rigid posture and cool tone clearly indicated her annoyance with Anna's lack of punctuality.

"How's Sasha?" Anna asked, sliding into her chair. She wanted to keep things light, and talking about her five-year-old niece was an easy ice breaker.

"Good. But since she started gymnastics, I can't get her to stop somersaulting."

Anna smiled. "I remember when we used to do that. It drove Mom crazy!"

"It sure did," Julia mused, a slight smile lifting one corner of her mouth.

As the waitress wrote down Anna's order, Julia took a drink of water from her goblet. Once they were alone again, she asked in a serious tone, "How come you didn't make it to my birthday party last night? Mom was really disappointed."

"I know. I'm sorry." Anna nervously twisted a skein of her long, auburn hair around one finger. "I had a dinner meeting with the partners to celebrate my tenth anniversary. I told you I might be late."

"You weren't late. You were a no-show and you never even called," Julia snapped.

"I forgot and, besides, the meeting didn't end 'til eleven." She paused. "Why? Did I miss something?"

Julia ran her hand across her forehead as though trying to calm her nerves. "You're never around for anything. Mom wanted to tell you something important last night. But do you even care?"

"Of course, I care. I don't need one of your guilt trips, Julia. How was I supposed to know that Mom was saving *your* birthday for something important to say?" Anna clenched her napkin in her fist. She was tired of everyone trying to make her feel guilty for working hard. Since when was that such a bad thing? "Why don't you just tell me what you came here to say?"

Julia sighed. "Mom fainted at the party last night. She was out for only a few minutes, and I called her doctor right away. He wanted her to take it easy and go in today for some tests."

A lump burned in Anna's throat. Her mother had passed out, and no one had bothered to tell her. Now who was being irresponsible?

"I took her to the doctor this morning," Julia went on. "We should have the results by next week."

"That's it? That's all you have to say?" Anna searched Julia's eyes for an answer. There had to be more to the story than that.

Drumming her fingers on the table, Julia glanced across the restaurant before meeting Anna's gaze. "What happened last night with Mom has happened before. She was diagnosed with high blood pressure a couple of months ago and has been taking medicine to keep it under control." Julia exhaled loudly. "I didn't mean to keep it from you, but Mom insisted. She knew you'd been traveling a lot for work and didn't want you worrying about her while you were away."

"Isn't high blood pressure something we have to

worry about?" Anna didn't like being kept in the dark about something this important. "Why wouldn't you tell me?"

Julia studied Anna for a long time. "I wanted to, but Mom was afraid she'd be a burden. The doctor said that if she took her medicine and remained healthy, things would improve. And they did, for a while." Julia fiddled with a button on her blouse. "But last week, the fainting episodes returned, so the doctor adjusted her medication. Mom and I were planning to tell you after my party. However, when you didn't come and Mom passed out again, I knew you needed to hear the truth."

Anna fell silent, letting the news sink in. The pit in her stomach grew as she imagined her mother being ill. She had always been so strong. She took care of herself and was fiercely independent.

"I'm sorry," Julia uttered. "It wasn't right that we kept the truth from you for so long. I guess I tried to tell myself it didn't matter because you were too busy anyway."

"It *was* wrong. But I'm sorry too," Anna said, her voice softening. "Work has certainly taken a lot of my time these days. It's a place where I can get away from everything and don't have to think about my life." She paused. "I need that right now."

Despite her indignation at being left out, Anna felt the familiar twinges of guilt. Last April, she had missed her mother's 60th birthday party because she was working in Madrid. Although she had sent a beautiful bouquet of irises—her mother's favorite flower—to the house, her presence was markedly absent from all of the family photographs taken that day. For Anna, burying herself in work was the only way she could survive. It helped dull the pain that never seemed to diminish. Even though Claire had died seven months earlier, it still felt like yesterday.

"I think that's the first time I've ever heard you admit that you work too hard," Julia said. "When Dad died, I wanted you to know that you could come to me with anything. I tried to be available and give you the chance to open up. Yet, somehow I pushed you away. Twenty years later, and you still won't share what you're feeling."

"Opening up is not one of my strengths, Julia. You know that. But I promise to try to focus a little less on work and help out with Mom some more. What does the doctor say?"

Julia took a sip of water. "The doctor switched Mom's medication and ran some more tests. He thinks we should know something by early next week."

"Why didn't Mom come with you today?" Anna tried to keep her voice steady. "Why wasn't she here to tell me this herself?"

"She was tired from all the chaos last night and having to go to the hospital this morning. She just wasn't up for it." Julia reached across the table and took Anna's hand in hers. "Mom loves you a lot," Julia said, emphasizing her words with a tilt of her head.

"I know she wishes I came around more. Work is just really busy."

"She understands." Julia's voice was kind. "It's been a hard year for you."

The waitress placed their food on the table. As Anna stared down at her favorite strawberry salad, she was no longer hungry. She pushed the spinach around on her plate. "I hope it's good news ... what you hear from the doctor."

"Me, too. She's in good hands. The doctors are some of the best in the country."

"I just sometimes wish Dad were still here."

"To take care of Mom?" Julia asked.

"To be with all of us. He always had a way of making

sense of things. He was a man of few words, but I always felt as though he understood things better than anyone else."

CZ

As Anna walked back toward the office that afternoon, the humidity was stifling. She had never liked the July heat. It made her feel as though she was suffocating from everyone's expectations. Claire was dead, but she wasn't ready to talk about it. Couldn't Frederick understand that? Now, her mother was sick. Why hadn't anyone told her? Why hadn't she made more time for her mom? That's what she should have done. That's what Julia always did. But for some reason, Anna ran the other way. She never seemed to do the right thing.

Hurrying along the sidewalk, she slowed when the children's boutique came into view. A man held open the door for his wife as she carefully maneuvered a stroller through it. He put his hand tenderly upon her back and followed her inside. Anna drew closer.

A tall, elegant woman peered at the jewelry in the window, her belly as round as a basketball. A wide smile crept across the expectant mother's lips as she caressed her stomach. When she entered the shop, Anna tracked her through the window. The woman selected a shiny trinket from a shelf. Slowly, Anna placed her hand on her own empty stomach. Regret and loss roiled her insides and she wondered what it would have been like to be a mother. Eight months ago, she felt such joy and expectancy, but now only sadness and loss remained. She dropped her hand to her side. Without a backward glance, she trudged up the street.

The first rays of sunlight streamed through her bedroom window when Anna awoke for her morning jog. She hadn't slept well. She had tossed and turned for hours. Exhausted, she pushed back the covers and forced herself to sit up. Glancing beside her, she noticed that Frederick was still asleep. His dark hair was disheveled, but he looked so peaceful.

Watching him, she thought about the fight they had the night before. He had criticized her for stopping at the gym after work and getting home well after ten o'clock. She explained that it was not only a busy time of year at work, but that the marathon she was training for took up all of her extra time. What she didn't say was that running gave her the chance to get away from everything. When she ran, she didn't have to describe her feelings or justify her actions. She could just be. Frederick focused so much on Claire and their marriage these days. But she couldn't revisit the past. It hurt too much. Instead, she focused on the race and her work. She missed Frederick. But this was the way it had to be. For now. She hoped he understood.

After dressing in a sleek tank and black nylon shorts, she tiptoed past the bed and hurried down the wooden steps that led to the beach. A fiery sun emerged fully from the horizon as Anna fell into a comfortable pace. Aquamarine waves careened toward the shore, cresting with white foam and crawling ever closer to the coastline until gravity drew them back to the churning sea. The sound of the ocean rumbling against the shore sparked a distant melody that reminded Anna of a lullaby she used to sing to Claire. Shaking her head, she quickened her pace and focused on her breath, determined to push that memory from her mind.

Anna ran along the water's edge for several miles, watching the sand slither like a snake as the warm breeze blew loose granules across the beach. The landscape was ever changing, and Anna still found it fascinating how the continual tides could dictate the topography of an entire coast, leaving various treasures for all who ventured upon its shores. The mystery and sheer beauty of the ocean calmed her like nothing else.

ଔ

That evening, Anna stood in the dining room among the sparkling crystal and fine china she had meticulously set on the mahogany table for their upcoming dinner party. Straightening the silverware, she looked up to watch the sun's myriad colors dance across the rolling sea. The long, narrow isle of Duxbury Beach reached into the bay. The lights of Plymouth could be seen on the distant shoreline.

"Wow, you've outdone yourself again," Frederick said, walking into the dining room. "Everything looks perfect as usual."

"Thanks," Anna said, turning away from the window and placing the last water goblet in place. "Entertaining is fun, especially here. Everyone loves this house."

"That's because of what you've done with it."

"No, what Martha Stewart has done," she corrected him, smiling. "She's where I get all my ideas."

"I'm glad our families are coming over to celebrate your mom's good news from the doctor. It'll be nice to have them all together again. It's been a long time."

Anna nodded. Carefully, she folded a cloth napkin into the shape of a bird of paradise. After examining her work, she placed it on top of the plate.

Frederick stepped toward her and gently touched her back.

Anna turned to face him. His dark hair was combed neatly back and his face curved into his usual half-smile. He watched her with kind blue eyes. She knew what he wanted but was unsure if she could give it to him. The closeness they had once shared seemed so far away now. She had to keep up her wall. If one emotion came out, they all might.

"We'll have to watch Julia tonight so she doesn't raise your mom's blood pressure," Frederick said, brushing Anna's hair out of her face. "I don't want anything to spoil that raspberry cheesecake you made."

"You always were one to eat your dessert first," she said with a laugh.

He smiled and leaned toward her. At the last moment, she turned her head so his soft lips fell upon her cheek.

Rigidly, Frederick straightened. "Is there a reason you don't like to kiss me anymore?"

"What do you mean? I kiss you." She strode over to the hutch and bent to grab the breadbasket from the bottom shelf. Guilt bloomed in her. She wanted to be close to Frederick, but it felt so foreign to her. She couldn't explain it. Not even to herself. But just because she didn't melt into his arms every time he came near her didn't mean something was wrong. She still loved him. Marriages change and theirs was no exception.

"You act like you don't even care if I'm here," Frederick asserted. "But if other people are around, then our marriage is another show for you, like entertaining. As long as things look fine, then they are."

"That's not true." She sighed as she approached him and placed her hand on his arm. "Our families are going to be here in a few minutes. This isn't exactly the time to talk about this. Why don't you go get a couple bottles of wine from the cellar while I finish folding these napkins? I want everything to be perfect when they get here."

Cଞ

Pillar candles flickered on the sideboard, dancing in the cool breeze through the open windows. A scent of baking brie infused the house with contentment. As guests filled the kitchen, Anna poured the wine and passed around the glasses. Gripping a tumbler of iced tea for her mother, Anna led the way to the porch and the twilight. With her guests settled in the fresh evening air, she returned to the kitchen for more guacamole.

Hushed whispers drew her to the doorway. She froze. The urgency in the voices evoked secrets and conspiracies. Anna hugged the wall, listening. Her mother-in-law, Louisa, spoke in a low voice.

"You can pretend all you want, Frederick, but I can see your marriage isn't working anymore. Anna has never gotten over Claire's death and I don't think she ever will. She runs away from everything, especially you. You deserve someone who will treat you better. Someone who can show you how to love again."

Anna tried to catch her breath. Louisa and she had their differences, but to tell Frederick that it was over … how dare she interfere like this? What right did she have?

"This isn't your concern, mother," Frederick retorted. "You need to back off and let me handle my own life. I don't need you butting into this."

"I only want what's best for you," Louisa went on. "You married Anna against my wishes and I've tried to be supportive, but to see her treat you with such indifference hurts me. No man deserves that from his own wife." She paused. "And don't even get me started on her sister. Julia dresses like a hippie and works as a landscaper. I mean, we use those people at our estate but to have one in the family ... it's just not right."

"She owns the company, Mom. She and Ben started it before he died. You know that."

"Well, she was never the quality we expect as the Sterling Family. We have certain standards to uphold."

"Hey, Anna, do you have some more Merlot?"

Anna whipped around, feeling as though she had been caught doing something illicit in her own home.

Julia was holding up her glass as she walked through the doorway.

Anna stood straighter and hastily smoothed her skirt, "Sure. Let me get it for you."

"Are you okay?" Julia asked. "You're as white as a sheet."

"I'm fine." But Anna's hands trembled as she tried to uncork the bottle.

Just then, Frederick walked in and, gently touching Anna's arm, took the corkscrew from her hand and opened the bottle. As Anna backed away, he poured Julia more wine.

Louisa entered the kitchen, looking predictably unruffled in her soft cashmere sweater and pressed pants. A grin was plastered across her made-up face. She touched the edge of her perfectly coiffed bob with her fingers. "Oh, Frederick, could you please get me a glass? I'm parched. This humidity just doesn't agree with me. Of course, I prefer the air conditioning to having the windows open, but to each his own."

She sighed and glanced pointedly in Anna's direction. "But if you ever do have a family, air conditioning will be the way to go. A baby just couldn't take this heat." She snatched up her glass from the counter and walked toward the porch. "I think it's time for me to visit with your mother, Anna. I'm glad she's doing so well."

As Louisa sauntered away, Anna clutched a towel in her hands before hurling it into the sink.

"Don't let her get to you," Frederick said, stepping toward her. "She doesn't mean to be so rude."

"Really? Is that why she just told you that I'm a lost cause? That you should get out of our marriage?"

"You heard that?" Frederick asked, tapping his fingers on the granite countertop.

"It's no secret she never thought I was good enough for you, but this is too much. And how dare she criticize my family."

"Anna, c'mon. Let's just get through dinner and then she'll leave. She's just overreacting as usual."

"Always defending her. Some things never change," Anna spat.

"This isn't the time for this conversation. We can talk about it later." He tilted his head toward Julia, who was still standing near the cucumber sandwiches, pretending not to be listening. "But we will talk about it," he insisted.

"Yeah, I'm sure we will."

Frederick looked at Anna one last time and then walked out the door.

"Don't say it," Anna said, glancing at her sister.

"I just think Louisa has a lot of nerve to speak to you and Frederick that way in your own home. I never liked her."

"I don't want to talk about it, okay?"

"It obviously bothered you. It would bother me," her

sister pressed. "Frederick will stand up to her though, just like he did when he married you."

But Anna knew what a bully Louisa could be. She had seen it far too many times before, and that woman never liked being wrong. Her plan was to wear Frederick down and the truth was, how long could he really resist?

"Frederick knows you just need more time," Julia said.

"I don't need you to tell me what I need," Anna said, her cheeks heating. "I just have to get through this dinner."

"It's okay to be mad at her, you know," Julia said, obviously trying to be supportive.

"Why do you have to comment on how I feel? Why can't you just stop talking about it? I need to get this salad on the table so we can eat." She gripped the cut crystal bowl so tightly that the etched edges of the glass bit into her fingers. "Please tell everyone to join me in the dining room. The meal is ready."

&#x2633;

After several hours, their last guests finally left. Anna took a deep breath and rolled back her shoulders, trying to loosen the stiffness. Despite the fact that she normally did enjoy entertaining—as Frederick had reminded her—she was relieved everyone had gone. She continued drying the last few dishes when he approached her.

"I'm sorry about what my mom said tonight."

"She's always unpredictable and she'll always hate me. Those two things will never change."

Frederick put his arm around her waist. "But it doesn't matter what she wants. Our marriage has nothing to do with her."

Anna shook her head. "She's right, you know. You're probably better off without me."

Frederick's arms tensed as he bristled at her words. "What exactly are you saying?"

"I don't know," she admitted. "Maybe you do deserve more. Maybe we both do. Perhaps this is one thing our marriage really can't survive."

Frederick turned her around to face him. He placed his hand tenderly under her chin. "It can survive. We just have to work through it *together.*" Caressing her cheek, he bent toward her. This time, as his soft lips met hers, she tried not to resist his touch.

But it was too much. She couldn't let him love her like that. She didn't deserve it. Her inability to deal with Claire's death had brought pain to them both. Pushing away from him, she accidentally knocked a crystal vase off the counter. It shattered on the wooden floor.

"I'm sorry," she whispered, tears forming in her eyes. "I have to get this." She crouched down and began to pick up the pieces of broken glass. Frederick watched her for a moment before bending to help. Collecting the shards of glass, Anna wondered how something so beautiful could now be damaged beyond repair.

&#x6161;

Anna was poring over her notes the next day and making last-minute preparations for her presentation when Frederick ambled into the living room.

"I found something I want to show you," he said quietly.

Looking up at him, Anna lowered the lid of her laptop. She arched an eyebrow and smiled. Regret over the way she had treated him the night before had consumed her all morning, and she wanted to fix it.

"Must be serious to bring you up from the depths of your photo lab," she teased.

Sitting down next to Anna, he held out a photograph.

"It's the last picture taken of us while you were pregnant with Claire. We were so excited."

Anna's stomach lurched. Resisting the urge to look away, she stared silently at the picture for a few minutes. With such a large belly, she looked like a totally different person, her eyes joyful and her smile wide. That seemed like such a long time ago ... part of her life she could never get back. Why did Frederick have to show that to her now?

"That was the day of our last dance lesson," Frederick recalled.

Anna nodded, inhaling deeply.

"Do you remember how you had the hardest time following me? You always wanted to lead."

"Tough to imagine," she said with a chuckle.

"Yeah," Frederick replied, smiling. "You never were one to do what you were told."

He stepped away for a minute. Soft jazz music filled the air and he reached for Anna's hand.

As they began to dance, Anna remembered the last time she had heard the song "Come Away with Me." It was nearly a year earlier. They had celebrated Frederick's birthday with a nice dinner out, but instead of lingering at the restaurant for coffee and dessert as they usually did, he had surprised her by suggesting they go home early. With the lights down low, they had danced in the living room, swaying to music for hours as though time stood still.

Moonlight cascaded through the windows, and it felt to Anna like the most romantic place on earth. As the sweet melody played, Frederick reached down and gently caressed her growing belly. He professed that the happiest day of his life had been in Italy when she had agreed to be his wife.

Now, as Anna stood in the same place where they had

danced all those months ago, she wondered if perhaps Frederick was right. Maybe it was time she focused more on her marriage.

Wrapping his arms around her slender waist, Frederick pulled her close. She leaned against his body, which was sculpted and hard beneath her touch. His tall frame always comforted her as though his powerful arms could protect her from harm. She wanted to connect with him again and feel the intimacy they once shared. He was thoughtful and sensitive. But above all, she knew he would support her through anything.

Frederick stroked her cheek, his breath warm on the nape of her neck. Tingles raced down her spine when he nuzzled her throat.

"I want you so much. Let's make love like we used to," he whispered.

Anna's body stiffened. She wanted him, but she couldn't let herself give in to her feelings. Closing her eyes, she backed away.

Frederick stared wide-eyed at her.

"I can't," she muttered. "I'm sorry, but dancing won't make things like they used to be. It just won't."

Frederick moved toward her with outstretched arms. "I know that. I just miss you."

Anna brushed away a tear.

"It's okay to cry," Frederick offered. "You don't have to fight how you feel." He was standing next to her now.

Anna wanted to reach out and embrace him, to tell him he was right. She shouldn't have to fight how she felt. But the truth was that she couldn't let herself feel anything. It would cause too much pain. She had to stay numb until she could finally face her grief. And as much as she wanted that to be right now, her walls were too high. Maybe she needed the counseling Frederick had talked about, but it would have to wait a few more weeks.

She couldn't take her attention off of work. She had to keep moving forward. She wrung her hands and leaned against the wall, choosing its support over his.

Avoiding his gaze, she said, "I have a lot of work to do. I leave for New York tomorrow and I need to stay focused."

Just as Frederick made a move toward her, her phone rang. Anna rushed toward it, needing space to breathe. "It's work. I gotta take this."

"Of course you do," he whispered. Wheeling around, he pounded his fist on the banister and headed back down to the basement.

# 3

With a spring in her step, Anna walked into her office, proud of her latest acquisition. After her trip to New York, she had spent over a week in Los Angeles and another week in London, but her hard work had paid off. Placing her briefcase on the polished oak desk and peering out at the Boston skyline, she smiled. It was good to be back.

"Good morning, Boss," Martha said. Anna's secretary stood in the doorway grinning. Her silver hair was pulled back and her red lipstick matched her polka-dot blouse perfectly. "How was your trip?"

"Long. But well worth it. The Bradford team is finally on board. This is a huge account for the firm."

"I'm glad it went so well." She pointed toward the desk. "Your messages are there next to the phone."

"Thanks."

Martha sighed. "You've been out of the office a lot lately. I hope they appreciate all the traveling you're doing. You didn't even get Labor Day weekend off."

"I usually don't," Anna admitted, turning on her computer. "Hey, would you mind getting me a cup of that delicious coffee of yours?"

"Flattery is almost as good as a bonus, but not quite." Martha teased. Smiling, she headed toward the break room.

As Anna pulled up the Bradford documents on the screen, she heard a knock on the door. Her co-worker, Sylvia Rogers, poked her head in the office. The bun in her dark hair had fallen sideways and was about to come undone, as if she'd been running there in a frenzy. "Is everything ready for tonight?"

"Yes."

"Good luck. I know it'll go well." Then she strode across the office and handed Anna a small stack of files. "Tom wanted me to give these to you. He knows you're busy, but he needs you to check on a couple of mergers that are happening this week."

Anna looked over at the growing stack of files on her library table and shuddered. The clutter was driving her crazy. "I'll get to them as soon as I can."

Sylvia nodded. "You should think about taking a break, you know. Your office light is on at all hours."

"Contracts have to be drawn up and mergers completed." Anna said. "You can't expect work to get done by having dinner at home."

Sylvia, twenty years older than Anna and very experienced in the field of law, opened her mouth as though to say something and then thought better of it. Looking at Anna kindly, she said, "I can't think of anyone who works harder than you do."

After Sylvia left, Anna sighed and leaned back in her chair. Maybe a break would do her some good. The Bradford deal was done. Perhaps she could afford to spend a little less time at the office. Glancing at the wall by her desk, she saw the yellow sticky note that was still on her bulletin board. It was the number for the counselor Frederick had told her about last spring. She didn't seem to be getting better on her own. Resting her chin in her hand, she thought of Frederick, imagining the patient look of his handsome face. She would do it for him.

Picking up the phone, she punched in the therapist's number.

Later that afternoon, Anna was still at her desk. She had made the appointment and couldn't stop thinking about Frederick. She hadn't been very good about keeping in touch with him during her time away. In fact, it was as if they were drifting even further apart. Tracing her finger across the photograph of them snorkeling on their honeymoon, she realized she didn't want to let Frederick slip out of her life. They had been through too much together. His kind heart, attentiveness, and love of travel were why she had fallen in love with him in the first place. Those things hadn't changed. He had tried to support her, but she wouldn't let him. Yet, somehow she had allowed all of those qualities to fade away beneath her anger. She wasn't angry with him, but with herself. She had gradually let everything take precedence over him.

Getting up from her desk, she began pacing the floor. She had to make things right. It wouldn't be easy, but she had to try. She owed them both that much. He had wanted to make their marriage work before, and hopefully he still did. She grabbed her purse. If she left now, she could make one stop and still catch him at his desk. Dashing through the doorway, she was determined to get there as soon as she could.

Her stomach fluttered on the cab ride to Frederick's office. He would be thrilled to see her, wouldn't he? She'd tell him about her appointment and her new resolve. They could start over.

Arriving at his company in the financial district, she peeked in her purse to be sure the lace-edged lingerie was still there. She exhaled nervously. The stop at the boutique on her way over was out of character for her, but she knew Frederick would be pleased. His secretary was away from her desk, so Anna knocked once and entered his office. Surprise lit his features when he looked up from his computer.

"Hey! What are you doing here?"

"I have to talk to you."

Frederick stood and walked around the desk to greet her with a kiss on the cheek. He then returned to his chair and motioned for her to sit down, his expression concerned.

"I've been thinking," Anna began. She leaned forward and straightened the picture frame on his desk. "I owe you an apology. A couple of months ago, when you showed me that picture where I was pregnant with Claire, I saw how happy we used to be. It reminded me of how much we've lost—first Claire and now us. I've been so hard on you, avoiding you when I should've been reaching out to you instead. I'm sorry. I called the counselor this morning. I'm ready to see her now."

"What do you mean?" he asked warily. "You told me you didn't need counseling."

"I know I did," Anna replied. "But I've been thinking about all the adventures we've had. It's time we tried to get our spark back. It's never too late, right?"

Frederick ran his fingers through his smooth black hair and shifted in his seat.

Anna's stomach plunged. Her gaze caught on his raised left hand. A white line on his ring finger where his wedding band should have been was like a beacon.

"Where's your ring? I haven't seen it off your finger since we were snorkeling on our honeymoon and you lost it in the coral reef. Once we finally found it, you swore you'd never take it off again. Has something changed?"

He rubbed his hands together and shook his head. "I was lifting weights this morning and forgot to put it back on. That's all."

Anna wanted to believe him, but something in his voice told her there was more to the story.

"Why did you decide to go to counseling now?" Frederick asked. "I tried to bring us back together months ago, but you weren't interested. You rejected me."

"I know and I'm sorry. But since then, I've realized some things about myself. When I went to the doctor this morning for a refill of my sleeping meds, he asked about counseling. While talking with him, I realized how angry I still was."

She clasped her hands together. "The accident was my fault. Claire died because of me." Her voice broke. "I dove headfirst into work and traveling so I could distance myself from the pain. But now I realize it also distanced me from you."

Frederick leaned back in his chair, placing his hands behind his head.

"Part of me died with Claire," Anna went on. "I know that now. I need to try to find that part of myself again."

The room fell silent. Finally, Frederick met Anna's gaze. "I wish it were that easy," he whispered.

"Of course it's not that easy. But we have to try."

Frederick sighed. "You've told me before that you wanted our marriage to last and promised to go to counseling. But you were always too busy and cancelled the appointments. Things never really changed. How do I know it'll be different this time?"

"Because I want to make our marriage last. Can't you see that?"

"Since our dance together, you've been traveling all the time and sleeping in the guest room whenever you're home. That doesn't seem like a woman who wants her marriage back."

"I was trying to figure things out," she reasoned. "After that day, so many emotions came back to me.

I needed my space to focus on what I had to do for work."

"Work always comes first," he said firmly. "I'm afraid it's too late for us."

"What do you mean?" Anna asked, her shoulder muscles tightening.

Frederick sat up and cleared his throat. "It's true that since Claire died, we've gradually been drifting apart, spending less and less time together. But that's not the worst part." He paused. "Claire's death changed our entire relationship. You stopped sharing your fears, your hopes, and your dreams with me. You completely cut me out of your life. I wanted to grieve over Claire and talk about what we had lost, but you wouldn't hear of it. I was left to suffer on my own. Never once did you ask how I was feeling."

He tugged at his collar, loosening his tie. "I tried to give you time, but you never let me in. You didn't seem to care about our marriage or me. Yet, today you say you want to make it last. You can't just pretend this past year never happened. Things aren't how they used to be. You made that very clear after our last dance." He stared at her, his eyes devoid of emotion. "I don't think you know what you want anymore."

Anna's jaw dropped. "Do you think I want out of our marriage?"

"I think deep down you do, and I can't live like this anymore. You're cold and distant all the time. I've tried to win you back, but you've resisted me at every turn. I've always loved you, Anna, but I've been lonely."

He paused and stared out the window for a moment before returning his gaze to her. "Now there's someone else."

"What?" Her heart pounded as she imagined Frederick in the arms of another woman. "You're seeing someone? How could you?" Anna clenched her fists. "After everything we've been through?" Her voice came out sounding shrill, desperate.

"You're never home. I tried to deny my feelings for her, but I can't anymore. I never meant to hurt you, but it's time we faced the truth. I want a divorce."

Anna could hardly breathe. This couldn't be real. Not after she had finally decided to go to counseling and get her marriage back on track. "How long have you felt this way?" Anna tried to keep her emotions under control. "Is that the real reason you took off your wedding ring?"

"I'm sorry. I didn't want it to happen like this." He stood and walked around the front of his desk and reached for her hand.

"You're sorry?" she rebuked, slapping his hand away. "Was our dance together and talk of happier times a sham? Was the photograph you showed me a cruel joke?"

"No, my feelings were real. But after you rejected me, I realized that our marriage was over. It has been for a while. I just never wanted to admit it."

"So, that's it? You're giving up on us? You, the one who always said we could make it through anything?" Her head hurt as she tried to grasp the fact that her husband wanted out. It was over. She had missed her chance. But she couldn't give up that easily. She had to tell him how she felt.

Searching his face, she went on. "Having a family with you meant everything to me. It may not have seemed that way initially, but that's the truth. When Claire died, she took a big part of me with her. That wasn't supposed to happen. You see, after my dad died, I promised myself something. I never wanted to feel that kind of pain again, so I closed myself off from everyone. But then I met you. You showed me how to love and be loved, how to open up and be vulnerable. But when Claire died, I felt all that pain and grief return. I was reminded of the danger that comes with loving someone so fully."

Her voice shook. "I stopped feeling because it was the only way that I could go on each day. I hardened my heart rather than allow it to break over and over again. Can't you see that I was struggling too? I should have been there for you, but I couldn't even be there for myself. I'm sorry I let you down. I was doing all I could just to survive." Tears flowed down her cheeks.

"I know," Frederick whispered. Bending beside her, he gripped her hand. "I tried so hard to be patient. But nothing I did seemed to matter. I couldn't keep hoping that things would change," he went on. "Too much has happened for us to go back."

"So, it's over between us? There's no hope for a future together."

His gaze fell to the floor. "I don't know. You aren't the same person you used to be and neither am I. The accident changed us. I also know you partly blame me for what happened. You never wanted a child in the first place."

"No, I didn't. But that changed. I wanted our family. And maybe you're right. I blamed you for showing me how to love again. I blamed you for all the grief I felt."

Frederick brushed a tear from her cheek. "You want us to move forward and forgive each other for everything that's happened. But the truth is, I don't know if we can. Anna, you hold on to things and never let them go. I'm afraid you will always resent me for loving you the way I did and causing you so much pain. That's something I can't live with or fix. You have to figure out what you want and who you are. I don't think you can do that being married to me. I deserve better and so do you. I'm sorry."

Anna clenched her jaw. How had their marriage come to this? But perhaps Frederick was right. Too much had happened. Maybe it was best to leave the past where it belonged. No more questions, no more concerns. Her marriage was over.

Rising from her chair, she nodded and rushed out the door, wiping away her tears as she went.

# 4

Walking up the stone steps and past the two large white pillars of their spacious Cape Cod-style home, Anna unlocked the front door.

"Are you sure you're ready to do this?" Julia asked. "You just found out about the divorce yesterday."

"There's no point in waiting. It's over." Yet, as soon as the words left her lips, the pit in her stomach grew. *Her love story was over … the one she had thought was strong enough to last forever.*

Seeing her reflection in the mosaic-patterned mirror, she winced and turned away. The dark circles under her eyes were certainly not doing her sallow complexion any favors.

"Baby steps. That's all you can do for now," Julia said, placing her hand lightly on Anna's shoulder. "I'll wait for you on the back deck. Take as long as you need."

Baby steps. Her sister's words couldn't have been more ironic, she thought.

Anna planned to select only a few things from the master bedroom, but as she neared the nursery at the top of the stairs, she slowed down. Maybe she wasn't as ready as she thought. Sighing, she stepped inside the room. Pictures adorned the pink walls while ribbons and bows embellished the slatted wooden crib. It looked as though a baby would be coming home any day. They had made the nursery picture-perfect. But now it reminded Anna of a museum. A place preserved to remember people we never had the chance to know.

Trembling, she opened the top drawer of the antique oak dresser. There, in the front corner, lay the light-pink paint sample, wrinkled and torn. Anna ran her finger across its tattered surface. Why had she kept this, of all things? Crumpling it up in her hands, she threw it across the room into the empty wastebasket.

Lip quivering, she peered into the drawer. Anna saw the posy print dress Julia had given them for baby Claire. Picking it up, she rubbed the smooth fabric between her fingers. It was the perfect dress for summertime. Anna clutched the material in her hands as though it was the last part of Claire's memory she would ever touch. Slowly releasing it, she noticed through the veil of her tears a small, silver charm bracelet. The one she had bought at the little boutique in Boston last November. The one she had hoped to fill with memories of Claire's life. Her heart beating fast, she reached down with shaking fingers and caressed the tiny charms. *I did this. I destroyed everything.* Her head pounding, she slipped the bracelet into her pocket and blew her nose. She had to find a way to let Claire go. But the truth was, she had no idea how she was going to do it.

Entering the master bedroom, Anna watched the sun's rays cascade through the oversized windows. She had loved decorating this expansive space, attempting to blend her and Frederick's distinctive tastes. The cherry furniture had been Frederick's idea, while the damask duvet cover was something she had chosen. The natural artwork upon the walls and toffee-colored paint were decisions they had made together.

Anna still remembered the day they painted this

bedroom. Frederick was carefully brushing along the trim boards when Anna jokingly wiped a streak of paint across his cheek. Frederick had jumped up and chased after her, brushing a tan stripe across her forearm. But Anna would not be beaten that easily. Back and forth, they dueled. Soon they were both covered in wet, sticky goo.

Remembering those happier times, Anna ran her hand along the smooth surface of her dresser. Next to a framed photo of her and Frederick, there was a white envelope with her name on it. Curious, she reached for it and pulled out a handwritten letter. She made her way to the edge of the bed. Sitting, she drew a deep breath and began to read.

> My Dearest Anna,
>
> I'm sorry for everything that's happened and how things ended between us. I know how hard this past year has been and I regret the pain I have caused you. I care about you so much. And deep down I know I failed you. That is a truth I will have to live with my entire life. You were always a bright light in my world. But now I fear that light has become only a flicker. Claire's death devastated our lives. We did all we could to survive, but our loss was too great for even our love to overcome. One day, I hope you're able to find what gives you joy and happiness. You deserve the greatest kind of love. When you are free from all this pain, perhaps you will feel love again. I wish you the very best and thank you for sharing the deepest part of yourself with me. You changed my world and will always be in my heart.
>
> Forever,
> Frederick

Anna held the letter against her chest and bowed her head. As the tears fell, she wondered why she hadn't tried to save their marriage sooner. Why hadn't she embraced the counseling they so desperately needed? Why had she been so selfish? Frederick had needed her and all she did was turn away. Sniffling, she reached for the box of tissues on the nightstand.

Several minutes later, she wiped her last tears with the back of her hand and glanced above the curved headboard of their king-sized bed. Her gaze settled on the large, silver-framed picture of the two of them on their wedding day. Studying it, Anna realized why it had always been her favorite. It not only showed how deeply they loved one another, but it also represented the hopes that they had for a long future together. Nine years earlier, when that photo was taken, she never would have imagined everything could disappear so quickly. She spun her diamond wedding band upon her finger before picking up a pen.

Dear Frederick,

As I leave this house for the last time, I feel a myriad of emotions. We built a life together here, but that's all gone now. I leave you the ring that belonged to your grandmother. Although it once symbolized the strength of our love, tragedy changed all that. Who would have guessed that we would experience such heartbreak and loss? I didn't give you the support you needed and for that I'm sorry. My own pain is what eventually tore us apart. I failed us too . . . I guess we were simply not meant to be. May you one day find laughter and happiness again.

Good-bye.

Anna

Anna removed her ring and placed it alongside the note in the envelope. After writing Frederick's name on the front, she set it on his pillow. Looking down at her bare finger, she realized how strange it felt. There was no ring, no symbol of the promises she and Frederick had made to one another. There was nothing left.

It took less time than she imagined it would to pack all of her belongings from the bedroom into a few suitcases. As she reached for her last piece of jewelry from the armoire, she paused. It was the tri-colored mesh necklace that Frederick had purchased for her on their honeymoon. He bought it on their first evening in Paris and said it symbolized her passion and zest for life, something he had always loved about her. Glancing at it now, she wondered where that passion had gone. Carefully, she placed it in its box. She put Frederick's letter in the outside pocket, lowered the suitcase off the bed, and wheeled it out the door.

Passing by a table in the hallway, Anna stopped. She noticed the small figurine of a mother and daughter that her mom had given her last Christmas. Not wanting to leave it behind, Anna opened her purse. Immediately, her heart plummeted when she noticed what was inside. The undergarments she had purchased only yesterday. The hopes she had for them to help rekindle her marriage were gone now. Reaching down, she felt the silky fabric between her fingers. She closed her eyes as tears stung her cheeks. Frederick didn't love her anymore, and nothing was going to change that.

Anna found Julia waiting on the back deck. Sunlight glimmered across the rolling waves.

"I'm ready," Anna told her, pushing open the screen door. "I have everything I need."

"You sure? Don't rush on my account."

"I think it's better if we just go." Yet, as she stared

across the vast ocean, part of her didn't want to leave. She loved this house. She and Frederick had so many happy memories here. And as strange as it sounded, Claire's spirit was somehow here too.

Leaning against the wooden railing, Anna met her sister's gaze. "I have to leave this part of my life behind, as hard as that is. I let so many people down."

"No one's perfect. You did the best you could," Julia said, reaching for her sister's hand. "You know you can stay with Sasha and me as long as you need. We're happy to have you."

"Thanks. It'll give me a chance to get back on my feet again. I appreciate it."

"Are you ready?" Julia asked.

Anna straightened her back and lifted her chin. "As ready as I'm going to be."

On a brisk October evening, Anna was halfway through her twelve-mile run when she found herself drawn to the verdant banks of the Neponset River. She slowed her pace and removed her earphones, placing them in her jacket pocket. Stepping through the tall grasses, she finally came to a stop alongside the river's edge. European starlings chattered in the treetops while smooth cordgrass rippled in the nipping wind. Anna glanced down at the churning river, mesmerized. Beautiful and powerful, its allure drew her closer. She imagined herself kneeling beside it. Then suddenly, she lost her balance and tumbled off the bank into the frigid waters. Sputtering and gasping for air, she tried to breathe. But gradually she sank below the surface into its depths, darkness consuming her.

Anna gasped. Frantically, she looked around. She was standing on shore, at the river's edge. Her running clothes were completely dry. How could that be? She clutched her chest. The drowning had felt so real. But it wasn't. Sweat poured down her forehead as she took a few deep breaths to calm her shaking body. Was she drowning in her own life? She shook her head. No. Everything was under control. She could make it through. Slowing her breathing, she took one last look at the river and shuddered. Turning around, she stepped onto the path. She wouldn't let her imagination get the best of her. Not now, not ever. Setting her jaw, she put in her earphones and dashed down the trail. It was time to focus on her run.

Exhausted, Anna trudged up the steps to Julia's house. It was in a quaint little neighborhood in the southern part of Quincy. Anna had always loved the character of the white colonial, with its black shutters and scarlet brick steps. And although darkness shrouded them now, pruned gardens encompassed the entire yard with beautiful mums in full bloom.

When Anna walked through the back door, Julia was standing near the sink in the kitchen. Her face was lined with agitation, and her arms were crossed tightly across her chest.

"I see you were out late running again," she quipped. "Were you so busy training that you forgot about Sasha's gymnastics meet today?"

"I did," Anna admitted, taking a sip from her water bottle. "It completely slipped my mind until I was a few blocks from here. I'm sorry."

"You'll have to explain to Sasha why you weren't there. She was devastated."

"I will. I'll talk to her in the morning." Anna opened the fridge and pulled out an apple. She knew how important the meet was to Sasha. Her niece had been talking about it for weeks. It was her chance to show off all the new moves she had been practicing. Anna sighed. She hadn't meant to let Sasha down. She just lost track of time.

"Did you know she cried herself to sleep tonight because she hasn't seen you for the past three days?" Julia went on. "You get up before she wakes and come home after she's asleep. You're always absent … either working or training for your marathon. She misses you."

"I miss her too," Anna said, biting into the fruit.

"Do you really?" Julia's tone was harsh.

"Yes, I do. How could you even question that? I love that little girl." Guilt seeped in as Anna pictured Sasha up in her room crying. She was a sensitive girl and was too young to understand that her aunt's absence had nothing to do with her.

"Lately, your actions don't show you care."

"What is that supposed to mean? I live here with you and try to help out whenever I can. I love Sasha, but I'm not available all the time." She paused and took a deep breath. "I'm not her babysitter."

"No, you're not. You'd actually have to be here for that."

Anna stared at her sister in disbelief. "How dare you? I have a million things going on right now. I don't need you to lecture me about how I'm once again letting you down. That seems to be my greatest strength these days."

"No, hiding from how you feel is. That isn't going to change anything, you know." Julia rubbed her hand on her forehead. "At some point, you have to face what your life has become."

"As if you're the expert. My life's just fine. I don't need you or anyone else to judge me. I'm going to bed."

But as Anna headed upstairs, her anger gave way to shame. She knew she had let Sasha down, the one person she didn't want to disappoint. She had to try harder to be there for her niece. She had to keep it together. Determination welled up within her. She had to keep trying.

☙

Anna curled Sasha's blond hair into an updo and put bright red lipstick on her lips. In her ruby red dress and black tiara, Sasha looked exactly like a vampiress.

"I can't believe Halloween's finally here," Sasha said, beaming at her reflection in the mirror. "It's the best day of the year!" She turned around in circles, her eyes shining.

"Endless candy and costumes," Anna said with a smile. She buttoned her long tan cardigan and patted Sasha on the head. "What's better than that?"

"Nothing!" Sasha exclaimed, running out the door. "Let's go!"

Her excitement was contagious as they walked around the entire neighborhood holding hands and laughing. Sasha told detailed stories of fairies and unicorns. She said that one day she was going to introduce Anna to the fairy that lived in their backyard.

"You know your mom is going to kill me when she realizes how much chocolate you've eaten," Anna teased, unwrapping another bite-sized peanut butter cup and handing it to Sasha.

"How will she find out? I'm not going to tell her. Are you?"

"Are you crazy? I value my life," Anna said with a grin.

"Then she'll never know."

Rounding the next corner, Anna popped her third mini Snickers bar into her mouth. The chocolate caught in her throat as she froze. A woman approached them. She was holding an infant dressed as a baby elephant. Anna couldn't take her eyes off the woman and child.

"What's wrong?" Sasha asked.

"Nothing," Anna lied.

The child was exactly the same age as Claire would've been, had she survived. Trembling, Anna leaned against a tree. *What is wrong with me? I've got to pull it together.*

"Isn't that baby cute?" Sasha cooed.

"She is," Anna confessed. Her chubby cheeks, button nose, and sparkling blue eyes were absolutely perfect.

Anna squeezed her eyes to hold back fresh tears. When they arrived home, she rushed to her room without a word.

An hour later, Julia came upstairs to find Anna sitting on her bed, arms wrapped around her knees.

"Are you okay?" Julia asked.

"I'm fine."

"Would you like something to eat or drink? Or maybe a little candy?"

"No thanks."

"What happened tonight?" Julia sat down on the bed next to her sister. Anna met her gaze. Julia's eyes were filled with concern. "Sasha said you seemed upset after seeing a little baby. Did she remind you of Claire?"

"I don't want to talk about it."

Julia paused. "Have you thought about making another appointment with that counselor?

"No. After what happened with Frederick, I never bothered."

"Maybe now would be a good time to think about it again," she suggested.

"Maybe."

"It's okay to miss him, you know." She reached for Anna's hand.

"I don't want to miss him." She looked away as a tear streamed down her cheek. "I just want to move on."

"But until you admit you miss the people you've lost, maybe you can't move on. At least that's what I've found."

Anna peered up at her sister. "You still miss Ben, don't you?"

"Every day. It's so hard to believe Sasha will never know the wonderful man her father was."

"She will. She hears the stories about him from all of us. And there are the letters that he wrote to you every week while he was overseas. You'll show those to her someday, right?"

Julia nodded. "I always knew the risk of marrying a soldier. I knew one day he could be gone. But I never believed it would really happen. It was his last tour. He was almost done. We had so many plans." Her voice broke. "But that roadside bomb changed everything."

Anna hugged her sister. Four years earlier when Ben died, it completely devastated Julia. Sasha provided the only light that helped her endure. "Does it ever get any easier?" Anna asked.

Julia sat up straight, her eyes moist. "Eventually. But the ache in your heart never completely goes away."

"I've been so focused on my own grief these days. I haven't thought about much else."

"That's what grief does. It's all you can do to make it through each day." Julia stood and touched Anna's shoulder. "I'm always here if you need to talk. But think about counseling. It might help."

"Okay. I will."

Julia walked across the room and turned around when she reached the door. "Sasha was hoping to see you before bed. Could you go in and say good-night?"

Anna leaned against the pillows. "I will in a few minutes."

Julia nodded and closed the door behind her.

Anna appreciated how much Julia was trying to help. She sometimes overlooked how much grief her own sister had suffered. But they were very different people. As much as the counseling sounded like a good idea, Anna wasn't sure she could do it. She had to shut out her feelings. The wounds were still too fresh. Love had failed her.

A few minutes later, she walked into Sasha's bubble-gum-pink bedroom. With colorful butterflies on the wall and a silver mirror and vanity, it looked like a room fit for a princess. Sasha was in her bed, snuggled under her butterfly comforter, hugging her stuffed puppy, Buster.

"Did you get enough candy tonight?" Anna asked, sitting on the bed.

"I did. Mommy said I can even take two pieces in my lunch tomorrow."

"Lucky you," Anna said, touching Sasha's nose.

"Are you sad?" Sasha asked, staring into Anna's eyes. "Why?"

"You just look sad a lot."

"I am sometimes. But I'll try to be happier. Okay?"

"Mommy says it's okay to be sad. That's what she tells me when I miss Daddy. I know she misses him too."

"We all miss him."

"Are you sad you came here?"

"No," Anna said, kissing Sasha's forehead. "Of course not. I love spending time with you and your mom."

"Me too," she said. Smiling, she wrapped her arms around Anna in a bear hug. "You know you can sleep with Buster if it helps." She pulled her white puppy out from under the covers.

"Thanks, but I think Buster likes it in here with you."

"I think so too," she said, hugging him tightly. "Can we have a tea party tomorrow?"

"Sure. I think that would be fun."

"I'll be a princess and you can be the queen. Okay?"

"That sounds perfect. Let's do it first thing in the morning."

After saying good-night, Anna remained awake in her room for a long time. At last, she drifted off to sleep.

The Neponset River swirled with turbulence. A figure washed up on the shore and, though she first saw it as from a distance, Anna realized with a start that it was her own body. Wounded and sore, she pulled herself out of the water's powerful grasp and struggled to her feet, looking around. A lush green forest stood in the distance. Among its dense foliage, she saw something move. Fear flickered for only a moment as she narrowed her eyes and watched a magnificent orange and black tiger emerge from the trees. The large cat sauntered toward a small gap in the undergrowth and turned its head toward Anna, resting its gaze upon her. Kindness and understanding emanated from the creature, and Anna yearned to follow it. Shivering, her clothes still soaked from the river, she stepped forward. As she moved, the tiger advanced toward the trees and vanished back into the forest from where it had come.

When Anna awoke the next morning, she wondered what her dream could mean. Desperate for answers, she grabbed her laptop and began an Internet search. She discovered that in some cultures, tigers represent strength and power. What did that have to do with her? She wanted to be strong, but why did she feel so weak? Perhaps inner strength was what she needed now more than anything.

She abruptly slammed the laptop shut. This was crazy. Dreams didn't really mean anything. Why was she so focused on this? She dressed in her running clothes and dashed down the stairs. Changing the song on her iPod as she walked through the kitchen, she nearly knocked Sasha over.

"Oh sorry, Sweetie. I didn't see you there."

"Where are you going?" Sasha's eyes were wide with curiosity. "I thought we were having a tea party."

"We are," Anna explained. "I'm just going for a short run."

Sasha's face fell. "But you're coming back?"

"Of course. I'll be back as soon as I can."

"I'll have everything ready."

"I can't wait." She kissed Sasha on the cheek and ran out the door. It was time to clear her head. The race was only days away.

 C8

As the days turned to weeks and the weeks to months, Christmas came and went, along with the cold days of winter.

On a rare afternoon that Anna was home, Julia approached her in the kitchen, where she was working on a new proposal for work, laptop humming.

"Are you planning on doing another marathon?" Julia asked.

"I'm not sure … maybe."

"Sasha loved coming to the last race. She still has the poster she made for you hanging in her room. She was so proud when you finished in the top ten. I've never heard her scream so loud!"

Anna looked up at her sister, smiling. "It was really great that both of you came to support me. It meant a lot to have you there."

"I know," Julia said, touching her arm. "But I can't believe you've already run in two marathons this year. I could never do it."

"It's fun."

"Doesn't look like fun to me," Julia said with a laugh. "I swear you run every minute you're not working."

"I love it." Anna sighed and returned her gaze to the computer screen. "I guess it helps me feel in control of something."

"You're in control of your job," Julia offered.

"I suppose," Anna said, typing on the keyboard.

"You know your life won't be like this forever. You'll make it through."

"I know. I've even taken your advice and seen a counselor a couple times. It's just hard to fit into my schedule.

"I can imagine. What are you working on there?"

"The Martinson deal," Anna said. "It's another big account Tom gave me."

"Have you done any writing?" Julia asked, nodding toward the journal she had given Anna as a birthday present earlier that month. It was still lying on the table where she had left it.

"No." Anna said, placing her hands in her lap. She still couldn't believe she was another year older. Time was marching on. She was inching closer to forty, and other than her job and a few gray hairs, she didn't have much to show for it. "I don't have time to write these days."

"You did it a lot when we were kids," Julia recalled, grabbing a bag of chips from the pantry. "I would always find you up in the tree house writing stories. Day or night, it didn't matter. It was your favorite hideout. Remember when you were in middle school and you surprised Ben and me when you came up there late one night?"

Anna smiled, remembering it like it was yesterday. "You practically jumped out of your skin. And Ben, he never let me forget that was the night he was planning to kiss you for the first time. I'm surprised he still stuck around after that."

"Yeah. I was so mad at you for interrupting us."

"You finally got over it. The cookies I made probably helped."

"I always had a sweet tooth." Julia stared out the window. "You were going to be a journalist, remember?"

"Didn't exactly work out that way, did it?"

"You enjoy it, right? I mean, for all the hours you put in, I sure hope so."

"Yeah, of course," Anna said, staring down at the floor. "Writing isn't exactly an easy field to break into. Law's a much more practical choice." But as she said those words, something stirred inside her, making her wonder about her writing. It had been so long since she had created anything.

Julia walked over and rubbed Anna's shoulder. "Dreams can always change," she whispered. "It's never too late to be the people we always wanted to be."

6

"This is the last of it," Martha said, walking in and handing her a thick file folder.

"You're sure there's nothing else?" Anna asked, opening the folder and skimming the financial report.

Martha shook her head. "Everything pertaining to the Martinson deal is in there. I checked it over three times," she said, rubbing her eyes. "Nothing is missing."

"Well, it took you long enough," Anna snapped, taking another sip of coffee. She hadn't left her desk for the past four hours and the stack of file folders next to her computer was mounting, along with the tension in her neck. Scanning the columns of numbers, she had to be sure everything was just right. "I could've used this information three hours ago."

Martha sighed. "You didn't ask for it until late this afternoon. I got to it as soon as I could." Martha's voice was strained. "I'd like to head home now, since it's well past dinnertime."

"Okay," Anna replied, looking up and tempering her tone. Martha always did what was asked of her. Anna appreciated that, but perhaps tonight she had pushed her a little too hard. There was no reason they both had to stay so late. "You can finish things up tomorrow. But we can't miss this deadline."

"I know," Martha muttered. "We never can." Martha gathered up her things at her desk and then returned to the doorway, wrapping a Kelly green scarf around her neck. "You do know what day it is today, right?"

Anna shook her head.

Martha pointed to her shamrock earrings. "It's St. Patrick's Day. Didn't you hear Tom invite everyone out for a green beer after work?"

Anna leaned back in her chair and set the folder on her desk. "No, I didn't. My door's been closed most of the day. Sorry you missed that."

"It's okay." Martha's voice softened. "I'm not much of a green beer fan anyway."

"Did you have plans though?" Anna hoped she hadn't spoiled Martha's entire evening.

"I'll catch up with my husband down the street. We usually do a little something to celebrate. No big deal. But we'll have more fun than you will." She smiled. "Try not to stay too late. Good night."

As Martha walked out the door, Anna pulled her hair back into a clip and kicked off her pointed toe heels. How could she have missed St. Patrick's Day? That was one of the biggest days of the year in Boston, one she used to look forward to celebrating with Frederick. But not anymore. Her heart ached at the thought of what Frederick might be doing tonight. He was definitely not sitting home alone. Pushing him from her mind, she glanced down at her cluttered desk. From the look of things, she was in for a long night.

Hours later, she paced the office floor in her bare feet, reading over the last few documents. Her pink blouse was untucked and her black slacks had a stain from the Pad Thai she had ordered in for dinner. Blinking, she tried to focus and stay awake. She had to be well prepared for her meeting in the morning. Mr. Martinson was an international businessman who had devoted his entire life to expanding his company. His contract would bring in over four million dollars for the firm. She needed to know every detail in order for the merger to be a success. As the clock struck midnight, she sat down at her desk with only a few more pages to go.

The next thing she knew, she was standing on the glimmering beach near the forest where the tiger had vanished. Glancing up, she noticed a large, tangled tree several yards away. Empty birdcages swung from the branches, swaying in the breeze like tiny cradles. They had rounded rooftops and creative wire designs. The metal cage doors hung open, as if to welcome both residents and guests. But where had the birds gone? Suddenly, the chirping and cheeping of different melodies drifted on the breeze until, gradually, the songs burst forth like wildfire. Vibrant birds fluttered in the gnarled branches higher in the tree. The tree's strength and majestic beauty—branches reaching toward the distant heavens—bored itself forever into Anna's memory.

Reveling in the splendor of the tree, Anna was startled by a figure slowly moving toward the base of the massive trunk. It was a woman dressed in a light blue robe. Her crinkled face was radiant and kind. As the woman moved closer to the tree, the birds remained perched on the branches, undisturbed by her presence. Her steps were unhurried, yet purposeful. She beckoned Anna to follow her past the tree and down a winding path through the woods. Curious, Anna obeyed.

A clearing came into view, where a large house with a wide wrap-around porch stood alone on a hill. Following the woman inside, Anna found a pile of rocks, a pen, and some paper set on a table. Books filled every shelf, and a warm fire burned in the hearth. As Anna approached its glowing embers, she heard a woman calling her name.

"Ms. Waters. It's morning. You must've fallen asleep here last night."

Anna lifted her head from her desk, blinking. She squinted into the bright sunlight that shone through the windows.

"You have a breakfast meeting with Mr. Martinson," Martha urged, her eyebrows drawn together. "You know he doesn't like to be kept waiting."

Anna jumped up and hastily glanced down at her watch. It was eight thirty, and she was already an hour late.

Groaning, she said, "Martha, get him on the phone now. I need to apologize. This deal is too important for me to mess up."

As Martha hurried out of her office, Anna's cheeks heated with embarrassment. She was losing her edge. She couldn't afford to make mistakes like these. Her boss and the other partners were bound to notice.

When Sylvia stopped by Anna's office later that afternoon, she realized with a sinking in her stomach that her failure to keep the meeting had been noticed. Sylvia's posture was even more stiff than usual. Lips pursed, Sylvia got straight to the point. "It sounds like you smoothed everything out with Mr. Martinson."

"I did. We're meeting at four o'clock today." Anna looked Sylvia straight in the eye. She was still angry at herself for falling asleep, but she didn't want to let Sylvia know that. The problem was resolved and that was what mattered. Composed, she folded her hands on top of her desk and said, "Luckily, he had a cancellation."

"I know. He called to see if you were doing all right. It's unlike you to miss a meeting. Even he knows that."

"It won't happen again," Anna said, lowering her voice to a placating tone.

"I'm sure it won't. We really can't afford to upset our clients."

Anna nodded.

Sylvia straightened her tailored suit jacket before turning on her heels and walking out the door.

7

**W**hen Anna's lawyer called in late March to announce her divorce was final, she didn't even flinch. Her mind was numb from work. It wasn't until several hours had passed that it actually sunk in. Their long journey had come to an end. No more fixing, no more repairing. It was over.

Sighing, she walked toward the window and stared across the vast harbor. The glistening water sparkled in the sunlight as the sailboats floated across the waves. The view was as beautiful as the first time she had seen it. But now her entire world was different. A lone tear streamed down her cheek, and she closed her eyes for a moment before brushing it away.

A knock on her office door jerked her from her reverie. Running her hands through her hair, she sniffled and cleared her throat. "Yes?"

"Do you have a minute?" her boss, Tom, asked as he entered.

"Sure," Anna said, taking a deep breath and trying to regain her composure. She didn't need Tom seeing her like this.

"Are you all right?" he asked. "You seem upset."

"No, I'm fine." She forced a smile and nervously straightened her skirt. "I'm waiting to hear back from

Mr. Rourke," she said. "As soon as I do, we should be all set."

Tom waved a hand for her to sit. He shook his head and sat in the chair across from her. "That's not why I'm here." He stroked his gray beard. "I know you've been working a lot of hours lately. You come in on the weekends, work long past dinner, and haven't taken a vacation in more than a year."

Anna nodded. "I want to help this firm succeed."

"And you have. But at what cost?"

"What do you mean?"

"Anna, you've become irritable and short with your co-workers. I haven't said much because I know things have been difficult in your personal life. However, I think it may be time for you to take some time for yourself."

Anna clamped her jaw and gripped the arms of her chair. What was Tom talking about? She couldn't leave work. Not now.

"When you missed your meeting with Mr. Martinson a couple weeks ago, I overlooked it," he said. "There have been a few mistakes on the contracts you've drawn up, but they've been rectified without any problems. However, for someone who has spent ten years with us, I've seen more mistakes in the last several months than I have in all the time you've been here. You work too hard and won't give yourself a break. It's affecting your performance, Anna. You need to take some time off."

"You're asking me to leave?" Anna heard the incredulity in her voice. She swallowed, blinking. "For how long?"

"Three months, at least."

She looked down at her hands, seeing them as though they belonged to someone else. Her knuckles were white from gripping her chair so tightly. Of everything in her life, she always depended on her job. That was her one constant and she was good at it. Yet, now that was being taken from her too?

Anna cleared her throat. "Are you going to fire me?"

"No," Tom assured her, his eyes sympathetic. "This is for your own good. You won't take time off, so I'm making you. A change of scenery will do you good. Terry will take your clients while you're away." He rose to his feet. "You're one of the best lawyers at this firm. You just need a break. Good luck, Anna, and I'll see you when you're ready to come back."

Anna shakily rose to her feet after Tom disappeared from the doorway. She glanced around her office as though seeing it for the first time. What had all that work been for? The long nights in the office when she cheated Sasha of her bedtime kisses. The weekend afternoons when she spurned Julia's plans for the family. She had been discarded by Frederick, and now she was being cast aside by the only place that made her feel as though she had value. Through a mist of tears, she gathered only the personal items she needed and stumbled from her office.

Without realizing how she got there, Anna found herself behind the wheel of her car. The sound of the ignition jolted her to her senses. She rubbed her hands over her cheeks, coming to life. Action. She needed to take action. She would do the only thing she could think of to do. Run. Tires squealing on the asphalt, she sped out of the parking garage and on the road to the beach.

Grabbing her gym bag from the back seat, she quickly changed. Mile after mile she ran, seething with anger. How could her job be gone? She had devoted her entire life to that firm and now they were asking her to leave? Even if it was only for a few months, it didn't seem fair. How could Tom do this to her?

As the salty sea breeze blew steadily across the water,

Anna raced along the shoreline. The waves crashed thunderously around her like the beating of a giant drum. Gaining speed, Anna realized she had not only given her heart and her soul to that firm, but her marriage as well. That had been her choice. She had to take responsibility for her actions. Even if she had no idea the damage they would do.

Now she had nothing left. Tears wet her cheeks as she pushed herself even harder. Sprinting across the sand, her legs began to throb. Staggering the last few steps, she dropped to her knees. Burying her head in her hands, she forced all the accusations from her mind. She had to make a change. But it wouldn't be for three months. She didn't need that much time. Of that she was certain.

Stomach grumbling, she made her way back to the car. There was only one thing that could appease her hunger and help lift her spirits: coffee ice cream with chocolate toffee pieces. She picked up a small container at the grocery store, headed home, and made herself comfortable on the back porch with the pint and a spoon.

Leaning against the floral pillows of the wicker sofa, she stretched out her legs and placed her feet on the coffee table. She dug into the soft ice cream and slowly licked it from the spoon, savoring the sweet flavor of mocha and candy. The sun's warmth radiated against her skin as she relished another sugary bite.

Clay pots brimming with purple pansies lined the outer edges of the deck and yellow daffodils decorated the picket fence. Taking in all the beauty around her, she thought of the rose gardens surrounding her old home, the home she had shared with Frederick for so many years. He was probably celebrating the divorce being final today. He was free to do whatever he wanted. He was no longer a part of her life. And watching the wind blow through the branches, she realized for the first time that *she was free too*. Excitement sprouted within her and she smiled, pondering the possibilities.

It was time for her to go somewhere for a while ... a change of scenery. Nothing was holding her here anymore. Eating her ice cream, she watched the chickadees flit among the trees. Like an unexpected breeze, her dream swept across her mind. Was it telling her to leave? Was that really its message?

Bringing her spoon into the kitchen and placing the leftover ice cream in the freezer, she thought about the tree from her dream. It was so beautiful. Perhaps there was one like it out there somewhere. Maybe that was where she needed to go. Seeing her laptop on the counter, she began searching the Internet for images of trees that resembled the one from her dream. After browsing through countless gardening and arbor websites, she finally found it ... a Southern live oak. The tree was indigenous to the South. One of its most famous specimens grew near Charleston, South Carolina. She stared at the picture on the screen for several minutes, her heart fluttering. That was it. It had to be. Grinning, she closed the lid. For the first time, she knew what she had to do.

Anna had moved to the sofa and was leafing through a travel magazine when Julia arrived home. She heard her sister enter the foyer and then stumble. With a grimace, Anna remembered that her luggage was in the hallway.

"Sorry, Julia," she called out. "I'll move those bags."

Julia's brows were knitted, her mouth tight when she appeared in the doorway. "Are you going somewhere?"

Anna nodded. "You'll never guess what happened to me today. I've been put on a leave of absence. Can you believe that?"

"What are you talking about?" Julia demanded. "They can't do that!"

"They can and they did. I found out a few hours ago." Anna still couldn't believe the suddenness of it all.

Julia gaped at her. "Why? You've done so much for them."

"Tom said I needed a break." She closed the magazine and placed it on the coffee table. "That I've been working too hard."

"You've always worked too hard," Julia said, sitting unsteadily in the rocking chair. "Why now?"

"I've made some mistakes lately."

"We all make mistakes," Julia insisted.

Anna shrugged. "They say it's the best thing for me."

"What are you going to do?" Julia leaned forward, concern written all over her face.

"I'm going to take a vacation. Get away from here for a while."

"Where will you go?"

"I'm heading south," she said. "Down toward Charleston."

Julia gasped. "Why Charleston? That's so far away."

Anna stared out the window and returned her gaze to her sister. "I heard they have some beautiful trees."

"Trees?" Julia's eyes searched Anna's face.

"Yes. Live oaks, to be exact."

"You're leaving everything because of a tree? I don't understand. Don't you want to be here with us?"

Her hurtful tone tore at Anna's heart. She knew how strange and irrational her actions must seem. But her life had been leading up to this for a while. She knew that now.

"There has to be more to it than this," Julia said. "This doesn't make sense."

Anna tilted her head. "Today, I received the call that my divorce is final, and I realized that I don't recognize my life anymore. My job, my marriage … it's all gone. I need to take some time to figure out what's next for me."

"By leaving?" Julia's voice broke. "Are you sure that's the best thing for you right now? Aren't you just running away?" She exhaled loudly and when she spoke again, her words were slow and controlled. "How long will you be away? How will you support yourself?"

"I received a fairly large settlement in the divorce, and I have some money saved. I'll be able to live on that for quite a while. I'm not sure how long I'll be gone, but it shouldn't be more than a couple of months."

"That's a long time," Julia whispered.

Standing, Anna walked over to the rocking chair and

kneeled down beside her sister, reaching for her hand. "I can't stay where all these memories are. I know it looks like I'm running. But leaving for a while is the only way I can face my past, as weird as that sounds."

"I just want to be sure you'll be okay." She squeezed Anna's hand. "You're my sister and I love you."

"I know. I love you too. But this is my choice," she declared. "I have to go."

Julia nodded. "Have you told Mom?"

"I'm going to stop and see her on the way out. I know it's going to be hard for her. She's never liked having us far away."

"Yeah. When you were in law school in New York, she couldn't wait for you to move back."

"I know. Hopefully, she'll understand." Anna sighed. "For me, it feels like the right time to go. If I wait, I might change my mind."

"So, this really is good-bye, huh?"

"Tell Sasha I'll send her postcards." Anna paused. "I know it's something you don't completely understand. But this is what I have to do."

Julia hugged Anna tightly. "Okay, but call me when you get there."

"I will. I promise."

ᙢ

The yellow house in the small village of Rockport hadn't changed much since Anna's childhood. Abundant tulips bloomed along the front walk and "Abner" the bearded gnome still stood prominently on the top step beside the potted pink petunias. Walking past him with her overnight bag, she patted his red hat. Her dad had given Abner to her mother as a housewarming gift over forty years ago. Seeing the little gnome now, she thought of her dad and smiled.

The sun disappeared beneath the horizon as Anna entered the doorway to the kitchen and placed her bag on the wooden chair. The hour-and-a-half drive had gone much quicker than she had anticipated. "Hey, Mom! You still washing dishes?" Anna joked. "That always seems to be where I find you."

Her mom turned away from the sink, her apron damp with suds. Long, silver hair flowed down her back and she wore the blue housedress Anna had given her for Christmas two years before. She greeted Anna with a wet hug.

"It's good to see you, Anna. Thanks for making the trip up. Dishes keep me out of trouble, you know."

"That explains why your house is so clean," Anna said with a grin.

"Did you see my flowers out front? Spring is finally coming."

"The tulips look great. There's even more of them than I remember. But somehow this place feels like I never left." Comforted by that thought, Anna leaned against the counter. "How are you feeling?"

"My new meds seem to be doing the trick," she said, hanging the dishtowel on the front handle of the oven. "Julia says you've been working hard at the office."

Anna looked down at the tile floor for a moment, not sure if she was ready to tell her the news quite yet. "I certainly was."

"You always did keep busy there."

Anna nodded. She sat down at the round table where she had eaten so many meals over the years. She always sat in the same place, next to the window. Her father's chair stood beside her. No one ever sat there. It seemed strange to preserve people's memories in the objects they left behind. Maybe that was all people had to hold onto. Anna pushed her hair off her forehead with a sigh.

"Did you do something different with your hair?" her mother asked, interrupting her thoughts.

"I got it cut and highlighted. I felt like trying something new."

"It'll always grow back," her mother said, patting her on the shoulder and handing her a glass of water.

"Sorry you don't like it, Mom," Anna said coolly. "But, it is my hair." She pulled a strand through her fingers, loving the way the blond highlights blended with her soft auburn tones.

"Oh, it's fine, dear. You just always look so nice when it's longer, that's all." She leaned forward and pushed a strand of Anna's hair behind her ear. "Are you still enjoying your time at Julia's? It's good that you have your sister to talk to during all of this. You shouldn't keep everything inside, you know. It's not healthy."

Anna took a sip of water. "I'm still working through things. But it's been nice to be at Julia's. Although I really didn't get the chance to see her that much with all the hours I put in at work."

"You can't keep running away from your feelings," her mother explained. "At some point, you have to face them. You should know that by now."

"I do."

Her mother placed a plate of homemade chocolate chip cookies on the table. Their tantalizing aroma made Anna's mouth water. Even after all these years, they were still her favorite. "You don't need Frederick or his rich family," her mother said, taking off her apron. "When all that money came into your life, it changed you. It was like you forgot where you came from. You don't need a big house. You were better off before you had any of it."

"Not this again," Anna muttered, rolling her eyes. "I've told you that I never changed when I got married.

You just thought I did. Besides, I have a law degree, remember? I have money of my own. It's not like I need anything from Frederick."

Her mother sat across from her, a serious expression on her face. "Yeah, but ever since you were young, you had to prove yourself. You never wanted anyone to be better than you. That's why you were the valedictorian of your high school class, went to an Ivy League school, and became a lawyer. You needed people to believe you had made something out of your life. It was always a competition. Yet, look where it's gotten you!" She reached for Anna's hand. "You don't have to be someone you're not. Faith and family are where it's at. Stick with that and you'll never go wrong."

Anna shook her head. "I am who I want to be."

"Are you sure? You seem to be making life harder than it has to be."

Anna had heard this lecture so many times. She had always bitten her tongue, but not today. Her mom, after all these years, still didn't get it.

"I had to prove myself because I never believed I was good enough for you, Mom." She pulled her hands away and clasped them in her lap. "You always tried to tell me who I was, instead of letting me find it out for myself." She paused. "Can't you see that doesn't work? I don't need your answers. I need to find my own." She sighed as she heard the intensity in her own voice.

Her mother's shoulders tensed, and her green eyes glistened with tears.

"I know this is hard to hear," Anna went on, her tone softened. "But I can't be who you want me to be anymore. I have to be myself."

"That's all I've ever wanted you to be. I'm sorry if you didn't get that from what I've always told you. But I wanted more for you than what I ever had."

Anna took a cookie off the plate and broke it in half. "I never felt like what I wanted mattered."

"How can you say that?" Her mother's voice quivered.

"It's how I feel, Mom," Anna whispered. "It's how I've always felt."

"Well, you're wrong. It's always mattered to me." She paused and with a shaky hand turned the wedding ring she still wore on her finger. "You just seem so lost. Ever since ..."

"Claire died. I know. Believe me, I know."

Her mother drew a sharp breath and fixed a sympathetic gaze on Anna. "Are you going to do anything about it? It's time, don't you think?"

"It is." Anna's stomach rolled. She needed to tell her mother why she had really come. "Tomorrow I'm leaving. I'm taking a vacation of sorts."

Her mother's mouth dropped. "Where are you going?"

"Charleston. I need to get away for a while and that seemed like a good place to go." There was no point in telling her about the tree or her dream. Her mother would never understand that.

"Are you sure about this?" Trepidation filled her voice.

"I am."

"What about work?"

"They want me to take some time off." Anna bit into her cookie.

Her mom stared at her, bewilderment in her eyes. Then she stood and walked over to the sink, her back to Anna. "That's a long way to go all by yourself."

"I know. But it's something I have to do." She paused. "I also found out my divorce is final today. That chapter of my life is officially over."

"I don't understand." Her mom's voice faltered. "Don't you want to be near us? Especially right now?"

Anna stood and walked over to her mother's side. "This has nothing to do with you and Julia. It's something I have to do for me. I need to leave for a while and clear my head."

"You're always leaving." A tear ran down her mother's cheek. "What have I done wrong?"

"Nothing," Anna whispered, wrapping her arms around her. "I have to do this for me."

"So, that's why you're here. To say good-bye?"

"Yes. I wanted to see you before I left. To let you know how much I love you and how much I'm going to miss you."

She gripped Anna's hand tightly. "I don't want you to go."

"I know," she whispered.

"But you've made up your mind, haven't you?"

Anna nodded.

Her mother bit her lip. "You need to find your answers, I suppose. I love you. Don't ever forget that."

"I won't." Anna embraced her mother. With a heavy heart, she pulled back and touched her mother's moist cheek. "I brought something for you." She walked over to her bag and pulled out a movie. "I saw this is in the store the other day and picked it up. I know *Casablanca* is your favorite. Since I'm staying the night, I thought we could make some popcorn and snuggle up on the couch. We can stay up as late as you want."

"It sounds like you're trying to cheer me up."

"I am," Anna said with a sly smile.

"I hate it that you're leaving, but since this *is* our last night together for a while, we better enjoy it." She grabbed a pot from the cupboard, "Let's have a few more cookies and pop some popcorn. I'll even splurge and melt some butter. I know that's how you like it best."

**9**

Brilliant sunlight filtered through cotton-ball clouds along a coastal highway somewhere near Charleston. Top down, the silver BMW convertible hugged the highway. A warm breeze whipped strands of Anna's hair across her face. This was her first road trip in more than five years and she felt free. She was ready for a new adventure.

Anna decided it was time to leave the interstate and drive wherever her instincts led her. Decelerating the car, she turned off the highway and onto a winding road lined with soaring cedars and fragrant pines. The vista shifted. Instead of overpasses and lanes of traffic, small streams etched their way across rolling hills. Anna inhaled, relishing the fresh, clean air and the majestic view of the countryside. She smiled. She was on her own schedule, free to travel anywhere she desired.

As she rounded the next curve, her cell phone rang.

Slipping on her headset and pushing the button, Anna heard her mother's voice on the other end. "How's the drive going?"

"Good. The weather's beautiful down here."

"I can't believe you're still on the road," her mother said, a note of concern in her voice. "It's been three days since you left. Will you stop soon?"

Anna shrugged. "I don't know … probably."

Her mother sighed. "Why do you want to be so far away? It was better when you were here. Then I could at least see for myself how you were doing."

"I just need some space." Anna's shoulder muscles began to tense. "Is that so hard to understand?"

"But you're not ready to be alone," her mother insisted. "You've been through too much too fast. I know you're looking for answers, but your family is what you need right now."

Anna tightened her grip on the wheel and took a deep breath. "I know you mean well, Mom, but I have to do this. It's what *I* need."

"That's what you said the other night. But I was hoping by now you would see things differently." She paused. "There's no changing your mind. I can see that. That's how you've always been." She exhaled loudly. "Well, be careful. You know there are a lot of strange people out there."

"Yeah, I've heard," Anna said, rolling her eyes. "I'll try not to do anything crazy."

"I'm serious, Anna."

"I know."

"Please call me when you get where you're going."

"I will. Bye." As an afterthought, she added, "Love you, Mom." But her mother had already hung up.

Nearing the bottom of the next hill, a loud pop sounded from the back of the car. Heart rate spiking, she chewed on her lip. *Oh no. Not now.* The car pulled dramatically to the right. Anna pressed slowly on the brake and guided the car to a stop along the edge of the narrow road.

With a heavy sigh, she stepped out of the car. The rear right tire was as flat as a deflated balloon. She peered into the trunk with a sinking stomach. Even if there were a spare, she wouldn't know how to swap it for the blown tire. She pulled out her cell phone, hoping for a signal. Triple A had to be good for something. But when there were no bars on the screen, she knew she had to come up with a different plan.

Hands on her hips, Anna scanned her surroundings. She noticed that the hilly terrain had now flattened to a few small knolls, and the trees were scattered among swaths of wild grasses. Vast fields of green spread for miles, and the only house she could see stood nearly a hundred yards away. Considering her options, she decided to find someone who could help. She grabbed her purse from the car and started walking toward the house.

As she drew near to the white Georgian-style home, Anna noticed a well-manicured lawn and trimmed hedges. Bushes with bright purple blooms skirted the edge of the long dirt driveway.

A distinguished-looking man in his early fifties stood on the front porch. His lean build and graying goatee reminded Anna of her father. "May I help you, Miss?"

"I hope so. My car blew a tire and it needs to be changed. Do you know someone I could call?"

"I do," he said, walking down the steps with his hands in his pockets. "Which way you heading?"

Anna shrugged. "How far is Charleston?"

"Not far," he answered. "Your accent tells me you're a long way from home." His laugh lines crinkled as he grinned. He held out his hand. "The name's Clark Benton."

"I'm Anna Waters. You're right about my accent. I'm from Boston."

"That's a beautiful part of the country. Very historic. I've been there a few times." He pointed toward her muddy high-heeled sandals. "From the looks of it, you must spend most of your time in the city. Those aren't exactly walking shoes."

"No." Laughing self-consciously, she looked down at her feet. Mud caked her toes. "They really aren't."

Clark smiled and Anna felt herself relax. Even though he was a complete stranger, his soothing voice calmed her. He seemed like the type of person who could handle anything that came his way.

"Why don't I call a tow truck so you can get that tire changed," he said, pushing up his glasses. "I have a friend who owns a garage."

"That would be great." Their gazes locked and Anna felt the warmth of his personality.

As Clark disappeared inside to make the call, Anna scanned the green landscape. From the corner of her eye, she noticed something moving among the tall vines and purple bushes. She strained to see what it might be, and realized it was a child.

"Hi there," a young girl with black pigtails said as she approached the porch. "My name's Lucita. Who are you?"

"I'm Anna."

Lucita scrunched her eyebrows together. "I've never seen you before."

"No," Anna admitted. "My car blew out a tire, and Mr. Benton is helping me out."

"I bet he's calling Charlie," she said, placing both hands on her hips. "He's the best mechanic in the whole county."

"I hope so," Anna said with a smile. "Can he get here quickly?"

"If anyone can do it, Charlie can."

"He's on his way," Clark said, pushing open the screen door and joining them on the driveway. "He said he can put on the spare tire so you can be on your way."

"Is the garage close by?"

"It's in Summerville. That isn't too far from here. I told him we'd meet him at the car."

Anna nodded as the three of them started walking down the driveway. Lucita hummed a happy tune as she jumped over a pothole in the dirt.

"It's really pretty here," Anna said, glancing at the wildflowers blooming among the vines.

"Yes, it is," Lucita agreed. "Clark's gardens are the best ones for miles around. You're lucky you found them!"

"I guess so," Anna said with a chuckle. "Does all of this land belong to you?" she asked, looking at Clark.

"Most of it. Gardening is a passion of mine. I find it quite healing."

"What sort of plants do you grow?"

"Vegetables, fruits, and flowers. I haven't always had so many plants, though. I've gradually increased my crop and transitioned to organic farming."

"That's a much healthier choice," Anna admitted. Yet, as she watched Clark in his neatly pressed polo shirt, khaki shorts, and brown stone necklace, she struggled to visualize him as a farmer. "Do you farm full-time?"

"No, it's more a hobby of mine. I'm a professor at a college in Charleston."

Anna nodded. That made much more sense. "So, how do you manage all the extra work involved in farming if you have another job?"

"We help him," Lucita said, as she picked up a stick from the driveway. "He lets our family take as many fruits and vegetables as we want. My favorite part is finding the ones hidden deep within the leaves."

"And she's good at it too," Clark said, patting her head. "I only work part-time at the college, and I'm lucky to have friends and neighbors, like Lucita and her family, that help me out whenever I need them. What about you? What do you do for a living?"

"I'm an attorney for a law firm back in Boston."

"What's an attorney?" Lucita asked.

"It's someone who studies the laws of our country and tries to help people with them," Anna explained.

"That sounds kind of boring," Lucita said, throwing the stick in the air and catching it with her hands again. "Do you like it?"

"Yeah, I do," she said, with less enthusiasm than she intended. *At least I used to.*

"Is that your car?" Lucita asked, as they stepped onto the shoulder of the road.

"It is," Anna said, proudly. She had dreamed of owning a convertible like this one since she was sixteen.

"Wow! It has an open top. That's so cool! Could you take me for a ride sometime?" Then her face fell and she looked down at her feet. "I mean, if you want to."

"That would be fun," Anna said with a smile. She wasn't sure if this was her final destination, but "sometime" was short term and that, at least, she could commit to.

Lucita looked up, her brown eyes shining. "Really?"

Anna nodded, wondering how anyone could refuse such an adorable face.

"Have you ever been to South Carolina?" Clark asked, as he leaned against the hood of the car.

"No, I haven't." Anna threw her purse into the passenger seat.

"Well, I hope you like it here. There's a lot to see, and the beaches are some of the best on the East Coast."

"I've heard that. I love the ocean, so I'll be sure to check them out."

Lucita leaned toward Anna. "So, besides the ocean, what else do you like?"

Anna eyed the inquisitive little girl, drawn to her innocence. She reminded her of Sasha. They were two girls full of curiosity and lots of questions. "I enjoy running, reading, writing stories, scuba diving, and traveling. What about you?"

"I like to play house, draw, collect bugs, and go fishing."

"Those all sound like fun, except for the bug part. I'm not much for creepy-crawlies."

"Not everything that crawls is an insect. Did you know that?"

Anna grinned. "I do remember learning that once. But it sounds to me like you're the expert."

Lucita beamed. She proceeded to chat about her favorite insects. "Bees and butterflies are fun to watch, but ladybugs and dragonflies are the best."

"Where do you and your family live?" Anna asked.

"Over that hill," Lucita said, pointing across the gardens to a clump of trees on the far side of Clark's house. "I live there with my mama and papa."

The sound of an engine drew their attention to the road. A battered blue tow truck pulled up behind Anna's car.

An older man with gray coveralls and a tattered red baseball cap stepped out of the truck. He lowered his tools to the ground and bent to examine the tire, probing the rubber with grease-stained fingers. "Looks like this tire has seen a few miles," he said in a slow Southern drawl. He stood and walked toward them.

"It hasn't been changed in a while," Anna confessed. "Probably should have checked that before I left."

"Well, I can take care of that for y'all right now. Give me a few minutes." He kneeled down in front of Lucita and peered into her dark eyes. "How are you doing this fine afternoon, young lady?"

Lucita giggled. "Great! How are you?"

"Just fine, thank you." He tipped his hat toward her and stood up. "Good to see you, Clark. How are those azaleas doing?"

"Fabulous. It's been a perfect spring for them."

"Let's hope they keep on blooming. They make everything look a little bit prettier."

As Charlie began working on the tire, Clark looked over at Anna with a grin. "Lucita and her family are great neighbors."

"It's fun living next to a gardener," Lucita explained. "The fruits and vegetables are yummy. I can have them every day and he knows more about plants than anyone!"

"I'm not sure about that," Clark laughed.

"Is that what you teach at the university?" Anna inquired, as she watched Charlie jack up the car and unscrew the lug nuts.

"No, my knowledge of botany is more recent. I've done a lot of reading on it, and Lucita's papa taught me some things, as well." He patted the girl's head. "I actually teach astronomy."

"A man who reads the stars," Anna said, tilting her head, assessing him. "How fascinating."

"It's an interesting job." He crossed his arms in front of him. "New discoveries are out there waiting to be found. Many people also look to the skies to find meaning. Even the earliest humans tried to read the stars."

"I look at them all the time," Lucita declared. "I wish on them."

"Do your wishes come true?" Anna asked, twirling her hair around her finger.

"Sometimes. But they won't if I never wish on them."

"Always keep believing," Clark said, grasping her hand. "That's what we all have to do."

Soon, Charlie was rubbing his hands together and walking toward them. "All right, Ma'am. Your car's ready to go," he said.

Anna took out her wallet and paid Charlie for the repair. Daylight was beginning to wane as subtle hues of deep ginger and golden flax stretched across the horizon. "Are you heading back into town?" she asked.

"Yes, Ma'am."

"Can I follow you? It's getting late, and I think I'll stay in Summerville tonight."

He adjusted his cap. "No problem. There's a place right up the road from my garage.

Anna nodded and turned toward Clark and Lucita. "It was nice to meet you. Maybe I'll see you around."

"I hope so," Lucita said and broke into a smile. "I still need to take a ride in your car!"

# 10

Vintage antique shops, specialty boutiques, and an old-fashioned ice cream parlor called *The Sweet Spoon* lined the streets of Summerville, adding to the charm of the quaint downtown. Hanging baskets blooming with butter-yellow flowers swayed in the warm breeze, and Anna smelled the scent of jasmine in the air.

Rounding the corner, she stepped inside a small coffee shop. At a table near the door, two businessmen intently discussed the cost of commercial property. Nearby, a teenage couple relaxed on the sofa cushions sipping their favorite brew. Instrumental music rose from the speakers. Inhaling the tantalizing aroma, Anna hastened toward the front counter. It was time for her morning caffeine fix.

With a mug of freshly brewed espresso in her hand, Anna turned around and smiled. There at a table in the corner near the window sat Clark.

"Hi!"

"Hey," Clark replied. "Fancy meeting you here. I wasn't sure if you'd even still be around."

"I decided to check out the local flavor," she said, holding up her mug.

"Well, have a seat." He picked up his leather bag from the chair and placed it on the floor.

"Thanks." She sat across from him and yawned. "Excuse me. I guess I need this more than I thought. Do you usually have coffee here?"

"No, I had a meeting with someone early this morning. I stayed to work on a few things."

"Are you an artist too?" Anna asked, nodding toward the spiral notebook lying open on the table.

Clark briefly looked down at his sketch before gently closing the cover. "No, I'm an inventor of sorts. I design things in my spare time."

"Do any of your inventions work?" She sipped her mocha, savoring the whipped cream and chocolate syrup on the top.

Clark smiled. "Of course. My house is filled with gadgets. Lucita loves playing with them. She's a great kid." He traced his finger across the top of his mug. "She really likes you, by the way."

"I like her too. She's got spirit."

"More than you know," Clark said thoughtfully.

Anna twirled her hair. "I'm thinking about staying in the area for a while. I'm kind of on a sabbatical. Do you know if there's a realty office close by? I'm looking for a place to rent."

"Yeah," Clark said. "There's an office a few blocks from here." He paused. "I happen to know of a specific place that's available, if you'd be interested."

"Where's that?"

"It's a house about a quarter mile down the road from me. It's vacant right now and could use a renter. I don't mean to be too forward, but it would be quiet, if that's what you're looking for."

"That sounds nice," Anna said. A house in the country would be different, but it might be the perfect thing. It was close to Charleston and she had already met Lucita and Clark. It was as good a place as any.

"Nick, the realtor, knows about it, so mention my name, and you two could go by and see if it would work for you." He gathered up his bag and slung it over his shoulder, nearly knocking over his tea. "I have to run, but it was nice seeing you again. Have a good day!"

As Anna watched him disappear out the door, she decided that she would check out this house he had mentioned. She had a sense that it could be exactly what she needed.

The real estate office was walking distance from the coffee shop, so Anna headed straight there. When she mentioned Clark's name, Nick knew just the house she was referring to. Fortune was smiling on her because he was also free to show it to her that morning. A glimpse of the old Victorian's corner turret and steeply pitched roof was all it took for her to fall in love with the house. It was positioned on the top of a small knoll overlooking several acres, and its wide wrap-around porch was encased with giant pink rose blossoms.

"Would you like to take a look inside the house and see if it would be suitable for you?" Nick asked. "It does come fully furnished."

Anna nodded. Butterflies tickled her stomach. She couldn't put her finger on it, but the house looked oddly familiar. The beveled-glass door opened to a spacious entryway where a brass-and-crystal chandelier sparkled from the ceiling. A broad wooden staircase with an ornamental railing and decorative crown molding curved elegantly up to the second floor.

Upstairs, long, narrow windows illuminated golden walls. In the corner of one of the rooms, a hand-painted dome trunk drew her attention. She traced the trunk's delicate floral image, wondering about its history. It looked more than a century old, with wooden slats and etched brass hardware. It was stunning and reminded

Anna of her grandmother's trunk where she kept her treasures. Sometimes, when it was just the two of them, her grandmother would sit next to her on the bed with the trunk between them. Inside, there were love letters her grandparents exchanged during the Second World War, old family photographs, baby blankets, and her grandmother's white lace wedding dress. The smooth fabric felt as soft as water between her fingers.

From the bedroom window, Anna gazed onto the expansive back yard lush with blooming flowers. Her breath caught in her throat. There, among the sprawling gardens, stood an enormous Southern live oak tree. *The* oak tree. Anna could hardly believe it. Immediately, she raced downstairs to get a closer look. As she peered up into its twisted branches, her heart stuttered. Birdcages of every size and shape hung from its sturdy limbs. These were the cages from her dream. How could this be? Could her dream really have brought her to this very house? Her mind struggled to make sense of it. For a few minutes she lingered, watching the birdcages swinging freely in the breeze. She realized this was the place. It had to be.

"What do you think?" Nick asked. He walked up beside her and smoothed his shiny blond hair.

"It's perfect," she said, turning toward him. But then her mouth dropped open. Clark was approaching them with an old wooden hoe in his hand.

"What are you doing here?" she asked, unable to hide her surprise.

"That's my place over there." He pointed to the lone white house across the field of green she visited yesterday. "Since I live so close, the owner asked me to keep an eye on this place until someone moved in. I was on my way over to pull out a few weeds along the front walkway when Nick pulled up."

"So you're the reason everything looks so nice?" She glanced around. Nothing seemed out of place.

"For now. Hopefully, a new owner will take over soon."

"You're in luck," she said, placing her hands on her hips and smiling. She turned toward Nick. "I'll take it."

"That's great!" Nick said.

This was her new home. It was so beautiful. Giddy, Anna spun around in a circle, her arms wide. "I can hardly believe it's mine!"

"Welcome to the neighborhood," Clark said with a grin. "Here's the key to the house." He handed her a brass antique skeleton key. "I'm not going to be needing it anymore."

"Thanks," she said, running her fingers along the smooth, etched metal and slipping it into her pocket. "Do I need to sign a lease or anything?"

"No," Nick said. "You just have to pay the utilities. The owner made that very clear before she left."

"Really? That's amazing! I've never heard of *that* before."

Nick shrugged. "That's how she set it up."

"Okay. That works for me. Now if you don't mind, I'm going to look around a bit more."

"It's yours now. Do whatever you like," Nick said.

Strolling through the brilliant flower garden, Anna recognized climbing roses and daylilies, but several of the plant species were unfamiliar to her. In the center of the garden, there was a fountain with a large marble replica of a Greek goddess. She had a helmet on her head, her eyes staring toward the horizon. The spear in her left hand pointed toward the heavens, while her long hair curled down her back. Her one-shouldered dress flowed elegantly over her body, and in her right hand was a small angel. Anna focused her gaze on the woman's

face. Although she was young and beautiful, she seemed
to possess great strength and wisdom. The striking figure
captivated Anna, until she had to force herself to look
away.

&#x2767;

The sun was melting into the horizon when Anna
returned to the house with all of her belongings. She
had chosen a few essential items to bring with her on this
trip besides her clothes: a family photo, Claire's charm
bracelet, a locket from her father, the mother-daughter
figurine, journals, and a laptop. That was all she wanted
from her former life.

When she arrived, Clark was watering the hanging
baskets of impatiens on the front porch.

"Do you water these plants often?" Anna asked,
walking up the steps.

"Usually once a day. I wanted to keep them looking
nice until someone moved in. The flowers are beautiful.
I couldn't just let them die."

"Hopefully, I won't kill them the first week I'm
here." She touched the soft pink blooms. "I'm not much
of a gardener."

"They'll be fine. I can give you some watering tips if
you'd like." He set down his sprinkling can.

"That'd be great. Thanks."

"Can I give you a hand with that?" He nodded toward
the large suitcase she was holding.

"There's a couple more bags in the car if you don't
mind getting them."

"No problem."

Anna unlocked the front door with the key Nick
had given her. Clark's key was still nestled in her pocket.
Standing in the living room, she surveyed her new
surroundings. A large picture window offered a view of

vast open fields. It was so quiet here. Exactly what she needed. Smiling, she headed toward the kitchen.

"You'll find things are a little slower paced around here," Clark said, walking through the doorway into the kitchen. "I hope that suits you."

"It will be a welcome change," Anna said. "Thanks for telling me about this house. Did its owners move away?"

Clark leaned against the counter. "It belongs to an old woman named Lydia. I met her when I moved out here five years ago. She loved to garden and, as you can see from all the flowers, she was quite good at it too. She could make anything grow."

"You two must've been quite the pair."

Clark laughed. "Oh, no. I didn't know anything about gardening back then. She taught me a lot about nature … and life. She is a very spiritual person who thinks all religions can teach us something."

Anna looked out the window before returning her gaze to Clark. "Did she also like birds?" she asked curiously. "It appears as though she had a whole flock."

Clark smiled. "Actually, she never kept birds inside the cages. They were merely symbols to her. She believed many people were locked within themselves, unable to be truly free. The cages helped remind her to stay true to herself."

"What happened to Lydia?" Anna asked. "She seems like an incredible woman."

"About three months ago, she came over to my house for tea, as she often did, and told me it was time for her to move on. She never said specifically where she was going, but she asked me to watch over the place for her. When I questioned her further, she said that soon someone else would need the house. I guess she noticed my confusion because she went on to tell me that one day a woman would come who needed a place to stay. I was to offer this home to her."

"That seems a little hard to believe," Anna said, raising her eyebrows.

"I know, but she asked me to befriend the woman and offer her a place to stay. Then she finished her tea and thanked me for my friendship. She returned home and I never saw her again. I was always skeptical of her notion that a woman would come. Yet, when you walked up my driveway yesterday, I wondered if you might be the one she was referring to. Lucita even said how much Lydia would have liked you."

"That really is extraordinary!" Anna whispered, trying to wrap her mind around Clark's words. The whole situation was strangely incredible. Yet, Anna had to admit it was possible. Between her dream and Lydia's premonition, it was more than coincidence that she had found herself in this house. The mystery of it all perplexed and intrigued her.

"Well, now that I know about the past, I better start thinking about the future," Anna said. "Thanks for helping me bring my stuff in, but from the look of things, I have an awful lot of cleaning to do."

"I'll leave you to get settled. If you need anything, let me know." He handed her his business card. "Here's my phone number. Don't be afraid to give me a call, and you're welcome to stop by anytime. Take care."

She watched Clark leave and cross the field, her excitement continuing to grow. She finally had her own place, her own sanctuary from the world. It was time for her new life to begin.

Lifting the sheets off the furniture, she instantly loved the cozy atmosphere. The sofa and love seat coordinated in soft, sand-colored canvas. A braided fringe rug cushioned the legs of the pine coffee table.

The methodic ticking of a large antique grandfather clock in the corner provided another source of comfort.

Anna set to work stripping the sheets from the beds, dusting the furniture, wiping kitchen counters, and mopping floors. When she finally finished, the house felt even more inviting and warm. A brick fireplace stood in the center of the living room, built-in wooden bookshelves lined the walls, and dozens of candles made Anna smile with delight. It was the perfect place to curl up and read—or maybe even write.

Anna chose the large back room facing the towering oak tree as her bedroom. The room was the color of lilacs, with four tall windows providing ample natural light. An elaborately carved wooden desk sat in the corner. Pictures of stunning gardens overflowing with vegetables and flowers hung on every wall. But the most interesting thing of all was the flowered stationery and small collection of pens on the desk. It was as if they were waiting for her.

As Anna unpacked her things, she noticed a three-foot-tall statue of what appeared to be the Virgin Mary next to the wooden dresser. Anna stepped toward the figure and examined its features closely. This statue was much different from others Anna had seen in the Catholic churches of her childhood. Intricately carved out of wood, Mary's skin was the color of almonds. Her flowing robe was red garnet with ornate gold designs, and her face held an expression of compassion and tenderness.

Anna stared at the figure for several minutes before purposefully putting the rest of her things away. Occasionally, her gaze wandered to Mary, but she quickly looked away. Mary represented everything Anna had been taught to believe in as a child. Yet, Anna wondered if any of it was real.

When everything was in its proper place, she sat on the soft mattress of the canopy bed. Feeling as though Mary's eyes were watching her, Anna stared at the statue. She tried to fight her fascination with this remarkable figure. Religion wasn't based on fact. It was based on stories. There was no way to prove it was real. So, how could people rely on faith alone? Yet, reflecting on the past few days, Anna realized she had done that very thing. Maybe she hadn't relied on faith in God, but faith in something. It had brought her where she was right now.

Drawn to this woman, she slowly rose and walked toward her. Falling to her knees before the statue, she folded her hands, closed her eyes, and began to pray.

"Dear Mary, it has been a long time since I've prayed to you, but your presence here has stirred something within me, and I feel I must share the concerns of my heart. I'm starting anew and ask that you please watch over me. I've found myself in a strange place and yet I somehow feel as if I belong here. It's time for me to stop running and look within, to face my past head-on. Please help in whatever way you can, and watch over Julia, Sasha, and my mother too. Thank you. Amen."

Anna opened her eyes, surprised at her own ability to pray so candidly. Not that praying to Mary was going to make a difference anyway. But, what could it hurt? She rose to her feet and pulled on her pajamas. Crawling into bed, she watched as moonbeams cascaded a silvery glow across the darkened shadows. Soon, her eyelids grew heavy and she drifted off to sleep.

# 11

The next morning, Anna awoke to the cheeping of tiny wrens. She stretched as she sat up in bed. The wrens perched on a thin branch outside the window, their energetic tweeting bringing a smile to her face. Today was a new day filled with endless possibilities. Feeling inspired, she padded to the desk and picked up her journal. It had been a long time since she had written anything. Too long. Movement outside the window, among the flowers of the garden, caught her attention. Squinting to see better, she realized it was Lucita.

Slipping on some capris and a T-shirt, she dashed down the stairs and out the back door. She found the little girl sitting near the edge of the garden, digging up dirt with a small spade.

"Good morning," Anna said. "What are you up to?"

"I'm looking for worms," she said, digging a hole in the moist earth. "I'm going fishing, and I was wondering if you had any juicy ones."

"I don't know," Anna said, placing her hand on her hip. "Do you usually look for them here?"

Lucita nodded vigorously. "Miss Lydia always let me take as many worms as I wanted. Is that okay with you?"

"I don't see why not."

"Great!" Lucita exclaimed, before reaching into

the dirt. A few seconds later, she pulled a long, slender earthworm from the soil. "I bet I'll catch a big fish now." Lucita inspected it carefully before placing it into her white plastic container.

"I'm sure you will," Anna agreed. "Would you ever consider taking me fishing?"

Lucita stopped digging and peered up at Anna. "Are you sure you'd want to come? You don't seem like the fishing type."

"Why would you say that?"

"Well, fish are kind of slimy and look at your pretty fingernails ..." She carefully examined Anna's manicured hands. "They don't have any dirt under them!"

Anna crossed her arms. "Did you know my father was a fisherman? He would go out on his boat every morning. When I was younger, he took me fishing all the time."

"I never would've guessed that," Lucita said with a giggle. "A city girl who likes to fish?"

"I may be a little rusty, but I think it'll all come back." Anna pretended to hold a fishing pole and cast a line out to sea.

"Your form's pretty good," Lucita said after observing her for a few seconds. "It must've been fun fishing with your dad." She pulled her knees up to her chin. "Can you tell me about him?"

"He was a wonderful man whom I loved very much." Anna crouched down beside Lucita and settled into the dark earth. "He taught me how to fish, to swim, and even to play the fiddle."

"You play the fiddle?" Lucita asked, her eyes wide.

"It's been a long time since I've played."

"Why did you stop?"

"I don't know," Anna said, her voice fading. She watched the tree branches bend in the breeze. Even though it had been a long time, her heart still ached every time she thought about playing the fiddle with her father. "I have many wonderful memories of making music with my dad. He died in a boating accident a long time ago. After he died, playing the fiddle reminded me of him, and it made me sad. So, I packed it away."

Lucita touched Anna's arm. "But you liked to play. Don't you want to do it again?"

Playing the fiddle always made her and her father smile. It was something they both loved. "Maybe you're right. I should think about the joy the fiddle brings me rather than the loss."

"I think you should play again. It'll make you happy. You'll see."

Anna didn't answer. But maybe Lucita was right. Music could help her heal. Anna inhaled the earthy aroma of fresh soil and stared at the blooming flowers all around them. "These gardens really are amazing. It's too bad I don't know more about plants. Do you?"

Lucita's face brightened. "I sure do. Would you like me to teach you?"

"I bet you'd be a fabulous teacher."

"I *am* one of the best."

Lucita's serious expression made Anna smile. That was something she was doing a whole lot more these days. "How old are you?"

"I'm eight. My birthday was last month."

"I have a niece who's a little younger than you. If she comes to visit, the two of you could play."

"I'd really like that. There aren't too many kids around here." She leaned down and lifted a red and black beetle from a leaf and placed it on her thumb. "I know you don't like bugs, but you know this one is a ladybug, right?"

"Yes," Anna said with a grin.

"Did you know that in some countries ladybugs are considered good luck?"

"No, I didn't. Let's hope it's lucky for us, as well."
Anna leaned down. "Ladybugs are kind of cute, even for
an insect. Maybe she's a sign of good things to come."
"I think having you here is already good luck."
Anna's heart warmed. "I hope so."
Lucita stood up and brushed the dirt off the knees of
her denim overalls. Taking Anna's hand in her own, she
said, "I want to show you something."
She led Anna along a curving path of wood chips
lined with charcoal pavers that wound among the towering
grasses of the garden. Eventually, they stopped in front of
a small pond with a trickling waterfall. A granite statue
of a man in a pose of meditation sat about twelve inches
from the water's edge. His hands were nestled together
while his legs opened into a perfect lotus position. A
flowing robe covered his arms and legs. Two climbing
rose bushes encircled him in streaming blooms of red
and white.
Lucita squeezed Anna's hand. "What do you think of
the statue?"
"He looks very peaceful."
"His name's Buddha and I love how he sits with his
feet in his lap and wears a necklace!"
"How do you know about Buddha?"
"Miss Lydia talked to me about spiritual things. She
said having Buddha, Athena, or Mary close by can help
me feel safe. I sometimes tell them my worries. Buddha's
my favorite because he looks so happy. But I think Athena
is the most like you."
"You do?" Anna glanced at the marble statue across
the yard that had captured her attention only yesterday.
"Miss Lydia said Athena was wise and knew lots of
things. She believed in the arts. And, she was known for
her strength." Lucita grasped Anna's hand. "Doesn't that
sound like you?"

Anna shook her head, wondering how she could be anything like Athena.

Lucita explained. "You know a lot of things and came here wanting to be wise, right?"

Anna nodded.

"You also play the fiddle because you like making music, and when your dad died, you had to be strong. See, you're just like her!"

Anna studied Lucita. "You sure do know a lot for being only eight."

"That's because of Miss Lydia. She taught me so much. I still miss her, but I know she sent me you."

Anna smiled. Whether or not Lydia "sent" her there didn't matter. If Lucita needed her, then that was exactly where she wanted to be. "Do you visit Buddha often?"

Lucita peered down at her dirty blue flip-flops. "I didn't used to but lately I've been coming more. Mama's cough has gotten worse, and sometimes Papa gets angry, so I like to be where it's quiet."

"Is your mama sick?"

Lucita's small fingers touched Buddha's robe. "Yeah. She used to help me pick our vegetables from Mr. Clark's garden, but now I do it myself. I don't mind, but it was more fun when she was with me. Mr. Clark's so nice. He always helps."

Lucita plucked a lone rose petal from the bush and held it to her nose. Then she offered it to Anna. Its fruity fragrance infused her senses, reminding her of the sweet aroma of her rose gardens back home. "Mama doesn't do as much as she used to," Lucita continued. "But she does cook some of our meals. She also knits. Otherwise, I help with everything else."

"Does your papa help too?"

"Not really. I think he's too sad. He usually goes

outside and sits on the porch or works in the barn. When he gets mad, I try to do whatever he says."

Anna touched Lucita's shoulder. "Are you scared of him?"

"No," she said, shaking her head. "I try to listen and respect him because that usually helps." Lucita's eyes sparkled. Excitedly, she grabbed Anna's arm and pulled her toward the pond. "Look, there are frogs and fish living in there! Isn't that neat?"

Anna took a moment to respond, still thinking about what Lucita had just told her. She glanced into the rippling water. "Yes, there are a lot of them in there."

"Miss Lydia let me feed them." She leaned forward and touched the water with her fingers. "Will you too?"

"Sure." Anna sat on a large boulder next to the pond. "You can be in charge of the fish."

Lucita jumped up and down, clapping her hands. "Thanks, Miss Anna! I know we're going to have the best times. I can even teach you a little bit about the birds around here. Do you know much about birds?"

"Other than seagulls, not really." She crossed her legs.

"I love hearing the birds sing. They make music that I could listen to all day long. I tell them my problems and they seem to understand. It's amazing all the wonderful creatures God made. She sure knew what she was doing."

"She?"

"Well, Miss Lydia believed God was like a Great Mother who gave birth to all the universe. It was her love that made the world such an amazing place." She touched a lily pad in the water. "I think God is a girl because girls are so good at creating beautiful things. It makes perfect sense to me."

"I guess it does." As Anna watched Lucita's exuberance, a twinge of sadness encircled her heart. This is what Claire would have been like: joyful and innocent.

Lucita twirled and started skipping back toward the house. "It's been fun seeing you again, but I'm going to Mr. Clark's to pick some vegetables for dinner tonight. It's always better to pick them in the morning when it's not so hot outside."

"Would you mind if I walked over there with you? I want to talk with Mr. Clark for a few minutes, and I'm sure you could teach me some more things about gardening."

"You can come with me anywhere," Lucita said, spreading her arms wide.

"I'm going to grab my sunglasses inside. I'll be right back." Anna ran up the porch steps and into the kitchen.

When she returned, Lucita was placing a holed lid on her worm container.

"I thought you were going to wear sunglasses?" Lucita stared up at her with a puzzled look on her face.

"I couldn't find them," Anna confessed. "So, I put this on." She rubbed her hand across the wide brim of the flowered hat. "What do you think?"

"I love it!" she shouted. "It will keep out the sun and the bugs!"

"It was hanging by the door. You don't think Lydia will mind if I wear it, do you?"

Lucita put her hand on her hip. "She probably left it there for you. She always knew what other people needed. That's what made her so special."

# 12

Anna and Lucita held hands as they left the gardens and wandered along a dirt trail, headed toward Clark's house. "Has this path always been here?" Anna asked, squeezing Lucita's hand and looking at the winding trail that snaked among the vines and flowers.

"For as long as I can remember. Miss Lydia and Mr. Clark made this path in the fields so we didn't have to walk on the road. She said it would keep us all connected."

"So, the trail goes all the way to Clark's house?"

"Yep. I even have one to my house too!" she exclaimed, picking a purple iris from the field. "It goes up that hill over there." She pointed toward the trees.

"You'll have to show it to me sometime," Anna said, peering at the small knoll.

"I will."

Clark was in the back garden hoeing the soil around numerous strawberry plants. He straightened and waved when he saw the two of them approaching. "Good morning, Lucita," he said, wiping his brow. "I see you brought a friend along. Is she here to help?"

"Of course," Anna said, although she wasn't exactly sure what she was going to do. Julia often did her gardening projects without Anna's help. She claimed Anna had a way of killing everything green.

Clark picked a red ripe strawberry off the stem and handed it to Lucita. "Thanks for bringing some extra hands."

"No problem," Lucita mumbled through the strawberry juice dribbling down her chin. "She isn't well trained ... yet."

"Let's see what we can do about that." He reached up his hand and gave Lucita a high five. "Together we can do anything."

"Exactly!" Lucita shouted. She ambled over to the porch and gripped the handle of a brown wicker basket. "I'm going to start with the asparagus and then pick some radishes and onions. Is that okay?"

"Of course. Take whatever you need." Clark turned toward Anna. He tried to keep a straight face, but had trouble containing the mirth creeping across his lips. "Nice hat. Are you trying to make a fashion statement?"

Anna's hand brushed lightly against its brim. "I found it in the house. Lucita likes it. She said it will help keep out the sun and the bugs."

"With that obnoxious flower print, I'm sure it will keep everything away," he joked. "You won't be hard to find out here. But it's a good look on you," he said with a wink.

Lucita spent considerable time showing Anna the proper way to tell if a vegetable was ripe and the best way to pick it. She even shared some of her mother's favorite recipes.

Anna would have loved to stay all day listening to the music of the little girl's voice, but her legs were cramping from crouching for so long.

"It's time for a little break," Clark called from the back porch. "I have some sweet tea if anyone's interested."

Lucita dropped her red radishes into the basket and

darted toward the steps. "I am. You know how much I love your sweet tea!"

Anna clambered to her feet and followed Lucita, trying not to wince every time pain surged down her leg.

"How are you doing, Miss Style?" Clark teased.

"Wonderfully, despite the fact that I can't feel anything below my waist." She hobbled up the porch steps. "But I'm guessing that's the life of a gardener."

"Don't worry, you'll get used to it," he empathized. "Remember, no pain, no gain."

Anna slumped into a padded rocking chair. "Yes, but I can honestly say that I never knew gardening could be so grueling."

Clark chuckled. "Maybe you should call it a day. I don't want you to be so miserable that you never want to come back again."

"It may already be too late," she said, rubbing her knees.

"Thanks, Mr. Clark," Lucita said after she took her last sip of tea. "I've had fun, but I need to be going back home now. Mama's probably resting and I'll need to get lunch ready for her. I'm going fishing with Miss Anna this afternoon. She's promised me a picnic. Isn't that great?"

"It sure is," he said, looking over at Anna with a smile. Then he turned his attention back to Lucita. "Say hello to your mama for me."

"I will. See you soon, Miss Anna. We're going to have so much fun!"

"We sure are," Anna laughed. "I can't wait to get my nails dirty."

"Me neither. Bye." She waved one last time and scurried up the small hill until she disappeared into the thick grove of trees.

"And there goes our sweet little Lucita," Clark said, pouring more tea into his glass.

Anna watched Clark for a moment. He struck her as the philosophical type, one who saw difficulties as opportunities. Someone Julia would call an *old soul.* "I found Lucita in my garden this morning. She's such a lovely girl."

"She's incredible. Her family has been through a lot this past year and yet she always has a smile on her face."

"She told me her mother was sick. Is she going to be okay?"

Clark sat down in the wooden rocker next to Anna. "Esperanza was diagnosed with stage-four lung cancer a few months ago. She was given just over a year to live and began chemotherapy and radiation. But the treatments made her very sick and didn't keep the cancer from spreading. She's decided to fight it on her own and wants to spend the rest of her time at home with her family."

"That poor girl." Anna remembered the pain of losing her father. But Lucita was only eight years old and that pain would be even worse. To lose her mother at such a young age would be devastating. Anna felt sick to her stomach. "What about her father? How's he doing?"

"Bernardo has really struggled with Esperanza's disease. He drinks heavily and lost his job a couple weeks ago. He rarely leaves the house. He used to help with the vegetables, but now he refuses to come by. Lucita has held that family together, but Bernardo's a very proud man. He refuses any help that's offered. It's a difficult situation. It shows what a blessing Lucita really is."

"How much longer does Esperanza have?" Anna's voice was barely above a whisper.

"I don't know. Bernardo rarely allows visitors, so I haven't seen Esperanza in a couple months. But from what Lucita has told me, she's getting worse. I wish Bernardo could pick up the pieces of his life. He loves his family so much, but he's in tremendous pain. It's sad to watch what alcohol can do."

"Is Lucita in danger?" Anxiety crept up her back as she gripped her hands in her lap.

"As long as Esperanza's around, things will be okay. Bernardo loves Lucita very much and she's a strong little girl. At this point, the best thing we can do is support Lucita."

Anna followed Clark's gaze to a ruby-throated hummingbird. It drank from a small feeder and flitted around the corner of the house.

Clark sighed. "Sometimes I think Lucita comes here to escape from everything going on at home."

"Will she come to you if anything happens?" Concern filled Anna's heart.

"I think she will. She knows I would do anything for her family."

Anna walked the winding path into her garden later that morning and stopped near the statue of Buddha. Placing her hand upon his shoulder, she whispered, "Please help Lucita and give her the strength she needs during the days ahead. Let her feel your guidance and love."

# 13

The afternoon sun warmed Anna's back as she walked among the flowering green plants with an old, white fishing pole slung over her shoulder. She had found it in the small shed behind the house. She also carried a red bag filled with goodies … turkey and cheese sandwiches, pita chips, apples, carrots and hummus, sparkling cider, and a package of Oreos for dessert.

Clark knelt beside a large group of potato plants, throwing weeds into the nearby wheelbarrow. Lucita sat beside him, eating a strawberry and talking animatedly.

"Are you ready to go?" Anna called out to Lucita.

"I sure am," she said, jumping up.

"I see you found Lydia's old fishing pole," Clark said, standing and brushing dirt off his knees.

"I'm hoping it brings me some luck."

"You'll definitely need it. This little girl can out-fish anyone." He patted Lucita's head.

"I'm taking Miss Anna to Pepper's Pond. That's the perfect place to catch them. Right, Mr. Clark?"

"It has lots of fish. But the bugs can be nasty."

Anna cringed. "Really?"

Clark laughed. "They shouldn't be too bad today. Besides, it's all worth it if you catch some big fish, right?"

Anna slowly nodded. *Maybe this fishing thing wasn't such a good idea.*

"Let's go," Lucita said, pulling on her arm. "Maybe you can have fresh fish for supper."

"Great. That's just what I was hoping for." Anna loved eating fish ever since she was young. Whether it was ocean or freshwater fish didn't matter. They were all delicious to her.

Anna grinned back at Clark as Lucita dragged her off by the hand. Clark waved, eyebrows raised as if to say she was in for a great adventure. They crossed a white wooden bridge that brought them to the banks of a large, tranquil pond. Swathed in green, the grasses steadily rose toward towering evergreens along the banks. Cypress and oaks surrounded the peaceful water while the bright sun cast its reflection upon the smooth, glassy surface. A translucent green dragonfly rested upon a floating log. A kaleidoscope of color reflected off its tissue-paper-thin wings.

"It's so beautiful," Lucita gushed, pointing toward the delicate insect. "Did you know adult dragonflies only live for a few months?"

"No, I didn't."

"Miss Lydia said it makes them live each day to the fullest and enjoy every moment. She said dragonflies know more about how to truly live during their short lifetimes than many of us will ever learn in ours."

As the dragonfly flapped its wings and took flight again, Anna uttered, "It seems even dragonflies can teach us something."

Lucita set her container of worms down on the grass and opened the lid. "This is the best spot to catch fish."

"I hope they're biting today." Anna knelt down and pulled out a worm. "Do you know why this place is called Pepper's Pond?"

"Papa named it."

"It's cute."

Lucita nodded as she cast her line into the water. "I used to love eating peppers when I was little. I ate them so much that Papa started to call me that. So when he brought me out here to fish for the first time, he said that it was my special place. Pepper's Pond."

"Your papa must love you a lot."

"I guess so, but it's been a while since he's called me Pepper."

As Anna watched Lucita brush a strand of hair away from her eyes, she suddenly felt something tug on the end of her line.

"Miss Anna, you've got one! Reel it in!" Lucita shouted.

Anna saw a glint of gold splash through the water before she lifted the pole and dropped the fish onto the bank.

"That's a big one!" Lucita exclaimed.

Excitedly, Anna eased the hook from the fish's mouth and showed it off to Lucita.

"It's a black crappie. Those taste so good!" Then Lucita abruptly ran toward the water and screeched, "My pole!" Quickly, she reached for her rod and caught it just before it slid under the surface. "It's another one! They're bitin' like crazy!"

Anna ran over to watch Lucita reel in another fish. Unexpectedly, Lucita swung the pole in Anna's direction, causing her to dart out of the way so fast that she lost her balance. She stumbled, splashing into the shallow water.

"Sorry!" Lucita screamed, still gripping her pole. "Are you okay?"

Anna laughed as she lifted her dripping arms and saw her soaked capris. "Are you so afraid I'd out-fish you that you made me fall into the pond?"

Lucita grinned as she grasped the fish with her hands. "No way! I'm going to beat you fair and square!"

Anna climbed out of the pond and kicked off her muddy flip flops. Water trickling down her arms and legs, she pulled her damp hair up into a ponytail. "We'll see about that. Now, how about you give me another worm?"

By the time the worms were gone, so was Anna's energy. Giddy with exhaustion, she pleaded with her new little friend to end the contest. "You weren't kidding when you said you could fish, Lucita."

Giggling, she reached for Anna's hand. "Okay, I'm ready to go."

As they strolled away from the pond, Anna smiled down at her. "Fishing was really fun today," she said. "Thanks for bringing me along."

"I can't believe you haven't fished since you were little. You caught two pretty big ones," Lucita said, pointing toward the long stringer of fish Anna was holding.

"Yeah, but yours is still the biggest," Anna said lifting up the large crappie on the bottom. "You really did beat me fair and square."

"That's because you fell in the water. Your form wasn't as good after that."

"You mean your pole nearly knocked me into the water," Anna said with a wink. "A little foul play, no doubt."

"Oh, no," Lucita insisted. "That was an accident, but I couldn't have planned it any better if I'd tried."

They reached a clearing occupied by a cute two-story blue house with white shutters. Yellow flowers decorated the window boxes and a small station wagon sat in the driveway.

"This is my house," Lucita said proudly. She raced down the hill, arms wide, and then came to a stop, waiting for Anna to catch up.

"It's very nice," Anna said, quickening her pace

until she was walking in-step beside Lucita again. Stone planters lined the front walkway and a floral wreath hung on the door. It was a welcoming sight, but Anna wondered just how welcoming Lucita's father would be.

"I've lived here all my life. Papa uses the barn for his workshop and Mama likes to garden, but she stays in the house now." Lucita placed her hands in her pockets.

"What about you?" Anna asked, touching Lucita's shoulder. "Where do you like to be?"

"Outside, but not when it's nighttime." She kicked a pebble across the grass.

"Are you scared of the dark?"

"I don't like being alone in dark places. Something might come out and get me." She shuddered.

"Well, then I'm glad the sun's still shining."

They trudged side-by-side up the front steps. Lucita set down their fishing poles by the front door. The screen door unexpectedly burst open. Anna jumped. An angry man, who could only be Lucita's father, glared at her from the doorway.

"Lucita, who is this?" he demanded. "I told you visitors are not welcome here."

"I'm sorry, Papa," Lucita said, staring down at her feet.

Anna swallowed hard and squared her shoulders. "I'm Anna Waters. I just moved into Lydia's house. Lucita said she was going fishing this afternoon, and I asked if I could come along. I just wanted to make sure she got home okay."

He crossed his arms in front of him. "My wife's very sick and cannot handle visitors. I think it's best if you leave."

"I understand." Anna held out the stringer of fish. "These are for you then."

Bernardo looked at the fish and then back at Anna.

"Set them over there." He pointed toward a small round accent table nestled between two Adirondack chairs.

Anna didn't like his domineering tone, but she walked over and placed them on the table anyway.

"But Miss Anna has to take her fish," Lucita said, peering up at her father. "We don't need all of these."

"If she can get 'em off the stringer, she can have 'em."

Anna's neck heated in irritation. She was determined to do just that. She selected one of her fish and tugged it from the stringer. These were her fish and she had every right to take them home. As she began twisting off the second fish, she heard the door hinge squeak behind her.

A petite woman with dark, tired eyes emerged from the house. Her breath was labored as she came forward, leaning on a wooden cane. She wore a modest cornflower blue dress that complemented the delicate features of her face. "I see you caught some fish today."

"Yes, we have plenty for supper tonight," Lucita said.

Bernardo stepped toward his wife and whispered, "You shouldn't be out here. Please go back inside."

The woman held up her hand, and Bernardo said no more.

She turned toward Anna. "You must be the new neighbor I've heard so much about."

"I'm Anna Waters," she said, extending her hand. "I just moved into Miss Lydia's old place."

"I'm Esperanza Martinez," she said, shaking her hand. "And this is my husband, Bernardo. Do you like Lydia's place so far?" Esperanza asked. A cough shuddered through her.

Anna nodded. "It's great. Clark and Lucita have been very kind. And who knew the fishing could be so good?" She winked at Lucita.

"It usually is," Bernardo interjected, "but my wife needs to go inside now, so it's time for you to leave."

"Bernardo, don't be so rude." Esperanza gently patted his hand. "She brought Lucita home. The least we can do is get to know her a little. Besides, I could use some fresh air."

"Please, dear, don't overdo it."

"I won't."

Anna watched as Bernardo helped lower Esperanza into the chair beside her.

"Bernardo, why don't you go inside and get a bag for Anna to take her fish home in? And also bring the washcloth. I don't want her fingers to smell all afternoon."

"Thanks," Anna said, pulling her last fish from the stringer. "I love fresh fish."

Bernardo returned to the porch and thrust the bag and washcloth in Anna's direction. "Here."

"Thank you." Anna carefully placed the fish inside the bag and washed off her hands.

"I hope your family will enjoy them," Esperanza said.

"Oh, I don't have a family here. It's just me."

Esperanza rested her cane upon the floor. "That means you're all alone in that big house?" Esperanza asked. "Now I'm very glad Lucita goes over to visit you."

"Me too," Anna said, smiling over at Lucita.

"So, what brings you to South Carolina?" Esperanza inquired.

Anna leaned against the side of the house. "I needed some time away from everything."

"I see." Her gaze lingered on Anna's face. "Are you planning to stay long?"

"I'm not really sure," Anna admitted.

"I hope so!" Lucita said exuberantly. "Miss Anna doesn't know much about gardening or birds or spiritual things," Lucita explained to her mother. "I'm teaching her!"

"That's great." Esperanza said as she eased back in her chair and took a couple of labored breaths.

Anna grinned. "And Lucita has been a wonderful teacher so far, but I fear there's much more I need to learn."

"I'm sure there is," Bernardo muttered.

Suddenly, Esperanza clutched the side of her chair and began coughing uncontrollably.

Bernardo was on his feet in an instant. He picked up his frail wife who appeared as light as a bird and carried her into the house. He set her gently on a blue suede sofa. He stroked her long black hair while she struggled to regain her breath. Anna stood in the doorway, watching.

Lucita dashed past her with several tissues that she dabbed against her mother's mouth and chin. Blood saturated the tissues. Bernardo and Lucita hovered over Esperanza, waiting quietly for the episode to pass.

Anna felt like an intruder on this family's private desperation. She lowered her gaze and turned away. The kitchen was across the tiny entry hall. Her gaze picked out a framed family portrait in the center of their square table. The faces appeared much different than those of the three people she saw today. They were sitting in the grass snuggled together. Bernardo's arms were wrapped lovingly around Esperanza, who held a younger Lucita in her lap, pigtails in her hair and wearing a bright pink sundress. The smiles and love on their faces revealed a family with no burdens and no sickness.

"Miss Waters, it's time for you to leave." Bernardo's voice was stern behind her.

"Of course," Anna whispered. "I'm sorry." Without looking again at the scene of quiet anguish, she retreated through the front door.

# 14

Thoughts of Lucita and her family's private pain absorbed Anna as she meandered along the path to her home. A voice from up ahead startled her. She inhaled sharply, then saw that it was Clark approaching, a smile on his face.

"I was coming over to see how the fishing was going," he said. "You two have been gone for quite a while. I figured the fish were either really biting or both of you had fallen in."

Anna wiped the tears from her cheeks with the back of her hand, trying to be discreet, but knowing that her distress was obvious.

Clark's smile quickly faded. "Did something happen? Are you okay?"

She nodded. "I'm fine." But she couldn't stop thinking about the Martinez family and the strain of Esperanza's illness.

Clark gazed at her inquiringly, waiting for her to say more.

Anna began walking again. Clark accompanied her. Neither of them spoke until Anna broke the silence. "Lucita and I had a great time today. After I walked her home, Bernardo met us at the door. He was not happy to see me. But then Esperanza came out and she was so kind. We talked for a while but before long, the coughing began." She paused. "Esperanza's sicker than I thought she would be. I dread the pain that is ahead for that family."

"Maybe that's why we're here," Clark said softly. "We can help them, for both of us know what it's like to lose someone close."

Anna stopped walking. Their gazes locked.

"This afternoon," he explained, "Lucita told me about your father. I'm sorry for the pain his death has caused you."

She nodded. "May I ask what loss you've had?"

"I've experienced the loss of a child."

Anna blinked, unable to speak. How was that possible? Goosebumps rose on her arms at the mention of this uncanny coincidence. "I'm sorry," she whispered. The lines of pain on his face were familiar to her ... she had seen that same expression in her own reflection.

"It was my son, Ethan," he whispered, staring off into the distance. "And not a day goes by that I don't think about him."

*And it never will,* Anna wanted to say.

They resumed walking in silence. The wind rustled through the tall cypress trees as Anna's fingers brushed against the slender grasses of the meadow.

"About twelve years ago," Clark began, "my wife, Jillian, and I wanted to have a baby. We had tried for several years to get pregnant and even went to a well-known fertility clinic in hopes that they could help us. Finally, after many months and procedures, we were thrilled to find out she was pregnant."

He paused, running his fingers through his short gray hair. "In August, our little Ethan was born and he was the light of our lives. He grew up quickly and inherited one thing from his father ... his curiosity. He loved to explore new things. Science was one of his favorite subjects." Clark smiled.

Anna nodded. Having just spent the day with Lucita, she knew what the curiosity of a child looked like. It was contagious and made life much more fun.

Coming to the bottom of the hill, Clark continued. "When Ethan was in kindergarten, I worked a lot, but tried to spend as much time as I could with him. One weekend in early June, the two of us went camping. We drove to a state park and Ethan eagerly helped me set up the tent." Clark paused and looked toward the horizon before continuing. "We built a blazing fire that night, roasting marshmallows and telling stories under brilliant stars. I began to feel my passion for the outdoors being awakened once again."

"I'm sure Ethan loved spending that time with you." She reached out and touched his arm. "I remember looking at the stars in the summertime with my father on his boat. It's still one of my favorite memories." She gazed up at the blue sky and sighed. Their path took them through the twisted vines of Clark's vegetable garden.

Clark continued speaking, but more tentatively. "The next morning, we hiked the trails for insects. Ethan loved to collect them, just like Lucita. He began chasing after a butterfly. I warned him to be careful and watch his step." Clark cleared his throat. "But he lost his balance and tumbled into a ravine."

Anna gasped, cupping her hand over her mouth. She wasn't sure she wanted to hear the rest.

"Immediately, I ran after him. But when I got there, I knew he wouldn't make it." Clark brushed a tear from his cheek. "He died in the hospital that night."

Anna felt numb. "I'm so sorry," she whispered. She knew the crippling grief of losing a child. Words were meaningless. The only comfort she found was silence.

Clark touched a rose blossom hanging down from the trellis. "I blamed myself for the accident. Jillian tried to offer her support, but she was so angry. We divorced less than a year later."

Anna's heart pounded in her chest. That was exactly what happened to her and Frederick.

"That spring," Clark went on, "I moved out here and began the process of healing. Lydia welcomed me with open arms and listened to me without judgment. Over time, she helped me realize that our experiences in life, the good *and* especially the bad, shape who we are. Although I will always bear some responsibility for what happened to Ethan, I must not let the guilt destroy me. I have to move forward. Going back is not an option."

"No, there's no going back," Anna agreed. She stepped onto Clark's back porch and set down her bag. It seemed unbelievable to her that this man she hardly knew had so much in common with her.

"Moving forward. It's my greatest struggle, as well." She paused and took a deep breath. "I've also lost a child."

Clark stared at her, concern etched across his face. "Would you like to talk about it?"

Anna unsteadily lowered into the rocking chair and leaned her head against the cushioned back. She watched the afternoon sun slip fleetingly behind the clouds before emerging on the other side. Collecting her thoughts, she interlaced her fingers and sighed.

"About two years ago," she began, "my husband Frederick and I discovered we were going to have a baby. It was an unexpected pregnancy, but he was ecstatic. He had always wanted children, but I wasn't so sure. A baby didn't fit into my career plans, and I didn't even know if I wanted to be a mother."

"No one's ever completely ready for a baby," Clark said sympathetically. He sat in the chair beside her.

Anna sighed. "Frederick said everything would work out and encouraged me to enjoy this special time of our lives. I wish I had listened to him." She stared at the clouds before continuing. "During the next several months, Frederick spent less time at the office and bought whatever crazy foods I was craving." She smiled. "When we found out we were having a little girl, my excitement grew."

"I remember that day too," Clark said. "When I found out I was having a son, I couldn't have been happier."

Anna nodded. "One evening, my mother brought over an oak bassinet my father had made for us as children. Since he'd already passed, it meant so much, knowing my daughter would have something from him."

"I gave Ethan my father's baseball that was signed by Hank Aaron. It made me feel as if he was still a part of his life somehow."

Anna stretched out her hand and looked at the vacant spot on her finger where her wedding ring used to be. "I was seven months pregnant when the accident happened. It was winter and we were on the expressway, returning home from our doctor's appointment. It was my fault. Here I was, finally excited about decorating the nursery, and I made Frederick look down to critique a swatch of paint color while he was driving. Just a split second—that's all it took. The car in front of us had come to an abrupt stop, and we rear-ended the car, causing a chain reaction." Anna paused and closed her eyes. She could still see the taillights in her mind as if it were yesterday. Her voice quivered. "The accident had caused a placenta abruption and, due to the loss of blood, I barely survived. However, the baby was not so lucky. Our little Claire didn't make it through the surgery."

Clark reached over and squeezed her hand. "I'm sorry. There are no words to describe that type of pain."

Anna rubbed her forehead. "After that day, I was never the same. I dove into work to avoid the guilt I was feeling for causing the accident. Frederick tried to talk with me about it, but I only became angry. It all seemed so unfair. I began traveling more, and the gap between us widened. A year and a half later, our marriage was over." Her words hung in the air.

"A divorce is never entirely one-sided," Clark assured her.

"I know, but I caused Claire to die because I was so concerned about the color of the nursery." She fisted her hands. "What if I had waited to show him the paint swatch? What if we hadn't lost the baby? Maybe we would still be together." Her voice shook. "Clark, my entire life changed forever in that split second. Yet, I know I brought this situation upon myself … and now I'm all alone without my baby or my husband." Tears spilled down her cheeks.

Clark rested his hand on her shoulder. "But you are facing your feelings now, and that's a good thing."

Anna sniffled.

"I'm sorry for what you've been through," Clark whispered, "but I've learned that 'what ifs' often paralyze our ability to heal. I wish I could tell you that it will be over soon. Time does help, but it's not an easy road. I think a fresh start is a good idea for you."

"I think so too. I was talking with Lucita this morning, and she reminded me how much I love to play the fiddle. I had forgotten the way music makes me feel. I think, in my attempt to control my emotions, I've drifted far away from my creative side, fearful of letting that part of me emerge. I now realize that needs to change."

"A creative outlet can be a huge help, and although it may not seem like it now, you will eventually heal. And I'm always here to listen." Clark leaned back in his chair and put his hands behind his head. Then he added, "The past is something we cannot change and the future is uncertain. We can only live in the present by trying to make the most of each day. Every morning, we are given the opportunity to wake up and try again. What we do with that opportunity is up to us."

"Thanks for listening," she said. Clark seemed like a caring soul. He made her feel at ease in the same way her father would have. His friendship warmed her. She rose to her feet.

"Before you go, there's something I want to give you." Clark went inside and returned with a tattered book in his hand. "You said you haven't explored much with different religions, but I know you're trying to get through this difficult time. Lydia gave a copy of this book to me several years ago, and I found it very helpful. Please take it. Whether you decide to read it or not is up to you."

Anna read the cover. It was a book on meditation written from the Tao tradition. "I don't know much about the Tao," she confessed.

"I didn't either, but I think it has a lot of value and offers incredible insights into our lives. You don't have to wholeheartedly believe everything it says, but I found it really helped me clarify my personal beliefs."

"That sounds interesting."

"And there's one more thing," he said. "If you are interested in learning more about meditation, I want to show you these."

He placed a long strand of assorted beads into her palm. She gently ran her fingers over them. Some were smooth as glass, while others were rough and coarse. There were stones in nearly every color, from deep amethyst to metallic turquoise to soft amber.

"These are wonderful," she said, examining their intricate patterns and carvings.

"They're prayer beads," Clark said. "Their imperfections remind me that life is far from perfect and can be filled with challenges. Each bead means something different to me. Some beads represent a specific person, like my Ethan, while others signify a particular feeling or emotion. As I meditate, I have these prayer beads in my hands. They're soothing and help me stay centered."

"They really do have a calming effect." Anna continued to massage the various stones, liking the way they felt.

"The round doughnut-like bead on this end goes inside the loop on the other end so that the strand makes a complete circle." Clark demonstrated this for her before continuing. "It reminds me how everything is connected."

"Where do you meditate?" She glanced around, trying to imagine where his meditation place would be.

"Upstairs. I have a special meditation room. But everyone is different. Some people prefer to meditate outdoors. It's really a matter of personal preference."

Anna nodded. "I could meditate in my bedroom but with the statue of Mary in there, it doesn't seem right. It makes me think of my mother and my Catholic upbringing. It just wouldn't work."

Clark stroked his goatee. "Why not? I think Mary was a strong, caring woman. She understood spirituality and what it meant. If meditation brings you closer to a God, a Creator, or a spiritual Source, don't you think Mary would understand that?"

"What do you mean by a spiritual Source? I've never heard that term before."

"I believe that all of creation comes from an abundant and loving Source that gives us life. Through meditation, we can connect with this Source and come to fully understand ourselves and our world."

"I like that," Anna said. "It's comforting."

"I like how connecting with ourselves is the way we also connect with God or our Source."

"Me too," Anna said. "But I still would feel better if I didn't meditate where someone was watching me. Even if it is just a statue," she said with a grin. "Perhaps I should try to find a place outside with the birds. Lucita says they're good listeners."

"Well, they won't talk back," Clark said with a chuckle. "Seriously though, you'll know your space when you find it. Open your soul to meditation and I think you'll be amazed."

Anna sighed and then handed the prayer beads back to Clark. "I'm glad you showed me these. I may have to make some for myself."

"If you decide to, there's a shop downtown that sells different kinds of beads. I think it will have whatever you need."

"Thanks for the book," Anna said. "I better be getting home." She was intrigued by the possibility of learning more about prayer beads and this "Source" Clark talked about. Straightening her shoulders, she stood a little taller, hopeful that her healing journey had finally begun.

As she bounded down the steps, Clark called after her.

"Anna!"

She spun around. "Yeah?"

"I just thought of something." He descended the stairs and joined her on the path.

"What's that?" She slipped the Tao book in her bag.

"This Sunday I'm going on a tour of homes in downtown Charleston. Would you like to come along?" He handed her a brochure. "There's some magnificent architecture and beautiful gardens, which of course, is my favorite part. It might be a fun way for you to become familiar with Charleston. What do you think?"

She glanced at the stunning pictures, her excitement growing. "That sounds like a lot of fun. I'd love to!"

"Okay, I'll pick you up around ten." He glanced down at her flip flops. "Be sure to have your walking shoes on."

"I will. Bye." She strolled through the twisting vines, thumbing through the rest of the brochure. Sunday was only days away, but it couldn't come soon enough.

# 15

Cozy coffee shops and authentic horse-drawn carriages created an atmosphere where modern conveniences intertwined flawlessly with Charleston's rich history and culture. Anna smiled at this large city's simple charm, where both colorful row houses and grand private residences lined the narrow streets.

"What do you think of our fine city?" Clark asked, slowing the car to turn the next corner.

"It's amazing. I've never seen anything like it."

"That's why we're here. I wanted you to have a chance to see beautiful homes and experience some of the South's majestic charm. This self-guided 'Tour of Homes' is one of the best."

"Well, if this is any indication of what's ahead, I can't wait," Anna said, returning her gaze out the window.

Driving past a traditional colonial church with a towering steeple, Anna noticed an abundance of dogwood trees in full bloom. "Springtime here is beautiful. I've never seen so many flowers."

"That's one of the things I love about Charleston." He lowered his window. "Along with its fondness for history and its relaxed atmosphere."

"It sounds nice," she said quietly.

"You Northerners tend to get caught up in the rush

of life," he teased. "Down here, we like to take time to smell the roses." He pointed to a young woman standing on the pier, staring off into the distance.

"All work and no play," Anna acknowledged. "I've been doing that for far too long."

"It's an easy habit to fall into," Clark empathized as he parked the car. "I did it once too."

Anna opened her car door and stepped onto the narrow sidewalk. The blossoming trees, rustic brick walls, and elaborate wrought-iron gates looked as though they had existed for centuries.

"The architecture is stunning!" Anna said as she stopped in front of the first house on the tour. "The pillars, the exquisite details, even the color!"

"Canary yellow certainly grabs your attention," Clark said, walking up the steps. "Architecture is an art form I enjoy because of its unique blend of both creativity and style. It's like inventing, only on a grander scale."

"I never thought of it that way." Anna stepped through large wooden doors and into a spacious foyer. She peered up at a three-tiered brass chandelier designed with more than twenty candle sockets and an elaborate pineapple-shaped base. "Wow, this place is remarkable!" she said aloud.

"It sure is," Clark agreed.

Anna moved to an elegantly carved antique sofa. "The furniture is gorgeous. This whole room looks as though it belongs in a magazine."

"The ornate décor is one of the things I like best, besides the gardens of course."

"Clark, is that you?" a man's voice called.

Anna turned to see a man with broad shoulders and bronze skin approaching them. His curly brown hair fell gracefully past his angular chin. Stubble peppered his jawline, giving him a rugged, unshaven look. An inexplicable thrill ran through her. With his casual style of carpenter shorts and an orange Henley, he struck her as someone who didn't feel the need to impress anyone.

"Simon, what a surprise!" Clark said, hugging him. "I didn't expect to find you here."

"I'm remodeling my kitchen and thought I might get a few ideas." His voice was smooth and rich.

"This is certainly the place to get some inspiration, that's for sure," Clark agreed.

Simon extended his hand toward Anna. "I'm Simon Russo."

"Oh, of course," Clark said, throwing out his hands. "Where are my manners? Simon, this is Anna Waters. She just moved into Lydia's old place."

Anna shook his hand. His grip was firm and strong. The touch of his calloused fingers sent tingles up her arm. "Nice to meet you," she said breathlessly.

"Are you enjoying the tour?" Simon asked, his brown eyes captivating her with their attentive gaze.

"I am," she said, nervously fingering her beaded necklace. "At least from the little I've seen so far." A soft breeze blew in through the window, awakening her from his spell. Self-consciously, she brushed her auburn hair behind her ear. She was suddenly aware and pleased that the green sundress she was wearing accentuated her curves as well as her eyes. "What about you?" Anna tilted her head as she spoke. *Oh God, am I flirting?* "Is it helping you come up with remodeling ideas?"

"It is, but I have to admit I like taking a break and walking around this part of Charleston." His gaze lingered upon her face. "The architecture and gardens are almost magical, even to those of us who have seen them before."

Anna could see why that was true. She didn't think she could ever grow tired of a setting like this.

"So, are you still coming over for dinner?" Clark asked.

"Yeah, I'm planning on it," Simon said, returning his attention to Clark. "When does John get back?"

"Friday."

"Then I'll see you at dinner Saturday night." Simon paused. "I'll let you two get back to your tour. It was nice to meet you, Anna."

When he smiled at her, warmth crept into her cheeks.

"You too," she said.

Clark and Anna strolled toward the formal dining room at the back of the house. Her heart still fluttering, she asked, "How do you know Simon?"

"He's John's little brother. We try to get together with him whenever we can, but with John's work schedule, that can be difficult."

"Who's John?"

Stepping outside and walking along the flagstone path through the gardens, Clark turned toward Anna. "He's my partner."

"Oh," Anna said. "I *see.*"

"You sound surprised."

"I am a little, I guess. I mean you just told me about Jillian and Ethan."

"Yeah, having a wife and son probably would throw you off a little bit. But that experience made me realize a lot about myself." He paused. "I'm still a very private person. Being gay is only part of who I am. It doesn't define me. Yet, when people find out I'm a gay man, that's usually what it ends up doing. Therefore, my personal life has become something I keep to myself."

Anna nodded. Even though she'd felt comfortable opening up to Clark, she normally wouldn't share much about her life with others either.

"John's one of the few people I've let get close to me since Ethan's death. He travels a lot for work, so most people don't even know we're a couple." Clark sighed. "I keep my relationship with him very discreet."

"You don't have to tell everybody everything. That's your prerogative." She studied the cool water rushing across the stones and pouring into a small pond below. A tiny frog jumped into the pool before its color disappeared into the depths. Even nature used camouflage to protect itself. Anonymity had its comforts. She knew that all too well. But Clark seemed more uninhibited than that.

"You appear so comfortable in your own skin. I figured you were an open book and didn't care what anyone else thought."

Clark nodded. "I know, and perhaps it's time I was more open about my entire life rather than only parts of it."

"Everyone's different, Clark." They continued walking along the path. "You have to do what works for you."

"Perhaps we're both getting a little better at sharing already," Clark said with a smile.

"Perhaps," she agreed.

"You know, John's an incredible man. I'd love for you to meet him." He reached for a nearby branch, smelling a stunning white magnolia blossom. He offered the bloom to Anna.

"I'd like that," Anna said, leaning over. The sweet aroma of sugary candy permeated her senses. The magnolia smelled good enough to eat.

"Why don't you join us for dinner on Saturday?" Clark asked, releasing the branch and meeting her gaze.

"Are you sure?" She blinked, surprised at his invitation.

"John would enjoy the chance to meet you," he said, sincerely.

"Okay. I'll be there."

Strolling in the back gardens of the next home on the tour, Anna stopped in front of an immense tree. "What's this one called?"

"It's a gingko tree. They have the most amazing leaves." He pointed toward one. "See for yourself."

Anna gasped as she examined the intricate leaf. "They look like little fans."

"Exactly. That's what I love about them." He gently rubbed the leaf as though polishing a precious gem. "Did you know the gingko is the oldest living tree on Earth?"

Anna shook her head. "I had no idea. It's so beautiful."

"It's the only type of its species left. It has no other living relatives."

Anna stared at Clark. Although astronomy was his field of expertise, she marveled at his knowledge of botany. "How do you know so much about gingko trees?"

"They interest me so I've read about them," he said with a shrug. "But as pretty as the tree is, stay away from the seeds. They really stink."

Anna stepped back and grinned. "I'll take your word for it. No need to prove that one to me." She walked along the iron fence and reached for a soft pink bloom nestled in a flowering bush. "This has to smell better than that, right?"

"That's a camellia flower. They're abundant around here, but smell different to everyone."

Anna breathed in a strong musky scent, powerful and pungent. She scrunched up her nose.

Clark laughed. "Not a fan, I'm guessing."

"It's just so strong," she said, rubbing her nose to weaken the lingering scent.

"Yes, but they sure are lovely."

Anna enjoyed touring the elaborate homes and

gardens with Clark for the next several hours. As they wandered through the last garden, Clark's face lit up when he saw a lone tree standing at its center. "Anna, come look! Do you know what this is?"

Anna ambled over, staring at the spiky leaves. "I have no idea. But I'm sure that doesn't surprise you," she said with a chuckle.

"It's a monkey puzzle tree." He felt the green blade between his fingers. "Its short, spiny triangular leaves and upward reaching branches are supposed to be representative of a monkey's tail. What do you think?"

Anna squinted, trying to imagine a monkey. "I don't really see it." She backed up to get a better view. "Well, the branches do kind of look like a tail, though it seems to be missing a body and a head."

Clark smiled. "Well, we can't have a monkey with no body and no head." He circled the tree several times, his eyes riveted on its branches. "You know I tried to grow one of these a couple years ago, but it never made it past its second year."

"Why not?" Anna asked, touching the rough spike of its leaf.

"I'm not sure. It even stumped Lydia."

"You could always try again," she suggested.

"I think I'll do just that." He patted its trunk. "It's time for another monkey to grow in the garden."

"It seems with Lucita and me, you have more than enough monkeys already." Anna winked.

Clark snorted. "You can say that again."

"So, what did you think of the tour?" Clark asked on the way back to the car.

"It was incredible. I can see why you love it here." She had never seen so many flowers. It had been an enjoyable and relaxing day. "Thanks for bringing me along."

"It was nice to have company."

As they drove past businessmen bustling down the sidewalks alongside gawking tourists, Anna's thoughts drifted to Simon. He seemed so nice and genuine. She looked forward to the possibility of seeing him again on Saturday. Maybe they'd end up being friends.

Her excitement began to dwindle as she noticed a man and woman sitting outside a small café. They were huddled together, talking. They seemed inseparable. Soul mates. Anna couldn't help but think of Frederick. What was he doing these days? Was he happy? Was he with someone else? That thought squeezed her heart. Maybe marriage really wasn't something she wanted after all.

"What are you thinking about?" Clark asked.

"I was wondering whether there are people in the world who are never meant to get married."

"That's an interesting premise," he said, taking a sip from his water bottle. "What did you come up with?"

Anna clasped her hands in her lap and stared across the bridge at the sparkling blue water. "I don't know. I guess it's possible. According to Frederick, I wasn't meant for marriage. He said it was something he didn't believe I wanted." She paused. "Do you think people sometimes get married because it's what's expected of them?"

"I believe many people get married thinking it's going to solve their problems or make them into the people they want to be. Unfortunately, that's not what marriage is. A spouse is not there to rescue you from your troubles. That's way too much pressure on someone, and it's bound to create disappointment and resentment when that person can't live up to that enormous expectation. In that instance, perhaps marriage isn't the best option. Now, whether that was true in your case, I don't know."

Anna nodded. She always had high expectations about everything. That was part of her problem.

"It's easy to believe in the happily-ever-after ideal,"

Clark went on, "but that's not the way life is. It's about learning from our mistakes and realizing that no one is perfect. We're human and, in the case of marriage, it's about two people coming together to share in both the joys and struggles of life. That's all it can be in order for any marriage to succeed. At least that's how I see it."

Anna leaned her head back against the seat and wondered why it was so easy for expectations to become unreasonable. It was as though it happened without a person even realizing it.

"Many people don't know who they really are when they embark on the journey of marriage," Clark continued, tapping his finger on the wheel. "They often present themselves as one person, when in truth they are actually someone quite different. I know that's what happened with me. When I failed to be who I really was upon speaking my wedding vows, it became impossible to keep them."

The branches of the towering trees reached across the road, draped with weeping moss the way a veil adorns a bride. Anna sighed. So many people wanted to get married. But maybe marriage was a false hope, a doomed reality. "Do any marriages really have a chance of succeeding?"

"If people are honest about who they are and realize that marriage isn't perfect, then there's a chance. Marriage isn't about simply loving someone else. In order to give love to another, you must first love yourself. For many, that's where the difficulty lies. Life is messy and complicated, yet that's what makes it worth living. Problems will come, but it's how we handle them that's important. When people focus on developing their inner character and truly loving themselves, contentment will follow."

Anna gazed at Clark, considering his words. When

she spoke, her voice was raw with emotion. "I know my expectations of marriage were unrealistic ... and that my false sense of self played into its destruction. Quite honestly, I don't think I like myself, much less love myself." She took a deep breath. "I'm trying to, but it's such a long road."

Clark was quiet for a moment. "Just by being down here, you're connecting with yourself more every day. Through that process, you'll come to accept the remarkable person you were made to be. You will come to believe in your worth." He adjusted the rearview mirror. "Have you had a chance to read the Tao book I gave you?"

"No, I haven't."

"It might be helpful."

Anna nodded, hope filling her soul. "Maybe I'll learn how to love myself. Perhaps that's possible. Even for me."

"It is. I did it and, believe me, it's well worth the effort."

# 16

Anna awoke to the low sounds of thunder rumbling far off in the distance. The sky was a somber shade of gray, blanketed by large clusters of thick clouds. Raindrops splattered against the windowpanes. Although the rain's gentle melody often comforted Anna, her mind was restless today. The tiger and the woman had returned to her dreams last night. She knew they had led her to South Carolina. But why?

Reaching across the nightstand to check the clock, her hand brushed the meditation book Clark had given her. She hoped he was right that it might help clarify some things for her. She sat up in bed and leaned against the pillows. A cool breeze blew in through the narrow opening of the window, and a streak of lightning flashed in the distance. Opening up the front cover of the Tao book, she read the introduction, which explained that the Tao was the source of all life. It had no beginning and no end, empty but also limitless. The Tao was indefinable and immeasurable. The only way for a person to truly see it was to stop trying to. Anna stared at the words on the page, trying to absorb their meaning. *How can the Tao be empty and limitless? How is that even possible?*

Anna turned the page and continued to read, wanting to learn more. To begin understanding the Tao, people had to accept every part of themselves and live in the flow of life. Meditation provided a way to silence the mind. When people focused on their breath, they could truly be one with themselves. But everyone's path to understanding the Tao was different. Since the Tao itself was indefinable, all people needed to discover it in their own way. Anna liked the sound of that.

Flipping the pages, she found a meditation on new beginnings. It explained that hope and optimism were essential parts of beginning again. But it was the commitment to connecting with their inner selves that mattered most. Through acceptance and exploration a new journey would begin – one where people live in the here and now.

Anna pushed aside the covers and kicked her legs over the edge of the bed. Taking a deep breath, she walked over to the window. The rain was falling steadily now, and the wind blew across the meadow, rippling the grasses. Reflecting upon her own new beginning, she wondered if perhaps meditation and the Tao would provide the clarity she sought. She was intrigued by the possibility.

Carrying the book downstairs, Anna decided to give meditation a try. It couldn't be that hard. She poured a glass of orange juice and stepped onto the back porch. Two padded wicker chairs and a matching settee sat along the edge of the house. On the opposite side, a round table with four turquoise sling chairs created a comfortable atmosphere for eating dinner or watching the birds. Potted plants surrounded the porch's perimeter and a small angel statue sat near the sliding glass door.

The rain slowed to a gentle sprinkle and Anna breathed in the fresh scent of moistened earth. Puddles dotted the grounds and as she peered up at the gloomy sky, a faint rainbow appeared. Sitting beside a pot of blossoming geraniums, she crossed her legs into a lotus position. She closed her eyes, struggling to clear her mind. Yet, as her thoughts drifted to her grumbling stomach and what she would eat for breakfast, she tried to refocus. *Breathe. I just need to breathe.* A fly buzzed near her ear. Frustration bloomed in her stomach. She wanted to ignore the annoying insect, but couldn't. *Why are there so many flies?* She shook her head. Making one last attempt to concentrate, she inhaled a deep, cleansing breath. But as she did, her mind drifted to Frederick ... his smile, his eyes, his touch. Sadness enveloped her. She opened her eyes and pushed him from her mind. Why couldn't she stop thinking about him? He certainly wasn't thinking about her. Exasperated, she realized her first attempt at meditation hadn't gone well. It was going to be much more difficult than she thought.

Stretching her arms, she stood on the edge of the porch. The rainbow had disappeared along with her hopes for a successful meditation. Walking over to the table, she picked up her journal and sat in the nearby chair, ready to write.

> *Meditating seems like such a simple concept, yet why is it so hard? I can't clear my mind, not even for a few seconds. Thoughts creep in and the more I try to stop them, the more they fester and grow. I don't want to think about Frederick. I want to move on. Isn't meditation supposed to reveal my future rather than my past?*

Closing the cover, Anna looked up and sighed. The rain had stopped and the sun peeked out from behind the clouds. A lull in the weather promised the freedom of a run. She stood and walked into the kitchen. Grabbing her sneakers, she laced them up and headed out the door.

# 17

Anna walked through Clark's front door into the foyer, carrying a plate of fresh bruschetta. A wooden bench stood against the far wall. Its open cubbies held various sweetgrass baskets like the ones Anna had seen at small stands along the roadway. A large candle flickered on the center of a matching wooden shelf, the flame reflecting in the gilded mirror hanging above it. A pair of boots and a fold-up umbrella rested on the nearby rug. Nothing was out of place.

"Let me take that," Clark said, dashing over to help her. "I'm glad you could make it. Why don't you join us in the living room?"

Anna loved the room's simple charm. It was painted the color of peacocks, brilliant and blue. A contemporary gas fireplace glowed along the opposite wall, and a glass coffee table rested on a cream shag rug. Two almond chairs and a coordinating diamond-patterned sofa were skirted by large, potted ferns and a lofty lemon tree, creating a warm and cozy atmosphere. Neatly stacked books lined the built-in shelves while several seascapes adorned the walls along with a lone portrait of a beautiful young boy, Ethan.

"So, this is the famous Anna I've been hearing about," a stocky man with round cheeks and a crooked smile said. "I'm John. I'm so glad to finally meet you." He walked toward her and gave her a hug. His gray beard scratched against her soft cheeks and the subtle smell of mint tobacco wafted through the air.

"It's nice to meet you too," Anna said, smiling.

"I hear you've already met my little brother," John said, pointing toward the almond recliner.

Simon stood, his snug shirt revealing well-defined shoulders and arms. "Hello. It's nice to see you again." His resonant voice hung on the air like smoke drifting from a fire.

"You too," she said faintly, her mouth suddenly gone dry. His penetrating gaze left her breathless. At last, she forced herself to look away, conscious of the attraction she felt and hoping it didn't show.

"You enjoyed the tour, I trust?" John asked. "Clark said it was fun."

"I did." She sat on the patterned brown sofa and adjusted the paisley pillow behind her. "There was so much to see."

"Great for remodeling," Simon said, settling into the recliner. His gaze still focused on Anna. "My kitchen will be all the better for it."

John stood and placed his hands on the rounded back of the empty chair opposite his brother. "The wooden doors and natural tile that you picked out will certainly give it a warm, inviting feel," John said approvingly.

Simon's face turned thoughtful. "That's what I'm going for, the natural look."

*That certainly fits,* Anna thought. With his longer hair and unshaven jawline, he seemed like the nature type. "John," Anna said, turning toward him, "Clark says you do a lot of traveling?"

"I do. Right now I have a few days off, which doesn't seem to happen all that often anymore. I'm in international sales so I'm in the air almost more than I'm on the ground. But I like it. It's part of the joy of the job. There's so much out there to see."

Anna nodded. "I've done my fair share of traveling too. But spending some time in the same place does have its benefits."

"You sound an awful lot like Clark." John sighed and hobbled around the front of the chair. His expression pained, he sat and rubbed his lower thigh.

"How's the old knee feeling these days?" Simon asked.

"Same as usual. Gets pretty ornery with the rain." He looked over at Anna. "It's an old injury," he explained. "I was in a car accident a few years back and my knee's never really been the same. Even after the surgery and physical therapy, it doesn't exactly work like it used to."

"The benefits of getting older," Simon teased, sweeping his hair away from his face.

"Yeah, enjoy being young as long as you can."

"Being young does have its perks," Simon said. "Don't you think so, Anna?" He raised his eyebrows and smiled at her mischievously.

She looked up at him, her gaze lingering longer than she meant it to. "Yeah," she agreed. "I always used to tease my sister that she'd be forty and have wrinkles long before I ever did."

"Age does eventually catch up with us all," Clark said, walking into the living room from the kitchen, carrying a tray of drinks and appetizers. He handed each of them a glass of sweet tea.

"But that doesn't mean we have to act over the hill," John said with a grin. "Isn't there a saying that you're as old as you feel?"

"Well, in that case," Simon said with a laugh, "you must be about twenty."

"And don't you forget it," John said, winking at Anna.

They continued to talk and laugh over bruschetta, southern pimento cheese, and Clark's specialty: boiled peanut hummus. Anna enjoyed watching John, Clark, and Simon interact. They were so comfortable with each other and teasing was a part of the fun. They were a family and her heart tugged as she thought of her own back home.

When they finally made their way to the dinner table, Clark served she-crab soup, shrimp creole over rice, and fresh Brussels sprouts, Anna's favorite. A bouquet of lavender tulips created a beautiful centerpiece and soft jazz music floated from the speakers.

The four of them laughed and chatted over dinner. John loved sharing his travel stories, particularly from overseas. Whether he was left stranded on an island with no money or being chased down a sidewalk by a monkey, he always managed to find his way out of trouble. And he definitely loved to keep people entertained.

"Dinner was delicious," Anna said, taking her last bite. "I could get used to Southern cooking."

"I'm glad you enjoyed it," Clark said. He sipped from a glass of sparkling water.

"So, Anna, what brings you to our fair state?" Simon asked, leaning back in his chair. His gaze locked intently with hers. "Clark says you're from Boston."

"I am," Anna said. His voice reverberated within her until every sound, even the music, faded away. "But I wanted a break from things there. This seemed like as good a place as any to go."

"It's actually better than some places you could've chosen," he said, favorably. "Many people like Florida, but it's too muggy for me. Here you get the benefits of a warm climate and the stunning views of the ocean, without the intense humidity year-round. And have you seen our beaches?" His gaze set her heart to palpitating.

"No, I haven't," Anna admitted.

"That would be a great place for you to show her," John interjected. He poured himself another glass of sweet tea.

Chills ran down her spine. Intrigued at spending alone time with Simon, she knew it wasn't a good idea. His presence aroused her senses far more than she was comfortable with.

"Simon loves spending time on the beach," John continued. "He even takes his dog, Magnus, down there sometimes."

"You have a dog?" Anna asked, glancing at Simon. She loved animals, but Frederick was allergic to them so they never had one of their own.

Simon chuckled. "Yeah, he's crazy though. He loves chasing after balls. He would do it for hours on end if I let him. He never gives up, that's for sure."

"Sounds like his owner," John said. Mirth crossed his lips.

Simon blushed. "I'm not that bad."

"If you get an idea in your head, there's no stopping you. You always were as stubborn as a mule."

"Thanks for mentioning my best qualities, Bro." Simon smiled sheepishly at Anna.

"That's what I'm here for," John said, patting Simon on the back.

"Stubbornness isn't so bad," Anna rationalized. "It's just another word for persistence."

Simon leaned forward and nodded. "Well said." His brown eyes riveted on her; it was as though no one else in the room existed.

Feeling the fire in her cheeks, Anna took a deep breath. She didn't know how to respond to these new feelings: desire, attraction, and guilt. Laying her napkin on the table, she pushed back in her chair. "Clark, let me help you with the dishes." She picked up the platters, and with her stomach tumbling, she followed Clark as he carried the last of the dishes into the kitchen.

Setting the plates by the sink, she collected herself and glanced around. There were odd trinkets scattered throughout the room: a two-handled bread knife, a silver teapot rack, and a gold clock with four rotating hands. "You have the most fascinating kitchen I've ever seen," she said.

"Thanks." He ran his fingers under the water and dried them on a towel.

"I've started reading the Tao book you gave me."

"What do you think?" Clark pulled a fresh strawberry pie from the fridge.

"It's helped me examine my beliefs about the world and God." Anna gathered four dessert plates and placed them on a wooden tray. "Made me question some things."

"An open mind can do that."

"I know." She paused. "But somehow when I question my faith, it feels like I'm doing something wrong."

"Questioning is how we learn," Clark acknowledged. "It's how we grow."

Anna nodded. "It's given me a new perspective. Maybe it isn't about finding God, but about finding myself and my connection with something spiritual, whatever that is."

"Your spirit is the essence of who you are. It helps you find the answers that you seek. I've always believed that," Clark said, placing the creamer and sugar on the tray next to the plates. "We're all looking for meaning, but everyone's journey to spirituality is different."

"And that's not a bad thing."

"No, it isn't." He smiled. "Now, how about we go have some pie?"

They returned to the dining room and after another hour of casual conversation, Anna finally stood up. "I think it's time for me to head home. It was nice to meet you, John," she said.

"You too," John replied, giving her a hug.

"Thanks for dinner. It was amazing," Anna said, embracing Clark.

"Come back anytime."

"I better be going too," Simon said, rising to his feet. He hugged first his brother and then Clark. Then he walked over to Anna, the warmth of his body only inches from hers. "May I walk you out?"

She nodded, a shiver coursing through her.

As Simon followed her out the doorway, he gently placed his hand on the small of her back, as though it were an instinct. Anna's heartbeat quickened. She placed her fingers against her chest. *Why is he affecting me this way?*

"Are you all right?" Simon asked.

"Yes," Anna said as she walked down the steps of the porch. "Just lost my breath for a second."

"I know what that's like," he whispered.

"Well, I better be going. It's late." She stepped toward the trail that led across the field to her house, thankful for the distance between them. She didn't trust herself to be any closer.

"Will you be all right to walk home alone?" he asked, concerned.

"Yes, I'll be fine," she said. "I've walked this path before."

"Perhaps we'll have the chance to see each other again," Simon said. His voice sounded confident, but his eyes revealed a hint of uncertainty she hadn't seen in them before.

Impressed by his humility, she smiled. "Perhaps

we will. After all, Clark and John do seem to enjoy our company." She smiled and waved before heading up the path alone.

As she walked, Anna gazed up at the luminous crescent moon that shimmered in the night sky, wondering how something she had seen hundreds of times could still be so beautiful. Entering her garden, she heard the gently flowing water of Athena's fountain. She considered meditating there, as she had at the statue of Mary, but it seemed too lifelike. She needed a more solitary place.

Her gaze was drawn to the giant oak standing a few feet away. Its branches reached toward the heavens. She stepped around the large furrowed trunk and listened. The breeze rocked the bird cages from side to side. The hollow sound of the wind whispering through the leaves was all that could be heard.

She thought back on her conversation with Clark and realized her entire life had been spent in a narrow mindset rather than one that was open to all possibilities. It seemed strange to her now that she had never noticed it before.

Anna wrapped her shawl tightly around her shoulders. The night air had quickly chilled. The tree's enormous roots flowed into the earth like a mighty river flowing into the ocean. Taking a few steps back, she surveyed the tree in its entirety, from its gnarled and twisted roots all the way up to the towering branches. Uninhibited and certain of its destiny, the tree climbed toward the skies, never questioning its role on this earth. Powerful and beautiful, it lived each day always reaching toward its full potential. A simple concept, Anna knew, but difficult to master.

Anna pulled a barrette from her hair and let her auburn locks blow in the breeze. Closing her eyes, she felt the gentle wind upon her face and listened to the subtle rhythms of the earth. This was the perfect spot, she thought. She would begin meditating here tomorrow. The loud hoot of an owl broke the stillness and Anna jumped in surprise. She looked up to find the source of the sound. In the upper branches of the oak tree, two eyes glowed like yellow lanterns in the dark night. Staring down at her, the owl blinked once, spread its brown wings, and flew away. Anna shook her head in amazement. She had never seen an owl that close before. Yet, having one in her tree had to be a good omen.

Chased inside by the dropping temperature, Anna prepared for bed. Settling under the covers, she propped against the pillows and opened her laptop to do a little research. When an image of an owl next to the goddess Athena appeared on the screen, she smiled. Somehow she knew there would be a connection. The owl was one of Athena's favorite creatures and was viewed by Greek armies as a great protector. It was also believed that whenever Athena traveled on the earth, she came in the form of an owl. Consequently, owls came to signify wisdom and watchfulness. It was believed that owls had extraordinary night vision because of a magical inner light.

Anna knew her glimpse of the owl wasn't a coincidence. It couldn't be. The connection with Athena had arisen once again and, of all places, it had occurred in the towering oak tree. Maybe there really was something to this spirituality thing after all.

# 18

The next morning, Anna had just finished a short run and was straightening up the kitchen when her sister called. "Thanks for the postcard you sent Sasha," she bubbled. "She loves the palm trees."

"They're everywhere down here," Anna said, wiping off the counter. "It's crazy!"

"Well, in that balmy weather, I can see why." She paused, her voice tentative. "Don't get too used to it, okay?"

Anna smiled at her sister's concern. Julia always liked having Anna close by. "How's Mom doing?"

"Pretty well, but she misses having you around."

Anna rinsed out the dish rag at the sink. The familiar guilt unfurled in her stomach. "She did even when I lived there."

"Yeah," Julia agreed.

"I'm sorry you're taking care of her on your own again," Anna said. "I guess I didn't really follow through on that one."

"I know you need to take care of yourself. You've been through a lot. Mom does keep mentioning how much she hopes you'll be home by the middle of summer, though. But after talking with you the other day, I try to remind her of the possibility that you might not be back by then."

"At this point, I really have no idea," Anna said. But she knew that Boston was the last place she wanted to be right now.

"What are you up to today?"

Anna hesitated, not sure if she wanted to share her new morning routine with her sister. Then she decided to feel Julia out. "I've started meditating. I've read it can help with both spiritual and personal growth. This morning, I'm trying a new spot for my meditation to see if I like it."

"That's interesting," Julia said, a hint of cynicism in her voice. "I didn't know you were so into spirituality."

"I'm just trying to be open to different things," Anna replied.

"I see. Well, do what you have to do. But remember when it comes to religion, people can sometimes get carried away. You and I have always thought that." Her last few words were laced with conviction.

"I know we have," Anna said. She opened the kitchen window and felt the tension in her shoulders. She didn't need Julia to remind her of her past views on religion.

"Mom was always disappointed because we didn't go to church," Julia said, her voice taut. "Especially after Ben died. It looks like I'm the only delinquent one now."

"Meditating is hardly the same as going to church," Anna reasoned, feeling the warm breeze upon her face.

"You know how religious people are," Julia asserted. "They are right and everyone else is wrong. Mom's been that way forever."

"But I'm not Mom," Anna countered. "I don't think spirituality and religion are the same thing." She sighed. "I just need to see if meditating might make a difference for me. The Tao book I've been reading has really been enlightening."

"The Tao book?" her sister scoffed. "Since when are you into *that*?"

Anna wished she hadn't said anything. Her sister wasn't going to understand this. "It's just a book that was recommended to me."

"Well, maybe you want to watch whom you're getting recommendations from." Julia paused. "Are you going to mention this to Mom? If she hears you're studying the Tao, she's not going to be happy."

"I don't see the point in telling her right now," Anna whispered. "It's nothing she needs to know."

After hanging up the phone, Anna inhaled a few deep breaths. Julia had really hit a nerve. She didn't have to approve, but a little support would have been nice. Heading upstairs, Anna grabbed her journal and began to write.

> *Today is the big day. I'm going to meditate outside for the first time next to my oak tree. I don't imagine a vision will come my way, but I guess I have to start somewhere. Last night, an owl appeared in my tree signifying the search I have begun for my own inner light. Is being an attorney really what I want to do? Or is my light trying to lead me somewhere else?*

Later that morning, as Anna walked past Athena's fountain, she wondered if meditating would feel different today. When at last she stopped in front of the giant oak tree, she reached her arms around its massive trunk to see how big it was. She could only reach halfway around its girth. Selecting a level spot of grass in the shade overlooking the field of heather, she sat down "pretzel-style," as Sasha would have said. She smiled at the thought of her young niece.

Inhaling deeply, she closed her eyes and uttered, "Ah." She repeated this mantra, attempting to keep her mind clear.

She continued to breathe deeply, trying to relax every muscle in her body. After several still moments, a blue light became visible in her mind's eye. Gradually, thoughts about where she was going in Charleston that afternoon and what she might eat for lunch intruded. The light disappeared. She shook her head. *Focus. Stay focused.*

Anna quieted her mind again for several minutes until she heard the creaking of metal. Slowly, she opened her eyes to see a small bird perched on the top of an iron birdcage. Its wings fluttered as it opened its tiny beak to chirp. After singing a chorus or two, the bird flew to a branch higher in the tree.

Anna sighed. Meditating outside was a lot harder than she thought it would be. She stood up and brushed herself off. Silently, she thanked her tree and went inside.

ભ

Later that day, Anna walked into the quaint little beading shop Clark had told her about. Colorful seashell lights adorned the ceiling and strands of gems lined the walls. There were dozens of containers filled with beads in every size, shape, and color imaginable.

Wandering among the narrow aisles, Anna noticed something. When she fingered particular stones, they instigated certain emotions within her. Some beads drew upon her memories of the people she loved while others reminded her of places she had been. It was as though the stones were speaking to her. She knew logically that didn't make sense, but she couldn't deny it.

Her browsing over, she was pleased with her

collection of stones. Nearing the sales counter, Anna scoured through one last pile of painted wooden beads before placing four of them in her palm. Still peering down at them, she took a step and promptly bumped into someone. The beads slipped through her fingers and bounced across the floor.

"Oh, no!" Anna gasped. She quickly bent and tried to catch them before they rolled away.

"I'm sorry. Let me help you." A young woman crouched next to her.

"That's okay. I got it," Anna said as she reached for the last one.

They stood at the same time.

"I'm sorry for standing in the middle of the aisle," the woman apologized. "I was so busy looking around the store that I didn't even see you there."

"Well, I should've been watching where I was going," Anna said, looking at the woman. Her dark hair was pulled back in a ponytail and her luminous green eyes were bright and friendly. She wore black yoga pants and a patterned racerback tank top.

"Did you find your beads?"

"Yes," Anna said, peering down at the loose stones in her hand. "They're all here."

"Good. I don't want to be the one responsible for your losing them."

"Don't worry about that. I have exactly what I need." She dropped them inside her cloth bag.

"I'm Emily, by the way."

"Oh, I'm Anna." She met her gaze. "Nice to meet you."

"You have quite a collection," Emily said, tucking a loose strand of hair behind her ear.

"Yeah, I'm doing a project. It's my first time here. I can't believe how many beads they have!"

"That's what I love about this place. I make my own jewelry." She showed Anna a bracelet on her wrist. "I find it soothing to hold the beads in my hands. It helps me stay centered."

Anna nodded. She felt the same way. "Can I ask you something?"

"Sure."

"Is there a yoga studio nearby? I noticed your pants." She opened her palm toward them. "I read an article about yoga and it sounds like something I might like."

"Sure is," Emily said, picking out a clear bead from a nearby basket and glancing back at Anna. "I'm an instructor at a studio down the street. It's called Gentle Moves. You can stop in to find out about our classes or check them out online."

"Do you have a recommendation for me?" Anna inquired, stepping aside as another customer walked by. "I've never done yoga before. I'm more of a runner."

"Many runners find that yoga is beneficial for their workout routine," Emily explained. "I teach a beginner's class in Vinyasa yoga if you want to come and check it out." She smiled. "It's on Thursday mornings."

"Thanks." Anna liked the sound of the word "Vinyasa." It was soothing somehow. She stepped toward the sales counter.

Emily inspected another bead before looking over her shoulder at Anna. "I'm also leading a Soul Sister group once a month on Saturday nights. It's a group of women who come together in an open environment to connect with each other. We're meeting in a couple weeks if you're interested." She reached into her workout bag and handed Anna a flyer.

"What does the group do?" Anna asked. She placed her beads down on the counter so the cashier could ring her up.

"We do visualization exercises." She pointed toward one of the headings on the pamphlet. "They give us a chance to connect with ourselves and, if we choose, share our insights with others."

"That sounds interesting." Anna handed the cashier her credit card.

"It's a great experience. I've been doing it for many years. It's my favorite thing to teach."

"Okay, maybe I'll check it out." Anna placed the flyer and the bag of beads in her purse.

"Great. Nice meeting you, and good luck with your project."

# 19

Clark and Lucita were sitting on Anna's back porch steps as she came around the corner.

"Hey there, what are you doing?" she asked, surprised to see them waiting for her.

"Oh, we're talking about life, bugs, and spirits. Just the usual stuff," Clark said.

"Nothing strange about you two, that's for sure," Anna joked.

"Miss Anna, Miss Anna, what did you bring?" Lucita excitedly asked. "Mr. Clark told me you went to get something for a project for us. What are we going to do?"

Anna bent down in front of Lucita and opened up the bag. "Tell me what you see."

Lucita's eyes sparkled. "Beads. I see lots and lots of beads! What are they for?"

"I thought it would be fun for us to make prayer beads together."

Lucita stared up at her. "Can I use them to pray for Mama?"

"Of course you can. I will as well," Anna said. "They'll give us a chance to pray for the people we love and remind us of our connection with them."

"Miss Anna, thank you!" Lucita hugged her waist tightly.

Anna met Clark's gaze. Appreciation shone in his eyes.

"You know Clark also believes in angels," Lucita said with a wide grin.

"Does he?" Anna asked, arching an eyebrow.

"He believes they watch over us, offering their light and love."

"That's a comforting thought," Anna said.

"Comforting indeed," Clark said, patting Lucita's shoulder as he rose to his feet. "It looks like you two better get to work. I'll see you both a little later."

Anna retrieved a red-checkered tablecloth from the kitchen and spread it on the lawn so Lucita could dump out the beads.

"Pick out whatever ones remind you of your mama or speak to you in some way," Anna instructed. "I bought many different kinds, so you should have lots to choose from."

"This is great!" Lucita said, picking up a jessamy yellow bead. "I think this is going to be the best day of my life!"

Anna's heart warmed at Lucita's enthusiasm. She wanted to brighten up that little girl's life as much as she could.

The two of them made their selections and soon Lucita announced proudly, "I have mine!" She pointed toward a small pile of colorful beads in front of her knees. There were tiny circles and small rectangular stones in every color of the rainbow. It was a beautiful collection. "Can we do the next step?"

"Sure," Anna said

Over the next hour, the two of them carefully placed their beads onto the string and created the doughnut on the end to clasp it all together. When they were finished, Lucita was beaming.

"Look at the ladybug! I put it right in the middle,

between the ocean bead and the sunshine bead. It fits perfectly there!" She considered her handiwork before continuing. "I love how every bead feels different in my hands. This rough one reminds me of Papa because sometimes he can be rough around the edges, even though he means well. The red one reminds me of Mama because of her big heart and how much she loves me. This green crystal reminds me of you, Miss Anna, because you are starting a new life and trying to grow. The wooden leaf reminds me of Mr. Clark because he loves to garden. Finally, the lotus flower reminds me of Miss Lydia and her faith in all things."

Anna set down her beads and stared at Lucita. She had such insight for being so young.

"What are you thinking about?" Lucita asked, tilting her head and squinting with curiosity.

"That your beads are wonderful. I can see how they were each chosen with great care. You are a special girl." She squeezed Lucita's hand. "Always remember that."

Lucita shrugged her shoulders. "Of course I'm special. Aren't we all?"

Anna laughed. Lucita certainly had a way with words.

"Okay, Miss Anna, now it's your turn. Tell me about yours."

Anna rubbed her fingers along the smooth stones, as well as the ones that were irregularly shaped and slightly chipped on the corners. "I'd be happy to share them with you. Just like your prayer beads, the rectangular blue one with the wavy line reminds me of the ocean. The purple nugget of amethyst is my birthstone. The chipped wooden one reminds me that life is not perfect, and that we are all broken in some way. Yet, our flaws make us who we are. The metal one with many colored stones reminds me of my niece, Sasha, since she loves rainbows. The bright-blue crystal reminds me of my sister, Julia, and her blue eyes filled with concern and care, despite her own struggles." Anna then rubbed her fingers across the small angel and paused. *This one is for Claire.*

"Why does the angel make you sad?" Lucita asked. "Does it remind you of your dad?"

"No," Anna whispered. "It reminds me of a little girl I never had the chance to know."

Lucita touched Anna's hand. "Angels are everywhere. Miss Lydia taught me that. Maybe the girl is watching over you right now."

Anna smiled and hugged Lucita. "Maybe she is." Returning her fingers to the beads, she continued. "The owl reminds me of the wisdom that I seek. The smooth, brown stone with a cross etched in the middle reminds me to stay connected to my spirit. The yellow one reminds me of you, because you are a bright sunshine in my life."

Lucita's face broke into a broad grin.

"The small round bead with different hues of brown and white running through it reminds me of Clark and his love of the earth and nature. The clay bead with a turtle drawn on it reminds me of my mother. The painted dragonfly reminds me to live life from moment to moment, relishing every day as my father did. I was simply drawn to the amber, jade, and resin beads that remain. I can't explain it any more than that."

"I guess you know more about spiritual things than you thought," Lucita concluded. "Today you were the one teaching me!"

"We're all teachers of different things. When we learn something, we should share it instead of keeping it to ourselves."

"You sound an awful lot like Mr. Clark. Has he shared all of his ideas on life with you already?"

Anna grinned. "Not yet. But he's made me think

about the importance of staying true to who I really am. Does that make sense?"

Lucita nodded. "I've been hearing that my whole life from Miss Lydia and Mr. Clark. They always encourage me to do the things I love, even when they're hard."

"They're both very wise," Anna said, looking off into the distance. "Did I tell you I saw an owl last night?"

"You did? What did it look like?"

"He had brown and white feathers with tufts on the top of his head. His eyes glowed like amber against the dark night and he stared down at me before he flew away."

"Wow! Where did you see him?"

"Right up there in those branches," Anna said, pointing to the tall limbs of the oak.

"I bet he really liked you," Lucita said, placing her hands on her hips.

"Why?"

"Because owls are really smart and so are you." Satisfaction filled her voice.

Anna laughed. Somehow, Lucita's simple logic always made perfect sense.

"Miss Anna," Lucita said, standing up. "I want to show Mr. Clark my prayer beads. Do you want to come along too?"

"Sure, why don't we go show him?" Anna accompanied Lucita to Clark's house. He was in the flower garden by his back porch. The purple irises were in full bloom. "You aren't working too hard, I hope," Anna teased.

"Oh, nothing I can't handle," Clark said with a grin.

"Mr. Clark, look at what Miss Anna and I made!" Lucita thrust her prayer beads toward him.

Clark took off his worn, tan gloves and inspected the bracelet. He whistled in admiration. "Wow, this is beautiful."

"Miss Anna let me choose whatever beads I wanted. Each of them reminds me of someone, even you!"

"What an honor! I'm a bead on your bracelet." He held out the bracelet in his palm. "May I ask which one?"

"Sure. You are the wooden leaf," she said, pointing to the brown bead. "It shows how much you love to grow things!"

Clark nodded and stroked his goatee. "Well, that sure sounds like me."

"They're my special prayer beads, and now whenever I see them, I will pray for people. Isn't that a great idea?" She jumped up and down, clapping her hands.

"Yes, it definitely is."

"Miss Anna made one too. Do you want to see it?"

He smiled and turned toward her. "I'd love to see your handiwork."

Anna opened up her hand to reveal the string of nearly twenty beads. The distinctive circle of stones was slightly bigger than a bracelet and dangled over the edge of her palm. "Here it is."

"May I hold it?"

"Go ahead."

Clark ran his fingers along the beads and closed his eyes. "It has a good feel about it. I think it will serve you well."

"I hope so."

Lucita tugged on Clark's other hand. "Did you know Miss Anna also has a bead on there to remind her of you?"

"She does?" Clark asked with surprise.

Anna fingered the brown and white bead. "I figured you were the one who introduced me to prayer beads and meditation. You also encouraged me to open myself up to new experiences. It was only right to have a bead on there that reminds me of you, so your kind spirit will never be forgotten."

"I appreciate that. You've become more relaxed since I first saw you. You seem more open to things."

"That's what I think too!" Lucita exclaimed. "She seems different somehow. Better though, definitely better."

"There might be hope for me after all," Anna said, smiling.

"Miss Anna, do you think maybe these beads will help my mama heal if I pray hard enough?"

Anna shared a concerned glance with Clark. "I don't know, but it can't hurt to try."

She nodded her head fervently. Then she hugged each of them. "See you tomorrow!"

Together, Clark and Anna watched Lucita prance and twirl up the hill singing until her joyful melody was lost on the wind.

"I hope the beads make a difference for her, but I'm afraid time is not on Esperanza's side."

"No," Clark agreed. "It doesn't appear to be."

"Do you think making the prayer beads gave Lucita false hope about her mama getting well again?"

Clark folded his hands. "It's never wrong to give someone hope."

Anna sighed. "Thanks for showing me your prayer beads last week. Mine are special to me already, and I know how much Lucita's mean to her."

Clark pulled on his gardening gloves. "Did you do any meditating this morning?"

She nodded. "I tried to keep silent, but thoughts kept creeping into my mind."

"That's because your mind is not used to being still. Thoughts are always running through our minds. That's why silencing them becomes so important. It's the only way we can connect within and attain inner peace."

"I know I have to keep trying."

"You'll get the hang of it," he said, reaching for his hoe. "You'll see."

# 20

Large picture windows lined the outer walls of the Gentle Moves studio. Twilight had descended upon the city, and a thin crescent moon hung low in the lavender sky. In her keyhole tank and yoga capris, Anna felt a pleasant warmth douse her bare skin. Soft New Age music and shimmering candlelight imbued the studio with tranquility. Several women were relaxing in contented postures on soft pillows and bolsters.

Anna settled into a space within the circle and surrounded herself with soothing cushions and a cozy wool blanket. Rolling back her shoulders, she closed her eyes. *Source, please open my mind and my spirit to whatever experience awaits me. Help me learn something about myself, no matter how difficult it may be.*

Anna opened her eyes and watched Emily lower herself onto her yoga mat.

"Good evening, everyone. My name is Emily and I want to welcome all of you to our Soul Sister Circle tonight. I'm thrilled to have you here on this beautiful May evening," Emily said. "As I glance around our group, I notice a few new faces, as well as some familiar ones. So to begin, I'm going to share what circling is all about."

She clasped her hands. "Circling is an opportunity for women from all walks of life to gather together for a time of connection, inspiration, and healing," Emily explained, readjusting her pose. "It provides a place where women can unconditionally support one another."

She glanced at Anna. "In our world, there are two interconnected energies. They are the yin, or feminine energy, and the yang, or masculine energy. The yin represents connection, intuition, and nurturing, while the yang represents aggression, action, and accomplishment. Each of us possesses both of these energies, and when they are balanced, we live in harmony."

Emily took a deep breath and then continued. "However, in our culture, many of us have been taught to value the yang at the expense of the yin. We base success solely on our material accomplishments, always striving for more. We never take the time to reflect upon the things we have achieved, causing intuition to fall to the background where its importance is devalued. This yang-dominated thinking comes at an incredible cost for women, and for society as a whole."

From what Emily described, it was clear that Anna had spent her life focusing on the yang. She had valued success and achievement above all else. The focus on the yang had cost her dearly in her relationships. It was time for her to connect more with the yin.

Emily glanced at each of the women in turn. "Our circle tonight is for all women, regardless of age or faith. It's a place for renewal in a supportive and compassionate community. As the famous poet Matthew Arnold once wrote, 'If ever the world sees a time when women shall come together purely and simply for the benefit of mankind, it will be a power such as the world has never known.' May you feel that power within you."

Anna's heart swelled as she thought about the power that resided within all women, even herself. Their strength, compassion, and love were unparalleled. If women combined their efforts, they really could change the world.

Emily rose to her feet and collected a small stack of papers from the floor. "To open our circle, we'll call together the four corners of the earth and all the elements of nature, welcoming them into our sacred space. As each of the passages is read aloud, I'll light a small candle to represent nature's presence here with us tonight."

Anna adjusted her position on the mat and looked at the group of women around her. They represented a diverse range of ages, ethnicities, and socio-economic backgrounds. The youngest woman had thick dreadlocks and a shiny nose ring. She looked like a college student still trying to find her way. An elderly woman sat next to Emily. Her short, gray hair and glasses could not hide the many laugh lines she had earned over the years. Across the circle, a plump woman with black hair was dressed in bold colors. Beads hung around her neck and her jaw was strong and chiseled. She looked like a leader who knew how to captivate a room. Finally, next to Anna sat a tall, slender woman. Her posture was rigid and she wore a serious expression. Anna wondered what was troubling her, and whether she had been to the group before.

"We'll start with the east and go around the room with each woman reading her passage aloud," Emily explained. Then she knelt down in the middle of the circle, ready to light the first candle.

"To the east," the young woman began, "the time of the crescent moon, the season of spring, the element of air, and the dawn of the new day. We are grateful for the creative inspiration each new day brings during this season of renewal and rebirth. We give thanks for the warmth of the new morning sun and the continual opportunity to start fresh again in our lives. Let inspiration and vision come forth in new and beautiful ways, ever enriching the essence of our own potential."

Anna was struck by the connection between the moon, the seasons, the elements, and time. She had never heard of anything like this before. Yet, it intrigued her. Could all of those things really be connected? And if spring were the time of new beginnings, then her journey was aptly timed. Could it be that she was given rebirth during the very season her daughter would have been born? Was that somehow significant or was she crazy to think so?

"To the south: the time of the full moon, the warm season of summer, the element of fire, and noontime each day," the older woman said. "We are grateful for strength to take action and bring thoughts into fruition during this most active of seasons. We give thanks for the illumination of the sun and full moon that enable us to see what needs to be seen and do what needs to be done. Our spirit is fueled by the fire of our passion and the power of our will. We take action to fulfill our calling and honor that which our heart aches for most."

Anna tried to process the words that she was hearing, but it was all so new. Were passion and will connected? Did her heart really have a calling? That seemed so strange. She always believed her career was supposed to be her passion. But being a successful lawyer had nothing to do with her heart. She worked hard whether she loved it or not. It wasn't about what she wanted to do. It was about what she needed to do.

"To the west," the dark-skinned woman read, "the time of the waning crescent moon, the season of autumn, the element of water, and the time of dusk each day. We are grateful for this season of transition and change. We embrace its uncertainty and know it helps build strength and faith. It is a time of preparation for the upcoming winter, when we turn inward. We practice forgiveness for others and ourselves as we flow with the ups and downs of life. Emotions come and go, and we are open to the love and acceptance that comes from this understanding."

Thinking upon her recent transition, Anna wondered what it had been for. She had needed to take time away and now that she had, would she be able to face her past? Would she allow herself to lose control long enough so she could feel again? She let out a deep breath.

"To the north," the woman beside her began, "the time of the new moon, the cold season of winter, the element of earth, and the time of midnight. This is the period where the outer world is the darkest and we must go within. Listening and reflecting, we connect with the center of our beings, trusting that like the light that always returns in the spring, we too will come through dark times with newfound wisdom and strength. We give thanks for this truth and know we are unconditionally supported even in the darkest of nights."

Anna exhaled. She had been trying to go within for the past month. But whenever she did, it reminded her of the shame and inadequacy she felt. In her life, she had hurt everyone she loved ... Sasha, Julia, her mother, Frederick. She had gradually become numb to everything. A tear streamed down her cheek. Anna knew she wasn't worthy of love. She simply didn't deserve it.

"Every time we meet," Emily continued, "we have the opportunity to hear our chant. It is the song, 'Love, Serve, and Remember,' written and performed by John Astin. Feel free to sing along, if you like."

*Why have you come to earth, do you remember?*
*Why have you taken birth, why have you come?*

*To love, serve, and remember.*
*To love, serve, and remember.*
*To love ...*

Anna listened to the words and thought about her purpose for coming into this world. Was it really that simple? She sighed.

The room fell silent once again as Emily smiled. "Each of you has come to the circle tonight with your own intention or reason for being here. I'm going to ask you to place your hands over your heart and take a few moments to reflect upon your intention and what you need from our group tonight."

As Anna rested her hands upon her chest, she knew at some point she had to stop being afraid. There was hope that she could change.

"Now," Emily said, glancing at Anna, "let's go around the circle and have each of you state your name and your intention for the evening."

Anna listened as the other women in the circle mentioned connection, balance, and wisdom. When it was her turn, she breathed in deeply and said, "My name is Anna, and my intention for the evening is acceptance." Anna needed to accept the person she was right now, even if she wasn't who she wanted to be.

"Thank you," Emily whispered.

As the other women continued to share, Anna stared at the small flames burning in the center of the circle. Continually beating herself up for the past wasn't going to change it. She had to stop hating herself for the things that couldn't be undone.

"We've all shared some things that are in our hearts," Emily said quietly. "For tonight's circle, we're going to focus on the inner light that burns within each of us. This light is always aflame, trying to guide us on our way. Yet, sometimes due to life's circumstances, it can be reduced to barely a flicker. As a result, during our time together tonight, each of us will have a chance to reconnect with our inner light and listen for its guidance."

Anna's mouth dropped open in surprise. Frederick had used that same language in his letter. He had said her light had become only a flicker and that he wanted her to find happiness again. But maybe the happiness she needed wasn't about finding something; it was about finding and loving herself.

Emily glanced at a large white candle in the middle of the circle. Its wick crackled as the flame burned brightly.

"Scattered around this large candle are several smaller votive candles. Each of you will have the opportunity to use the existing flame to light one of these." Emily's eyes scanned the group. "The votive will symbolize your inner light."

For the next few minutes, Anna watched as the sea of lit candles steadily began to grow. Walking toward the center, she bent and lit the wick of a candle and placed it back upon the wooden floor. The flame flickered and danced. Returning to her pillow, she focused on the candle she had just lit, the symbol of her inner light. She had to somehow find her light and let go of everything that kept it from burning ... her need for control, anger at herself and Frederick, hurt from the divorce, and shame over Claire's death. All of this burned within her, but it consumed her in darkness, not in light. These were the reasons she couldn't go within.

"As we look upon the array of candles burning before us," Emily said, "we are reminded that the light within us is always present, leading and guiding us along life's journey. It's through listening to this light that we're able to find our passion, the very thing we're placed upon this planet to do. So tonight, I'm going to lead us in a visualization exercise where we'll have the opportunity to relax and reflect upon our inner purpose and passion. Please take a few moments to make yourself comfortable."

Settling herself upon her yoga mat, Anna closed her eyes as the hollow sounds of the sitar rose from the speakers. She listened to its gentle melody and placed her hands on her heart. Focusing on her breath, she attempted to prevent intrusive thoughts. When those thoughts did come, she imagined them as clouds drifting across a clear, blue sky fading from view.

"As you relax," Emily began, "find yourself in a place where you love to spend time. Perhaps it's near the ocean or the forest or even a garden. As you visualize this place, let it offer you comfort and peace."

Anna visualized her place immediately. It was the oak tree from her dream. She saw its gnarled roots digging deep within the earth and its twisted branches climbing toward the heavens.

"Now envision the thing in this world for which you have the most passion. What brings you great joy? What helps you feel alive? Visualize this passion residing within your heart. Can you feel its presence? This passion is your guide. Let it lead you."

Anna hoped if she listened to her heart, it would tell her something. She reflected upon the things that brought her great joy and began to visualize the heart that was pounding steadily beneath her hands. As she remained focused upon that image, she observed a white letter being engraved upon her heart. Anna held her breath as another letter was formed, and then another. When at last she read the word, a warm sensation filled her chest and permeated her entire body. She had gotten an answer. The letters had spelled the word "write."

"Now take a moment to reflect upon your passion," Emily said softly. "When you are finished, please sit up and open your eyes." Anna remained motionless for a few moments. Writing was something that had gradually faded from her life. She buried her feelings in hopes they would fade away. But a life devoid of feeling was no way to live. The Tao book explained that struggle made life have meaning. Metal did not bend without the fire. Change could not come without effort and reflection. A tear streamed down her cheek. She had given up creating a long time ago. It was time to create once again.

Opening her eyes, she sat up with her hands still placed upon her heart. The candles cast a soft glow around the room. In the silence that surrounded her, Anna felt a peace within herself she had never known. She had finally learned how to mediate and quiet her mind. Only then had her purpose become clear.

The exercises compelled Anna to go immediately to her journal when she got home. When her father had died, she wrote a poem about her greatest memories of him. The thoughts had poured from her onto the paper. It was time she tried it again.

> *I'm lost in the caverns of my own thoughts,*
> *Held captive by their chains of reason.*
> *Thrashing, pulling, I try to escape,*
> *But the bonds hold firm their grasp.*
> *Panting, crying, my body tires,*
> *And slowly comes to rest.*
> *As quiet stillness fills the air,*
> *Doubts pervade my mind.*
> *Will this torture ever end?*
> *Can I survive the pain?*
> *At long last, a gentle sigh,*
> *And the torments start to fade.*
> *With each breath comes new hope,*
> *Awareness settles in.*

*Who is the warden of these chains?*
*It's purely and simply me.*
*I'm the keeper of the keys,*
*Will they unlock my soul?*
*Searching, probing, will I find*
*The answers that I seek?*
*The bonds are off, the bonds are on,*
*When will my heart be free?*

Reading it over, Anna realized she needed to let go and start listening to her inner light, believing that she was worthy. She had become a prisoner to her negative thoughts, and the only way to break free was to love and accept herself, unconditionally.

# 21

The garden was flourishing with flowers by the time May turned to June. Anna knelt by the path, tugging the weeds that had grown in through the dark mulch. A stone paver at the garden's edge caught her attention. Imprinted upon the brick was the yin-and-yang symbol, subtle yet distinct. The irony of its location shot a thrill through her. She had learned about the energies of the yin and the yang at her Soul Sister Circle and here it was, right in her own backyard. She looked toward her tree. It seemed spirituality was everywhere around here. As she smiled to herself, Lucita appeared in the distance.

"Miss Anna, Miss Anna, guess what?" Lucita shouted as she skipped across the yard, wearing a bright green rain jacket. Not watching where she was going, she nearly tripped over the stone birdbath.

"Be careful, Sweetie. What are you so excited about?"

"I found a ladybug outside my window this morning, and I'm going to bring her with us on our trip today."

Anna considered the cloud-covered sky. "I'm not sure it's the best day to go down to the beach. It looks like we're in for some rain."

"Oh, please, Miss Anna. School's finally out for the summer. I've been waiting for this day all year!"

"I know you have, but the weather is supposed to be better tomorrow."

Lucita frowned. "But I was really hoping we could go today."

"Okay," Anna relented. "We can go." She traced the yin-and-yang symbol with her finger before she stood up.

"I see you found Miss Lydia's favorite symbol," Lucita said, pointing down at the paver.

"That was her favorite?"

Lucita nodded. "Miss Lydia said the circle of this symbol stood for unity. She loved the wisdom of the yin-and-yang symbol so much that she placed it around the entire garden."

"Everywhere?" Anna asked with surprise.

"Oh, yes. Miss Lydia said we could never be exposed to too much harmony. And she believed unity could be found even among people who were different from each other."

"If only everyone saw things that way," Anna said. Her gaze fell on the tiny ladybug that was now crawling across Lucita's knuckle. "Are you really going to take that ladybug to the beach?"

"She'll bring us good luck. Besides, she fits perfectly in my pocket." Lucita slipped the ladybug into the pocket of her denim cut-offs. Patting it gently, she said, "Can we go now?"

Anna nodded. When Lucita tugged on the sleeve of her jacket to pull it closer to her wrist, Anna noticed that it was even more snug than the last time she had worn it. "Follow me. I have something for you." She beckoned to Lucita with a wink.

In the foyer, Anna reached into the coat closet and pulled out a pink, polka-dot rain jacket. "What do you think?"

"That's for me?" Lucita gasped.

"I found it in a shop when I was in town the other day. I know how much you love pink, so I couldn't resist. I especially love the ruffle on the bottom."

Anna helped Lucita put her arms into the sleeves before buttoning it.

"Thank you, Miss Anna," Lucita gushed. "I love it. It's the nicest coat I've ever had!" She ran her hands along the edges.

Anna pinched her cheek. "You're welcome. Now, we'd better get going."

Anna drove them to Sullivan's Island and when they arrived, the sandy shoreline was deserted. Thick blankets of clouds blocked out any sign of the sun. Walking alongside the churning water, Anna held Lucita's hand.

"I used to love coming to this beach," Lucita said, her voice distant. "The seagulls and shells, the wind and waves. I've really missed this place."

"Did you come here often?" Anna asked. Ashen waves rolled toward shore. She loved the hypnotic rhythm of the surf.

"When I was younger, Papa used to throw me in the air and build sand castles with me. Mama made our picnic lunch. Afterwards, we would all go swimming." Lucita took the small ladybug from her pocket and studied it. "The beach reminds me of those times."

"It reminds me of happier times too, Lucita," Anna whispered.

A cool drop of rain fell from the dismal, gray clouds, splashing on Anna's skin. Then several more raindrops fell onto her cheeks. Studying Lucita's sad expression, Anna felt sorry for her and wanted to lift her spirits. Suddenly, she had an idea.

"Would you like to dance in the rain with me?"

Lucita gaped at her. "Really?"

"Yeah, I think it'd be fun."

"Okay, let's do it!" she cried, carefully placing the ladybug in her coat pocket.

Anna grabbed Lucita's small hands and the two of them began prancing along the shoreline on their tippy toes, raising and lowering their arms as if they were flying. As they frolicked across the sand, Lucita began to sing. Her rousing melody was quiet at first, until it gradually grew into a boisterous song. They splashed through the waves, clasped hands, and twirled faster and faster until at last they let go and fell to the ground laughing.

Elated, Anna let the cool raindrops sprinkle her face. Who knew basking in the rain could be so much fun?

After catching their breath, they grasped hands and helped each other stand up. Lucita was beaming, her cheeks flushed.

"That was awesome!" she exclaimed.

"Maybe we'll have to dance in the rain more often," Anna said with a chuckle.

"Sounds good to me."

It continued to drizzle as they walked along the shore.

"Can I hold the umbrella?" Lucita asked.

"Sure, hopefully it will help keep us dry."

Lucita twirled the rainbow-striped umbrella as they strode across the damp sand. "I know one thing for sure."

"What's that?"

"We'll never get lost today."

"Why do you say that?" Anna asked.

"With your canary-yellow rain jacket, people will see us coming from a mile away."

Anna's lips curved into a smile. "Well, I happen to like it. Sorry if it's a little too loud for your taste," Anna teased.

Lucita squeezed her hand. "Can we come here every week now that school's out?"

"That sounds like fun. But hopefully it won't be raining every time."

"If we get to dance, that would be okay with me."

Anna laughed. "I think we could make just about anything fun."

"As long as it's exercise, you'll like it." Lucita spun around in a circle. "Is that why you like running? You do it almost every morning."

"It helps me stay in shape and get out my frustrations," Anna admitted.

"What do you mean?"

"When I get upset or angry about something, I go for a run. It calms me down and lets me forget about things for a while."

"Does that help?"

Anna was quiet for a moment. "Sometimes."

Lucita shook her head. "Miss Lydia said that it's wrong to run away from problems."

"She's a smart lady," Anna said, watching the large waves crest in the distance. "I'm still learning that."

"She said even if they're hard to fix, you should at least face them." Lucita paused and kicked the sand with her rain boot. "I think that's why it's hard for Papa to see Mama so sick. It's something he can't fix."

Anna put her arm around Lucita as heavy raindrops fell from the sky. "The most difficult problems are the ones we can't find a solution to. They can hurt us for a really long time."

Lucita twirled the umbrella between her fingers. "That's why you have to let them go. Otherwise, they'll keep making you sad."

"That's true, but sometimes it's hard." Anna breathed

in the damp sea air. It stirred her soul like a haunting melody.

"That's what makes it worth doing. At least that's what Miss Lydia always said."

"She's right." But letting go of past hurts was more difficult than Anna had imagined, even now.

"We have to take chances and believe," Lucita said, picking up a seashell. "I've heard that my whole life."

"That's really good advice," Anna admitted, hearing a rumbling of thunder in the distance. "That's what I did when I came down here, and I'm so glad I took that chance."

"Me too," Lucita said with a grin. "You're one of my best friends."

Anna grabbed Lucita's hand and started running as the rain poured from the skies. "Well then, this best friend is going to get you home and out of the rain."

Even though Anna drove back to Lucita's house, they were both soaked when they got there. Water pooled on the deck around their feet.

"We look like we went for a swim," Lucita laughed.

"You're home!" Esperanza was gasping for air when she opened the front door. "It sure is a wet one out there."

"Yeah," Lucita said. "But we still went to the beach, and it was so much fun!"

"Hello, Anna." Esperanza said after catching her breath. "Thanks for bringing Lucita home safely."

"Of course," Anna said. "We had a great time."

"Is that a new jacket?" Esperanza asked, touching the slippery fabric with her fingers.

Lucita twirled around and nodded enthusiastically. "Miss Anna gave it to me. Isn't it beautiful?"

"It sure is. You look like a princess. I hope you said thank you."

"I did," Lucita said, rolling her eyes.

Esperanza looked up at Anna. "That's a nice gift."

Anna patted Lucita's head. "I knew it was perfect for her when I saw it in the store. I couldn't resist."

Esperanza nodded. "Will you please come in for some tea and warm up? I don't want you to catch a cold."

"Are you sure?" Anna asked.

"Of course." Esperanza said kindly. "It'll just be us girls. Bernardo's out working in the barn."

"I'll fill the kettle, Mama." Lucita unbuttoned her coat and hung it on the hook next to the door before dashing into the kitchen. Esperanza followed her.

Anna slipped off her coat, hung it beside Lucita's, and walked into the living room. On either side of the blue sofa stood two blue chairs that faced a corner brick fireplace. Brass table lamps cast a soft glow around the room while beautiful glass vases and bowls added a touch of charm. Sitting in the blue chair nearest the fireplace, Anna stared at the welded metal tree scene that hung on the wall. Their branches bare, the winter trees were a symbol of desolate beauty.

A few minutes later, Lucita and Esperanza entered the room with a tray of tea cups, napkins, and Oreo cookies. Lucita set the tray on the wooden coffee table before sitting beside her mama on the sofa.

"Oreos are my favorite," Lucita declared. "Do you want one, Miss Anna?"

"Double-stuffed are the best," Anna agreed. As she popped one into her mouth, she stared at the glass figurine on the wooden mantel. "I love that hummingbird. Looks like it's drinking nectar from a flower. The pink and green colors are so vivid."

"Papa made it," Lucita said proudly. "He makes things out of glass. He even lets me watch him sometimes."

"He's a glassblower?" Anna asked, unable to contain her surprise.

"Yeah. He used to work for a glass company." Lucita twisted apart her Oreo and licked the cream filling. "But now he makes his own stuff."

"That's incredible." Anna stared at the hummingbird, still struggling to believe Bernardo had made something so beautiful.

"See that purple, yellow, and blue vase on the table?" Lucita pointed across the room. "He made that for Mama after they got married. We put flowers from the garden in it."

Anna glanced at the vase. With its scalloped edges and swirl of color, it looked as though it belonged in an art gallery. "Is his studio in the barn?"

Lucita nodded.

"He spends hours out there," Esperanza explained. She smoothed out the napkin on her lap. "It helps calm him when he's troubled."

Anna imagined he spent a lot of time out there these days.

Esperanza let out a small cough. She gripped her cup of tea with shaking fingers. "It brings him some happiness, even now."

Esperanza's pale face made Anna wonder why sickness had to happen. Her heart heavy, she reached for her own cup of tea. A woman so young shouldn't have to struggle for breath.

"Do you know what I like to do with Mama?" Lucita asked, trying to get Anna's attention.

"What's that?"

"Sewing. It's so much fun! Can I show you a couple of things I made?" She stood up and clapped her hands excitedly.

"I'd love to see them."

"I'll be right back!" she said as she raced for the stairs.

Once she was gone, Esperanza slowly turned toward Anna. "She's loved spending time with you these past months."

The mention of time was like a splash of cold water. Nearly three months had passed since she arrived. She had promised her boss, Tom, she would check in with him. He had been right to make her take some time off. It had helped clear her head. But, surprisingly, she still wasn't ready to go back. Guilt seeped in. It was time to give him a call.

"Lucita talks about you all the time," Esperanza continued. "Every night she sleeps with her prayer beads."

"She's a joy to be with," Anna confessed. "She reminds me how much fun life can be."

"A child can do that. They're easy to love," Esperanza said quietly.

Anna nodded. It was true. She had come to love Lucita. She couldn't imagine not seeing her face every day.

"These next few months are going to be very hard on her. They're going to be hard on all of us." Esperanza paused and twisted the wedding ring upon her finger. "I saw the doctor yesterday, and he said the cancer is continuing to spread." A raspy cough suddenly erupted from her.

Unsure what to do, Anna anxiously jumped up and sat next to her on the sofa. She rubbed her back as she had seen Bernardo do months ago.

Esperanza struggled for several minutes to regain her composure. At last, her breathing returned to normal.

"I'm sorry the cancer is spreading," Anna said. "Please let me know if there's anything I can do." But her offer sounded so hollow. It was what everyone said when they didn't know what to say. She wanted to do more for them, but she didn't know what.

"I don't want my family to be a burden to anyone," Esperanza whispered.

Anna shook her head. "You're not a burden. I'm happy to help, and I know Clark and John are too." She wanted Esperanza to believe they would be there for her.

"If only Bernardo would let you." A troubled expression crossed Esperanza's face but before she could continue, Lucita sprinted into the living room, her hands full of fabric.

"Look, Miss Anna! It's a purse, two sets of clothes for my dolly, a skirt for me, and a blanket. What do you think?"

Anna smiled at the pile of treasures Lucita brought in. "Your mama has taught you well."

Lucita's eyes shone as she placed the pink blanket over Anna's shoulders. "You could even use this for a shawl. That's the best thing about sewing. You can make anything!"

The front door swung open. Bernardo stood in the doorway, his hair and jacket wet from the rain.

"Papa! Have you finished the pitcher you were making? The one with different colors?"

"Yeah," he said as his eyes settled upon Anna. "It's cooling now."

"Hello, Bernardo. How are you?" Anna asked, hoping her presence wouldn't upset him.

"Busy," he snapped. He wiped off his work boots on the rug and turned toward the kitchen without another word.

"Oh, Bernardo," Esperanza said, unsteadily rising to her feet. "Where are your manners?"

He nodded and turned apologetically to his wife. "I best be grabbing some water and finishing up." He disappeared into the kitchen for a moment and then returned with a bottle of water in his hand. "Please don't overdo it, Esperanza. You know how visitors can tire you out. That's why I prefer they don't come over. After they leave, you have to sleep for hours just to recover."

"It's nice to have the company," Esperanza replied.

"I'm sure it is," he said, glaring at Anna before walking out the door again.

Esperanza sighed. "Don't mind him. It takes him a long time to warm up to people."

"Do you have family nearby to help out?"

Esperanza shook her head. "All of our parents have passed away."

Anna nodded. That was all the more reason for her and Clark to stay close. "If you need anything, I'm here. Even if it's just for a little company."

"Thank you," Esperanza said, reaching for her hand. "I may just take you up on that."

# 22

The following afternoon, Anna drove along the bustling streets of Charleston. With the sun reflecting upon the clear blue water and a warm breeze blowing in from the coast, it was a perfect summer day.

After parking the car, Anna marveled at the towering palmetto trees and the exuberant tourists flocking to purchase souvenirs at the open-air market. Strolling along Waterfront Park and the Battery, she inhaled the fresh sea air and relished the lush gardens blooming with color. Boats glided peacefully along the harbor and children climbed the majestic branches of the giant oaks. Meandering along narrow roadways, she discovered quiet neighborhoods that smelled of freshly-mown grass and quaint little shops hidden away like precious jewels. Humming to herself, she passed by a small, locally owned coffee shop and decided to stop.

An old-fashioned bell on the door chimed when she entered. Canisters filled with assorted coffee beans lined the long counter beside the back wall. Several comfy couches and chairs, along with a few tables, created a cozy and inviting atmosphere. Local artwork filled the walls. Hand-painted mugs, engraved journals, and artisan jewelry were tastefully displayed on various wooden shelves.

Closing her eyes, Anna breathed in the aroma of freshly roasted coffee.

"May I help you?" an attractive woman asked from behind the counter. She had blond curls and looked to be around Anna's age. Her silver hoop earrings and jeweled necklace sparkled in the sunlight.

"I would like a white chocolate mocha, please."

"Whipped cream?"

"Yes, but only a little."

The woman handed a wide, ceramic mug to a young man who was standing near the espresso machine. His dark dreadlocks hung halfway down his back and a thin horseshoe mustache accentuated his full lips. Placing the mug under the machine, he flexed his muscular bicep, partially revealing a tattoo hidden beneath his black T-shirt.

"I don't think I've seen you in here before," the woman remarked, looking Anna over.

"No, you haven't," Anna said, trying not to let the woman's curious gaze bother her. "I'm new to the area."

"I see," she said. "I'm Jillian, the owner."

"Did you decorate the place? I like the antiques, and the sea paintings are gorgeous."

"Yes, they are," Jillian replied as she grabbed a container of milk from the small fridge.

Anna stared back at Jillian. Where was *her* Southern hospitality?

"Here's your coffee, Miss," the young man said, handing her the large mug with whipped cream and chocolate shavings.

"Thank you." Anna left the counter to weave past a group of college students huddled around a laptop and an older gentleman reading the local newspaper. She sat at a round table next to a row of windows adorned with panels of stained glass.

She watched Jillian for a few moments, wondering why she wasn't very friendly. It seemed that if you owned a business you would want to treat all your customers well. Shrugging it off, Anna pulled out her journal and began to write.

> *Charleston is an enchanting city filled with bountiful treasures. Lavish gardens, historical mansions, and breathtaking vistas create a perfect setting for solitude while the lively marketplace invites even the weariest of travelers to explore its riches. Yet, despite the splendor all around me, I can't get Esperanza's face out of my mind. She struggles so much. Her shallow breaths signify the sickness hidden deep within. Seeing her in such pain, I despair that there is nothing I can do. But, as difficult as it is to watch her slowly fading away, I can't let her suffering prevent me from visiting her. I have a way of avoiding things that I don't want to see. I've been doing that for far too long.*

As the door jangled open, Anna was startled to see Simon walk in. She hadn't seen him since dinner at Clark's. She watched him brush a curl behind his ear as he walked over to the counter.

Jillian waved to him with a big smile. She was talking and laughing, a very different person from the one who had taken her order. Jillian gently touched Simon's arm, but he didn't seem to notice.

He grabbed his coffee and turned to leave. Anna quickly looked down at her journal, pretending to write.

"Hey Anna, it's nice to see you again."

She looked up, feigning surprise so that he wouldn't

know she had been watching him. "Oh, you too," she said. His royal blue polo and khaki pants flattered his slender frame. "Do you work around here?"

He nodded. "Just up the street, actually. I come in here quite a bit." He put his hand in his pocket. "What about you? Are you working on something important?"

"No, just doing some writing."

"Mind if I join you?"

"Not at all." A shiver ran through her. But she shook it off, determined not to let him affect her the way he did at Clark's house. As Simon sat across from her, Anna couldn't help but notice the scowl that crossed Jillian's face.

"You have an awfully fancy drink there," he said, pointing to her half-empty mug. "Are you a high-maintenance coffee drinker?"

"Yes, I guess I am. My sister always told me I liked my coffee to be more like hot chocolate than anything else. If coffee is black, I can't stand to drink it. But add some cream and sugar, and I'm good to go." She tilted her head and looked down at his mug of steaming black coffee. "What about you? Have you always liked it straight up?"

"Yeah, I'm not much for adding anything to coffee. The stronger the better, if you ask me." He took a sip from his mug.

"No, thanks," she said, making a sour face. "Liquid tar just doesn't appeal to me."

Simon laughed. "I guess you'll have to be the sweet one and I'll be the ... straight-up one."

"Well, that's better than being the bitter one," she teased.

"Yes, I suppose it is."

From his tanned complexion, Anna figured he enjoyed spending time outdoors. His cheekbones were chiseled and his brown eyes were warm.

"Why are you looking at me like that?" he asked quizzically.

"I'm trying to read your face," she said, as if people did that kind of thing all the time.

He leaned back in his chair, his gaze curious. "What's it telling you?"

"It's telling me you're a kind man who doesn't try to be someone he isn't."

His expression turned thoughtful. "You must have a knack for reading faces because that seems to about cover it. Do you do this type of thing for a living?"

"Not exactly. Although as a lawyer, reading people's faces does come in handy."

"I imagine it does." His eyes danced as if he enjoyed their little banter.

And the truth was, Anna enjoyed it too. It made her feel desirable again. That type of attention was hard to turn down. She took a slow sip from her mug. "How's Magnus these days?"

"He's good. Still crazy, but he loves running with me along the beach."

"You run?"

"Yeah, a little." He shrugged and stroked his chin. "I like to stay in shape."

"I can see that," she said, looking at his lean, athletic build. He was sexier than she cared to admit. "You seem like the outdoor, adventurous-type."

"Again, you have me pegged," he said with a grin. "You're really good at this. Anything else about me you want to guess?" His eyes dared her to say more, much more.

"No, I think I'll let you take it from here." She looked out the window for a moment, her stomach fluttering. When she gazed at Simon again, a smile curved his lips.

"Wise decision, I'd say."

Anna glanced to the counter where she was pinned by Jillian's icy glare. She looked away, puzzled. What was that all about? She was just talking to Simon. Jillian didn't even know her.

"How's Clark doing?" Simon asked.

"He's great," Anna replied, turning her attention back to him. "He's so much fun to be with."

Simon took a sip of his coffee. "I know you and Clark have become friends. He said you two have talked a lot about meditation. I'm curious … do you find it helpful?" He leaned forward, his wavy hair framing his narrow face, high cheekbones, and those captivating almond-shaped eyes. The small dark mole beneath his left eye captured her attention.

Anna shifted in her seat, her breaths shallow. She thought back on her meditation practice and some of the discoveries she'd made at the Soul Sister Circle. Did she really want to share those details with Simon? He seemed nice enough, but she didn't even know him. However, her past experiences of keeping everything locked inside hadn't exactly worked out well. She just had to make it clear where she stood on things. She would establish the boundaries so he would know exactly what to expect.

Rubbing her fingers around the rim of her coffee cup, she said, "I'm going to be honest with you from the very start. That way you'll have no false pretenses about me. Ten months ago, my marriage to my husband, Frederick, abruptly ended. It was something I didn't foresee, but that didn't matter."

She shrugged and stared down at the table. "It was over. I threw myself into my work and tried to forget. Eventually, I realized that wasn't enough, and I needed some time to clear my head. So one afternoon, I got in my car and left everything behind me: my job, my family, my past … and I drove south. That's how I ended up here. I found Lydia's place and met some incredible people, including Clark and Lucita." She gazed steadily at Simon. "My time down here is about finding myself. The last thing I want is a relationship. I want to be sure you're clear on that."

Simon nodded. "I understand if you aren't looking for anything more than friendship. Besides, I believe all I did was ask you about meditation." His lips curled into a sly smile.

"Yes, I guess you did," Anna said, feeling her muscles relax. She tucked a strand of hair behind her ear self-consciously. "Sometimes I have a way of getting ahead of myself. As for the meditation," she continued, "that's something Clark introduced me to, along with prayer beads. They help me stay focused during my meditation, and I definitely need that. My mind tends to wander quite a bit. I'm learning a lot about myself, though. About some of the things I need to face and accept. I still have a long way to go." She swallowed the lump in her throat. Admitting weakness had never been her strength.

"What do the prayer beads mean to you?"

"They signify someone or something, and show me how everything is connected." She met his gaze. "They demonstrate how life has flaws and that's part of what makes it interesting. Meditation has become a deeply personal experience for me and helps me connect with a Source much deeper than myself."

"A Source?" he asked, knitting his brow.

"Yes," she explained. "A loving Source is where all creation comes from and this abundant Source gives us all life. Through meditation I connect with my Source, and it helps me better understand myself and the world."

He looked at her, contemplatively. "Would you say you're on a spiritual journey?"

"I am." Anna said. Yet as she said the words, it was as

though she was saying them for the first time. She was on a spiritual journey. That was why she was here.

Simon sighed. "I'm not much for spirituality, although I hear about it a lot from Clark. I don't believe in much of anything. Religion and spirituality seem like smoke and mirrors to me. They keep people from seeing that this life is all there is."

Anna leaned back in her chair, studying Simon.

"I'm guessing you weren't expecting that type of response," he said.

Folding her hands in her lap, Anna took a moment to reply. "Truthfully, I'm not used to sharing this type of conversation with anyone other than Clark. It seems strange to me that I'm even sharing it with you."

He took another sip of his coffee. "Maybe that's a sign you're making progress."

"Yeah, maybe it is." Simon was so easy to talk to. She opened up to him like a blossoming flower. That was so unlike her. But he had his share of surprises. He was a skeptic when it came to spirituality. She would not have guessed that. Maybe he was not everything she expected him to be.

"What do you do for work?" Anna asked. She absentmindedly fingered the spiral binding on her journal.

"I'm a social worker." He finished his coffee and placed the mug on the table, his fingers dangerously close to hers.

"Do you have a lot of clients?" she asked, her voice steadier than her shaking fingers.

"I do. I devote as much time to them as I can, but I try to give extra attention to the families that are going through a particularly hard stretch." He adjusted the leather bracelet on his wrist. "Their lives are a lot tougher than most of us can even imagine."

She fidgeted with the spiral binding for a moment longer before folding her hands and placing them in her lap. "I'm sure you see a lot of suffering in your line of work."

He nodded. "So, you said you're a lawyer?"

"I'm a partner at a firm back in Boston." She paused, muttering, "Well, at least I used to be." Her last words were drowned by the whirring blender.

"Wow, that's great. You seem so young to be a partner though. Is that an accurate perception or is my ignorance of the field of law showing through?"

"When I became a partner three years ago, I was pretty young," Anna admitted. "But I made a lot of sacrifices along the way to make it happen."

The door of the coffee shop opened, and Anna looked up to see a young couple with an infant come inside. The baby was bundled in a pink blanket, sleeping soundly in the stroller. As they neared the front counter, an older woman bent to admire the little girl and began cooing over her. The parents beamed with pride. Anna's heart grew heavy.

"Are you sorry that you made the choices you did?" Simon's words broke through her reverie.

"Some of them, yes." She wrung her hands and looked back at Simon. "I've learned that you can't be successful at everything in life. Something has to give. In my case, it was my marriage, and that's a truth I'll always have to live with." Anna blinked back a tear.

"Breakups are difficult, but it seems they're never entirely one-sided," he said sympathetically.

"That may be true, but I know how much Frederick loved me. If I would have tried harder and made different decisions, our relationship would have lasted."

His gaze steady on her, Simon said, "Regretting past decisions won't change them. In fact, it will only fill us with guilt and disappointment. The past is a learning experience for us all, and the best thing we can do is try to move on."

"I know," she muttered. *If only it were that easy.*

Jillian suddenly appeared at their table with a piece of lemon pound cake. "This is on the house, Simon," she said sweetly, leaning in front of him and touching his shoulder. "I know it's your favorite. Enjoy."

"Thanks," he said, smiling.

Jillian stepped behind his chair and laid her hands on his shoulders. Gaze fixed on Anna, she pulsed her fingers into his shoulder mounds, massaging him.

"My pleasure," Jillian said, releasing her grip. "Keeps you coming back for more." Then she winked at Anna and walked away.

Reaching for her purse on the nearby chair, Anna said, "Great to see you, Simon. Enjoy your cake."

"Would you like some?" He pushed the plate toward her.

"No, that's okay. I think Jillian wants you to have it." Her cheeks heating, she kicked herself for letting Jillian get under her skin like that. But Jillian had made her point. She was clearly interested in Simon, and Anna had gotten the message. Not that she cared. Simon wasn't her type and, anyway, she wasn't in the market. In spite of that, her stomach plummeted when Jillian touched him.

Simon set down his fork and met her gaze. "Jillian and I are friends," he explained as if sensing her irritation. "We go back a long way."

Anna nodded. But she didn't know many friends that looked at Simon the way Jillian did.

"You're a good listener," Anna said. "I apologize for pouring my heart out to you. I'm not sure that's what you had in mind when you sat down."

Simon placed his hand over hers. "It was fine. You can always talk about anything with me."

A surge of electricity raced up her arm, but she forced herself to pull away from his touch. "That's good to know," she said, fiddling with the button on her chiffon tank.

"Would you consider getting together sometime?"

"I don't know," Anna said, searching for her keys. She had enjoyed spending time with him, but she didn't need an attractive man in her life. It was a distraction. "You're a nice guy, but I'm not sure it's a good idea."

"How about this," he began. "Why don't we get together as friends, talking, and nothing more? That way, we can enjoy each other's company without any expectations. Would that work?"

"I'll have to think about it," Anna said. She didn't want to make her life more complicated. She had enough to deal with without adding Simon to the mix.

"How about I call you in a few days?"

"Okay. I'll talk to you then." She hurried toward the door, passing the baby, still asleep in its stroller. She glanced away and pushed the door open against an unexpected gust of wind. She longed for her memories to stop haunting her.

# 23

Anna dripped with sweat and her hair curled up on the ends as she did her last downward-facing dog of the morning. Since joining Emily's yoga classes, Anna had incorporated several of the positions into her daily routine.

She was so engrossed in concentrating on her breath, the ringing phone startled her. She straightened so quickly that she nearly knocked over a clay pot filled with fragrant petunias that sat at the edge of her back porch … currently an outdoor yoga studio. Geraniums and impatiens also bordered her stretching area. Her yard, with its flourishing gardens and soothing waterfall, created a serene atmosphere that was perfect for her yoga practice. She reached for the phone on the glass patio table.

"Hello."

"Hi there. What are you up to?" her mother chirped.

"Doing some yoga. What about you?"

"I'm dropping Sasha off. She started her theater camp yesterday."

"I bet she loves it," Anna said, wiping her face with a towel.

"She's excited for the performance they're doing in a few weeks. I told her you'd probably be back for it."

Anna gasped. "You told her that?" The last thing she wanted to do was disappoint Sasha.

"Of course," her mother said. "You've been down in South Carolina for over three months. That was your deadline. I figured after you talked to Tom, you'd be heading straight home."

Anna sighed and fingered the pink impatiens blooms that cascaded from a nearby hanging basket. This wasn't going to be easy.

"You talked to Tom, right?"

"Yeah."

"And?" her mother urged.

Anna took a deep breath. Even as old as she was, she still dreaded this type of conversation ... the one where she disappointed her mother. Anna didn't need her approval, but somehow she always felt a little better when she got it. She peered up at the brilliant blue sky. *I might as well get this over with.*

"I asked for an extension on my leave. I told Tom I wasn't ready to come back yet." She grasped the porch railing with her fingers, bracing herself for her mother's reaction.

"What? How could you not be ready?" she demanded.

"I just need more time," Anna explained, lowering herself onto the porch steps. "I'm still trying to figure things out."

"You've had three months." Her mother's voice lifted an octave as it always did when she was indignant. "I never got time away to sort things out when your father died. I had two kids to raise. And Julia. You didn't see her running off when she lost Ben. She dealt with her grief sensibly *and* she had a baby besides." Her mother heaved a sigh. "Why are you doing this? You're being so irresponsible, Anna. You have a career and a life in

Boston. How can you give that up? Stop questioning so much and come home."

Anna closed her eyes. "I know you had to work hard, Mom. And I know Julia faced her pain head-on like she always does. But my life is different than both of yours. I have this time and I'm going to take it. I'm sorry if it isn't what you think I should do." Her voice trailed off.

"This isn't about me," her mother snapped. "I can't believe Tom is letting you do this. I mean, what kind of career will you have when you get back?"

"I don't know," Anna admitted, guilt welling up in her chest.

"And not only that," her mother continued, her pitch rising higher with every word. "What about your family? We miss you terribly and want to see you. Have you even given us a second thought?"

"Of course I have," Anna said. A lump formed in her throat. She stared at the proliferating orange rose blooms entwined in the decorative porch railings. Leaning toward them, she inhaled their scent, a delicate fusion of lemon and clover. She closed her eyes and breathed in their alluring aroma until her shoulder muscles relaxed and her breathing slowed. "I need more time," she whispered. "Coming down here has been good for me. It has helped me face some things."

"I'm glad to hear that," her mother said, her voice tempering.

"I do know what I'm doing." Anna affirmed, staring at the branches of her oak tree. Healthy and strong, the tree changed with the seasons and grew sturdier with each passing year.

"I hope so," her mother said, doubt lingering in her words. "We're counting on you to come back home."

"I know."

Her mother meant well, but why did she have to make it so hard? It wasn't like she was choosing South Carolina over her family. She just needed to be away from her past for a while longer. She shouldn't have to explain that to anyone, not even her mother.

# 24

"I can't believe we're at a real carnival," Lucita squealed, staring up at the colorful Ferris wheel. "There are rides and games everywhere. I could play all day!"

"Isn't that the point?" Anna asked as she felt the sun warm her back. "The Fourth of July only comes once a year. We wouldn't want you to miss all the fun."

"The fried dough's my favorite part," Clark interjected with his mouth full. "I had to stand in line for ten minutes, but it's well worth it. Anybody want some?"

Lucita reached out and grabbed a piece with her fingers. "You know this isn't good for you, right?"

"Once in a while it's okay to splurge, even for me," he said with a wink.

"Maybe they'll fry you up a vegetable if you ask them," Anna teased. "How about broccoli on a stick?"

"Yuck!" Lucita said, making a sour face.

"Maybe it'd be good," Clark said, thoughtfully.

"Not likely," Anna replied.

"Hey!" Lucita shouted. "Look who's with Mr. John!" She pointed toward the lemonade booth, waving her stuffed pink monkey in the air excitedly.

Anna turned, peering through the crowd. When she saw Simon approaching, her heart skipped a beat. She'd wondered if she would see him today. She smoothed the fabric of her peasant skirt and twisted a loose strand of hair with her finger before tucking it behind her ear. Then taking a deep breath, she smiled.

"I'm glad I caught up with you guys," Simon said. "It's always nice to be here with friends." His gaze lingered on Anna. "And the food's even better than I remember." He popped a mini doughnut into his mouth. "I might just eat all day!"

"I'm deciding between the chocolate chip cookies and French fries," Anna said. "I've been smelling them all afternoon."

"Why don't you get both?" Lucita suggested. "I'll help you eat them."

"Great idea. I'll be right back." She ambled toward the cookie stand, aware of Simon's penetrating gaze on her. Enticed, she peeked over her shoulder. Their eyes met for only an instant. His lips curved into a sensual smile and Anna's knees weakened.

Anna stole a few glances in Simon's direction as she waited in line for her cookies and French fries. He mingled so easily with people. Casually attired in a white button-down shirt, cargo shorts, and flip flops, he chatted with Lucita.

Lucita spoke animatedly. Stretching her arms wide in a circle, she giggled. Simon laughed and spun her around as if they were dancing. Watching them, Anna's heart warmed. He had a natural connection with Lucita … something special indeed.

When Anna returned to the group, she was munching on a warm cookie. The sweet chocolate lingered on her taste buds. She held a brimming cup of piping hot French fries and carried a plastic yellow bucket filled with fresh cookies.

"Do you want some fries?" she asked, stopping in front of Lucita.

"Of course," Lucita exclaimed, grabbing a handful. "I'm starving!"

Lucita devoured the fries as though she hadn't eaten in days. Yet, her pink T-shirt revealed remnants of fried hot dog, chocolate ice cream, and caramel apple from earlier that afternoon.

"Would you like some?" Lucita asked her pink monkey. She pretended to give her monkey a bite and then placed the last fry into her own mouth.

"Who are you feeding?" Simon asked, watching her.

"Cuddles," Lucita said, holding up the monkey.

"Are those hearts on her belly?"

"Yeah," Lucita said as she gave Cuddles a squeeze. "It makes her extra loveable."

"Just like you," John said, patting her shoulder. "Now, how about that game of skee ball you promised me? Remember, it's my specialty."

"We'll see about that," Lucita countered. "I've been practicing."

Lucita led Clark and John to the nearby skee ball lane, past an older woman who was handing a bright blue snow cone to a little girl.

"Thanks, Nana," the girl said, grinning as she bit into the mound of ice. "Blue raspberry is my favorite!"

Blue snow cones were Sasha's favorite too, and she loved it whenever her nana took her to the fair.

"What are you thinking about?" Simon asked as they passed by a table where a woman was selling handmade jewelry.

"My niece, Sasha. She'd have a lot of fun here."

"I bet you'd spoil her rotten."

Anna nodded, wishing she had made more time for her niece when she had lived so close.

"Do you miss your family?" He popped another doughnut into his mouth.

"Sometimes. The Fourth of July is Sasha's favorite holiday, after Christmas, of course."

They stopped in the expansive shade of a large oak tree. She set her cookies and half-empty cup of fries on a blue picnic table.

"It must be great having a niece," he said longingly. His eyes stared toward the horizon.

"It is. Do you have any nieces or nephews?" She dipped a fry into the ketchup before eating it.

"No, John's my only brother and I don't see that happening." He shrugged and met her gaze.

"I suppose not. Do you want to have children some day?" As soon as the words were out, she regretted them. It seemed so intimate. But Simon seemed unperturbed.

"I do. I want to have that special relationship." His voice resolute, as if that was something in life he wanted above all else.

"You'd make a great dad," Anna said. "I can tell." He deserved someone who could give him a family. Anna looked away. She was not that person. Inexplicably, her heart grew heavy.

"I hope so." He smiled. "What about you? Do you want kids?"

Anna turned her attention to a family standing in line for the Ferris wheel. A little girl with pigtails pulled off tufts of pink cotton candy while her older brother devoured a vanilla ice cream cone. They huddled close to their parents, faces filled with anticipation as they stared up at the rotating white wheel. It was the picture perfect family.

"I don't know. I try not to think about kids too much. We never know our future anyway." She finished her last fry and threw the container in the garbage.

Simon was quiet for a moment. "That's true. We don't know the future," he said. "Besides, before I think about having kids, I need to meet the right woman."

"That sounds reasonable," Anna said. Music from the nearby carousel floated through her mind like a daydream.

"Or at least get to know her better." Simon's gaze held her.

Anna's cheeks warmed. He couldn't mean her. She wasn't ready for that. And besides, she wasn't who he thought she was. She came with too much emotional baggage.

"Hey, you two! Having fun?" Jillian ambled over and squeezed her slender body between them. Her orange tube top and scalloped mini-skirt revealed a woman who knew the value of making a first impression. There wasn't a man there who wouldn't have noticed her lean legs and toned abs. "You both look awfully serious for being at a carnival."

Anna stepped away from Jillian's touch, her stomach lurching as she watched Jillian snake her arm around Simon's shoulder.

"We're just talking about family," Simon said matter-of-factly.

"Oh, come on. You two can't think of something more exciting to talk about on the midway?" She ran her manicured fingers across Simon's bronzed arm. "You could always tell her about the time you and I came here together. We made out just over there." She pointed toward a narrow opening between the balloon and dart booths.

Anna folded her arms over her chest. *So, those two had been more than friends once.* Somehow, that wasn't surprising.

"That was a long time ago," Simon said. His furrowed brow warned Jillian to leave it alone. But of course, she wouldn't be stopped that easily.

"I don't suppose I could convince you to come with

me over there, for old time's sake." She peered at Anna and leaned in close. "I promise it won't take long."

Anna stared back at her, gaze unwavering. Was Jillian really that desperate?

Simon straightened his shoulders. "I'm talking with Anna, if you don't mind."

"I see," she said with a tilt of her head.

"Hello, Jillian," Clark said, approaching them.

"Nice to see you," Jillian said stiffly. "But I better be going. There's not nearly enough excitement over here." She scoffed and glared in Anna's direction. Then she grabbed a mini doughnut out of Simon's bag and sauntered toward the ring toss.

"Does Jillian always come on so strong?" Anna asked.

Clark and Simon looked at one another and chuckled.

"Jillian's always had a way of getting her point across," Clark said. "I should know. I was married to her for eight years."

"*That's* your ex-wife?" Anna stared at him wide-eyed. A loud bell rang in the distance like a game show accompaniment to this new revelation. *Wow!*

Clark nodded.

"I knew Jillian wasn't a very common name, but the two of you seem so … different. I never would have put you with a woman like her. I guess that's why I never suspected."

"As they say, opposites attract." Clark gazed in the direction Jillian had gone. He breathed a heavy sigh. "She hasn't always been this way." He paused before continuing. "Circumstances changed her. Ethan's death, our divorce, and my coming out were extremely difficult for her."

Jillian's laugh suddenly burst through their conversation. She stood next to the ring toss booth flirting with a cute, young carny. He couldn't have been more than twenty-one, and his short dark hair was gelled and spiked in a tall peak. His long denim shorts hung off his narrow hips, and his white tank revealed sculpted and inked arms. Wrapping them around her tiny waist, he lowered his hand until it settled on her toned buttocks. Jillian pressed her body tightly against his and whispered something in his ear that made him smile with pleasure.

Anna turned away, flabbergasted, but also a bit pitying, in light of what Clark had just revealed.

"Look everyone," Lucita shouted as she walked up holding John's hand. "I won a blowup pig!" she squealed. "Isn't he cute?" She pointed to the life-sized animal in John's arms.

"He's something," Simon said with a chuckle.

"It's so much fun to win stuff here," Lucita went on. "Mr. Simon, would you play a game with me?"

"Sure. How about a little fun with the ducks?" He reached for her hand.

Lucita jumped excitedly. "But we have to bring the pig. He wants to watch."

John shook his head. "I guess it's back to the farm for us."

As Simon led Lucita and John toward the duck pond, Clark leaned against the fence. "You and Simon seem to be getting along well."

"Yeah, he's nice." She dropped her gaze guiltily.

"Anything else?" Clark raised his eyebrows.

Anna fingered her ruffled tank. "He's a friend. That's all."

"I'm sure you've made that clear," he alleged.

"Right from the start." Her tone sounded more adamant than she had intended.

"Was he cool with that?"

"Yeah. I even told him about Frederick." She paused. When she spoke again, her voice was only a whisper. "It's too bad he was so great about it." She kicked the dirt with her sandal.

"Why's that?" Clark asked with a puzzled expression.

"Because he's cute and he's nice. I can't keep myself from thinking about him sometimes. But I just want to be his friend. That's it." She paced in front of the wooden fence. "I'm just not sure that's all he wants."

"Is that a problem?"

Anna sighed. "I like spending time with Simon, but I don't trust myself to be alone with him. What if something happens between us that I can't take back? I don't want him to get the wrong idea."

"But Simon's someone you want to get to know better, right?"

"Yeah." Her voice optimistic, she looked up at Clark.

"So, have fun with him. You haven't forgotten how to do that, right? Don't put so much pressure on yourself. Just live in the moment and stop trying to control everything."

Anna nodded. "I'm working on that."

Clark squeezed her hand. "Let things happen as they will, one day at a time. Friends can have a lot of fun together, whether or not it ever leads to anything more."

# 25

L ucita entertained everyone by playing carnival games and riding the rides for the rest of the afternoon. As the last rays of golden light cascaded across the sea, John led the way to the beach. Anna, Simon, and Lucita followed close behind with Lucita playfully jumping over the cracks in the sidewalk. When they arrived, the beach was abuzz with excitement. Small children chased after seagulls that danced among the waves or burrowed tunnels in the soft sand. Young lovers cuddled close on their blankets, whispering secrets in one another's ears. Older couples meandered along the shoreline hand in hand. Laughter rose from people settling into chairs and blankets in anticipation of the evening ahead.

Simon squeezed Anna's hand. "I'll be right back."

Checking her watch, Anna noted that Clark had left about an hour earlier for the Martinez's house. He had promised Esperanza he would get her and Bernardo at nine.

"I can't believe Mama's coming!" Lucita beamed as she sat on a blanket next to Anna. "She loves fireworks!"

"And this should be quite the show," Anna said, letting the sand slip between her fingers.

"Here we are," Clark said, appearing through the crowd and pushing the wheelchair up to the edge of the sand. "The best seat in the house."

Esperanza smiled. "It's beautiful. I love how the sunset reflects upon the water. It's so majestic. It nearly takes my breath away every time I see it."

"Where's Papa?" Lucita asked, moving to stand next to her mama.

"He had a lot of work to finish."

"So, you came without him?" Lucita asked, her shoulders drooping.

"We couldn't change his mind." She looked over at Clark and sighed.

"He's going to miss everything!" Lucita's voice cracked.

"I know," Esperanza said, brushing her daughter's hair with her fingers. "I'm sorry."

"Why doesn't Papa ever have fun anymore?" She traced her finger along the arm of the wheelchair.

"He will. The old Papa will come back one day, you'll see." Esperanza wrapped her arms around Lucita and hugged her.

Anna hoped Esperanza was right. But Bernardo's anger had distanced him from everyone. He was blind to everything but his own feelings. She knew all too well what that was like.

Esperanza smiled as she listened to Lucita tell her something about the fair. Anna's heart clenched. They all knew this might be the last fireworks show she would ever see. And Bernardo was going to miss it all.

"Special delivery ... boiled peanuts, popcorn, and candy!" John shouted as he strolled toward them. His arms were filled with boxes of sweet treats, buckets of salty kernels, and steaming hot peanuts.

"That's enough sugar for a week!" Clark exclaimed,

placing his hand on his hip. "You know you need to be careful with that. You're supposed to lower your blood pressure, not raise it."

"I know," John replied. "But what's it gonna hurt for one night? That's what holidays are for." He tilted his head down and looked up at Clark, his lip protruding.

"I just want you to be around for lots more of them." Clark said, his jawline softening.

"I will. Don't worry." He squeezed Clark's arm. "You can't get rid of me that easily."

As everyone grabbed their favorite snack, John grinned. Then he leaned over and whispered to Anna, "If everyone eats these, then I can buy more for myself next week when Clark isn't looking."

Anna smiled as John stuffed a box of Milk Duds into the pocket of his shorts.

"Are all these treats from you?" Simon asked as he rejoined their little group.

"They sure are," John boasted.

"I realize you're usually the life of the party," Simon confessed, "but there's one thing I think you forgot." He grinned mischievously. "Lucita, this is for you."

"What is it?"

He pulled out a glow-in-the-dark wand from behind his back. "I know how much you like magic. I thought maybe this would come in handy."

"That's for me?" She grasped it in her hands and began waving it feverishly in the air. As she twirled in circles, she bumped into Clark and nearly knocked him off balance.

"Whoa!" He laughed. "Be sure not to cast any of your spells on me!"

"I won't. I'm saving them for something very important." She looked over at her mama and smiled. "Maybe this is just the kind of magic I need."

An hour later, the fireworks show began. Lucita was snuggled up on Esperanza's lap. Clark and John were enthusiastically visiting with some people nearby while Simon and Anna sat next to each other on the blanket.

Anna had seen spectacular fireworks many times in her life, but she realized that this Fourth of July felt different somehow. She couldn't quite put her finger on it, but it was as though the hole in her heart that had been there for so long somehow didn't feel quite as vast.

"This is the greatest night ever!" Lucita exclaimed.

"I agree," Simon said as he leaned back on his elbows and stretched out his legs. His thigh nudged against Anna's. "Tonight, this is the best place in the world."

The warmth of Simon's body next to hers felt strange. She had been with Frederick for so long. To be with someone other than him, a man she really didn't know, was more alluring than she had suspected. As he leaned in, she noticed a small scar shaped like a salamander on the back of his left hand. That was a mystery for another day.

"Thanks for being here," he whispered. His hot breath tickled her ear and sent shivers down her spine. "This has been an incredible day."

*It sure has.* The clap of thunderous fireworks made Anna jerk against Simon. Laughing, their shoulders pressed together as they settled back on the blanket. There was nowhere else she would rather be.

# 26

"Mama's still talking about the fireworks," Lucita said as she sat down on the ground beside Athena's fountain. "She said it was one of the best nights she's had in a long time."

"The show *was* amazing," Anna said, still remembering the tingling feeling of Simon's touch.

"Papa felt bad he didn't go." Lucita pulled her knees up to her chin. "I heard him talking to Mama about it the other night."

"I'm sure he did," Anna said, sitting down next to her.

"Maybe he'll come with us next time." Lucita's voice was hopeful.

"Maybe he will."

Anna wrapped her arm around Lucita and, in the silence that settled between them, they watched a little chipmunk scurry across the grass and dart behind the base of an old beech tree. He peered at them through beady black eyes and then scurried into a hole near the tree's large roots. Seconds later, he poked his head out and steadily chewed on an acorn, still watching them.

"I think a chipmunk would be a perfect pet," Lucita said. "They're exactly the right size."

"They're pretty cute and plenty small, but I'm not

sure I would want one in my house. If it ever got loose, I don't think I could catch it!"

"All you have to do is make sure it doesn't get loose," Lucita said, smiling.

Thinking she heard something, Anna turned her head, listening. The phone was ringing in the kitchen.

"I wonder who that could be?" she asked aloud. She had called both Julia and her mother the day before, and Clark had already stopped by earlier that morning.

"Why don't you answer it? Maybe it's something important. I'll keep my eyes on our furry friend."

Anna dashed across the yard and up the back porch steps. In her haste, she stumbled into the green cabinet that stood near the door. The tarnished mercury vases on the top shelf teetered. Instinctively, Anna extended her arms to catch anything that fell. Luckily, nothing did. Breathing a sigh of relief, she picked up the phone. To her surprise, it was Simon.

"I have a question for you," he said, after she'd greeted him.

"What's that?" Anna asked, her heart racing from the dash and from the voice on the other end of the line.

"Are you available tomorrow morning?"

"I think so. Why?" Goosebumps ran up her arms.

"There's a place I want to take you to. It will involve a bit of hiking, but it really is South Carolina at its best."

"That sounds interesting," Anna said, leaning into the cabinet and twirling her hair with the excitement of a schoolgirl. A way she hadn't thought she'd ever feel again. "Are you going to tell me where it is?"

"I'm afraid not. I think you'll enjoy it more if you don't know where we're going. And as extra incentive, I promise to be on my best behavior."

"Best behavior, huh? With an offer like that, I don't think I can refuse."

"I'll meet you at Garris Landing. It's about thirty-five minutes northeast of Charleston. I'll text you the address. Do you think you can find your way there okay?"

"I'll do my best," she said with a smile.

"Promise me you won't Google Garris Landing for our destination?" His voice slightly apprehensive, he continued. "That would ruin all the fun."

"For you or for me?" she asked playfully.

"For both of us."

"Okay, I promise," she affirmed. "See you then." She hung up the phone and danced around the kitchen. Simon had asked her out. It seemed so strange to be going on a date. But Clark was right. It was just for fun. At least that's what she tried to believe. The fireworks must have made an impression on him too.

Outside, Lucita stood near the statue of Buddha.

"What happened to the chipmunk?" Anna asked, looking around the yard.

"Oh, he went inside his hole. I waited for a while, but when he didn't come back out, I figured he must have taken a nap." Lucita leaned over and sniffed one of the nearby rose blossoms. "Who called?"

"Simon. To ask if we could get together tomorrow morning."

"Where are you going?"

Anna shrugged. "I don't know."

"But it's a date, right?" Lucita wiggled her body with excitement.

"Simon's just showing me around. Don't get any ideas, okay?" She wagged her finger at Lucita, but couldn't keep herself from wondering what it would feel like to be alone with Simon.

Lucita's eyebrows rose as she smiled. "Okay, I won't."

**ᗉᗉ**

Simon escorted her down a long wooden pier the next morning. Inhaling the salty air, she was anxious to discover their destination. She glanced around at the expansive salt marsh, quiet and serene. Brown pelicans soared overhead, and a lone wood stork waded in the shallows near the shore. Excitement flooded through her. It was a gorgeous morning. The sun reflected off the clear blue water and a gentle breeze blew through her hair. Several other people boarded a small, white ferry, passing their tickets to a young sea captain who stood on the bow with a jovial smile.

"Where are you taking me?" Anna asked curiously.

"A place you can only get to by boat." Simon reached in his pocket and pulled out his wallet.

"Is that so I can't run away?" she teased.

"The thought crossed my mind," he said with a wink. Simon handed their tickets to the captain and then stepped onboard to lead Anna to their seats.

The boat roared across the salt marsh, yet Anna was struck by the pristine beauty all around her. Spartina grasses edged up to the unspoiled waterways. Ospreys, pintails, and loggerhead turtles meandered through the wetland as though civilization had not yet touched their world. Uninhabited, this was a lush wilderness unlike Anna had ever seen.

A family with young children around Lucita's age sat on the opposite side of the ferry. The kids pointed wildly at the large turtle bobbing in the water while their dad was doing his best to capture the moment on film. Another family, with two lanky teenage boys, chatted excitedly at the back of the boat. The boys ogled a rectangular table packed with animal skeletons and interesting seashells at the center of the ferry. An elderly couple sat beside Anna and Simon. They wore lightweight sunhats and matching olive hiking pants.

Two pairs of blue trekking poles rested beneath their boots.

As the captain emphasized the importance of this estuary and its abundance of healthy oyster beds, the distinct smells of suntan lotion and bug spray wafted through the air. Sitting comfortably next to Simon, Anna emitted a contented sigh. This was going to be an incredible day.

The boat slowed, and Anna saw a lone egret standing on the grassy shore. Watching and waiting, the egret remained perfectly still as though the rest of the world didn't exist. *Now that's a way to meditate*, Anna thought.

The boat came to a gradual stop. A secluded island with short grasses and clusters of emerald trees spread out before them. Other than a few wooden signs, there was no trace of civilization. The view nearly took her breath away.

"Here we are," Simon said, stepping off the boat and onto the dock.

"You never said we were coming to an island," she said, staring at the vast sea of green before her.

"I wanted it to be a surprise. What do you think?" He took her hand as she disembarked.

"It's amazing." She squeezed his fingers gently before reluctantly releasing his hand.

Leaving the dock behind, Simon led Anna up a dirt trail lined with palmetto trees. When she gazed up at their massive fronds, she caught sight of a bald eagle soaring through the sky. "It's so remote," she marveled.

"That's part of the reason I like it." He trailed his fingers along the dry grasses. "There's something about spending time outdoors. When I'm not working, I try to be outside as much as I can."

"I can see why. Since I've come down here, I've been outside more than ever before. It helps clear my head."

"Do you meditate outside?" he asked, crumpling up a leaf in his hand.

"Next to a tree," Anna confessed. "One I saw in a dream, if you can believe that."

Simon raised his eyebrows.

"I know it sounds strange, but it's part of the reason I ended up down here."

"That's something I've never heard before."

"I know. You probably don't believe in that sort of thing." She kicked a pebble down the path.

"Do you?" he asked.

"I didn't used to, but now I'm not so sure."

He nodded. Then he opened up his hand and held it to her nose.

"What's that?" Anna asked, pulling away.

"It's a red bay leaf … smell it."

She leaned down and was surprised at the sweet fragrance of spice and cinnamon. "You know about plants too?"

"I know enough. It comes in handy when you spend time outdoors."

She looked at him suspiciously. "So, what's that?" She pointed toward a tree along the path with prickly green leaves and a twisted trunk.

"You're testing me already," he said with a grin. "That's a juniper tree. Do you see the dark blue berries?" He pointed to one of the branches.

She nodded.

"They're used as a spice and an ingredient in gin."

"Really?"

"Even I couldn't make that up," he said with a chuckle.

As a group of bikers passed by them on the trail, she asked, "Are you some kind of adventure guide?"

He smiled. "Actually, yes. I did that when I got out of college. I met a lot of interesting people."

"Where'd you go to college?"

"Clemson. On a football scholarship. My dad wanted me to be a doctor, but that didn't exactly work out. He always said medicine was where the money was. Too bad I went into social work instead. Not exactly the most lucrative of careers, but it's rewarding. Anyway, when I finished, I came back here. I missed the waves and the surf. The ocean gets in your blood somehow."

Anna nodded. "I'll always have to live near the coast, too. The ocean draws me in. I could never leave it." She paused. "Did you like being a guide?"

"Yeah, I did it for a few years." He touched the bark of a nearby magnolia tree. "I wanted to be outside, to live life. I never really thought it through more than that. But eventually, I had to take a day job like everybody else." He paused and looked over at Anna. "What about you? You seem like you would've been a planner when it came to your future."

"I was, but it didn't exactly work out the way I thought it would." Anna watched as a turkey trotted across the trail and headed toward a nearby pond. "I was pretty much living the American dream: successful lawyer, married, first child on the way…. But then in an instant everything changed. My entire world crumbled."

"I'm sorry," Simon offered. "That must've been really hard."

She nodded. "It was. But, it eventually led me here. My family thinks I'm crazy to be so far away from home, and maybe I am. But it's here where I discovered that I need to accept the things that have happened in my life. Even when that means facing feelings and choices I don't want to face. I have to stop hating myself for things I can't change. I have to move on."

"A hard lesson for us all, no doubt."

Anna looked up to see a black squirrel frantically

racing up the bark of a nearby tree. It was clearly trying to get somewhere in a hurry. "So, what about you? It still seems strange to me that you and John are brothers. Were you close growing up?"

"Since John's fifteen years older than I am, by the time I was in school he was already out on his own. He began traveling early on in his career and he seems to thrive on it. It has become a part of who he is. That's why Clark is such a good match for him. He keeps him grounded. I don't know how Clark manages with John away so much, but somehow it works for them. I think John feels better knowing you and Clark have become so close."

Warmth radiated through her. She was equally grateful for Clark's friendship. "I can relate to John with the traveling thing," she said. "I used to enjoy flying all over the world, and I even believed I was somehow making a difference. The problem was that I was making such a difference for the firm that I ended up losing myself in the process."

"I fear that a little bit for John, but he insists that he loves what he does. Part of me thinks he's afraid to stop because he's concerned that he won't be needed anymore. Many people believe if no one else needs them, they no longer serve a purpose."

"It's interesting how many of us spend so much time focusing on our outward significance in the world that we forget about our inward one. We come to base our success solely on someone else's point of view rather than on our own."

Simon was quiet, seeming to form his next words. "That's where the danger lies. Being yourself is always the best way to go."

Anna nodded.

"It sounds like you've learned a lot about what you

want from life." Simon wiped off his sunglasses with his T-shirt.

"I have, but I need to keep the focus on myself." She paused. "That's why I can't be in a relationship right now."

"I know," he said, his lips curving into a smile. "We've already had this conversation." He placed his sunglasses back on his nose. "So, besides working on yourself, what else do you like to do?"

"I've started writing again. That's a big one for me. I also read, scuba dive, hang out with friends, do yoga, run, and recently started hiking."

"That's quite a list." He placed his hand in his pocket. "I could tell you were into the hiking thing, though."

"How?"

"The shoes were a dead giveaway. Hiking boots are always a must, and the Nalgene you brought along also confirmed my suspicions. But the real clincher for me," he said with a smirk, "was the wool socks you have pulled up to your knees."

"They're not pulled up to my knees," she refuted, staring down at her legs. Then pushing her socks down slightly, she added, "The truth is, I'm deathly afraid of poison ivy."

"I see. As long as we stay on the path, you should be fine." Then he let out a small gasp. "Oh, no! There it is!" He pointed to a small plant on the edge of the trail.

"Where?" she asked, frantically searching the ground.

"I'm just kidding," he said, with a mischievous grin.

She hit him in the arm. "That's not funny."

"It was for me! Now, how about I race you to that tree over there? Let's see how fast of a runner you really are."

"You're on," Anna said, settling into a starting stance. "After what you just did, I'm taking you down."

"Go!" he shouted.

The two of them dashed down the trail and raced neck and neck until they reached the tall pine.

"That was a valiant effort," Simon said, panting hard. "Too bad I still beat you." He placed his sunglasses on top of his head, his dark curls pulled away from his face.

"Are you kidding? I clearly won." She placed her hands on her sides, out of breath. "You don't mind getting beat by a girl, right?"

"Not when she legitimately beats me," he said with a gleam in his eye.

"Well, this girl not only beat you, she kicked your butt."

Simon laughed. "It was close, I'll give you that."

Watching him, Anna was enchanted by his gaze. His chestnut brown eyes radiated warmth and passion. They drew her to him like a bright light in the darkness.

"You reading faces again?" he teased.

"Yeah. Something like that." She moistened her lips before turning around and continuing down the path. Suddenly, she came to a stop. Hundreds of downed trees were scattered across the sand, bleached by the sun and salt water. It was a melancholy but breathtaking view.

"They call this the 'boneyard,'" Simon said quietly. "It shows how the ocean's gradually eroding the sand on this side of the island."

The trees spread all along the beach, haunting remnants of the forest that once thrived there. In the distance, a lone oak stood strong against the steady line of surf that pounded its trunk.

"I don't imagine that tree's going to make it much longer," Anna said, mesmerized by its humble beauty.

"No, but it stands as a reminder of the strength that can exist even against incredible odds."

"True strength in adversity," Anna whispered.

Comforted by the significance of these words for her own journey, she stared at the rolling surf. "You know, that almost sounds spiritual."

"Nice try," Simon said, stepping toward her. "But it's really all about standing strong on your own."

"I don't think that's all of it," Anna said. "It's also about connecting with something inside yourself ... a force that's always there."

"You mean God?"

"God, a Source, something. I know it's there because I feel it."

"Is that what you write about? This connection you feel?" He was close to her now. She could feel the heat of his body inches from her own.

"Sometimes," she said, her breath hitching. "But I mostly love writing because it centers me."

"That sounds like something Clark would say. As for me, I'd rather live in the moment and not think so much about my life's path. Pre-planning life seems way too complicated." He faced her, his eyes touching every part of her body.

Anna's skin burned. "I can see that, but I also think when you find something you love, you know it."

"So I've been told," he said, brushing her hair out of her face.

Anna tilted her head toward his touch and closed her eyes, the intensity between them mounting. She tried to stop herself, but couldn't. For once, she wanted to let herself stay in that moment.

Simon leaned down and kissed her tenderly. The warmth of his mouth on hers aroused her senses, making her forget where she was. His lips were salty, firm, and wet. She roved her hands along his arms and back. His skin was like fire. Anna folded her body into his, yearning for more. The kiss deepened. His breath was hot against her own. She wanted him, every part of him. Drifting to a place driven only by her desire, she felt Simon pull away from her touch, breathing hard.

Anna met his gaze and asked, "Are you okay?"

"Yes, of course," he said. "I didn't mean to rush things. It's just ... I couldn't help myself. I promised you I would be on my best behavior, and I'm afraid that I may have overstepped my bounds."

"Perhaps you have. But I can let it go this time," she teased, pulling her tangled hair back into a ponytail. "After a kiss like that one, it's hard to be too upset."

Simon let out a relieved laugh. "But what about the whole relationship thing? I didn't think this was what you wanted."

"It isn't," she shrugged. "But I can't help how I feel when I'm around you. It's something I can't really explain."

"You don't have to." He caressed her cheek. "It's a sort of connection, right?"

Anna nodded. "I guess you could say that." Then she reached for his hand. "But whatever is happening between us, I need to take it slow. I can't lose focus on working on myself too."

"Of course." He squeezed her hand and winked. "I'll give you whatever time you need."

# 27

Anna closed her journal and walked down to the kitchen to make a breakfast burrito. Her stomach rumbled. She had been up for hours, too excited from her adventure with Simon to sleep in. She had already finished her morning run and meditation, although quieting her mind had been nearly impossible. The memory of their passionate kiss still sent tingles down her spine. While the eggs sizzled in the pan, there was a knock on the back door.

Anna opened it to find Clark smiling at her.

"Did you come all the way over here to check up on me?" she asked, motioning him to come in.

"As a matter of fact I did," he said, entering the kitchen and grabbing a small tomato slice off the counter. "I heard you had a date with Simon yesterday. I was on my way into town, so I thought I'd stop by and see how it went."

"News travels fast," she said, raising her eyebrows. She opened the cupboard and grabbed a mug. "You thirsty?"

"Yeah. Tea would be great." He sat on a cushioned high back stool and placed his elbows on the counter.

She heated the kettle on the stove and placed two tea canisters in front of him. "Can I get you anything else?"

"Oh no, this is perfect. I already had breakfast." He popped one more tomato in his mouth.

"Let me guess," she said, leaning against the counter. "Lucita told you."

He smiled. "It's hard to keep secrets around here."

"Yeah," she laughed. "I can see that."

He pulled a bag of Earl Grey from the canister. "So, how'd the date go?"

"It was fine," she said, taking a sip of her coffee and spreading cheese on her tortilla. "I tried to take your advice and have fun without any pressure."

"Did it work?"

She nodded, scraping the eggs onto her plate. "We had a nice day. He took me to Bulls Island."

"That's one of his favorite places. He spends a lot of time there."

"I can see why. It's beautiful." She took a bite of her burrito.

"So, it was fun then?"

"It was." Definitely. She still couldn't get that amazing kiss out of her mind.

She lifted the kettle off the stove and placed his tea bag in the mug before pouring in the steaming water. "Do you want any honey or milk?"

"No, this is fine."

In the silence that followed, Anna felt her cheeks warm. "Why are you looking at me like that?"

"I'm curious. Are you still just friends?"

Anna shrugged, but couldn't keep herself from smiling.

"I think I have my answer," Clark said. "Maybe you two have more in common than you thought."

"Maybe we do."

Once Anna finished her breakfast, they walked onto the back porch drinking their coffee and tea. From across the field, Lucita ran toward them.

She shouted, "Mr. Clark, Miss Anna, something's wrong with Mama!"

They hastily set their mugs on the patio table and sprinted down the porch steps, meeting her by the fountain.

Anna's stomach twisted into knots. "What's going on?"

"She can't stop coughing," Lucita said, trying to catch her breath. "It's like she can't get enough air. I ran over here to get some help. Please … you have to do something!"

"Let's get in the car," Clark ordered. "We need to get her to the hospital as quickly as we can."

Minutes later, the three of them entered Lucita's house and found Esperanza curled up on the sofa, gasping for breath. A succession of wet, raspy coughs erupted from her chest and ceased for only a moment before resuming. Her dark eyes were glazed with exhaustion. She shuddered in pain when Clark lifted her into his arms. He carefully carried her out to the car and placed her on the back seat. Lucita climbed in next to her mother, and Anna took the front passenger seat.

"Lucita," he said, slipping behind the wheel. "Where's your papa?"

"He went into town to talk with someone about a job," she began slowly, pulling the seat belt across her. But as she continued to explain, her voice quivered. "Then Mama started coughing and I couldn't get her to stop. Please, Mr. Clark, you have to help her!"

"I will, Lucita. I will."

Clark sped down the gravel driveway. Anna dialed the hospital from her phone and explained what was happening. Before she hung up, the nurse assured her that Esperanza's doctor would be notified right away.

In the back seat, Esperanza continued to wheeze with every labored breath. Anna watched her, squeezing her fists so tightly that her nails tore into her palms. Esperanza was in so much pain. Anna hoped she could hold on.

"It'll be okay, Mama," Lucita repeated like a mantra. "We'll be there soon."

After pulling up to the front entrance of the hospital, Clark lifted Esperanza into his arms. Two nurses met him at the door and rushed her into the emergency room.

"Where are they taking her? Mama needs me!" Lucita sobbed as she watched her mother disappear around the corner.

Anna pulled Lucita into her arms. "The doctors need to help her right now. You'll see her soon."

Lucita hugged Anna tightly. Clark knelt down and looked into Lucita's eyes. "I have to ask you something," he said gently. "Do you know where your father was going today?"

"No, but I know he has a friend down at Casey's Garage." She swallowed hard. "Maybe he would know where to find him."

"I'm going to look for him. You two stay here and call me if you find out anything. I'll be back as soon as I can." Clark hurried through the emergency room doors.

Waiting for some news, Anna stroked Lucita's long hair and repeatedly glanced at the clock. Different people streamed in and out of the waiting room, old and young alike, all wanting a diagnosis for what ailed them. For over an hour, she read children's books with Lucita. Finally, she was relieved to see Clark and Bernardo burst through the door.

"Papa, I'm so sorry," Lucita sobbed, breaking from Anna and running to her father. "Mama wouldn't stop coughing and I didn't know what to do!"

Bernardo picked up his daughter. "You did the right thing, Lucita. It's going to be okay." He unsteadily sat down in a chair, his arms still wrapped around her. "You were a brave little girl today," Bernardo whispered. "Your mama's lucky to have you."

"I was so scared, Papa. Do you think Mama will be able to come back home with us?"

Bernardo rubbed Lucita's shoulders gently. "I hope so. Mama's a strong woman. You remind me a lot of her."

Lucita smiled and leaned against Bernardo's chest.

But when Bernardo met Anna's gaze, it was clear that his affection was only for Lucita. His icy stare told Anna to keep her distance.

When a nurse approached Bernardo, he slowly rose to his feet. In a low voice, she said, "Mr. Martinez, the doctor would like to see you now."

After several minutes, Bernardo returned and motioned for Lucita to join him across the waiting room.

She ran over while Anna and Clark stood within hearing distance.

"Is Mama going to be okay?" Lucita asked.

Bernardo placed her small hands in his. "The doctor said they have stopped the coughing and that we can go see her now. Would you like to come along?"

Lucita nodded, biting her lower lip.

"Let's go."

Clark and Anna went to the cafeteria. Drinks in hand, they sat at a table near the back.

"Lucita's really going to need you now," Clark said. His brow furrowed.

Anna had never had a child depend on her like this before. What if Lucita needed more of her than she could give? Her hands shook like the freshly caught crappies from the pond. Remembering that enjoyable afternoon they spent together, Anna felt some of her worries fade away. She had to support Lucita however she could. "I love that little girl. I'll do whatever I can."

"I know you will."

"It just doesn't seem fair," Anna added. "Esperanza's so kind and giving. Why does she have to be sick?"

"I don't have the answer," Clark said with a sigh.

Anna fiddled with a napkin in her lap, her heart heavy. "Lucita's going to lose her mother. That's a type of pain that never goes away. I still think about my father and how much of my life he missed. Lucita has so much ahead of her. She needs her mother. It's just not right."

"Try not to think about what Lucita and Esperanza are going to lose. They've been blessed with each other, and Lucita will always remember her mother. We're all watching over her. She'll never be alone. In a way, she can be like the daughter you never had."

Anna closed her eyes for a moment, barely able to breathe. How could she be like a mother to Lucita? She couldn't even be there for herself, much less for another human being. She left her family behind. They were over a thousand miles away. How could she be responsible for raising a child? She wasn't ready. Her lip quivered. Perhaps there was a reason Claire didn't survive the accident. Maybe Anna wasn't meant to be a mother.

Placing her head in her hands, she ran her trembling fingers through her hair. When she spoke, her words were only a whisper. "I don't know if I'm ready for that."

"I understand," Clark said tenderly. "But there is a special connection between you." He looked at her, concern in his clear blue eyes. "No matter what happens, remember we will all be there for her. This isn't something you have to do alone."

Anna nodded and took a slow sip of her water. "You know, I still mourn for Claire. Writing about it helps, but it doesn't take away the pain."

"No, it doesn't. Time is the only thing that can do that." He touched her hand. "And I can attest that the hole never completely goes away. Yet, we have to keep living."

"I know." She covered Clark's hand with her own. "And if Lucita needs me, I'll be here. I'll do whatever I can."

# 28

"What are you doing way over there?" Anna asked. She poured fresh sunflower seeds into an old wooden bird feeder.

"I'm picking some flowers to take home to Mama," Lucita said, peering out from behind a row of lavender phlox at the far edge of the garden.

"I'm sure that will brighten her day."

"I hope so. Now that she's out of the hospital and back home again, I want to show her how much Papa and I love her."

Anna folded down the top of the bag and walked over to join her. "She's very lucky to have both of you."

Lucita nodded, adding a freshly cut flower phlox to her small pile on the ground. "I want her to be with us for a long time, but I don't know if that's possible." Her voice faded. After a few moments, she looked up at Anna, her face filled with concern. "Was it hard for you when your father died?"

Anna knelt down and touched Lucita's shoulders. "It was very hard. But don't give up on your mama yet. You never know what might happen."

"I know," she said, lowering her gaze. "But I sometimes wonder what losing Mama will feel like."

Anna sat down on the grass and patted the ground next to her. "Can you sit with me for a minute?"

"Sure," Lucita said, crisscrossing her legs.

"I want you to try something for me. Focus on enjoying whatever time you've been given with your mama. Show her all the love you have for her and live out each day as much as you can without worrying about the future. Then, if the time comes for you to know what losing a parent feels like, we'll talk about it more."

"Okay, I'll try," she said, resting her head on Anna's knees.

Anna wrapped her arm around Lucita's shoulder, wishing she could take away her pain.

"How's Mr. Simon?" Lucita asked.

"He's good. He's coming over this morning to help me with a leaky faucet."

"That's nice of him."

"Yeah, it is." Her heart fluttered at the thought of seeing Simon again.

"Hello," a deep voice called out from the distance. "Is anyone here?"

Anna's back immediately stiffened and the hairs on her skin prickled. It couldn't be. Slowly, she turned her head and saw a familiar figure standing on the back porch.

"Who's that?" Lucita asked, shading her eyes with her hand to keep out the sun.

Anna's jaw dropped. *Not anyone you need to meet.* Quickly, she collected the pile of phlox flowers and handed them to Lucita. "Why don't you take these home to your mama before they wilt?"

"Okay, see you later!"

As Lucita ran across the fields, Anna stood up, her knees wobbling. She tried to breathe. What was he doing here?

"Hello," Frederick said, walking down the back steps. Dressed in a navy button down shirt and white chinos, he looked even better than she remembered. His shiny dark hair was longer and neatly combed with a deep side part. The look suited him. "I'm sorry to have surprised you like this. But I was afraid you wouldn't see me if I called."

"You were right. I wouldn't have," she said, turning away, her stomach tight.

"Anna, wait. Please. There's something I need to tell you."

As he approached, her heartbeat quickened. But she knew she had to keep her feelings in check. She didn't want another complication in her life.

Awkwardly, he handed her a box of chocolates.

"What are these for?" she asked, tucking her hair behind her ear and wishing she was a little more dressed up than her worn cotton shorts and faded tank top.

"For you. Please take them. They're your favorite, all the way from Boston." His penetrating eyes pleaded with her.

Reluctantly, she took the box from him. It was a long way to come just to give her some chocolates.

"How did you find me?" Anna asked, studying him. His smooth, clean-shaven face was just as she remembered it. Even the creased wrinkles of concern on his forehead hadn't changed. His eyes were still as electric blue as a macaw feather and hidden, for the moment, was his alluring half smile ... the one she had fallen for so long ago.

"Julia's worried about you," he said. "I talked to her a few weeks ago and she said you had no plans of returning. She wants to make sure you're taking care of yourself."

"I am. Not that you need to know that." She still couldn't fathom what he was doing there. This was so unlike him. He didn't stop by unannounced. He didn't leave work in the middle of the week to fly across the country. At least not the Frederick she knew.

"I know it isn't fair for me to drop in on you like this," he said, placing his hand in his pocket. "But the truth is, I had to see you. Can we sit down somewhere? There's something I have to say."

Anna nodded and led him toward the porch, not sure she was ready to hear his reason for coming.

"This is an incredible place," he said, looking around the expansive gardens. His eyes lingered on her tree. "I can see why you like it here. Although this August heat might do me in." He wiped his brow with his arm and rolled up the sleeves of his shirt, revealing his taut muscles.

"South Carolina's been good for me," she whispered as they sat down on the steps.

"I can tell," Frederick replied. "You look happier than I've seen you in a long time."

"I am," she sighed. "So, what brings you here?"

"An apology," Frederick began. "I've messed up both of our lives. I was wrong to let you go. I should've fought harder for us. I gave up way too quickly." He paused. "That night when we danced together, I believed you were shutting me out for good. I thought that you had given up on our marriage so I decided to give up too. When you came to me a couple months later wanting to save our relationship, I took the easy way out. I asked for a divorce. I was angry and upset about everything. I couldn't take the pain of losing Claire and the pain of watching you struggle with your grief alone." He shook his head. "I was a coward, Anna." He reached out and touched her hand. "I was afraid to keep fighting for something that I thought I was going to lose anyway. But I was wrong. Blinded by my own grief and pain, I ended up doing exactly what I told you not to do. I pushed you away and pretended that I no longer loved you."

Anna pulled her hand away and tried to make sense of what he was telling her. "Don't you think it's a little late for apologies? You said our marriage was over. It couldn't survive. Has any of that changed?"

"I was scared," Frederick admitted. "I knew I was losing you, and the harder I tried to get you back, the more you seemed to be drifting away. You wouldn't talk to me." He ran a hand over his hair. "That, above everything else, was the worst part."

"I came to you wanting to change, remember? But then you surprised me by asking for a divorce. You told me there was someone else. You said you couldn't fight how you felt about her. What happened? Let me guess. That didn't work out and now you're lonely."

His voice cracked. "There was never anyone else. My mom tried setting me up with someone, but nothing ever came of it."

Anna drew back, narrowing her eyes. "You lied to me? How could you? I trusted you."

"I thought it would be easier than telling you I was giving up. But I was wrong."

"Easier for who? For me?" She stood up, her stomach heaving. "How dare you!"

"Anna," he said, rising to his feet and facing her. "I didn't mean for it to happen. It's just you were so angry all the time, and my mother kept pressuring me to end our marriage. I didn't know what to do!"

"Your mother," Anna scoffed. "You're going to blame this on her? Frederick, you need to take responsibility for yourself." She folded her arms in front of her. "You have to be your own person. Why can't you do that?"

"That's why I'm here," he said. "I don't care what

anyone else thinks anymore. I tried to move on without you, but the truth is, I can't. I still love you. I should never have rushed into the divorce as a way to escape my own failures as a husband. I want us to give our marriage another chance." He met her gaze, his eyes filled with remorse.

"It's too late," Anna said, throwing out her arms. "Like you said, we're not the same people anymore."

"But it's only been five months since the divorce."

"Five months? You ended things a year ago." Her voice wavered as she stared at the clay pot of petunias. "I haven't heard from you for all this time. You can't just erase what's happened."

He stepped toward her and grasped her hands in his. Their gazes locked. "I know you still love me, Anna," he whispered. "I want to make this work. I want to dance and travel with you like we used to. I miss your laugh and your sense of humor. I miss you. Don't we owe it to ourselves to try again?" He blinked back a tear. "We've shared so much. How can you just walk away from that? We can be a family again." He gently stroked her cheek, his face inches from hers.

Comforted by his caress, Anna closed her eyes and thought back on all they had been through: the pain, the joy, the loss. Slowly, her anger began to fade into regret as she wondered what it would be like to go back to how things used to be. Was that even possible?

Before she knew what was happening, Frederick leaned down and kissed her. His lips were tender against hers, slowly caressing her open mouth. Anna tried to stop herself, but the taste of his lips and the heat of his skin against hers drew her back to what had once been. He brushed her hair with his fingers and stroked the nape of her neck. His touch sent shivers coursing through her body. Anna kissed him back. His tongue probed deeper and she melted into him. When at last she forced herself to pull back, she could hardly breathe.

Opening her eyes, she was surprised to see Simon standing beside the wicker settee with a stunned expression on his face. Mouth agape he remained motionless as if in a trance. His stubbled cheeks flooded with color. After what seemed like an eternity, he shook his head. Then, without a word, he turned the corner and was gone.

"Simon!" she shouted, walking across the wrap-around porch and following him to the front of the house. "Please, stop!"

He halted at the base of the steps, but did not turn around to face her.

Anna leapt off the porch and stood directly in front of him. "It's not what you think. It didn't mean anything."

"It looked like something to me," he said, clearing his throat.

"No, it wasn't. I didn't expect him to kiss me," she said.

"You didn't seem to mind."

"Please. You have to hear me out. I didn't even know he was coming. He showed up on my doorstep ten minutes ago. I still can't believe he's here!"

"Is he who I think he is?"

Anna sighed and gazed into Simon's eyes. "It's Frederick."

Simon exhaled forcefully as though he'd been punched in the gut. Crossing his arms, he said, "That's what I thought. What's he doing here? He has a lot of nerve showing up after what he did to you."

"I know. Lucita and I were in the garden when he came onto the back porch."

"What did he want? Was that a good-bye kiss? Because it looked like much more than that to me."

Anna tilted her head to the side and returned his gaze. "I think for me, it was."

"What does that mean?" Simon asked. His mouth tightened to a line.

"It means that Frederick wants me to come back with him to Boston, and I'm going to say no."

Simon looked at her warily. "I'll let you get to it then." He strode to his Jeep and drove away.

Slowly, Anna walked around the side of the house. Still bewildered by Frederick's sudden appearance and confession, she tried to understand Simon's reaction. She had never seen him so angry. But then again, she had kissed Frederick. Why had she done that? What was happening to her? Frederick's unexpected return should not make her lose control like this. He couldn't waltz back into her life that easily. She couldn't let him. She had to end this now.

Rounding the corner, she searched the porch, but Frederick was no longer there. Where had he gone? Panicked, she glanced around the gardens hoping he hadn't witnessed her confrontation with Simon. That was the last thing she needed. Her life down here was none of Frederick's concern. At last, her eyes settled on him. He was staring at Athena's fountain and appeared lost in thought. Clenching her fists in determination, she marched down the steps. It was time to settle this once and for all.

Approaching him with her arms crossed, she said. "You know, you can't just show up here and pretend that things are fine between us. That our divorce never happened."

"I know, but you have a life back in Boston." He faced her. "Your career, your family, us. Are you really willing to turn your back on everyone who loves you?"

Anna rubbed her forehead with her hand. "It's not

that simple. I've started a life here. A life I've built on my own."

"A life with him?" Frederick asked, his tone accusing.

"What difference does that make to you? The people I've met here are none of your business. You have no right to come down and question any relationship I have."

"So, you do have a relationship with him?"

Her shoulders tensed. "This isn't about him. This is about me."

"I'm sorry." Frederick stepped toward her. "You're right. But, I don't want to see you give up so easily on what we've shared. I made a hasty decision that has proven to be the worst one of my life. You're the only person who really understands the pain I feel every time I see a little girl." His voice broke. "You know about the endless aching in my heart for a daughter I never had the chance to know. Please give us a second chance." He touched her shoulder gently, his face pained. "Let us be a family again."

"I don't know," Anna said, shaking her head. "I have to think. You can't just come here and expect me to jump back in your arms." Her voice quivered. "It doesn't work that way."

"I know, but I can't deny how I feel when I'm with you." He leaned toward her. "You make me feel passionate, creative, and alive. It's like I could do anything when I'm with you. But what I really love the most is your smile. It has always melted my heart. I want you back, Anna. All of you. Don't you want that too?" He wrapped his arms around her waist and drew her into an embrace.

Closing her eyes, shivers ran up her spine as she felt his breath on her neck. He kissed her cheek softly and she leaned against him. His hands caressed her back, but when they dipped lower, she pulled away. "I can't," she said.

He nodded, straightened, and placed his hands loosely around her waist. "I get it."

Anna let out a heavy sigh. "I need some time."

"Okay," Frederick whispered.

"I've been angry for a long while," Anna admitted. "At you, at me, and over Claire. I've started to let it go, but I'm not there yet."

"I think we both need to look ahead rather than behind. We've made mistakes. But maybe it's time to fix them and move forward together." He kissed her on the forehead. "I love you, Anna, and I will give you whatever time you need to think things through. I'm staying at a hotel in Charleston. I'll be there as long it takes. When you're ready, give me a call."

Anna nodded. She knew she needed to face her past once and for all: her mistakes, her regrets, and her pain. She had to find herself. Only then could she finally move forward with her life.

# 29

Anna studied a picture of Clark and John that hung on their living room wall. They were posing near a leafy garden of vibrant vines and trees along the waterfront, each holding a slender baguette as though it were a sword. The Eiffel Tower rose prominently in the background.

"John surprised me with that trip several years ago," Clark explained, standing beside her. "It's still one of the best I've ever taken."

"You both look so happy." She traced her finger along the metal frame. "Are you still?"

He shrugged his shoulders. "Happiness is overrated."

"What do you mean?" Anna asked.

"No one's happy all the time. That's not the way life is. So I don't base my relationships on whether I'm happy. I base them on whether I'm content. But true contentment isn't about whom you're with; it's about knowing who you are."

Anna nodded. It sounded so simple.

"This doesn't have anything to do with John and me though, does it?" he asked.

"No," she admitted. Her shoulders drooping, she walked over to the almond armchair and plopped into it. She had tossed and turned all night reliving Frederick's visit in her mind and thinking about his request. But there were no simple answers. Her eyes weary with exhaustion, she stared at the collection of seashells in a wicker basket on the table beside her. She used to have a collection like that back home in her living room. It consisted of shells and unusual rocks that caught her eye when she was on the beach. But she had left it behind, along with so many other things she no longer needed.

"Yesterday, Frederick showed up at my house out of the blue," she began. "I had no idea he was even in town. He apologized for everything that's happened, and said divorcing me was the biggest mistake of his life." She sighed. "He wants us to give our marriage another try."

Clark settled into the recliner across from her. "It sounds like he cares for you a great deal," he attested.

"I know," she whispered. "But that's not all. Frederick kissed me. Passionately." She clasped her hands in her lap. "Unfortunately, Simon walked around the back porch at that exact moment and witnessed the whole thing. I ran after him and told him that it meant nothing, but seeing the sadness in his eyes made me feel so ashamed for what I'd done." She stared out the window, unable to meet Clark's inquiring gaze.

"So, you returned Frederick's kiss?"

"I couldn't bring myself to pull away," Anna admitted. "I'm not really sure what came over me."

"Then I can understand Simon's concern."

Stomach plunging, she looked back at Clark. "Why?"

"Simon arrived at your house yesterday expecting to fix your faucet and, obviously, to spend time with you. Instead, he found you kissing your ex-husband. Don't you think that must have been hard for him?"

"He happened to come around the corner at the wrong time," Anna insisted. "It was only one kiss." *At least that's what I keep telling myself.*

"Yes, it was," Clark agreed. "But would you have told Simon about the kiss if he hadn't seen it for himself?"

Anna thought about it. "I don't know."

Clark pushed his glasses on top of his head. "Simon does care about you, Anna. He came over here yesterday after he left your house. He was hurt and angry. He's afraid your regrets about the past will keep you from letting go of Frederick for good."

"Simon came here?" Anna asked, her eyes widening.

"He stayed for quite a while."

"So, he saw Frederick talking to me in the garden?" *And our long embrace,* she thought.

Clark nodded. "Even though your house is across the field, he saw the two of you from my back porch."

Anna's heart dropped to her knees. "I tried to say good-bye to him for good," Anna said. "But I just couldn't. After everything Frederick told me, I needed time to think."

"Simon's a sensitive guy. He saw how much Frederick's arrival affected you. I think it scared him."

"I don't want to hurt Simon," she said, tugging her knees toward her chin. "But right now I don't have any answers."

"Then that's what I'd tell him," Clark concluded. "He only wants the truth."

Anna sighed. "Do you think it was wrong of me to kiss Frederick?" She had been asking herself that question ever since it happened. She knew Clark would tell her the truth. At least she hoped he would. Lowering her head onto her knees, she held her breath waiting for his reply.

Clark grew quiet, his eyebrows knitted in thought. When he finally spoke, his voice held no trace of judgment. "That's not for me to say."

Anna sat up, knowing he was right. She was the only one who could answer that. "It's just that when he kissed me, it was like I lost control," she explained. "I couldn't keep myself from wanting him, especially when I thought he was someone I could never have again. It made me question the divorce and whether we gave up on each other too soon. But I never let it go further than a kiss."

"You've got a lot to sort through right now," Clark said. He glanced at the portrait of Ethan on the wall, as if lost in thought. Taking a deep breath, he returned his gaze to Anna. "And I'm here to listen, but only you can decide what to do about Frederick. All I know is you came down here to find yourself. But you haven't talked much about home since you've been here. You've missed your family, but I haven't heard you mention your career. I think you've really learned some things about who you are. You're connecting with yourself and facing your shame from both the accident and the divorce. You've begun to accept yourself, even the parts that you don't like. And that's not easy to do." He paused. "Yet, new beginnings are never easy. Sometimes they make us question our past decisions. I know you and Frederick have a strong history together and the loss of Claire will always connect you. But the question you have to ask yourself is whether going back to your life in Boston is really what you want."

Anna shook her head. "It's been so hard lately. Whenever I talk to Julia, she keeps asking me when I'm coming home. My mom gives me reports of her health and reminds me that she's not going to be around forever. The career I've worked so hard for is back in Boston, and although Tom has been wonderful in supporting me, at some point I have to go back. Massachusetts is where my life is." She chewed her thumbnail. "But what I didn't expect was how much I would fall in love with this place too. I've found you, John, and Lucita, who always makes me smile. Meditation has helped me develop my creative side and I have begun to write. I've actually started to like myself again." She paused. "And I'd be wrong not to mention Simon. He's become a good friend to me too."

"It's not an easy decision," Clark empathized.

Anna ran her fingers through her hair, frustrated at her own indecision. "I was able to be honest with Frederick last night and it felt good. I think we're both finally beginning to heal. He told me how much it still affects him whenever he sees a baby girl. I couldn't believe it. That's something he's never shared. But as we get past our anger, I think we can see how everything fell apart. We were two ships passing in the night that never found each other until now."

"That's a positive sign," Clark acknowledged. "But is this encounter with Frederick giving you an opportunity for a new beginning with him or a new beginning for yourself?" He paused and met her gaze. "Be honest as you consider that. After everything you've been through, you owe yourself that much."

Clark seemed to understand her fears better than anyone else. Wiping a tear from her eye, she asked, "Why did Frederick have to come now?"

"Because this is the point in your journey where you need to decide which path you're taking," Clark advised. "You need to focus on your own dharma, your purpose in this life. Whether that finds you in South Carolina, Boston, or somewhere else, is entirely up to you."

03

Clark's words still hummed in her mind when Anna walked up the back steps of her house. Could she really clear her mind? It was clouded with so many emotions. How could she sort through all of them? How could she find her inner voice?

The phone started ringing. She felt trepidation before answering. It might be Frederick or Simon, her mother, or Tom, inquiring about her return. She answered it anyway.

Julia said, "How are you?"

"I've been better," Anna said, hanging her keys on the hook next to the door.

Her sister paused. "Is something wrong?"

"Frederick stopped by yesterday," she chided. "I wasn't exactly expecting to see him." She kicked off her sandals, which landed haphazardly next to the door. Hastily, she leaned down and repositioned them on the rug.

"Oh, that," Julia replied.

"You told him where I was?" Anna asked, her voice incredulous. Of all the things Julia had ever done, this was by far the worst. "You know I needed time for myself," she said, walking into the living room.

"You've had five months for yourself. I've been worried about you," Julia said. "Since you left, you've made no plans to return. Your life is here. You can't leave and pretend that everything will be fine when you come back."

"What if I'm not coming back?" Anna slumped onto the sofa, shocked by the honesty of her own words.

Julia drew an audible breath. "What are you saying?"

"I don't know." She leaned against the soft cushion. "My life was just beginning to make sense again, and then Frederick showed up."

"I know this is difficult for you to hear, but you can't keep living in limbo. You have to make a choice," she declared. "Frederick's sorry for what happened and he wants to reconcile. Initially, when he approached me about it, I was doubtful." She paused. "You know I haven't always approved of the way his family acts, particularly his mother. But Anna, I've talked to him at length and he's sincere in what he's saying. He loves you ... of that I'm certain."

"But it's not that simple," Anna countered. "Frederick and I are divorced."

"That was because you both worked too hard after losing Claire and didn't talk to each other anymore. But we both know you never stopped loving him."

"Things have changed, Julia. I'm not the same person." She placed a pillow behind her head, exhaustion setting in. Why did Julia have to interfere like this?

"Of course you are. I know you say you went down there to find yourself, but you should've done that by now. People don't change who they really are."

"Yes, they do," Anna refuted. But she knew where Julia was coming from. She had once believed that too.

Julia gasped. "Wait a minute. Is this about that social worker guy you met? He's a fling, Anna. You can't tell me you're in a serious relationship with him. I thought you went down there to find yourself, not hook up with some guy."

"This isn't about him," Anna muttered.

"Then can you honestly tell me that you want to give up on Frederick? He wants you back. Isn't that worth at least considering? If I had a chance to be with Ben again, I'd do it in a heartbeat. But that's not going to ever happen for me." She sighed. "That's why when Frederick told me about his regrets, I really wanted this for you, and I thought you'd want it too ..." Her voice trailed off.

Anna took a deep breath. Julia cared about her so much. How could she be mad at her for that? "I don't know what to do," Anna whispered, fingering the locket around her neck that her father had given her. She wished she could talk to him. He would help her figure things out.

"Think about your options," Julia said. "You know Frederick won't make the same mistake twice, and he understands you. Your entire life is here, and we all want you back home. We miss you." Her voice broke. "Sasha asks about you all the time, and Mom hasn't been the same since you left. She's edgy and regrets that she didn't spend more time with you when you were here. In her mind, she failed you as a parent and thinks she's to blame for you living so far away."

"That's not true," Anna contested. Closing her eyes, she felt the guilt seep in. Why did her mom have to make everything personal? Her decision to go to South Carolina had nothing to do with her.

"Please, Anna, patch things up with Frederick and come home. Let's be the close family we always wanted to be."

# 30

Anna spotted Clark in his garden as she walked up the path two weeks later.

"I haven't seen you in quite a while," Clark called out good-naturedly. He was surrounded by flowering tomato plants, busily picking the ripened fruits.

"I know," Anna said. "I've been doing a lot of thinking lately."

"Has it helped?" he asked, placing a handful of tomatoes into a large bucket.

She shrugged, coming to a stop beside him. "I talked to Frederick last night. We're getting together tomorrow. He really wants things to work out between us, and he's been here all this time." She stared at the tiny green tomatoes on the vines, not yet ready to be picked. "He's been so patient."

"I know what *he* wants," Clark replied. "But what do *you* want?"

As Anna was about to answer, she heard Simon's voice, calling from a distance. "Clark. Are you here?"

Anna's heartbeat quickened. She hadn't seen Simon since the day she had kissed Frederick. She wanted to give herself space and wait to talk to him until she had made her decision. Unfortunately, that was taking longer than she had anticipated. Clenching her fists, she steeled herself. She had to tell him something.

"We're over here," Clark called out.

Simon appeared around the corner of the house, holding a long slender tree trimmer over his shoulder. "I wanted to return this."

"Thanks," Clark said, setting the bucket of tomatoes on the ground. "I was hoping to use it tomorrow."

Simon's face fell when he saw Anna. "Oh, I didn't realize you were here."

"I just stopped by to see Clark," she muttered. She wanted to say more, but after hearing the disappointment in his voice, she remained quiet.

Clark reached for the trimmer. "Let me get that."

Awkwardly, Simon handed it to him, his attention still focused on Anna.

"I'm going to put this in the shed," Clark said. "I'll be right back."

As Clark walked away, Simon ran his fingers through his curly hair. "Well, I guess I better be going."

He headed back toward the house.

Anna's breathing grew shallow. She didn't know if she should call out to him or let him go. "Simon, wait!" She hurried after him.

He stopped near the porch and turned around. His face held no expression, but Anna saw the hurt in his eyes. She knew she was the reason for it, and it made her physically sick. Simon had always been so kind to her. He made her feel alive again and believe that, despite the scars of her past, she was still beautiful. Standing next to him now, she felt her skin tingling with desire. She shook her head, not wanting to focus on that. She had to explain and help him understand.

"I need to tell you what happened with Frederick," she blurted out.

"You don't owe me an explanation, Anna."

"Yes, I do. I thought things were over between Frederick and me. But after seeing him, now I'm not so sure. I've needed some time to think about everything, and that's why you haven't heard from me."

She looked up at the cloudless blue sky and then back to Simon. "You know I wasn't looking for a relationship when I came down here. But somehow, one started between us."

"I know," he said flatly.

"Well, it's made me realize that I have to think about things more before I do them." She interlaced her hands and pressed her palms together tightly. "I have to be sure that I'm going down the right path."

"Planning out your life, you mean?" He leaned against the porch railing and crossed his arms, his eyes narrowing. "I thought you were trying to get away from that."

"I am," she admitted. "But maybe it isn't such a bad thing when it's about something as important as relationships."

"Our relationship or your relationship with Frederick?" Simon asked, his voice cracking.

"Both," she conceded. "As well as my relationship with myself."

"So, you didn't end up saying good-bye to Frederick that day. I figured as much."

"I felt he deserved some consideration," she insisted. "We were married for almost ten years."

Simon placed his hands behind his head. "Did you feel I deserved any consideration? Or don't I matter?" He kicked the dirt. "I'm not the one who divorced you."

"This is about me, Simon," she said, annoyed at his response. "I have to decide what I want to do for me."

"Now everything's about you. So, maybe you're

right. It's not like we're in a real relationship. We hardly know each other. I wouldn't think walking away from it would be real hard for you." His tone harsh, it was as if he had completely written her off like she had never mattered to him at all.

"How can you say that? You don't know what I want." She crossed her arms, her frustration mounting.

"No, I don't. But you don't owe me anything. We've shared a kiss, an incredible kiss. But that's all. So, don't feel like you need to stay with me. Let's end this now before it goes any further."

"You're just going to leave?" She couldn't hide her surprise. "Not even give us a chance."

"I'm not the one who's walking away. You've had two weeks to think things through and I haven't heard from you. If anyone's decided to leave this relationship first, it's you."

His words tore through her heart. How could he be saying this? She knew he was hurting, but this wasn't fair.

Simon continued, "If you want me to be the nice guy who says everything's fine and we can make it through this, I'm sorry. I can't do that. You have no idea what you want."

He gripped the porch railing with his hands. "If your past is something you want back so badly, then go home and don't feel guilty about it. Now's your chance to take back all of those regrets you have. You won't have to wonder what might have happened. Good-bye, Anna. I wish you the best." He turned and walked away.

Anna couldn't move. She wanted to chase after him and tell him he was wrong. She wanted to explain that she was still figuring things out, but somehow her feet wouldn't budge. There was nothing left to say that would change his mind. As he disappeared around the corner fading from her life, a palpable void filled her chest. He was gone.

"Is everything all right?" Clark asked as he returned. "Simon seemed upset."

"He ended things with me. He said good-bye." A tear trickled down her cheek.

Clark put his hand on her shoulder. "What did you expect him to say? He saw you kissing Frederick and then didn't hear a word from you for weeks. Simon believes that you're leaving and he's accepted it. For him, it's easier to reject you than wait for you to reject him. He's protecting his heart."

"But he doesn't know for sure that I'm leaving."

"In his mind, you already left."

୯୫

Anna was still thinking about her interaction with Simon when she walked out of the Soul Sister Circle that evening. She had struggled to stay focused during the group meditation, still unsure of what she should do.

Wanting a coffee, Anna decided to go to the closest place. She just hoped Jillian wouldn't be there. She walked up to the counter, relieved to see the young man with dark dreadlocks that had served her before. Politely, he took her order and as she looked at the assortment of coffee mugs along the back wall, she cringed at the sound of a familiar voice.

"I'm surprised to see you alone in here," Jillian said. "I figured you'd be spending every minute you had with Simon. You two seemed pretty chummy at the carnival."

Anna knew what Jillian was trying to do. She was digging for any information she could get. But Anna wasn't in the mood for games. "Simon and I aren't spending much time together anymore."

"I find that surprising," Jillian said. "He really seemed into you."

"Well, not anymore. That's what you wanted, right? You've never liked me anyway."

"I can see why you'd think that," Jillian admitted. "But it was nothing personal."

Anna grabbed her mocha off the counter. "I don't know how you could say that. Anyway, it looks like Simon's all yours." Her heart sank as she said those words, wishing they weren't true.

"You're going to give up that easily?" Jillian asked with surprise. "You seem like more of a fighter than that."

Anna walked toward a booth in the corner. To her surprise, Jillian followed with a cup of coffee in her hand. "Maybe I don't have the energy to fight anymore."

Jillian sat down across from her. "Why not?"

Anna wasn't sure why Jillian was so interested in her life, but it didn't matter. "Things have changed, that's all."

After a brief silence, Jillian spoke first. "I know I haven't been very kind to you. I guess for me, Simon was the guy who got away. Simon and I have known each other since we were kids. We dated in high school and had a lot of fun together. When I went off to college, I knew Simon still cared for me. But we lost touch. Years later, I came back here and thought Simon and I might reconnect. But he never showed any interest."

Anna took a sip of her mocha, surprised at Jillian's forthright confession.

"Anyway," Jillian went on, "enough about that. I wanted to ask you something. I know you and Clark have become friends, so I'm guessing you know our history."

Anna nodded.

"I think about him sometimes and wonder how he's really doing."

"He's well. You should stop by and see him sometime. Maybe you two could smooth things over."

"It's been a long time since I've visited him," Jillian said, flipping her hair over her shoulder and looking at her reflection in the window.

"Perhaps it's a good idea, then," Anna said, taking another sip of her mocha.

"You know, finding out your ex-husband is gay does something to your psyche. It messes you up."

"I can imagine," Anna said sympathetically. When she married Frederick, it felt like she knew him better than anyone, at least until the end. To find out your husband was gay would feel like the ultimate betrayal, as though you never really knew him at all. Your entire life would feel like a lie.

"Maybe it's time I stopped hating him. He's always been a caring person," Jillian said, tapping her manicured nails on the table. "More caring than most men I've been with since. Perhaps it's time I told him that."

"I'm learning that talking things through usually makes me feel better." Anna thought of Frederick, knowing that was what she needed to do with him.

"So, what about you?" Jillian asked. "You look like you have a lot on your mind."

Anna nodded, a lump forming in her throat. "Somehow, the past I was trying to get away from has followed me here."

"Troubles have a way of doing that." Jillian's voice became distant, as though she were lost in a memory.

"I know," Anna said, tracing the handle of her mug. "But I didn't expect my ex-husband to show up and want to reconcile. I didn't see that coming."

"Which explains your troubles with Simon," Jillian said. "What are you going to do?"

"I don't know. I've taken time to meditate and have

tried to stay centered. But it's not an easy choice. I don't want to give up on Frederick, especially when I see how much he wants our life back. I know how happy it would make him. Yet, when I think about leaving, my heart hurts. I've made some good friends here."

"Is that what Simon is? A friend?"

"I don't know," Anna admitted. "We connect, but it's not right. It's too soon for me. I don't want to lose myself again." She sighed.

"Would you lose yourself if you went home?" Jillian asked.

"I don't know that I would this time." Anna met Jillian's gaze. "And, since I've been given a second chance at love with Frederick, perhaps that's where I'm supposed to be."

"Perhaps," said Jillian. "Or maybe your second chance isn't about being with a man, but about discovering who you are."

Anna nodded. She had wondered that too.

Jillian sipped her coffee and then stood up. She walked over to one of the corner bookshelves filled with stationery and gifts. Pulling down a lavender journal, she handed it to Anna. "This is for you. Maybe it will help with your decision."

Anna looked down at the spiral bound journal with the inscription, "Love the life you're living."

"Thank you," she said, squeezing Jillian's hand.

Jillian seemed to instinctively stiffen at Anna's touch, but then her face relaxed. "I hope it helps you sort through your thoughts." She paused. "May I write something in it?"

"Sure," Anna said.

When Jillian finished, she snapped the journal shut. "Food for thought," she said, handing it back to her with a smile.

Anna cracked open the front cover and read the inscription.

> *Dear Anna,*
> *As you look for guidance along your path, listen to your heart. May this journal offer you whatever clarity you seek and the tranquility that can only come from being at peace with who you truly are.*
> *Best wishes,*
> *Jillian*

"Now," Jillian said with a wink, "how about a piece of chocolate cake?"

ભ

Anna stepped from the steam-filled shower and slipped into a pair of short-sleeve, pink-and-white-striped pajamas. The rain on the leaves outside offered a sweet melody. When Anna cracked her bedroom window, she inhaled the sweet scent of jasmine. Settling onto her canopy bed, she leaned against a pile of oversized pillows and opened her new journal.

Anna read Jillian's note again. She had been so kind to her. It was as though she were a different person. Would the change last? She wasn't sure, but she hoped it would.

She would be seeing Frederick tomorrow and she needed to sort out her thoughts. When at last she put down her pen, she read over the words.

*Listening to the quiet solitude of the rain, I reflect upon all of life, feeling disconnected and sad. My emotions rage, questioning everything I once knew. Frederick's return has wreaked havoc in my life—more than I could have ever imagined. It's as though I'm suddenly in a foreign land with nothing familiar, and clarity is beyond my grasp. Do I stay or do I go? I have arrived at a crossroads, and though I yearn to hear, there's not a whisper of sound. The stillness is deafening. My misery and uncertainty swell like the waves of a hurricane, and I'm left gasping for breath.*

# 31

Anna strolled across the soft sand as the rhythmic waves crashed onto the shore. The gentle rumbling had the power to calm her spirit, no matter what turmoil gripped her.

"I figured you might be here already," Frederick called out, walking toward her. In his plaid shorts and designer white polo, he was the perfect blend of casual sophistication. No surprise there. His face relaxed, he looked very different from the man she had seen on her back porch. The tense shoulders and crinkled brow were gone. It looked as though his time in South Carolina had done him some good. He stared at her, his eyes caressing her tanned skin.

Feeling self-conscious, Anna twisted her hair back into a ponytail and fingered the embroidered hem on her short, black linen sundress. "I wanted to come a little early and take a walk."

"I see you still love the beach," Frederick said, falling in step beside her. His lips curved into his usual half smile.

Her stomach fluttered. "It centers me somehow."

"Do you come here a lot?"

"When I can. That's one thing I miss about living right along the ocean. I can't go to the beach as often as I used to." She looked out over the vast sea, remembering how much she loved running along the shore. "But," she added, "the country has its own rhythms too."

Frederick nodded. "I'm sure it does but, hopefully, you'll be living along the beach again soon."

Anna sighed and bent to pick up a small white rock partially submerged in the sand. She would like living near the ocean again, smelling the sea air each morning. It would be like coming home. Yet, somehow she knew the country was home to her too. Standing, she held the rock in her open palm. "These are still your favorite, right?"

He reached for the translucent stone. "Yes. They are so pure and white as though nothing has tarnished them." He touched her palm, his body close to hers.

Anna shivered as she inhaled his familiar scent of vanilla, cumin, and sandalwood. "Why don't you take it?" she suggested. "Maybe it will remind you of your time here."

"A time of reconnection," he said, grasping the stone and placing it in his pocket. "That's something worth remembering."

They resumed walking along the shore, following the seagulls as they pranced along the sand. "You know we've had a lot of great memories together," Frederick said. "Like in Aruba when you thought you were invincible. Remember when that rip tide almost did you in?"

Anna laughed. "You had to come and rescue me. I learned my lesson though. The ocean's nothing to mess around with, that's for sure." She kicked the sand with her toes.

"Hawaii's still my favorite," Frederick went on. "When we were swimming and the clasp on your top broke."

"You grabbed the back of my suit awfully fast that day," she said, chuckling. "I never did get that clasp fixed."

"That was okay with me," he said, nudging her arm.

Her cheeks warmed.

"Remember what we used to dream about?" he asked. "What we wanted our lives to be?"

"I was going to use my law degree to help people," Anna began. "Single mothers, specifically, because I saw how much my mom struggled after my dad passed away. I wanted to make a difference in their lives ... but I guess that never really happened."

"My dream never did either," Frederick said. "Remember when I told you about my brother's heart defect and how we spent endless hours in hospitals when I was young. I used to dream about raising money for families plagued by illness. I planned to build a house where they could stay or set up a fund to help pay for medical bills. I had forgotten about that until now."

"We had so many hopes and dreams back then." Anna's voice trailed off as she watched a brown pelican dive head first into the surf. It broke the surface and rose again in a spray of gray water and white foam, a wriggling fish in its beak. It seemed so certain of what it needed, a certainty Anna no longer seemed to possess.

"It's never too late to have hopes and dreams, you know," Frederick said, putting his arm around her shoulders. "Even if you lose them for a while, you can still get them back."

Anna nodded and leaned her head against his chest. It always fit perfectly there. "That's what happened when Claire died."

"What?"

"I lost sight of everything I ever wanted. I let my dream of a family die with her instead of fighting for it."

"When we lose someone that's important to us, I think it's hard not to lose a part of ourselves too."

Anna watched the waves crest in the distance. She had let Claire's death nearly destroy her, like the stormy surf of a hurricane.

"With Claire gone," she said, "it felt as if I didn't need to make a difference in the world anymore. Nothing mattered, not even me. I stopped caring because it was easier not to. I became hollow, someone without a heart." She paused, her throat tightening. "But I guess this shouldn't surprise you, right? You saw it happen." A tear streamed down her cheek.

Frederick shook his head. "You've always had a heart, a beautiful heart. When Claire died, you just did what you had to do to survive. Everyone handles grief differently. I should have been more understanding about that. I should have been more patient."

Frederick stopped and gripped Anna by the shoulders. Compassion flowed from his gaze and he brushed the loose strands of hair from her face. "You do make a difference in this world every day. You care about people and what happens to them. And your smile lights up a room. That's never going to change."

He touched her cheek. "You're an incredible woman and I hope you know how much you mean to me. Even though we've lost Claire and our marriage ended way too soon, I know we're both stronger people now. We've learned how to face our pain. We can make our relationship last this time. I know we can."

Anna's heart squeezed. She wanted that to be true. She wanted to have the closeness they once shared. But could they really go back to how things used to be? Or had too much happened?

"I know you came down here to figure things out, and I don't want to rush you," he continued. "But I want to remind you of the love I feel for you. It's a love that's never left and will be there through the good times and the bad. I want you back, Anna. Will you please come home with me to see if we can make our relationship work again?"

"I don't know," she whispered.

Frederick stroked her neck with his fingers. "It's okay. Take as long as you need." He moved his hand to his pocket and withdrew a shiny ring. It was the platinum engagement ring she had worn for so many years. "I would like you to keep this. May it be a reminder of the love we've always shared."

She stared down at her shaking fingers and clasped the ring in her palm. It felt so strange to hold it again.

Frederick placed his hand under her chin to tilt her face toward him. Tenderly, he lowered his lips to hers in a kiss that was familiar and comforting.

Tasting his salty lips, Anna wanted to forget all her troubles. She wanted to stay in that moment with the man she had loved for so long. But how could she do that? She had to keep moving forward on her path, not go backwards. Why did reconnecting with Frederick feel both natural and unnatural at the same time? Uncertainty engulfed her. Somehow, she had to find a way to make a choice.

&#x2767;

Anna leaned down and breathed in the sweet aroma of the bouquet of yellow roses Frederick had brought over to her house that morning. He set them on her front porch and drove away without a word. It had been two days since their trip to the beach and Anna could hardly think of anything else.

She glanced at the clock. It was eleven forty and Frederick would arrive at noon. She ran upstairs to her bedroom, knocking her journal to the floor as she rushed past the nightstand. Anna paused to gaze at the open pages. Her heart thumped in her chest. She wasn't sure if she wanted to read what she had written. Giving in, she lowered herself to the floor and placed the bound pages gently in her lap. Running her fingers across the paper's smooth surface, she looked over the two lists she had made yesterday. Since trusting her emotions had gotten her nowhere, she had hoped two objective lists side by side would finally reveal the answer she needed.

| *Going Home* | *Staying in SC* |
|---|---|
| *Frederick* | *Clark* |
| *Julia* | *John* |
| *Mom* | *Lucita* |
| *Sasha* | *Esperanza* |
| *Work* | *Simon* |
| *Travel* | *Writing* |
| *Living at the beach* | *Living in the country* |
| *Being with my family again* | *Finding myself* |
| *Getting my life back* | *Soul Sister Group* |
| *Fixing past mistakes* | *Having Claire forever in* |
| *Having Claire's memory close* | *my heart* |
| *Having someone to love* | *Having me to love* |

As Anna stared at the lists, she knew she had let the numbers decide. There were twelve for leaving and eleven for staying. Taking the emotion out of the equation, she was able to make her choice. Yet, as she examined the last entries on either side, the same gnawing feeling that had been bothering her all morning returned.

Upon a closer look, Anna realized she had actually chosen loving someone else over loving herself. Why hadn't she seen that before? She was giving up her own contentment in order to provide it for someone else. Somehow that didn't feel right. She had to learn to love herself before she could truly love anyone else. And honestly, she hadn't figured out how to do that yet. If she went home now, she would end up hurting Frederick again and that was the last thing she wanted to do.

Reaching for a pen, she wondered if she had been wrong about everything. Taking a deep breath, she opened to a new page and, as her emotions poured out of her, began to write:

> *This decision has haunted every crevice of my mind and driven me nearly mad. Worrying, wondering, I wanted to do the best thing for us all. So, in desperation, I made my final choice. The list complete, the numbers tallied, reason led the way. My life in Boston was filled with promise. Why would I let it go?*
>
> *Yet, sitting here reflecting, my soul is not at peace. I fear the loss of myself and that I'm not enough. The storm is strong, my voice is faint. Will I hear its call?*
>
> *But that's not all, for there is more that plagues me to the core. My friends are here. They are family whom I have come to love. But there is sadness surrounding them and suffering ensues. How can I turn my back on them and simply walk away? Lucita is a special girl who needs me more than ever. I have to try to ease her pain and help her find her way. That is my path. I have to trust. Here's where I need to stay.*

Reading over her entry, Anna reflected upon her path. She couldn't leave Lucita and quit a journey she had only just begun for a path that seemed familiar and safe. She had to keep moving forward.

Spinning the silver engagement ring she had placed upon her finger, she carefully pulled it over her knuckle. *I can't do this. I can't go back.*

Tentatively, she placed the ring in the drawer, and it came to rest alongside her prayer beads. Somehow they seemed like an odd pairing, as if they represented two parts of her life that didn't quite fit together. That was the truth. She had become more connected to herself during her time in South Carolina. She was a different person. How could she go back to how she used to be?

The doorbell chimed. Anna closed the drawer, along with the notion that her two lives could become one. Passing the statue of Mary, she sighed. *It's time to be honest with myself and believe in me.*

Frederick reached for her hand as they strolled among the garden's abundant blooms. Her tall oak towered above them.

"This morning," Anna began hesitantly, "I had every intention of going back home with you. But the decision I waited so long to make didn't ease my mind. It ended up doing the opposite." She sighed. "It's too late for us, Frederick. There will always be a part of me that loves you, but it's time to move on."

He stopped walking and faced her, his expression a mixture of bewilderment and concern. "What are you saying, Anna? We made a mistake. But we can fix it. We can fix us." The desperation in his voice made her stomach ache.

"No, we can't. I'm not the same person I once was. I've learned what I need and this is no longer it." She bit her lip, hating that she was the reason for his pain.

"So, you're choosing that other guy," Frederick demanded. "The one who saw us kiss?"

Anna shook her head. "No, I'm not. This isn't about choosing between you and him. This is about what I need." Her voice broke. "It's about *my* journey."

"So, that's it? That's all you're going to say?" Frederick threw out his hands in disbelief.

"I know this doesn't make sense to you." She clasped her hands, her tone vacillating. "I'm sorry for what I've put you through. You are an amazing person. But you deserve someone who can love you with her whole heart and, right now, I can't. I'm not ready. I need to be here. I need to go my own way." She reached for his hand as her throat burned. "It's time for us to say good-bye."

Frederick's jaw clenched and his gaze hardened. "Good-bye then, Anna. I hope you find whatever it is you're looking for." He whirled around and left her standing there alone.

Guilt bloomed in her chest as she stared at the oak tree. That part of her life was now over. Peering across the vast gardens, she hurt for Frederick but, at the same time, felt free. The birdcages swung in the breeze, and she thought back upon her life. *It's finally time for me to stay true to who I really am.*

# 32

"What are you two doing up here?" Anna asked, climbing the wooden stairs to Clark's attic. Empty cardboard boxes lined the edges of a few steps and although the air was humid, it had a sweet earthy bouquet. "Clark, you told me to come up here when you called, but you never said why."

"We're looking at Jupiter in the sky tonight!" Lucita exclaimed. "Do you want to see it?"

As Anna reached the top step, she froze. There on the balcony stood a five-foot-tall telescope. "Wow! Did you build this?"

Clark peered out from behind the long tube, a toothy grin on his face. "Of course I designed it. That's why it works so well!"

She walked over and touched the metal tube with her fingers, a gentle breeze blowing in through the open windows. "How long did it take you?"

"About three years," Clark said. "Being an astronomy professor does have its advantages. I've seen many telescopes over the years, and now I've come up with my own design."

Anna studied him, smiling. He was a collector of things, but in an organized kind of way. The conversion of the attic to an astronomy tower certainly proved that.

An extensive moon rock collection occupied a table in the corner, a pile of old astronomy magazines was stacked up neatly near one of the windows, and a large bucket of metal strips rested behind a door. But what struck her the most were the potted plants scattered around the room. There were geraniums, impatiens, and petunias. That explained the sweet loamy scent. An astronomy tower with flowers—that was definitely a new twist.

"What's this?" Anna asked. She pointed to a gold pocket watch resting on Clark's desk.

"Oh, it stopped working the other day. It's on its last leg. I imagine I'll have to replace it pretty soon."

"You don't wear a wristwatch?"

"No, I like to keep time in my pocket." He patted his pants. "Speaking of which, here it is. I knew I had it!" He reached into his front pocket and pulled out a long silver bolt. Placing it through a hole in the metal frame, he reached for the matching nut on the top of his desk. He slowly screwed it in place until the bolt was secure. Then he flipped the switch and the telescope whirred to life.

"Can I look now?" Lucita asked with excitement.

"You sure can."

Lucita held on to the big black handles and looked carefully into the eyepiece. "It's awesome!" she declared. "The rings are so dark and it even has moons!" She focused her gaze on it for a few more minutes and then pulled away. "Do you want a turn, Miss Anna?"

"It's been a long time since I've looked through one of these," she admitted. She walked onto the balcony and peered into the lens. "What did you say we were looking at again?"

"Jupiter," Clark replied. "It's in perfect position tonight."

The clear beige color of the large planet and the

clarity of its belts took her breath away. "It actually looks like it's flattened," Anna observed.

"That's because it's not a solid planet and it rotates so fast," Clark explained.

Anna stepped back and stared at Clark. "This telescope is amazing! You can see so much!"

"There are whole other worlds out there," he said, gazing up at the sky.

"What's your favorite constellation, Miss Anna? Mr. Clark has most of them up on the ceiling if you aren't sure." She pointed at the ceiling covered with glow-in-the-dark stars in the shapes of various constellations. It must have taken Clark weeks to put them all up there.

"I'd have to say Orion, the Hunter. When I used to stargaze with my father, I always believed Orion was there to protect me."

"Kind of like the eagle for me," Lucita said. "To watch over you?"

"Yeah," Anna agreed, rubbing Lucita's shoulders and staring up at the ceiling. "Like the eagle."

Clark pushed a button and the telescope moved into position. "Did you know that some legends say Sagittarius is a centaur who protects Orion from the Scorpion?"

"I didn't," Anna said. "I guess even Orion needs protection sometimes."

"Would you like to see Sagittarius? It's the perfect time of year for it."

Anna smiled. "I would." As she looked through the lens one more time, bright stars came into focus. Watching them, she realized that maybe Orion didn't have to be her protector. Maybe he was more like a guide to help her along her way.

She stepped away from the telescope still lost in thought. Lucita wrapped her arms around her in a giant hug.

"What's this for?"

"For staying in South Carolina with us. I'm glad you didn't leave."

"Me too," Anna said, pinching Lucita's nose. "Somehow, this place has become my home."

cg

After hours of stargazing, Clark and Anna walked Lucita back home. Standing on her front porch, Lucita hugged them both good-night and tiptoed inside. Before she closed the door, Anna caught a glimpse of Esperanza sleeping soundly on the blue sofa, a wool blanket pulled over her. She looked so peaceful.

"Lucita says Esperanza sleeps quite a bit these days," Anna said, walking down the porch steps.

"Hopefully, that will help her stay as healthy as she can," Clark said optimistically.

Anna nodded. But she worried no amount of sleep would be able to heal Esperanza's cancer.

"Bernardo must be working late," Clark said, tilting his head toward the soft light glowing from the barn window.

"I've seen his artistry in the house," Anna said. "I can't believe he can do that with glass."

"It's an amazing process to see." Clark said, waving her over. "Do you want to take a look?"

Anna followed Clark across the freshly mowed lawn. The grass crunched beneath her feet and the scent of pine and rosemary lingered in the air. She came to a stop beside a large window. Inside, Bernardo blew air through a metal pipe, expanding a bubble of glass on the end. Then, while still rotating the pipe, he shaped the hot glass on a steel table before placing it back into the furnace. He did this for several minutes until at last it took the shape of a large bullet.

A young man stepped into the light next to the table. He was tall and thin and was wearing thick, dark glasses. Bernardo said something to him, but Anna couldn't make out what it was. He grabbed the tube carefully from Bernardo and knelt on the floor. He began blowing air in the tube while Bernardo continued to shape the glass on the other end. They worked cooperatively, one blowing and the other shaping, like a well-oiled machine.

"Who's that?" Anna asked, her nose pressed up against the windowpane.

"Gerard," Clark said. "He was a student in one of my astronomy classes who wanted to learn about glass blowing. He started assisting Bernardo last year when Esperanza got sick. Glassblowing often requires two people. And ever since Bernardo and Esperanza were married, they have done it together. They have made many beautiful designs over the years. I think that's why it's been so hard for him to do it without her."

Bernardo scored lines at the neck of the glass piece with large tongs and then separated it from the original pipe. Carefully, he inspected the curved design of an exquisite round bowl. Its color was the deep blue of a sapphire.

"I'm glad he's still making his designs. They really are stunning," she whispered.

"He loves to blow glass," Clark said, staring through the window. "He told me once that it's like creating something magical."

"Does he sell them?"

Clark shook his head. "Bernardo believes when you sell something you love to do, it cheapens it."

"But doesn't he realize it's also a way to share his gift? By letting others enjoy his workmanship?

Clark smiled and met her gaze. "Perhaps you should

tell him that sometime. Maybe he'd hear it if it came from you."

"I doubt it," she muttered. "He doesn't listen to me." She tugged Clark lightly on the sleeve and whispered, "Let's go."

They walked along the path that wound up the hill and through the cypress trees, guided by the light of the full moon.

"Why does Bernardo keep to himself so much?" Anna asked, letting her fingers brush against the tall grasses. "Has he always been that way?"

"No," Clark said thoughtfully. "He used to laugh and joke. It's like he's become a whole different person."

"All because Esperanza's sick?"

"She's everything to him. I think he fears he'll lose himself once she's gone. And he doesn't ask for help. He never has."

"Then maybe we'll have to offer him some," Anna suggested. "You can't turn down what you don't ask for."

Clark laughed and put his arm around her. "I'm glad you're still here."

"You didn't think I'd leave that easily, did you?" she asked, placing her head on his shoulder.

He shrugged. "I wasn't so sure, I have to admit."

"I finally listened to what I needed. It feels really good to have made a decision that I know is the right one for me." She picked her head up and looked at the stars still twinkling in the nighttime sky. "You know, I figured something else out this week."

"What's that?" he asked, dropping his arm to his side.

"I'm going to start a new writing project about some of the things I've discovered here," she said, meeting his gaze. "I think it will help me heal. And who knows? Maybe it will help others as well."

"That's great." He nodded his head approvingly.

"I feel like it's what I'm supposed to do." She couldn't explain it any more than that.

"You're starting to trust yourself more."

"It's still a challenge, though. I mean, look how long it took me to decide not to go back home." She rolled her eyes.

"You discovered it eventually. Don't be so hard on yourself," he encouraged. "You're doing just fine."

The cicadas sang their nightly song and Clark picked up their tune, humming to himself as they entered his gardens. After a few minutes, he asked, "Does this mean you're going to be spending more time by yourself?"

"I'll be writing every day, but I promise not to be too much of a stranger." She gently elbowed his arm.

"Lucita will miss your fishing adventures, you know." His expression grew serious.

"I'll be sure to get those in. Now that it's September and she's back in school, we'll probably have to fish more on the weekends."

Clark nodded. "So, you'll try to squeeze people in?"

Anna wasn't sure why Clark kept pursuing this subject. She tilted her head and asked, "Are you thinking of someone specific?"

"Maybe." The corner of his mouth lifted into a smile.

"Listen, if you mean Simon, I just want to leave that be for now. We both need time to figure things out. Besides, I don't think he even wants to see me." She stared at Clark's back porch, visualizing the last time they saw each other. Her heart heaved.

"You never know," Clark offered.

"You want me to get involved with him again? Have us pick up where we left off?" Her voice trembled slightly.

Clark shook his head. "I'm not saying that. I don't even know if that's possible." He paused. "I know you're focusing on yourself and starting your new writing project.

That seems like enough to keep you busy for a while. I was just curious if you were still interested in him."

"He's the furthest thing from my mind right now," she said. But as the words left her lips, she knew they weren't entirely true. Simon had a way of creeping into her thoughts, and she couldn't help but wonder if she did that to him too.

# 33

A brisk breeze blew across the fields as Anna lit the jack-o-lanterns on her front porch. She and Lucita had carved them earlier that afternoon. Lucita loved taking out the pumpkin's "guts" and carefully choosing the design she wanted to carve. Anna decided to go with the scary look for her own pumpkin, but Lucita had other ideas. When she finally finished, Lucita's pumpkin not only had a carved face, but earrings and a fancy hairdo as well.

Anna thought of the pumpkin that Sasha carved this year. Julia had texted her a picture of a cat jack-o-lantern complete with pointy ears and whiskers. The last twelve months had gone by so fast. It seemed like yesterday when she had dressed Sasha up like a vampiress and walked her around the neighborhood. Anna sighed. She hated being so far away from her niece.

FaceTime allowed them to stay connected in a special way despite the distance. Maybe this Sunday they would have a Halloween tea party via their iPads. They could even dress up in their costumes. Smiling at the thought, Anna told herself that she would tell Sasha how much she missed her.

The jack-o-lanterns glimmered, and Anna stepped back to take in the scene. Beyond the pumpkins, the sky was streaked with blazing orange, deep crimson, and rich magenta. The view was breathtaking. She missed her family, but she also wondered how she could ever leave a place as beautiful as this.

Turning back toward the house, she saw Lucita running across the lawn toward her. "Trick-or-treat!" she shouted, bounding up the stairs.

She was a little forest fairy, dressed in glistening green. From her sparkling wings to her glittery sandals, she appeared as though she had come straight from an enchanted land. "You look fantastic!" Anna said.

"My mama helped me with everything. She even let me put on the makeup you gave me."

"Well, turn around and let me get a good look at you," Anna said.

Lucita eagerly spun around in circles, her short skirt poofing out with every turn.

"Clark did a remarkable job on the costume. I love the wings and the way the fabric sparkles and shines. You really do look just like a fairy."

Lucita twirled around one more time. "I know, and look at the fairy dust Mr. Clark gave me!" She pulled a small, sequined, lime-green sack off her shoulder and opened it to reveal pink and green fairy dust that sparkled in the soft glow of the light.

"Isn't it fabulous?" she asked. "I'm going to try out some of its magic tonight."

"I hope all your wishes come true," Anna said.

"Me too," she said, bringing the sack toward her chest.

"How about a caramel apple?" Anna offered. "I know you've been waiting all afternoon."

"I sure have! I'd love one!"

She ran into the kitchen with her wings fluttering behind her. She sat carefully on the high back stool, pulling out the fabric of her skirt so it wouldn't get wrinkled.

"Here you go!" Anna said, handing her a caramel-coated apple with chopped nuts sprinkled on the top.

Lucita bit into the apple and as she pulled it away from her mouth, caramel hung from her chin in long, thin strings. "These are de-lish!" she said with her mouth full. "You have to have one."

"Sounds good to me." Anna grabbed an apple off the plate and took a crunchy bite.

"Is that your costume?" Lucita asked, pointing to Anna's short-sleeve black dress.

"It is." Anna set down her apple and lifted the short skirt. "Don't you remember picking it out?"

Lucita nodded. "But what about the hat? You can't be a witch without a pointy hat." She took another bite of her apple.

Anna walked over to the closet beside the back door. She pulled down her black witch's hat from the shelf. "You mean like this one?" She placed it on her head, her auburn hair draping past her shoulders.

Lucita gasped. "You look like a real witch! Especially with your high-heeled shoes!"

"I'm glad you think so." Anna said, placing her hands on her hips and sauntering back over to the counter.

"The sparkling buckle on your belt matches the one on your hat!" Lucita exclaimed.

"It's the rhinestones," Anna said, fingering the buckle on her waist. "They're the real reason you picked out this costume, right?"

Lucita giggled. "You can never have too much sparkle!"

When they had finished eating, Lucita leaned forward on her stool and said, "I better go visit Mr. Clark and Mr. John now. They haven't seen me yet tonight. Do you want to come?"

Anna washed the caramel off her hands and dried them on the towel. Pulling her sheer gloves onto her arms, she said, "Sure. I'd be happy to come. I got all dressed up, didn't I?" She paused. "But you know there's one thing I can't forget."

"What's that?" Lucita asked, walking toward her.

"My broomstick, of course." Anna picked up a mini broomstick from beside the door. It was made from a wooden dowel and had dried straw on the end.

Lucita's mouth gaped as she ran her fingers over the prickly bristles. "You couldn't be a more perfect witch, Miss Anna. We're going to be the best dressed girls Mr. Clark and Mr. John have ever seen!"

We sure are, Anna thought.

Lucita pointed up at the sky as they walked. "Look at the stars!" she shouted. "There's a group of them shaped like an eagle. Do you see it?"

"I do. That's the one you told me about, right?"

Lucita nodded. "Mama says the eagle means someone's watching over us from the heavens."

"I like that," Anna said. "It's comforting to know there's someone up there looking out for us and keeping us safe."

Lucita ran ahead of Anna, dancing across the fields, wings fluttering in the wind. Anna loved watching her. She had so much spirit and a love for life that Anna hoped would never change.

Clark's house was decorated with brilliant orange and white lights. Fake tombstones surrounded the yard and he even had a large inflatable pumpkin in the back garden. Ghosts hung from the tree branches and bat silhouettes could be seen through the glowing windows.

"Trick or treat!" Lucita sang when Clark answered the door.

Standing there, he wore a navy wizard's robe and

matching velvet hat. The soft fabric was embroidered with silver stars and moons. Satin trim adorned the edges. He had a long flowing white beard and his blue eyes twinkled through his silver spectacles. "Hello, my forest fairy, don't you look amazing?"

"You're a wizard!" Lucita shouted, clapping her hand over her mouth.

"I am." He extended his arms dramatically in front of him. "And you're a fairy."

She laughed and spun in a circle, her shimmering wings whooshing in the night air.

"You're everything I imagined you would be," Clark said glowingly. "Do you have your fairy dust?"

"Right here," she said, patting her sequined sack. "Remember, I have special plans for it."

He nodded, stroking his long, curly beard. "I remember."

"Do you have any candy?" she asked, jumping up and down excitedly.

"Yes. I happen to have some right here." He reached inside the door and grabbed a porcelain bowl decorated with ghosts and pumpkins. "Take as many as you'd like. Otherwise, Mr. John's going to eat it all."

She plunged her fingers into the bowl and grabbed a handful of snack-size Snickers and Reese's, along with several Blow Pops. Carefully, she placed them in her plastic orange pumpkin. "Thank you. I also got a homemade caramel apple from Miss Anna. I think this is going to be the best Halloween ever!"

Lucita walked over to the edge of the porch, reached into her sparkling bag, and threw a handful of green and pink dust high into the air.

"What are you doing?" Clark asked.

"I'm sprinkling magical fairy dust upon your home, so the eagle will always watch over and bless you."

"That's very kind of you," Clark said and bent to embrace her.

When he straightened, Lucita pointed to the glitter all over his navy robe and smiled. "Now, you can have some extra fairy dust for yourself!"

"I'm sure it will be quite useful when I'm casting my spells." He winked. "Thank you!"

"Wow!" John bellowed from the doorway. "Look at this little lady! She seems to grow every time I see her. Happy Halloween, my dear!"

"Mr. John!" she said, running into his arms. "Happy Halloween! I'm so glad to see you!"

He picked her up and spun her around before setting her back down on the porch. In his brown pants and brown button-down shirt, he reminded Anna of a giant teddy bear. He smiled warmly at her.

"Hi there, little fairy," Simon called out as he emerged from inside the house.

"Mr. Simon!" Lucita screeched. "You're here too. This is the best night ever!" She ran over and hugged him.

Anna could hardly breathe. She hadn't expected to see him there. Why had she let Lucita talk her into dressing up? This was not the outfit she wanted to be wearing when he saw her again. The dress's sleek fabric didn't leave a whole lot to the imagination. She never should have come.

"You are a beautiful fairy!" Simon raved. "Here's a bag of Skittles for you. I know they're your favorite!" He handed them to her, the red bag crinkling in her hands. "Thank you," she cried, placing them carefully into her pumpkin.

Simon stood and stuck his hands in his pockets, shifting his weight from one foot to the other. "Hello," he said to Anna.

"Hi," was the only word Anna could get out. Simon's

hair had gotten a little longer. He pushed it back from his face, looking even more handsome than she remembered. Those captivating chestnut brown eyes showed some apprehension, which made her wonder if he still cared about her. Her stomach flipped.

Lucita walked over and sprinkled some fairy dust on Anna's shoes. In a low whisper she said, "Remember, this dust has magical powers and will help you with Simon. You can thank me later." Then with a wink, she put the package back into her green sack and skipped over to the top of the porch steps and looked at Simon. "Don't you think Miss Anna makes a great witch?"

"Yes, definitely," he muttered, his gaze lowering to her formfitting dress.

Anna stood a little straighter, suddenly very aware of her curves and oddly pleased that he looked at her.

Lucita nodded with satisfaction. "I have to go now so I can show Mama what I got, and then I'm heading to the school carnival with a friend."

"Let me take you home," Clark suggested. "I don't want you walking by yourself at this hour."

"That means I get to walk home with a wizard! Maybe we'll even get to practice some spells."

"Do you have any in mind?" Clark reached in his sleeve and pulled out a plastic wand.

"A real wand!" Lucita squealed, touching it with her fingers. "Let's see what it can do!"

She pranced down the stairs and twirled toward the trees as the moonlight shimmered off her sparkling wings. Clark walked beside her, waving his wand in the air.

"It was sure nice to see that little girl again," John said, watching her disappear from view. "She has so much energy and joy."

When no one else spoke, John cleared his throat.

"Would you like to come in, Anna? We were just going to sit down to some chai tea."

"No, thanks. I think it's time for me to head back home."

As she turned, Simon asked, "Would it be all right if I joined you? It's a nice night for a walk."

"Sure, that's fine," she said, looking over her shoulder at him. She spoke calmly but a shiver ran down her spine. The tight-fitting T-shirt he wore emphasized a sinewy body that was hard to ignore.

"How have you been?" Simon asked, falling into step beside her.

"Good," she said, her heart beating faster. She inhaled deeply, willing it to slow down. "I've been doing a lot of writing lately."

"Clark said something about a new project?"

She nodded. It wasn't right that being this close to Simon still affected her so much.

"Is it going well?"

"It is," Anna said, bringing herself back to the conversation. "I'm enjoying it. What about you? How's your remodeling coming?"

"I finished it a couple weeks ago. The kitchen looks better than I thought it would."

"Did you do all the work yourself?" She twirled her broomstick in her hand and met his gaze.

"Most of it. I like doing projects and working with my hands, especially when it involves wood. There's something freeing about creating something out of nothing." His eyes lingered on her face. "I guess you know something about that."

"Yes, I do," Anna said, smiling. "I'd love to see your work sometime."

"I'd like that too."

They continued walking across the field in silence.

Like an unexpected breeze on a hot summer day, Simon reached for her hand and held it.

"Anna, I'm sorry about everything. I was wrong to push you away when Frederick came. I should've known you would do what was best for you. I was being selfish."

"No," Anna countered, stopping so that she could look into his eyes. "I was blind to what I needed. My own fears nearly convinced me to leave a place I've come to love."

Simon touched her arm gently. "I've tried to stop thinking about you," he admitted. "But the truth is, I can't. You make me want to be a better person, a better man. I want to be with you. I want us to see each other again."

"I don't know," Anna said, chewing on her bottom lip. "I love spending time with you, but I can't rush into something I'm not ready for. Besides, I need to spend time writing and focusing on me."

"I know that. We can go at whatever speed you want." He reached up and stroked her throat with a sensual touch that started a fire deep in her belly. "I just want to be able to be with you, to touch you."

Anna closed her eyes, savoring his caress. "I want that too."

Pulling her close, Simon kissed her hungrily, as though he'd been waiting his entire life for this moment. Her breath quickened. Anna's mouth opened to the gentle probing of his tongue. Desire warmed every inch of her body. His hands trailed up her arms and over her bare back. His touch was electric against her burning skin. His scent of ginger and oak moss filled her senses. She pressed herself against the length of him, not wanting to think about anything but them.

When at last she thought her body would ignite, Simon pulled away, but he continued to stroke her cheek.

"If you want to take this slow, I think we better say goodnight." His voice shook. "I don't trust myself."

"I know what you mean," she whispered, breathing hard.

He gently pushed the sleeves of her dress back into place and traced his finger down her arm.

She moistened her lips at his touch.

"You are the sexiest witch I've ever seen," he said with a smile. "I think you have me under your spell."

Anna chuckled as she straightened her hat. "That's what I was going for."

"I thought so." His gaze held her, longing in his brown eyes. "I'll call you tomorrow." Then with a wave, he was gone.

Anna stared after him, her body still tingling from his touch. She had to take things slow with Simon. She just hoped that was possible.

# 34

The days of autumn were passing quickly and Anna had to admit she enjoyed her new life. She spent her days writing, fishing with Lucita, chatting with Clark, and the occasional sightseeing trip with Simon. Their tour of the Magnolia Plantation last Saturday was like taking a walk back in time. The magnificent gardens sprawled over acres of secluded land with majestic trees and a meandering river surrounded by golden rice fields. Strolling along the winding paths with Simon, she felt as though they were the only two people on earth.

The daily stress of deadlines, clients, and contracts was a distant memory, almost as if it had never existed. Her world was carefree and relaxed like she was living a perfect dream. And she didn't want it to end.

Now, sitting up in the front seat of Simon's Jeep, she scanned her surroundings. A quaint brick bungalow on a quiet residential street seemed to be their destination. Looking at him sidelong, she asked, "We're eating here?"

The corner of his mouth curved up in a knowing smile. "Yep. Come on inside. You wanted to see my new kitchen. What better way to check it out?"

Anna smiled. He was taking her to his house. She would get to see a whole new side of him and she couldn't wait.

Stepping out of the Jeep, a warm breeze blew across her skin like a gentle whisper. It rustled the lean branches of a crepe myrtle tree standing in the center of his front yard. The boughs teemed with leaves in vibrant shades of copper, brilliant against the darkening sky. The dazzling foliage was a reminder of the changing seasons. But Anna wanted to enjoy the temperate November weather as long as she could.

A gabled roof and a wide front porch with over-hanging eaves and tapered columns added character and charm to the house. Natural shrubs in shades of vivid burgundy and yellow bordered the porch. A pair of wooden rocking chairs stood in front of the large window. The house's simple design definitely matched Simon's own relaxed style. It was exactly the type of home she would have pictured for him.

She followed Simon up the steps that led to the porch and when he opened the door, Magnus jumped up on Anna, greeting her. He pressed his forepaws on her belly and she scratched his ears. Magnus licked Anna's cheek as though she were a cheesy beef snack. She laughed, giddy from the retriever's exuberance. She wasn't used to so much attention from an animal.

"He loves company," Simon said. "In case you couldn't tell."

"He's adorable," Anna chuckled, stroking his fur.

"He's something." Simon walked across the room, Magnus at his heels. "Go ahead and take a look around. It's cozy, but we like it. Right, boy?" He patted Magnus's back and opened the sliding glass door. Magnus darted outside, sniffing the grass alongside the fence.

The living room was spacious and inviting with pecan-colored walls. Wide wooden planks lined the vaulted ceiling while a speckled hardwood floor added a natural elegance to the room. Smooth river rocks were set into the wall surrounding a grand fireplace, like diadems in a majestic crown. Tall windows provided ample natural light and a brown leather sectional rested on a patterned burgundy rug. The trunk of a twisted tree was fashioned into a rustic coffee table. An intricately carved pirate ship sat at its center.

"I hope you like seafood." Simon said, placing his keys in a carved wooden bowl that sat at the center of a small end table. "I mixed-up some fresh crab cakes this morning."

"Yeah," Anna said, awestruck at the elaborate ship. "I'm not much for lobster, but crab's perfect."

"How are your muscles doing?" he asked.

"They're fine. You did give them a pretty good workout though." She touched the ship's sail. "I still can't believe we kayaked in the harbor for over four hours. It was a gorgeous view, but it was a lot of work."

"No one said adventures were easy." Opening the door, Simon let Magnus back into the house. He bounded over to Anna. Once she scratched behind his ears, he trotted over and curled up beside the fireplace.

"How'd you know I'd make it?" she asked, walking toward Simon and following him into the kitchen.

"I think once you set your mind to something, you don't let anything stand in your way." He met her gaze and smiled.

"You got me there. But, the rock climbing wall, what was that all about?" She placed her hand on her hip.

"I just wanted to see what you were made of. You actually climbed pretty well for an amateur." He pulled a baking pan from the cupboard.

"An amateur, huh? Well, considering I couldn't feel my arms at that point, I was glad we only did one climb."

"Me too." Simon brushed his hair out of his eyes. He was so easy to be with. He encouraged her to have fun again and explore life. He opened up her world to a place she had long forgotten ... a place where she was spontaneous and free.

The polished almond countertops and hickory cupboards gave the kitchen a contemporary appeal. Pots and pans were suspended above the large island and patterned tiles in soft earth tones lined the walls. "This kitchen is amazing," she said, running her fingers over the smooth counter. "You really outdid yourself."

"I wanted it to have all the modern conveniences, but still be warm and welcoming." He reached in the refrigerator and pulled out a glass bowl.

"You like to cook then?" she asked.

"When I have the time." He took off the plastic wrap and stirred a mixture of crab, peppers, onions, bread crumbs, and a few other ingredients with a spoon. "I can cook a pretty mean steak if I want to."

"I'll stick with seafood." She inhaled the sweet smell of fresh crab. It reminded her of the evenings in her youth when her mom used to make crab cakes for dinner. They were Julia's favorite. "Red meat is really not my thing."

"You don't know what you're missing," he teased, shaping the mixture into thick cakes.

"Yeah, I do." The slaughter of innocent animals had never been her thing. She leaned down and examined a small dolphin carving that was sitting on the counter. "So, you're a woodcarver?"

"I am."

"Did you make all of these?" Anna pointed at the collection of animals that lined the ledge of a bay window.

"Everything you see here. I even made the dining room table." He finished placing the last cake on the baking pan.

Anna glanced into the next room. A large rectangular wooden table stood in the center. Its caramel top was smooth as ice and the knots and grooves along the bottom gave it a unique visual appeal. "You're very talented," she said. "I'm always amazed by people who can make something that beautiful with their own hands."

"Thanks. I always enjoy exploring new surfaces." He met her gaze and grinned mischievously.

Anna fanned her face. *I'm sure you do.*

He placed the pan in the oven and washed his hands in the sink. Pulling down two stemmed glasses from the cupboard, he asked, "How about a glass of wine? I think after all your hard work today, you've earned it."

"I think we both have."

After pouring them each a glass, Simon made sautéed asparagus while Anna mixed together a Southern Caesar salad. When everything was ready, they ate in the dining room by candlelight. The crab cakes were delicious. The best Anna had ever tasted. And when Simon served key lime pie for dessert, its tart and tangy flavor left her speechless. He was an excellent cook, another surprise.

Once they finished eating, they cleared the table and carried the dishes into the kitchen.

"I enjoyed kayaking with you today," Simon said, placing the plates in the sink. "You said you've done it before, right?"

"Several years ago, in Kauai. It was beautiful there." She paused and set the salad bowl on the counter beside him, still remembering her voyage along the steep cliffs of the island with Frederick. Kauai was where Claire had been conceived. Bringing herself back to the present, Anna added, "But it's beautiful here too."

"Yes, it is," he said, his eyes caressing her face.

Anna felt the blood rush to her cheeks. "How often do you kayak?"

"I take my kayak down to the harbor a few times a

week. It's relaxing and helps me clear my head. In the past couple of months, I've been out there even more than usual."

Anna nodded, wondering if that had anything to do with their time apart.

"Down here, you can be outdoors all year round. Even if you get wet, you don't get too cold." He turned on the faucet to rinse his plate and playfully splashed water on her bare arm.

She shrieked in surprise but then challenged, "You sure you want to mess with me?"

"I'll take my chances," he mocked.

Anna grabbed the sprayer from the sink and pushed the lever. She sprayed Simon right in his face. Without looking back, she sprinted into the living room, knowing he wouldn't stop chasing her until she was caught. At least that's what she was counting on.

By the time she reached the sectional, he was right behind her. Water dripped from his wavy hair, which only served to make him sexier.

"Turns out you're more dangerous than I expected," Simon said, catching her around the waist. He wrapped her in an embrace.

His face inches from hers, she inhaled his sweet breath. Their hearts pounded through their shirts as though ready to explode. "I warned you not to mess with me," she whispered.

"You did. I'll keep that in mind from now on." He kissed her, slow and soft.

She felt as though she was melting, that if he didn't hold her so strong and intimately, she would puddle to the floor.

Magnus trotted over to them and began to bark. Simon pulled away reluctantly. "I guess he's used to getting all the attention around here." He scratched

Magnus' ears and reached for her hand. "Why don't we head out to the patio and I'll build us a fire?"

Stars sprinkled across the heavens as they stepped outside, Magnus leading the way. The temperature had dropped several degrees, and Anna shivered in her long-sleeve T-shirt. Rubbing her arm gently, Simon reached for a fleece blanket that rested on the back of a cushioned wicker sofa. He placed it over her shoulders and said, "This should keep you warm until I get back."

"Thanks." She squeezed his hand.

Anna sat on the sofa with Magnus curled up beside her. Soon, small flames burned in the fire pit until they gradually grew into a roaring blaze. The scent of burning wood lingered in the air. Simon came over and joined them on the sofa.

"Magnus is so friendly," Anna said, rubbing his back, his amber fur soft between her fingers.

"Yeah, you'd never know he was a rescue dog."

"Have you had him long?" She stared at the crackling flames, continuing to stroke Magnus' fur.

"About a year. He went through a lot of suffering before he came to me. I don't know how people can treat an animal that way." He reached across her lap and patted Magnus' head gently.

"He's lucky to have found you," she said, her breath quickening at his touch.

"We're lucky to have found each other." He held her hand in his. Their gazes met. "But when it's a good match, you know it." His eyes were filled with desire.

*Yes, I guess you do.*

"So, what is it you like so much about the outdoors?" Anna asked, looking around at the landscaped yard in the silvery light of the moon.

"Being close to nature. I feel as though it's a part of me somehow."

"I know what you mean. When I'm outside, it's like I feel the rhythms of the earth." She tucked a loose strand of hair behind her ear.

"Exactly. That's why I try to be outside as much as possible, even at home. This patio is my favorite place. Sometimes I even sleep out here." He patted the sofa's soft cushion. "It's actually quite comfortable."

"I prefer a softer bed myself," Anna said.

"That's good to know." Simon leaned forward and grinned, adding a piece of wood to the fire. Then he wrapped his arm around her shoulder. "How's the writing going?"

"Pretty well, but it's a long process. There are so many ways to say the same thing. The words have to be just right." She had spent over an hour on one paragraph yesterday afternoon. No matter what she did, it didn't seem to fit together. Finally, after reworking the whole thing, she moved on. But she still wasn't sure it said exactly what she wanted.

"I can imagine that's challenging, especially when you're a perfectionist," he said kindly.

"Even though it's frustrating sometimes, I do love it." She looked up at him.

"I can tell," he said. "You light up whenever you talk about it. I look forward to reading your work someday." The flickering flames of the fire reflected in his brown eyes, their intensity smoldering.

"Hopefully, you'll be able to."

Simon stroked her neck and tilted her chin toward him. She closed her eyes. As his lips met hers, Magnus popped his head up and licked her cheek like a kitten lapping up milk. Anna laughed.

"I think I'm going to have to work on his manners." Simon smiled.

"He just wants to keep you out of trouble."

"But I like trouble," Simon replied, raising one eyebrow.

"It can sometimes be a bad thing," Anna reasoned, patting Magnus' head. "You just want to keep him safe, right boy?"

"Then maybe next time, we'll have to do this at your house." Simon rubbed her shoulder and rose to his feet. "Speaking of which, it's getting late. I better take you home. It's been quite a day."

As Anna stood up, Simon placed his hand on the small of her back. Her body tingled at his touch and she swallowed, trying to get a hold of her desire to kiss him one more time.

"Thanks for coming today," he whispered.

"You're welcome," she said breathlessly. "Even if I can't use my arms for two days, it was worth it."

"That's the life of an adventurer." His breath was hot against her bare neck.

"Then I guess I better get in shape," she professed, reaching for his hand. "I'm thinking we have many more adventures ahead."

# 35

The ringing phone startled Anna awake. She had been snuggled beneath several warm blankets, but threw them off in the reflex of jumping out of bed.

"Good morning! Merry Christmas!" Julia exclaimed when Anna brought the phone to her ear.

"Merry Christmas to you too," she mumbled, rubbing her eyes.

"We got a few inches of snow last night. Sasha's outside playing in it as we speak."

"I bet she's enjoying that. Did my presents arrive in time?" She stared over at the clock. It was 8 a.m.

"Yes, thank you for Sasha's doll. She absolutely loves her. With her long blond hair and freckles, the two of them look like twins. Sasha gave her a new hairstyle this morning and can't wait to show you tomorrow over FaceTime," Julia gushed. "We also loved the framed photo collage. There are a lot of great pictures in there from when you stayed with us. And the sister ornament was a nice touch. Thank you!"

"I'm glad you liked them," Anna said. She had spent several days putting the collage together, wanting it to be just right. "How's Mom doing?" she asked, putting on her black leopard print robe and matching ballet slippers her mother had sent her.

"She was over here for Christmas Eve last night. It's hard for her, not having you here for the holidays." Julia's voice hung in the air.

"I know. It's hard for me too." Anna walked over to the window and took a deep breath. "I'll give her a call later this morning. What are your plans for today?"

"We're going over to Ben's parents this afternoon. They always love seeing Sasha, and it's nice spending time with them." Julia's tone was hushed as it always was when she tried to suppress her emotions.

"I'm sure Sasha enjoys it as much as they do," Anna encouraged.

"Yes, the three of them get along very well."

Anna knew Julia appreciated Ben's parents keeping his memory alive for Sasha. It wasn't the same as Ben being there, but at least it was something.

"Anna," Julia whispered. "I miss Ben. Christmas was his favorite holiday, and he never got to share the joy of that season with his daughter. She's at such a fun age." Her voice quivered. "I wish he could've seen Sasha grow up."

"I know," Anna replied, staring at the towering oak tree. She thought about Ben and what his devotion to his country had cost him. Yet, somehow she knew he wouldn't have done it any other way. "Ben's memory will always live on through the stories we tell," Anna explained.

"I know."

Anna leaned against the wall, wishing she could say more to ease her sister's pain. "He loved you, Julia. He always did, even when we were kids."

Julia sniffled.

"Christmases aren't easy," Anna went on. "They can remind us of the people we've lost like Ben and Dad. But they also are a celebration of the people who are in our lives right now." She crossed her arms and sighed. "I know I'm not there, but you, Sasha, and Mom mean so much to me."

"We know," Julia assured her. "Are you doing anything special today?"

"Clark invited me over to help him prepare for his dinner party tonight." She stared across the meadow, its long grasses blowing in the wind. "I'm looking forward to it."

"I'm glad you have him for a neighbor. He's a great guy."

"I know," Anna replied. "When you and Sasha came down here for Thanksgiving, it was nice you got to meet everyone. Now, at least you know the people I'm talking about."

"Exactly," Julia agreed. "I feel more connected with your life, you know?"

"I do." She closed her eyes for a moment, the sun's rays warming her face. "And Lucita still talks about Sasha. Those two had a lot of fun together."

"Two peas in a pod." Julia laughed. "How's Simon these days? He's really cute. Not that I need to tell you that."

Anna chuckled. "He's great. We went kayak fishing a couple days ago and that was a new experience for me. I even caught a large Red Drum that was twice as big as Simon's fish. Not that I reminded him about it, of course."

"Yeah, I'm sure you didn't," Julia said sarcastically.

"All I know is every day is an adventure with him." She smiled.

"And the writing project? How's that coming?" Julia asked. "You certainly are in the perfect setting to write it."

"Some parts are more challenging than others. When you write about what you know, it isn't always easy. There's still a lot of hurt I have to work through." She bit her lip. "I've discovered it's easier to write about someone else's pain than my own."

"I can believe that," Julia empathized. "But I'm sure the writing process has been healing for you."

"I've cried a lot, but I love it, Julia. I really do."

"I'm glad. You deserve to find something that fulfills you. It's been a long time in coming."

Anna nodded, knowing how true that was.

Julia sighed.

"Is something wrong?" Anna asked, turning away from the window.

"You aren't ever coming home for good, are you?" There was a certainty in her voice Anna knew all too well.

"No, I'm not," Anna confessed. Even though it was what she wanted, it sounded so strange to say it out loud. She had made the decision a couple weeks earlier, but saying it to Julia now made it so final. "This is the place where I belong."

"I'm assuming you've told Tom. What did he say?"

"He was sad to lose me from the firm, but supportive of my decision." She ran her finger along the top of the wooden desk and walked toward the bed. "He said that if I was ever back up there visiting, or needed anything, I should give him a call."

"It's hard to believe you're giving all that up," Julia replied, matter-of-factly.

"It is for me too. But it wasn't what I ever really wanted. I just thought it was. I was too scared to leave the only thing I ever knew." Her voice trailed off as she sat on the back of the bed. "But somehow I'm not so scared anymore."

"It sounds like you're where you need to be."

"Do you mean that?" Anna asked, wanting to believe her sister's sincerity.

"I do. I've always wanted what's best for you. I thought that getting back together with Frederick was what you wanted, but it wasn't. It turns out you knew what you were doing. I can see that now," she said. "I'm sorry if I made it difficult for you."

"Thanks," Anna said. "Your support means a lot." Hope filled her heart. Maybe Julia finally understood. She was where she belonged, and they could still be a close family. That's what Anna had always wanted.

"I'm here for you. Never forget that," Julia affirmed.

"Well, I better get going. Merry Christmas. We miss you."

"I miss you too, and give my love to Sasha and Mom. Maybe next year I'll be able to be there." That would be a nice holiday for them all.

"Yeah, maybe you will," Julia said hopefully.

Anna ended the call and looked around her bedroom. She had never been away from her family over the holidays. Yet, this would be a good Christmas, she resolved. She was going to spend it with Clark and her new friends. She rushed into the shower.

# 36

Her expectations for a fabulous Christmas meal were validated by the succulent aroma of cumin and sautéed garlic that radiated from Clark's house when he opened the back door.

"Hey there, stranger. Merry Christmas!" Clark was wearing his bright blue apron.

"Merry Christmas to you too!" She gave him a hug. "It smells like you're already hard at work."

"No time for rest when you have guests," he said in a singsong voice.

Anna laughed and hung her party dress in the closet beside the door. "So, you have everything we need for today?"

"I hope so." He pointed toward the kitchen counter. There were two large baskets teeming with assorted peppers, parsnips, potatoes, and cabbage. A lone pumpkin rested beside them while a relish tray brimming with fresh vegetables sat near the counter's edge.

"Are we just having vegetables for dinner? That's fine with me," she mused. Selecting a crisp carrot from the tray, she took a bite.

Clark grinned. "We're actually having honey baked ham, meatless stuffed cabbage rolls, roasted carrots and parsnips, sweet potato muffins, homemade pumpkin cheesecake, and my specialty, garlic mashed potatoes."

"That sounds wonderful. My stomach is growling already!"

"But that's not all," he said, pulling out his crock pot from the cupboard and placing it on the counter. "For appetizers we're having bell pepper soup, cocktail shrimp, crackers and cheese, roasted chestnuts, and raw vegetables with dipping sauce."

"I think I'm coming here every Christmas," Anna declared, finishing her carrot.

"You sure can. The more the merrier!"

"So, what can I help you with first?" She grabbed a striped apron from the drawer near the sink.

"Why don't you cook up the pumpkin we're using for the cheesecake? Here's the recipe you'll need." He handed her a fruit-patterned recipe card.

Anna read over the card. "I'm going to cook an actual pumpkin?"

"Yes," he said, patting the pie pumpkin on the counter. "It will taste better than you can imagine."

Anna looked at him skeptically and then read over the instructions one more time. Following them line by line, she carefully cut the pie pumpkin in half and then scraped out all of the *guts*, wishing Lucita was there to help.

Clark showed her how to place the raw pumpkin in a steamer on the stove to cook it. While it was heating up, she prepared the graham cracker crust. Once that was ready, she scooped the cooked pumpkin out of the skin and pureed it in a blender. Cooking a pumpkin really wasn't as hard as she had thought. After mixing up sugar, eggs, cream cheese, and a few other ingredients, she cooked the cheesecake in the oven. When it was finished, her dessert creation looked and smelled delicious.

"I can't believe I made that!" she said, feeling pleased with herself.

Clark laughed, walking over to inspect the cheesecake. "I thought you liked entertaining back in Boston. Didn't you cook up there?"

"Sometimes," Anna said with a shrug. "But I also had a good caterer."

"I see." He carefully placed the ham in the hot oven. "Cooking can be quite enjoyable. What I love is that almost everything we're eating tonight came from my gardens. Growing things and having them provide me with the nourishment I need gives me a very gratifying feeling."

"I imagine it would," Anna said as she set the cheesecake on the bottom shelf of the refrigerator. She, herself, had come to love gardening. Her connection with the earth and all its beauty gave her a sense of peace unlike anything else.

Anna prepared the pepper soup and made the muffins while Clark busily cut up the rest of the vegetables and finished preparing the cabbage rolls. Once everything was nearly ready, Anna went upstairs to change before the guests arrived.

She slipped into the smooth fabric of her sleeveless red dress, still loving its scooped neckline and narrow straps. She had bought it at a small boutique in Charleston a few weeks ago. Pulling half of her hair into a beaded clip, she let the rest flow down her back. She stepped into her silver pumps and applied a fresh coat of red lipstick.

Descending the stairs, Anna held her breath. She couldn't wait to see Simon, and she hoped he liked her dress as much as she did.

The dining room table was beautifully arranged with white china, crystal stemware, and cranberry-colored cloth napkins decorated with wide, golden rings.

Each place setting was adorned with sprigs of fresh holly. Glowing candles encircled a centerpiece of blossoming red roses.

Making her way to the living room, Anna admired the towering Christmas tree festooned with golden ribbons and white lights.

"The tree is beautiful," Anna said as Clark emerged from the den.

"I love decorating the tree with a different theme each year," he said, touching the branches with his fingers. "But it pales in comparison to how fabulous you look."

"Thank you and you're also looking mighty handsome this evening, especially with that snowflake tie."

"I don't get to wear it that often," he said, chuckling. "Now, all we need are the other guests."

As if on cue, John opened the front door, his suit coat disheveled and lines of concern etched on his face. "I'm sorry that I'm so late," he said, embracing Clark. "Did you get my text about the flight delay?"

Clark nodded.

"Good to see you, Anna." He kissed her on the cheek. "But I better get cleaned up." Then without another word, he dashed upstairs.

"Typical John," Clark said, shaking his head. "Blowing in just before the fun begins."

Minutes later, with John still upstairs, Simon arrived. He wore a fitted gray sweater paired with a collared shirt. Tailored dress pants hugged his body. When he smiled, Anna's heart melted.

"I'm glad you could make it," Clark said, shaking his hand.

"You know I wouldn't miss it," he said. "The food is always spectacular and ..." His voice trailed off when he saw Anna standing in the living room.

"Hello, Simon," she said with a grin.

"Hello ... it's nice to see you," he said. "Merry Christmas."

"Merry Christmas."

"Why don't I go check on dinner and give you two a chance to chat?" Clark said before disappearing around the corner.

"You look beautiful," Simon said, kissing her cheek and then eyeing her sleek-fitting dress. "Red is definitely your color."

"Thanks. It seemed perfect for tonight."

"Were you able to get any more writing done?" he asked. "I know you had a little writer's block the other day."

"That's bound to happen after spending time going on an adventure with you," she teased. "It's hard to focus after that."

"I know what you mean," he said with a wink.

The doorbell rang and Clark came back into the room.

It was Jillian. She wore an elegant form-fitting black dress and a matching, wide-brimmed hat. Carefully removing it from her silky curls, she handed it to Clark. "The house looks great. You've outdone yourself as usual."

Surveying the room, she spotted Anna and sauntered over. "I'm glad to see you two are here together," she said, looking over at Simon with raised eyebrows. "It must mean things are going well."

"They are," Anna said, squeezing Simon's hand. Then she leaned toward Jillian and whispered, "Your journal helped me more than you know."

"There's my little brother," John announced as he descended the stairs. "Merry Christmas!"

"Merry Christmas to you too," Simon said, giving John a hug. "How was the flight?"

"Delayed, of course. But I'm here now, and that's what matters." He had changed into black corduroys and a red sweater that matched his rosy cheeks.

Smiling, John turned toward Jillian and gave her a hug.

"It's nice to see you again, John," Jillian said.

"You too," he replied. "It's been a long time. You haven't changed a bit."

"You, either," she said, straightening her dress and smoothing her curls with one hand. "Charming, as always."

Anna watched Jillian force a smile. Clearly, she still wasn't pleased that her ex-husband had chosen a man over her.

"Well, I better head into the kitchen and help Clark," John said with a sheepish grin. "I think he's losing patience with me."

The guests visited over appetizers and eventually sat down to a delicious Christmas dinner. Anna couldn't remember ever eating a more succulent holiday meal. Once the plates were cleared, John invited everyone to join in the festivities in the living room.

Standing next to Clark in front of the fireplace, he said, "First of all, I want to thank each of you for coming to dinner this evening. It's a very special time of year and it's wonderful that you chose to spend it here with us." He raised his flute of champagne. "A toast to friends and family. You are truly what make the holidays so extraordinary."

Everyone clinked their glasses as Clark cleared his throat for one more toast. "I want to thank Anna for coming over earlier today and helping me prepare our meal. I couldn't have done it without you," he said, looking at her and holding up his glass. "To you, Anna, a wonderful neighbor and friend."

Clark continued, holding his glass upraised. "As you know, this is Anna's first Christmas with us, and so I have a special gift I would like to give her. Anna, would you please come up here?"

Seated in a chair across the room, Anna felt everyone's eyes upon her. She slowly stood and made her way to the front of the room. Clark handed her a long rectangular package wrapped in shiny red and green paper. She arched an eyebrow at him. "Go on, open it," he encouraged.

She tore away the paper and peered inside the cardboard box. Wrapped in white tissue was the familiar outline of a black instrument case. She opened the silver clasp and lifted the lid. Inside was a brand-new fiddle.

"Clark," she gasped. "I don't know what to say! I haven't held a fiddle in twenty years! Thank you!"

"You're welcome. Do you think you can still play?"

"I think so," Anna said, pulling the perfectly polished instrument out of its case. Her fingers caressed its slender neck. As she touched the smooth strings, her stomach fluttered with excitement. It was like seeing an old friend again.

Clark led her over to the antique upright piano and sat down on the bench. "How about you give it a try?" He placed his hands over the keys and soon the melody of "Up on the Housetop" filled the air.

As the bow soared across the strings, Anna realized this was the first time she had played Christmas music since her dad died. The music filled her soul.

Clark and Anna continued to play carols and the rest of the group sang along. They took requests and sang as many verses as they could all remember. Finally, their voices hoarse from so much laughter and singing, they finished their last song.

"How did it feel?" Clark asked, rubbing his hands together.

"Really good." She had forgotten how much fun playing music could be.

"Well, it sounded great."

"The fiddle was a very generous gift." She leaned against the piano and held her hand to her chest. "My soul thanks you."

"Seeing you play is all the thanks I need." He stood up, grinning. "Somewhere, your dad is smiling down on you right now."

*I'm sure he is.*

After putting her new fiddle away, Anna sat next to John on the couch. "This is quite a night," she said.

"Yeah, it's another great Christmas. I appreciate what a good friend you've been to Clark," he said sincerely. "He's lucky to have you."

"And I him," Anna said, and she gave John's hand a squeeze.

Simon joined them. "I hope I'm not interrupting anything." he said, placing his empty wine glass on an end table.

"Not at all. I better go see Clark and Jillian. I don't want them to have too much fun without me." John winked and left them alone.

"You were amazing on the fiddle tonight," he said, sitting down beside her. "It sounded like you never stopped playing!"

"Thanks."

Simon stroked his stubbly jawline, a curious gleam in his eye. "I was wondering something."

"What's that?" she asked.

"My cousin is getting married in a couple of weeks in Minnesota. Would you consider coming along as my date?"

Anna stared at him. "It would be nice to meet your family, but that's a long way to go."

"I know it is, but I thought it would be fun. Clark and John are coming too."

Anna clasped her hands nervously in her lap. Was she ready for a trip like this? It could elevate their relationship to a whole new level. Yet, she couldn't deny the excitement she felt at spending a weekend with Simon.

"Okay," she finally said, her tone steady. "I'll go."

"Great!" Then, grabbing her by the hand, he pulled her toward the door. "I have something for you. Come outside for a minute."

On the porch, a cool breeze ruffled her hair and Anna pulled her shawl tighter around her shoulders. Even in December, the temperature felt mild to her.

Simon pulled out a small silver package from his pocket. "When I saw this, I thought of you." He placed it in her palm. "Please open it."

Anna stared down at the small box for a few moments. What could he have gotten her? It looked like jewelry, but was that really what it was? With shaking fingers, she opened the lid. Inside was a silver, heart-shaped locket set with a luminous opal that glistened like a dewdrop in the morning sun.

"Simon, it's beautiful," she said breathlessly.

He leaned toward her. "I know you came here hoping to find yourself. Opals are supposed to reflect our inner light. I thought maybe this necklace would help you find yours."

Anna's heart swelled. This was one of the most thoughtful gifts she'd ever received. "Thank you." Staring into his eyes, she knew Simon was a good man. The kind who cared about a woman and never wanted to see her get hurt. The kind who loved with his whole heart.

"You're welcome," he said, kissing her softly on the cheek.

"Can you put it on me?" she asked eagerly.

He carefully placed the chain around her neck.

"That's a pretty spiritual gift, Simon."

"Nah," he said, securing the clasp. "I did a little research, that's all."

She smiled. "I have something for you too." She handed him a small paperback book. An illustration of a pastoral scene decorated the cover.

"What's this?"

"It's what started me on my spiritual journey. A book on the Tao. I know you aren't spiritual, but maybe it will help you understand me a little better," she explained.

He nodded. "A year ago, I never would've even considered reading this. But maybe I'll learn something."

She wrapped her arms around his waist. "That's what I love about you, your openness to things. It's a very endearing quality."

"I have a lot of qualities you'd like," he said, his eyes twinkling. He pulled her close. "But I am open to all kinds of things. Don't you worry about that."

Tilting her face toward his, he kissed her tenderly. The touch of his lips against hers was like melted chocolate, soft and sweet. He caressed her lips, her cheek, her neck with his mouth. His hot breath against her skin sparked a fire inside her. She moaned as he backed her against the wall of the house. His hips pressed hard against hers and his hands ran down the length of her dress to the hem, where he gathered up the fabric, sliding it high on her thigh. The heat of his touch made her moist with desire and his cheeks whiskered against her skin. About to surrender to temptation, Anna felt Simon suddenly pull back.

He was breathing hard. "I have to stop kissing you

because pretty soon I won't be able to," he confessed, sensually stroking the back of her neck.

"I know," she whispered with a shaky exhale. "We should get back to the party. We wouldn't want anyone to wonder where we are."

"No, we wouldn't want that," he teased. Looping his arm around her waist, he escorted her back inside.

With everyone seated in the living room, John served coffee and Anna's pumpkin cheesecake for dessert. The smell of cinnamon and cloves permeated the air as Anna took her first bite. It was an explosion of tantalizing flavor, a perfect blend of spicy and sweet. The kind of cheesecake you would buy at a restaurant and relish every morsel.

After clearing their plates, Clark convinced everyone to play a game of charades in front of the fireplace. Animated and boisterous, John was the life of the party. He really couldn't have been more different from his brother. After Simon and Jillian said their good-byes and the clock struck nine, Anna was the only dinner guest who remained.

"Can I help clean up a little bit?" Anna asked. Coffee mugs and wine glasses were scattered around the living room.

"No need. I got it," John replied, carrying a stack of dishes toward the kitchen. "Besides, aren't you and Clark supposed to go over to Lucita's tonight?"

"Yes, we were hoping to bring them some holiday cheer," Clark responded. "We shouldn't be too long."

"Please give them my regards and wish them a Merry Christmas."

# 37

White icicle lights illuminated the roofline of the Martinez's house. "It looks as if Bernardo wants to make this Christmas extra special for Esperanza," Clark said, as they pulled up. "I know it's hard on him, but he wants her to enjoy it as much as she can."

Lavish red bows decorated the porch railings and a wreath hung on the front door. The thick shrubs and dense branches of two young evergreens glimmered with colorful lights. And a bright star hung in the front window.

"Hopefully, we can add some more joy to their holiday," Anna replied, stepping out of the car. "The goodies we brought should help."

"They can't hurt," Clark said, opening the trunk. He slipped the handles of two cloth bags over his shoulders. "And to think, you wanted to walk."

"Yes," she chuckled. "I'm glad I listened to you." She reached down, lifting up the last heavy bag and looping the handle over her arm.

"You might be the first," Clark concluded.

"The first what?"

"The first woman who's glad she listened to me," he joked, walking up the porch steps.

"That's not true," Anna countered. "Lucita listens to you every day and she seems pretty happy about it." She nudged his arm.

He laughed. "Even though she's only eight, I'll take what I can get."

Clark knocked and Lucita flung open the door. "Mr. Clark, Miss Anna, you came over! Merry Christmas!" She threw her arms around both of them. "Come in."

They set their bags inside the door and Lucita excitedly grabbed each of their hands, guiding them into the living room. Pine boughs hung on the fireplace mantel, and burning logs crackled in the hearth. The room was toasty warm. In the far corner, the tip of an eight-foot-tall fir tree bore a beautiful golden angel.

"What do you think?" Lucita asked, spreading her arms wide. "Papa and I decorated the tree yesterday. We put on all our ornaments and I even made a few myself."

The scent of pine and citrus perfumed the air. "It's lovely!" Anna exclaimed, inspecting the various decorations hanging from the branches. A glass spiral ornament with swirling stripes of ruby red and evergreen shimmered in the soft glow of the lights. Mesmerized by its beauty, Anna wondered if it had come from Bernardo's workshop.

"Do you see the fairy?" Lucita asked, touching Anna's arm and eagerly pointing toward the middle of the tree. "Mama and Papa gave her to me for Christmas."

"Wow!" Anna said, spotting the small fairy with amber hair and large butterfly-like wings. Her orange flowing gown had silver jewels along the ruffles of its skirt. "She's beautiful."

"I hope she can use her magical pixie dust to heal Mama," Lucita said as she rubbed the fairy's gentle wings. "I know if anyone can do it, she can."

Anna stroked Lucita's long curls that hung down her back. "A fairy will always try her best."

Clark walked across the room and picked up two of the bags from beside the door. He placed them carefully on the kitchen table. "We brought some treats for you and your family. It is Christmas, after all." He grinned.

"You brought us something?" Lucita asked as she clapped her hands together.

"We sure did," Anna said, picking up the last bag and setting it on the wooden chair near the table. Glancing toward the kitchen, Anna inhaled sharply. Bernardo was leaning against the stove, his arms crossed in front of him and his jaw set. A half-empty bottle of whiskey sat on the counter beside him.

"Bernardo, it's nice to see you," she stammered. She had wanted this to be a pleasant Christmas for everyone. But judging from Bernardo's expression, she wondered if that was possible.

"What are you two doing here?" he demanded.

"We stopped by to bring over some presents and a little dinner that was left over from our get-together today," Clark said kindly. "I'm sorry your family was unable to make it."

"You know I have no interest in stepping foot inside your house. We don't need your pity on this day or any other," he said, staring at the bags on the table. "Please finish what you came here for. Esperanza's resting, and I don't want her disturbed."

"Is someone there?" Esperanza's raspy voice called faintly from the back bedroom.

Anna stared down the empty hallway, her stomach heaving. She desperately wanted to see Esperanza again, but she knew Bernardo was upset at their intrusion. Glancing over at Clark, she frowned.

"Look what you've done. You've woken her," Bernardo chided.

"Mama, Mr. Clark and Miss Anna are here. They brought us treats!" Lucita cried.

They heard shuffling, and soon Esperanza appeared in the hallway with a carnation-pink bathrobe draped over her clothes. Her hands grasped the handles of a walker decorated with green and red ribbons.

As she came into the light, Anna's heart sank. Esperanza's collarbones were protruding above her faded black sweatshirt, and her eyes were sunken deep in her face. Her movements were labored, and when a harsh cough suddenly erupted, her entire body shook.

After she regained her breath, Bernardo extended his arm and helped her sit in a chair.

Smiling, she patted his hand. "It's nice to have visitors on Christmas, don't you think?"

"Thoughtful of them, I guess," he mumbled, sitting in the chair beside her.

Lucita walked over and stood next to her mother, massaging her arm.

"Why don't we see what we have here?" Anna asked, rummaging through one of the bags. "I believe this is the leftover pumpkin cheesecake," she said, pulling out a plastic container.

"That's a very special dessert," Clark chimed in quickly. "Anna made it from scratch this morning and it's quite delicious. For the filling, she even baked a real pumpkin in the oven. She discovered that pie filling doesn't have to come from a can."

"That's true," Anna laughed. "Who knew my country friends could teach me so much?"

As Lucita began devouring the cheesecake, Anna looked in the bag at the remaining items. "We also have some ham, mashed potatoes, bell pepper soup, and muffins. I hope you enjoy them as much as we did. Clark definitely knows how to make a tasty holiday meal." Anna placed each of the containers on the table.

"Clark has always had a generous heart," Esperanza said. "We've missed his spirit around here, but are so thankful for the kindness and compassion he shows our little Lucita every day."

"Thank you," Clark said as his voice cracked. "Your family has always been special to me."

Anna pulled out a rectangular box wrapped in sparkly red paper with a wide bow. "This is for Lucita."

"Mama, may I open it?"

"Go ahead," Esperanza said, motioning her hand toward the package.

Lucita meticulously removed the wrapping and gasped when she opened the box. Inside was a doll that looked exactly like her, with deep brown eyes and long, black, curly hair. She ran her fingers down the doll's rosy cheeks, across its pink lips, and over its black dress, which had little red roses and lace embroidered on the fabric.

"I love her!" Lucita jumped up and hugged the doll in her arms. "Thank you so much!" She danced around the table. Lucita's green velvet dress twirled as she spun around.

"You're welcome." Anna replied. "But that's not all." She handed her another gift.

Lucita sat on the chair beside Anna and tenderly placed the doll on her lap. She opened up the large snowflake-patterned bag and pulled apart the two pieces of white tissue. Grinning, she held up a tiny, red-velvet dress. "It's so pretty," she said, smoothing the fabric and carefully placing it on the table.

Reaching back into the bag, she removed two outfits of ruffled black capris and ladybug embroidered T-shirts.

"Wow, they're matching outfits for my dolly and me! Thank you!"

She set them on top of the dress and grasped the last item inside the bag. It was a small wicker basket filled with wooden fruits and vegetables.

"The red dress is for your doll to wear every Christmas," Anna explained. "The ladybug outfits and the basket are so both of you can go outside and collect berries, flowers, or whatever you like. And the wooden fruit and vegetable set was Clark's idea because he thought you should be able to have a picnic anytime, rain or shine."

Lucita hopped up and nearly bowled Anna over with the force of her hug. "Thank you, thank you! I've never had a doll so beautiful! She'll go with me everywhere!" She released Anna and turned toward Clark, wrapping her arms around him in a tight embrace. "You're the best!"

"So are you," Clark said, stepping back and pinching her nose.

"Mama, Papa, look at her, isn't she wonderful?" She held the doll in front of Esperanza and Bernardo, stroking her long hair. "I'm going to name her Lola!"

Esperanza smiled at the doll. "That's an incredible gift. These two must love you very much."

"They do and I love them too." She beamed at Clark and Anna. "I'm going to go show Lola my room! Is that okay, Mama?"

Esperanza nodded and Lucita dashed out of the kitchen and up the stairs, singing softly to her little Lola.

"This one is for you," Anna said, placing a square package in Esperanza's lap. "It was Lucita's idea. Clark and I helped her put it together."

Esperanza unwrapped the shiny golden paper and peered down at a cranberry cloth scrapbook. In the small cover window was a family photo of Bernardo, Lucita, and Esperanza at Pepper's Pond. Esperanza showed the scrapbook to Bernardo and she smiled, as if remembering more carefree days. Then she slowly began turning each page of the album. There were photos of Lucita picking vegetables, carving a jack-o-lantern, and eating pumpkin pie, along with pictures Lucita had drawn of princesses, fairies, flowers, and Christmas trees. Esperanza placed her fingers over each of these little masterpieces while Bernardo touched her arm, captivated by the pictures before him.

"Thank you," Esperanza whispered.

Anna smiled. Then, with a hopeful heart, she handed Bernardo a package.

"What's this?" he asked in surprise.

"We know this has been a difficult year for you and that you're trying to do what's best for your family. Please accept this gift and know that Clark and I are here to offer our support."

Opening the contents of the package, Bernardo drew a deep breath. Lying in the box was a dual silver picture frame. One side contained a photo of Esperanza and him walking along the sandy shore, hand in hand, while the other side showed a picture of him carrying Lucita on his shoulders. Written along the bottom edge were the words, *The love of a family will never fade away.*

Bernardo stared at the pictures for a long time, a stunned expression on his face. Then he glanced over at Anna and whispered, "Thank you."

Relief flooded through her. Maybe they were finally making progress with him.

Bernardo turned his attention to Clark. "Did you take these pictures?"

"Yes, last year while you were picnicking on the beach. I never had the right time to give them to you until now.

"Thank you." Bernardo brushed away a tear. "This is a kind thing you have done, and I will not forget it."

Bernardo wrapped his arm around Esperanza's shoulder. "We better have you rest for a while. This has been quite a night."

She looked over at her guests. "Thank you for everything you've done. You are very generous, and our family has been blessed by your kindness. Merry Christmas!"

"Merry Christmas!" Clark and Anna said in unison.

Anna picked up their empty bags. "Thank you for welcoming us into your home, and please say good night to Lucita for us."

Anna was quiet on the drive back to her house, reflecting upon the evening's events. Clark pulled into her driveway and shut off the engine.

"What happened with you and Bernardo?" Anna asked. "John told me you were like brothers once. What changed?"

Clark rested his hands on the steering wheel. "When Esperanza was diagnosed with cancer last winter, Bernardo couldn't accept it. She was his entire life, and he could not imagine his world without her. Wanting to help, I offered to take them to a doctor friend of mine. I hoped he would be able to suggest some natural alternatives. Esperanza went through months of chemotherapy and radiation before trying my friend's alternative therapy. However, when the tests came back confirming the cancer had actually spread, Bernardo lost his patience. The treatment hadn't hurt her. But Bernardo said it gave everyone false hope, and maybe even made Esperanza worse. He blamed me."

"I'm sorry. That must've been really hard," Anna empathized.

"It still is. I miss his friendship. But I think tonight

was a big step for both of us." He sighed. "Now, why don't I walk you up to the door? It's the least I can do for all of your help today."

Anna nodded.

When they reached the porch, Anna grasped his hand. She wanted him to know what a special friend he was. "Thank you so much for the fiddle. You have no idea how much your gift meant to me."

"I have some idea. When I watched you play tonight, a spark ignited within you."

"That spark is there because of you."

"No, Anna." He shook his head. "It's always been there."

She smiled and reached into her purse. "Now, it's my turn to give you something. I hope you didn't think I forgot," she said, handing him a small square box.

"You never forget anything." Clark ripped off the paper and opened it. Inside was a shiny gold pocket watch. As he pulled it out and examined it closely, he noticed that it was engraved on the back with the words, *Friends make the best teachers.*

"I know your watch broke a few months ago and you've been meaning to fix it. When I saw this one, I couldn't pass it up. You've taught me so much about life. I've begun to look at things from a new perspective. Thank you for that."

"I'm glad, but you've also taught me a few things. It was through your encouragement that I went to Bernardo's tonight and gave him a gift. You also have shown me that keeping our lives safe isn't being who we truly are." He slipped the watch into his pocket. "I think our friendship has been a benefit to us both."

They embraced and Clark walked slowly to his car. Anna waved as he drove off then strolled around back and paused in front of the oak tree.

"Angels, please watch over the Martinez family. May they feel the love that surrounds them each and every day. Help them know how much we care and send them our light and love."

Turning around, she saw the electric candle lights glowing brightly in each of her windows. They reminded her of Christmas in New England. In her neighborhood as a child, every house had candles in their windows for the holidays. And now seeing their brilliant glow against the darkness, they comforted her.

# 38

Anna and Jillian stepped into the spacious waiting room outside the yoga studio. A casual seating area with four round tables and chairs created a genial environment where a group of young women chatted while waiting for the next session.

Flourishing umbrella plants and a towering bamboo tree swathed the room with natural beauty. Photographs of coastal landscapes hung on the sage-colored walls, and a wide wooden cubby stood near the studio door. On its top rested several books about dreams and the connection between poetry and spirit.

"How'd the class feel?" Anna asked, reaching inside the cubby for her keys.

"Pretty good," Jillian said. She slipped on her jeweled flip flops and shrugged. "It wasn't nearly as bad as I thought it would be. It was actually quite relaxing."

"It can be," Anna said, pulling on her turquoise sweatshirt. "You did great for your first time. Your body's really flexible."

"I think it helped you knew the instructor," Jillian said matter-of-factly. "She probably went a little easy on me."

"Hardly," Anna countered. "I think you're already ready for Bikram yoga."

"Not me," Jillian said, holding up her hands and walking toward the door. "Intense heat is not my thing."

"It might surprise you," Anna said with a grin. "Anyway, thanks for coming tonight."

"That's what New Year's resolutions are for ... supporting a friend, trying something new. I'm just not sure why mine had to include spandex and a mat, but whatever." She winked and placed her plum wrap over her shoulders.

"Spandex can be sexy," Anna quipped.

"I know." Jillian smiled like a Cheshire cat. "That's why I wear it to the gym."

When they stepped outside, the afternoon sun warmed Anna's face. The breeze carried cries of cooing pigeons. They walked together for a few blocks past elite boutiques, an authentic local grocery store, and several charming cafés. At last they stopped outside Jillian's condo. The towering brick building had large windows and black metal balconies and dominated the harbor's edge.

"Do you have a minute to come up?" Jillian asked. "I have something for you."

"Sure," Anna replied, excited to see the indoor architecture and style of Jillian's place.

When Jillian unlocked the door, Anna was immediately drawn to the loft's open floor plan. Fuchsia-colored pipes ran through the ceiling and ten-foot-high windows lined the far wall. The sound of ocean waves splashing against the sea wall in the distance was like rumbling thunder.

"This place is great. I love the view!"

"Yeah, the windows provide a lot of natural light. That helps my mood."

Anna walked into the expansive room and gasped when she saw the large mural on the wall. "Did you paint this?"

Jillian nodded.

"It's incredible. Where is this place?"

"It's a small coastal village along the Amalfi coast in Italy. It's one of the most amazing places I've ever been."

"I feel as if I'm there," Anna said, studying the towering bell house, the gardens, and vast mountains that plunged into a foaming sea.

"Sometimes I wish I was."

"You're very talented. Did you study art?"

"That's what I went to school for. Now, it's more of a hobby." Jillian walked over to the window and picked up a canvas that was draped with an old pillowcase. "I've done a few exhibitions, but I don't have a lot of time with the café."

"I know how that can be." Anna stared at the mural for a few more minutes, admiring its rich color. Looking around, she noticed a wooden easel standing in the far corner of the room with a splattered apron hanging on the corner. Behind it stood a tall table with jars of various brushes and paints. When she moved closer, she saw a small portrait of a young boy around the age of three hanging on the wall.

"Is that Ethan?" Anna asked, gently tilting her head toward the painting.

Jillian nodded. "I painted that while he was playing on the beach one afternoon, with the waves crashing around him and a sand castle at his feet. It's always been one of my favorites."

Anna stared at the little boy with blond curls and rosy cheeks. The painting was so lifelike. Her stomach wrenched at the thought of Jillian's grief. She knew all too well the unrelenting pain and anguish that still resided in her own heart. "He's beautiful."

"Yes," Jillian whispered. "He really was." Taking a deep breath, she pulled the pillowcase from the picture she had been holding.

"This is for you," Jillian said. "It's something I want you to have." She handed the canvas to Anna.

She glanced down at the painting. Two women sat at a small round table amidst a blooming garden. They were sipping coffee with a plate of half-eaten chocolate cake between them. They were both smiling.

"They look just like you and me," Anna observed.

"That's the whole point," Jillian said. "It reminded me of the night we talked at the coffee shop. I titled it *Friendship*. I finished it last week."

Anna brushed away a tear. "Thank you."

"You're welcome." Jillian hugged Anna tightly. "Now, you better get out of here before you have us both crying like babies."

Anna laughed and held the painting close. "Thanks for being such a great friend."

○8

"When are you leaving for the wedding?" Lucita inquired as she put the finishing touches on her gingerbread house.

"Two days," Anna said, rinsing out a bowl of white frosting in the sink.

"Are you excited?" Lucita asked, her voice animated.

"I am." Anna turned off the water and brushed her damp fingers on her jeans. "But I don't have a thing packed."

"I can help you with that." Lucita pushed the last gumdrop into place. "I'm an expert packer."

"Great!" Anna exclaimed. "Do you want to pick out the dress I'm going to wear to the wedding?"

Lucita jumped up. "Of course. Let's go!"

She raced up the wooden stairs and down the long hallway. Anna could hardly keep up with her. Gasping for breath, she followed Lucita into her bedroom. Suddenly, Lucita came to a stop in front of the statue of Mary.

"What's wrong?" Anna asked.

"This statue," Lucita said, lowering herself to the floor. "I haven't seen her in a long time. With her long, dark hair, tan skin, and kind eyes, she reminds me of Mama."

Anna sat next to Lucita and studied the statue closely. "She does look a lot like your mama. I've never noticed that before."

"Do you mind if I pray to her?"

"No, of course not. Go ahead."

In a hushed whisper, Lucita began her prayer. "Dear Mary, it's been a while and I almost forgot your face. But when I look at you now, you remind me of Mama. She's sick and needs some healing. I know there are many people out there who need your help, but if you could do anything, I would be so thankful. Mama is very important to Papa and me. Every day, she's in pain. Is there any way you could give her strength? Also, please help Papa to drink less. I know he's sad, but when he gets angry, that makes me sad too. Thank you for listening. Amen."

Anna draped her arm around Lucita's shoulders. "Do you feel better?"

Lucita nodded. "I know that God and Mary are listening. I only hope they can help."

Sitting beside Lucita in silence, Anna too wished whatever power Mary possessed could help Esperanza get well.

Lucita rose to her feet, bowed to Mary, and helped Anna stand up. Together they walked over to the large, white armoire standing against the wall. Lucita opened the wooden doors and ran her fingertips over the delicate fabrics. "Miss Anna. You have so many beautiful clothes. How do you decide which ones to wear?"

"It's how they make me feel that helps me decide. Sometimes I want to wear something fun or something that will make me happy. Other times I need something more subdued or sophisticated. Why don't you give it a try?"

Lucita looked through the clothes once again. "This short pink dress makes me smile."

"The one with the ruffled skirt?"

"Yeah. It's so soft."

"Let's see how it fits." Anna carefully pulled the dress over Lucita's head and took a few steps back. "Wow! It's very fancy. Why don't you go look in the mirror?"

Lucita pranced over to the tall wooden mirror in the corner of the room. As she looked at her reflection, the bottom ruffle of the skirt brushed against the tops of her toes and the narrow straps hung off her small shoulders.

Pushing one of the straps back up, she said, "This dress is so pretty. I absolutely love the color pink. I feel like a princess."

"You look like one too," Anna said, smiling. She pulled out a pair of high-heeled black shoes with satin bows. "Should we see how these look?"

Lucita slid her tiny feet into the elegant shoes. She grinned as she glanced at her own reflection. "I look like a grownup!"

"Now let's try a new hairstyle for the occasion." Anna grabbed some bobby pins out of an egg-shaped china dish on the dresser. She pushed them into Lucita's thick, dark hair one at a time. After the last pin was put into place, Anna drew out a strand of hair, curled it around her finger and let it hang loosely beside Lucita's face.

"Wow, Miss Anna, I look beautiful!" She clasped her hands and twirled in front of the mirror.

"You sure do. Would it be okay if I took a picture of you?"

Lucita nodded.

Anna took out her phone, and Lucita eagerly modeled the dress for her. Loving the attention, she even grabbed a pair of Anna's sunglasses before flashing another big smile. When Anna finally put down the phone, Lucita was glowing.

"Do you want to try on another outfit?" Anna asked.

Lucita nodded. This time, she selected a fitted royal blue dress with a low neckline. Anna picked out shiny silver pumps and a sapphire necklace that matched perfectly. Lucita leapt around the room and then, after eyeing herself in the mirror, posed for another picture.

The fashion show continued for another half hour until Lucita walked over to Anna wearing a long rainbow-striped sweater.

"Thank you for letting me try on your pretty clothes, but don't you think we should figure out what you're going to pack?"

"I suppose we better."

What to wear on special occasions always posed a challenge for Anna. So, a wedding where she was going to meet Simon's family only made it more difficult. She had procrastinated on packing all week. She wanted to make a good impression, but not overdo it. And, of course, she wanted Simon to *really* like the dress she wore. Grateful for Lucita's help, she hoped the little girl's enthusiasm would not only make packing more fun, but calm her fraying nerves as well.

"Let's see what we have in here," Lucita said, standing on her tiptoes and looking through the closet one more time. Then she pointed to a long, black dress with a plunging V neckline and thin straps.

"What about this one?" She held it up so Anna could see.

"Excellent choice. I've always loved that dress." She had bought it years ago, but never had the chance to wear it. It was sexy and fun, a way Anna hadn't felt in a long time. She hoped it still fit.

Anna slipped out of her jeans and lime-green sweater and stepped into the smooth, satin fabric. She turned her back to Lucita and asked her to zip it up. "What do you think?" she asked, turning around.

"You look like a movie star!" Lucita gushed. "Now, all you need are the right shoes."

"Which ones would you suggest?" Anna asked, pointing toward the neatly arranged shoes at the bottom of the armoire.

"The sparkling silver sandals. They would be perfect!" She reached in and grabbed them between her fingers.

"Don't you think my toes will freeze?" Anna picked up the skirt of the long dress and looked down at her feet, wiggling her bare toes.

"Only on the way there and on the way home," Lucita said with a giggle as she placed the shoes on the floor beside Anna.

"All right. If I'm wearing sandals, then I better polish my toes." She touched Lucita's shoulder. "Would you like me to polish yours too?"

"Absolutely," Lucita said, kicking off Anna's high-heeled boots. "Can you paint a pattern of pink and purple on mine?"

"I sure can," Anna laughed, thinking of Sasha. They had played "spa" many times over the years where Anna had patterned her toes. They had even done it with Lucita when Sasha visited over Thanksgiving. By now, she was an expert at painting patterns.

Anna padded into the bathroom. Catching her reflection in the mirror, she froze. She almost didn't recognize the woman looking back at her. The smile, the dress ... she had become someone new ... someone better. Lucita joined her, immediately picking through a basket of assorted nail polishes on the shelf. "What about you? What color are you going to choose?"

Anna read the bottom of an egg-shaped bottle. "Romantic Red sounds perfect," she said. "It should be a weekend to remember."

# 39

Simon surprised Anna by taking her to a frozen lake on the southern side of Minneapolis. Snow-covered evergreen trees and glass skyscrapers dotted the landscape. On the glistening ice, small children whizzed through the crowd while young couples held hands, basking in the sunshine, despite the frigid wind.

After renting skates, Anna zipped her long navy coat up to her chin and sat down on the cold bench next to Simon. She took off her mittens to lace up her skates. When she finished, Simon was rubbing his gloved hands together.

"Are you ready?" he asked, grinning.

"I think so," she said, standing up unsteadily.

He grabbed her hand, and they stepped onto the ice. Gripping his fingers tightly, Anna held her breath.

"It's been awhile since I've done this," she admitted, trying to keep her ankles stable. Her sharp blades glided over the icy surface. As she coasted around the first corner, her stomach flipped. *What if I fall? What if I run over someone?* Her knees wobbled wildly.

"Don't worry, it'll all come back," Simon assured her, squeezing her hand. "It's just like riding a bike."

"Yeah well, I rode bike a lot better than I ever ice

skated," she said. But, as Simon continued to skate beside her, Anna deepened her breaths and slowly began to relax. The support of his strong body comforted her, providing a sense of safety and protection. Gradually, Anna increased her speed. She gained more confidence as her balance improved. Releasing Simon's hand, she glided smoothly across the ice.

Simon observed her for a few minutes before he took off around the lake. Circling past her, he skated backward on the inside edges of his blades, weaving effortlessly between people.

"Hey, I thought you played baseball, not hockey!" she shouted after him. "How does a boy from South Carolina get to be so good at ice skating?"

He flashed a big smile and then disappeared into the crowd. On his next pass, he grabbed Anna by the waist, making her shriek in surprise.

"Are you trying to give me a heart attack?"

Coming to an abrupt stop in front of her, he placed his ear near her chest, listening. Then he met her gaze. "Your heart sounds fine to me, just a little excited," he said with a smirk.

"Can't imagine why that would be." She placed her hand on her hip, knowing his presence alone was enough to make her swoon.

He leaned toward her and whispered, "It's my charm, isn't it?"

As his warm breath caressed her skin, she knew it wasn't just his charm that affected her. It was his love for life, his laugh, his heart filled with hope, his acceptance of others, and his acceptance of her exactly as she was.

Grabbing her hand, Simon settled them into a comfortable pace. "I used to come to Minnesota to visit my cousins. Ice skating was something we did for fun. I guess it kind of stuck."

"I'm excited to meet your dad and your family," she said, pulling her ivory crocheted hat over her ears. She was eager to meet them but, like the cold wind, her apprehensions lingered.

"My dad's great," Simon said, as if trying to assuage any concerns she might have. "But more stubborn than anyone I've ever known."

"Is that where you get it?"

Simon nudged her arm and she glided toward the edge of the rink.

"Are you trying to check me?" she said with a smile.

"Only if you need to be checked."

"You better watch yourself."

"I'd rather watch you," he said, raising his eyebrows.

Anna shook her head and grasped his outstretched hand. "Can I ask you something?"

"Sure, anything."

"Clark told me once that you've learned how to protect your feelings and your heart. What did he mean?"

Simon's expression saddened. "Several years ago, I was engaged to a girl I had known for a long time. We were planning the wedding, excited for our future together. Or at least that's what I thought. The night before the wedding, she suddenly changed her mind. She walked out on me, and I haven't heard from her since."

"That must've been difficult." She gently touched his arm.

"It made me doubt that relationships can endure. I think that's part of the reason I was so certain you would leave me when Frederick came. I didn't think our relationship could survive it. So, I let you go before you let me go." He sighed. "I guess that's probably what Clark was talking about."

"Well, I'm not going anywhere." She squeezed his hand.

"I know." Rounding the corner, he looked down at his watch. "It's time for us to head back."

"Already?"

"We don't want to be late for the groom's dinner, and showing up with skates on is probably not a good idea."

"Maybe we'd fit right in," Anna said, stepping off the ice onto solid ground.

"Yeah, but I'm guessing you left your skating costume at home." Grinning like a jack-o-lantern, he sat on the nearby bench.

"I can be creative in a pinch," she teased, sitting beside him and unlacing her skates.

"Of that, I have no doubt." He tilted her face toward his and kissed her softly, leaving her breathless.

**໖**

Back at Anna's hotel suite, she took a hot bath to warm her fingers and toes. Once she could feel her extremities again, she let the water out of the tub. She pulled on black dress pants and boots before buttoning her cardigan. Finishing up her makeup, she smiled at her reflection. This was the night she was going to meet the rest of Simon's family. Butterflies fluttered in her stomach. She hoped they would be as nice as Simon and John.

They arrived at the restaurant for the rehearsal dinner. The wooden ceiling was over twenty feet high with brick walls and tall windows. Patterned bronze pendant lights hung from the ceiling and a wide-plank hardwood floor added its own unique charm, giving it an eclectic feel. Across the room, a boisterous crowd was already gathered near the curved wooden bar where large television screens flickered with a variety of sporting events. Four long rectangular tables were set up near the back, decorated with plum-colored candles and fresh flowers. The smell of fried onions and peppers wafted through the air.

"Simon!" a young woman with short black hair screeched. "It's so good to see you! I can't believe you're here!" She was dressed in a long-sleeve teal wrap dress accessorized with a sparkling beaded necklace. The silky fitted fabric accentuated her athletic frame, and her suede ankle strap stilettos matched the dress perfectly. She wrapped Simon in a tight embrace.

"I wouldn't have missed it," Simon said, releasing her. "This is my girlfriend, Anna." He glanced down at her with a tender smile.

Anna felt her cheeks warm. He had actually called her his girlfriend. It had been a long time since anyone had called her that. As Simon placed his hand on Anna's back, her heart raced. He was definitely ready for the next step. But was she?

The young woman's pixie haircut highlighted her silky skin and steel blue eyes. She held out her hand toward Anna. "It's so nice to meet you. I'm Sarah."

"It's nice to meet you too," Anna said, shaking her hand.

"Did you two do anything fun today?" Sarah asked.

"We went ice skating," Anna said, leaning against Simon's arm.

"That's great. It's one of the highlights this time of year and my favorite sport." Sarah fingered her necklace.

"Apparently, it runs in the family," Anna said, peering up at Simon.

"It always has," Sarah said, "even for our southern cousins." She winked at him.

"It can be dangerous though." Simon pulled back the sleeve of his sweater to reveal the salamander-shaped scar on his wrist. "Do you remember when you gave me this?"

Sarah ran her fingers across the scar and looked over at Anna. "When Simon and I were kids, we were ice skating on a pond near my house. I showed off my new swizzle skills and, of course, he had to try them out. He was doing pretty well until he decided to challenge me to a race. He wanted to see who could do the fastest swizzles. I wasn't going to turn down a challenge." She grinned up at Simon. "We took off at the same time. He was faster than me until his feet got tangled up and he fell. I tried to avoid him, but my feet weren't quick enough. I ran over part of his wrist with my blade. There was blood everywhere."

"There sure was," Simon agreed.

Anna ran her fingers along Simon's long, slender scar. So, that's where it had come from. He was a daredevil even then.

"Well, now that you know a little more about Simon, I suppose I better go visit with some of the other guests. It was nice to meet you, Anna." Sarah turned around and strode over to a group of young women gathered near the far window.

"So, you've always had a competitive streak, huh?" Anna teased.

He smiled. "I don't show that side of me to everyone."

Anna cocked her head. *No, I don't suppose you do.*

"I'm going to order us some drinks," he whispered. "I'll be right back."

He walked over to the bar, striking up a conversation with the man beside him. Simon mingled so easily with people. It was like he could talk to anyone. His presence drew people in. She knew that well. Then Anna's gaze shifted to Sarah. Happiness exuded from her every pore. She was a typical blushing bride. Anna remembered feeling that way once. Her smile faded as she remembered her own wedding day. She had believed the love she shared with Frederick could conquer anything, and that it would last forever. Yet, as she thought about that now, she wondered if love really had the ability to conquer all.

Absorbed in her thoughts, she jumped at a tap on her shoulder.

"Hey there," Clark leaned down and kissed her on the cheek. "I didn't mean to scare you. Are you okay?"

"I'm fine. When did you get here?" she said, squeezing his arm.

"Just now."

Anna glanced around the room. "Where's John?"

"He's visiting with some family near the bar."

Anna spotted him and nodded.

"Is there something on your mind?" Clark asked with concern. "You looked lost in thought when I came in."

Anna hesitated. "This is the first wedding I've attended since my divorce. It makes me realize how different my life has turned out from what I thought it would be."

"Is that a bad thing?" He crinkled his brow.

"No, it's just that back then, I believed I could do anything if I set my mind to it." She sighed, remembering her sheer determination that not only got her through law school, but enabled her to graduate at the top of her class.

"You had a plan for your life, but it went off course. That's part of living," Clark explained. "Don't you think pain and suffering make us more human? It's how we learn our most valuable lessons. Cloudy days make us appreciate the sunshine all the more."

Anna glanced at Sarah before returning her gaze to Clark. "I suppose that's true. But even when things are going well, the pain's still there under the surface. Writing has helped, but the guilt lingers. Maybe I'm wrong to be here with Simon."

Clark was silent for a moment. "We have to learn from our past, but it's not the sole determiner of our future. I learned many years ago not to question fate or wonder whether you deserve the blessings you have. It isn't about fairness. It's about gratitude and making a difference with the things you've been given. You have to stop punishing yourself for the mistakes you've made. Simply be grateful for the second chance at love you've found with Simon."

"How do I know it's really love?" She gazed over at Simon. "Maybe it's a rebound romance where we're both destined to get hurt."

Clark took her hand. "There are never any guarantees when it comes to love. As hard as it is for you, open up your heart. Accept the possibilities, rather than constantly questioning what everything means. Live in the moment, Anna. You've said planning your life isn't something you want to do anymore. So don't pass up on someone as wonderful as Simon just because you're afraid. Stop thinking and start feeling. I know you've been hurt. But you can't live life on the sidelines. You have to play with all your heart. It's the only way to truly live."

His words rang true. She needed to trust herself more. She owed herself that much.

Simon emerged from the crowd with a distinguished-looking man in his late sixties. He had a neatly trimmed beard and the same strong jawline and brown eyes as Simon. "Anna, I want to introduce you to someone. This is my father, Vincent. Pops, this is Anna."

"It's nice to meet you," she said, shaking his hand.

"Oh, believe me, the pleasure's all mine," he said with a firm grip. "You must be awfully special for him to have brought you all the way here." His eyes sparkled.

Anna smiled and held her breath. She was starting to think the same thing.

"It's nice to see you again, Clark," Vincent said kindly. "I trust things are well with you."

"Yes, they are." He patted Vincent's back. "John said you are heading to California next week?"

"Yep, time to catch up with some old friends," he explained with a smile. "At my age, that's an important thing to do while you still can."

"I hope you have a good time," Clark replied. "Now I think I better go check up on John. He looks like he's swapping travel stories with Aunt Beatrice again. He could keep her there for hours." Clark headed toward an older woman in a stylish navy suit visiting with John.

Vincent turned his attention back to Anna. "I'm curious, did Simon take you on an outdoor adventure today?"

"He did." She glanced over at Simon, raising an eyebrow.

"I knew it," Vincent laughed. "Simon would spend his whole life outside if he could."

"It's those camping trips you used to take me on, Pops. They set me up for life."

"Yes," his father said, stroking his beard. "I can see that. A chip off the old block."

"Vincent!" An elderly man called from across the room.

Vincent turned. "Oh, there's my cousin, Teddy. I better go see what he wants before he has another glass of whiskey." He touched Anna's arm. "It was nice to meet you. I'll see you at dinner."

"Okay," she said. Vincent was a kind man. Anna could already see that, and she looked forward to getting to know him better.

When his father left, Simon's face turned serious. "It's difficult for him, being here without my mother. I think he still mourns the fact that he never had the chance to say good-bye. None of us did."

Anna rested her hand upon his arm. "That must've been so hard. It's been two years, right?"

"Yeah. I still remember when Pops called and told me she was gone. It happened so fast. A cardiac arrest, with no warning. I'll never forget that day. I still miss her so much." His voice cracked.

"You always will," Anna sympathized. She glanced at Vincent who was busily talking near the bar. Her heart grew heavy. A day didn't go by that she didn't miss her father.

"My mom would have loved you," Simon said, wrapping his arm around her shoulder. "Independent and strong, you remind me a lot of her."

Anna's lip quivered as she stared down at the floor. She wasn't sure she was as strong of a woman as he thought she was.

# 40

Anna pressed the silky poppy-colored lipstick over her puckered lips and checked her reflection one last time. Her auburn hair was swept up, with curls cascading down both sides of her face. The floor-length dress flowed elegantly as she walked, and its smooth satin fabric accentuated the curves of her breasts. She wanted to look perfect, and this was as close as she was going to get.

As she placed the lipstick in her beaded purse, she heard a knock on the door. *That must be Simon.* She held her breath and made her way across the room. With an anxious smile, she opened the door.

Simon's jaw dropped. "Wow!" was the only word that managed to escape his lips.

"So, you like the dress then?" she said, turning around once.

"Yes ... it's amazing," he said, staring with hunger and awe in his brown eyes. Entranced, he slowly walked through the doorway.

"You clean up pretty well too," she said, her voice soft and silvery.

Stylishly dressed in a charcoal, double-breasted suit with a slim-fitting jacket that hugged his sinewy body, Simon didn't look at all like the adventurer she was used to seeing. Sleek and sophisticated, he looked like he belonged on the cover of *GQ* magazine. Yet, his compassionate eyes and curly locks couldn't help but reveal his true down-to-earth nature. There wasn't a touch of arrogance about him. That was one of the things she admired about him most.

"I like the tie," she added. "Blue is one of my favorite colors."

"I'm glad you like it," he said, stepping toward her. "Ties really aren't my thing."

"At least you can still breathe. A slim-fitting dress definitely makes you suck it all in."

"Well, no one wears it better than you." He placed his warm hand on her arm. Then his eyes settled on the silver chain around her neck. "You're wearing the opal necklace I gave you."

Anna nodded. "It seemed perfect for today."

Simon smiled and picked up her black cashmere shawl that was lying on the arm of the sofa. Tenderly, he wrapped it around her bare shoulders and whispered, "Well, we better be on our way."

On the short drive across the city, Anna gazed at the frosty blanket of snow that covered the ground. Against the brilliant blue sky, bare tree branches cloaked in glistening white reminded her of winters in New England. It was a season of wonder and beauty all its own.

"The wedding's indoors, I hope," Anna said. "Otherwise, I'm going to freeze." She pulled her shawl tightly around her shoulders.

"It's at a synagogue just up the road," Simon said. "And if you get too cold, I can always warm you up." He grinned widely.

"I'll keep that in mind. For now, I'll count on the

heater." She reached over and increased the temperature on the console. "Is your cousin Jewish?"

"Sarah's a non-practicing Baptist," Simon explained. "But her fiancé Adam is."

"An interfaith marriage in a synagogue?" That was something she had not heard of before. Not that she was an expert.

Simon nodded and turned the steering wheel. "They went to pre-marital counseling and met with the rabbi a few times. It's a Reform synagogue."

"Oh," Anna said, rubbing her hands together as the heat warmed her skin. "That makes sense."

They sat beside Clark and John in the sanctuary. Outside, acres of evergreen trees painted with freshly fallen snow surrounded the wintry fields. Sunlight spilled through the small rectangular windows and reflected off lush bouquets of tea roses and calla lilies, creating a kaleidoscope of color.

Adam, in a classic black tuxedo, stood on the bimah, an elevated platform in the front of the sanctuary. His eyes were riveted on the entrance where his bride would soon appear. When she emerged, his face lit up, as though she was the only woman on earth. Traditional Jewish music filled the air.

Sarah's mother and father escorted her down the aisle, and she seemed to float in a strapless ivory gown with a long flowing train. Her face radiant, Sarah circled Adam three times. Then together they walked under the chuppah, hands clasped, prepared to make their promises to one another.

During the ceremony, Sarah and Adam drank their first cup of wine to symbolize that they would now be drinking from the same cup of life. They exchanged rings, flawless circles to represent the unending love and eternal joy the marriage would bring. The young rabbi read the ketuba, the traditional Jewish marriage contract, and recited the seven blessings during which Sarah and Adam drank their second cup of wine.

The ceremony culminated with the traditional breaking of the glass by the groom. When the loud *pop* was heard, Adam's face beamed as the congregation cried, "Mazel Tov!" He reached for Sarah's hand, and they dashed down the steps and out of the sanctuary as the congregation sang and clapped to an upbeat Jewish melody.

The receiving line went quickly and after congratulating the bride and groom, Simon and Anna drove back to their hotel where the reception was to be held. Exquisite rose centerpieces adorned the linen-covered tables of the grand ballroom while soft white lights instilled a feeling of romance and passion. Through the windows, an expansive marsh stretched across the landscape for miles, waving under a frigid wind. Tawny grasses and shrubs encircled a small rink of smooth ice that had been cleared for the evening's events.

Adam and Sarah made their way outside. Most of the crowd stood pressed against the windows along the back of the ballroom. But some chose to brave the weather and watch from the outdoor patio. They were all trying to catch a glimpse of the bride and groom in action.

"I still can't believe they chose to get married in Minnesota in January," Anna whispered, staring out the window. "They do have summers here, right?"

Simon smiled and leaned close to Anna. "They actually chose January intentionally. Sarah and Adam are both avid figure skaters who met four years ago while touring the country with an ice show. They wanted their wedding to be during their favorite season."

"Well, then they chose the perfect month for it."

Adam and Sarah sat on a wooden bench and laced

up their skates. Their faces were aglow with excitement. Sarah carefully placed her white faux fur cloak on the bench before she grasped Adam's hand. They flowed effortlessly across the ice, perfectly in sync as though they were dancing on glass. After a few minutes, the rest of the bridal party joined them in their plum chiffon capes and tuxes. Everyone laughed with delight. After one final combination spin by Adam and Sarah, the crowd cheered and the show was over.

Simon placed his hand on Anna's back as they made their way to their table. "It's not every day you see a bride and groom on skates," he said.

"It definitely made the wedding unique," Anna agreed. "Although I'm guessing it's much easier to skate if you aren't wearing a floor-length dress."

"I suppose that's true." Simon glanced at her gown. "But it must be good for something."

"I think I'll be able to dance in it just fine."

"We'll find out soon enough," he said with a mischievous smile.

After a delicious meal and touching toasts by the maid of honor and the best man, techno music suddenly blared from the speakers.

"May I have this dance?" Simon asked, reaching for Anna's hand.

"You may." She placed her hand in his and he guided her to the front of the ballroom.

On the dance floor, Simon jerked his arms like a mechanical robot. He encircled Anna with exaggerated mechanized moves, and she erupted with laughter.

The music slowed to an old Steely Dan tune and Simon pulled Anna close. Wrapped in the strength of his arms, she felt like the luckiest woman in the world. Dancing across the floor, Anna tried desperately to catch her breath.

The party went on until after midnight. Once they said their good-byes, Simon grasped Anna's hand and escorted her back to her room. Leaning against his arm, she wondered if he was thinking the same thing she was. Tonight was the perfect setting for their relationship to go to the next level. Heart racing, she stopped in front of her door and gazed up at him.

"What did you think of the weekend?" he asked. "Are you glad you came?"

"I am." She tucked the loose strands of curls behind her ear. "It was great to meet your family. And it turns out both John and your dad are good dancers. Who knew?"

Simon laughed. "I guess my family is full of surprises."

"You certainly are," she whispered, touching his arm. Her mouth went dry. "Would you like to come in?" she asked, her voice quavering.

He tilted his head. "Are you sure?"

She nodded, swallowing the lump in her throat. Unlocking the door of her suite, Anna pushed it open. Soft light from the lamp glowed in the living area. She reached for Simon's hand with shaky fingers. She led him into the bedroom without a word. It had been so long since she had been intimate with anyone. Was she ready? This would change their relationship. It would change everything.

Taking a deep breath, she faced him. The steady hum of the heater was the only sound that could be heard. She helped him take off his suit coat and then loosened his tie. Its fabric was smooth between her fingers as she placed it on a chair beside the window. With slow, deliberate movements, she unbuttoned his shirt, enjoying the warmth of his body against hers. Closing her eyes, she wanted to stay right here. She wanted to remember this moment.

Gently, Simon placed his hands over hers. "Are you

sure you want to do this? I know it hasn't been very long since ... you and Frederick ended things. I want you to be sure you're ready."

Gazing into his brown eyes, she whispered, "I wasn't looking for love when I drove to South Carolina, and I didn't feel as though I deserved it. But then I found you. Simon, I think I'm falling in love with you."

He stroked her cheek. "I love you too. I have since the first moment we met."

Shivers raced down her spine. He loved her? Wow! How was that even possible? She tried to breathe. That meant he loved her through everything: her indecision about her marriage, their time of separation, their trip to Bulls Island. Yet, he always gave her the space she asked for. He never pushed her. That was incredible. Her heart fluttered. Simon loved her. How could she not love him too?

His body only inches from hers, he slipped his hand down her back. Tingling, she felt his hands linger at her waist before he unzipped her dress. The soft fabric slid down her body like being immersed in a cool waterfall. Her opal necklace still glistened around her neck.

"You're beautiful," he whispered, his gaze easing over her body. He lifted her in his arms and placed her on the bed. He slipped off his shirt, revealing his bronzed body, sculpted and lean. As he lowered himself on the bed beside her, she moistened her lips. Tenderly, he stroked her arm while she caressed the hard curve of his biceps with her fingertips.

Their bodies entwined. His skin was hot against hers, like steam rising from a shower. Passion burned in her belly in a way it had not for too long. She wanted him like she had never wanted anyone. Her hands roved up his bare back, and she kissed him on the spot just over his heart. As he grasped her hair between his fingers, her eyes closed and she let all thoughts escape her. His tongue slipped expertly over her body, savoring every inch of her. She heard herself moan as though disembodied. He worked his lips up her body to her abdomen, her breasts, her neck, until they devoured her mouth with their salty essence.

Anna kissed him hungrily. She relished his scent ... oak moss and ginger. Arousal and desire overwhelmed her. She sank into an oblivion of pleasure in his arms.

∞

In the soft light of morning, they awoke wrapped in each other's arms.

"Thank you," he whispered, kissing her ear.

"For what?" she asked curiously, basking in his body's warmth.

"For helping me believe in love again."

She smiled, stroking the chiseled lines of his abdomen. "You helped me too. I never thought I could feel this way again."

He ran his fingers across the opal necklace still hanging around her neck. "Did this give you the guidance you were hoping for?"

"Yes. I'm learning to listen to my inner light. It's amazing what happens when I do." She squeezed his hand. Her passion had come full circle. She had found her spiritual path and finally trusted in its wisdom. Her writing was what she was placed on this planet to do. She knew that now. In addition to finding herself, she also found Simon. An amazing man who helped her rediscover her physical passion. A passion she had neglected for far too long. Contentment washed over her. She had finally found her way.

# 41

Anna's stomach roiled as she listened to the voice-mail on her cellphone. She was vaguely aware of Simon carrying her bags upstairs. Her fingers trembled. Lucita's words sounded hollow and distant.

"Anna, what's wrong?" Simon asked, entering the kitchen. "Has something happened?"

She couldn't answer.

He touched her arm. "Anna. What's going on?"

As if woken from a trance, she turned and gazed up at him. "It's Esperanza," she said, her voice brittle. "She took a turn for the worse while we were away. I just got the message. She's in the hospital." Her heart clenched. Saying the words out loud, Anna felt her anxiety intensify. "Simon, we need to be there. Lucita sounded so scared on the phone. We have to leave now!"

Not waiting for his response, she grabbed her purse and rushed down the hall to the front door. She knew they didn't have much time.

Simon climbed beside her in the Jeep and sped down the long, narrow driveway. His fingers laced tightly around the wheel.

Anna gripped her seat and stared at the clock. The minutes passed by slowly like molasses dripping from a spoon.

"Please don't blame yourself for being away this weekend," Simon said, rounding a curve. "You had no way of knowing this would happen."

"But I should have," Anna countered, her fears growing stronger. "Esperanza's been getting weaker for months, and just as we get back from our time away, she ends up in the hospital. I left Lucita when she needed me the most."

Her throat burned from the tears she tried to hold back as she pictured Lucita, nervous and afraid.

"We'll be with her soon," Simon assured her, navigating the Jeep through traffic that only added to Anna's panic.

When Simon finally pulled up to the front entrance of the hospital, Anna ran inside as Simon handed his keys to the valet and quickly followed her. Nearly out of breath, she inquired at the information desk about Esperanza's location. Reaching the fourth floor, she wiped her sweaty palms on her jeans. She hoped she wasn't too late.

Following the signs toward Esperanza's room, she found Clark worriedly pacing in a small waiting room. Blue cushioned chairs encircled a wooden coffee table piled high with magazines. A wall of windows overlooked an expansive river that spanned over a mile across.

"Where's Lucita?" Anna asked, approaching Clark. Simon was right behind her.

"With Bernardo and Esperanza." He tilted his head toward a hospital room door across the hall.

"Is she okay?"

"Lucita's all right." Clark paused. "But Esperanza's dying."

Anna felt her breath catch in her throat. This was the end. "When did they admit her?"

"This morning."

Anna shook her head. "I should've been here," she groaned, gripping her hair in distress. "I wish I had never gone to that wedding!" Turning around, Anna inhaled sharply. Simon stood there motionless, a shocked expression on his face. He had heard her. Guilt welled up in her chest. But her words were true. She should have been here.

Clark put his arm around Anna's shoulder and motioned for her to take a seat. "You're here now, and that's what matters."

Simon walked over and touched Anna's shoulder. Hastily, she pulled away and gritted her teeth. Why had she gone away with Simon? She should have known Lucita would need her. She had let that little girl down. That was the last thing she wanted to do.

She heard Simon draw a deep breath and then make his way across the room. She immediately regretted pulling away from his touch and buried her face in her hands. Why did she always shut out the most important people in her life in the midst of her own grief?

Clark knelt down in front of her. "Anna," he said in a hushed whisper.

She glanced up at him, her eyes brimming with tears.

"When we left for the wedding, we had no way of foreseeing Esperanza was going to get worse. It just happened. I understand you're hurting, but we need to find strength in each other."

Anna looked over at Simon, whose broad shoulders slumped forward. "I know," she said, nodding her head. She had to fix this. Easing into the chair beside Simon, she reached for his hand. "I'm sorry," she began. "I was angry at myself for not being here for Lucita, and I took that anger out on you."

Simon brushed Anna's hair away from her face. "Lucita's so lucky to have you in her life. You didn't fail her. You've been her rock during this time, and I don't anticipate that's going to change."

Anna smiled, despite the ache in her heart. "Thank you. You have an amazing ability to say exactly what I need to hear." She leaned her head on his shoulder, and he wrapped his arm around her. Comforted by his touch, she closed her eyes, wishing reality would fade away.

When Lucita emerged from Esperanza's room, Clark dropped to his knees and held out his arms. She rushed into them, sobbing.

Finally, she released her grip on him. His shoulder was still moist with tears. "Is Miss Anna here?" Lucita asked expectantly.

Clark nodded and pointed to the waiting area, where Anna was watching them. Seeing Lucita's grief, Anna thought about her dad and the pain of losing someone that you loved that much.

"I knew you'd come!" Lucita cried. She ran over and wrapped her arms around Anna's neck.

"Of course. Are you okay?"

She shrugged. "Papa says Mama's not doing very well and is probably going to leave us soon." Her voice broke and tears rolled down her cheeks. "What am I going to do without her?" She nestled her face against Anna's chest.

Anna held Lucita in her arms and blinked back tears. Glancing around, she noticed how sterile and cold the hospital seemed. Overworked nurses busily tended to their tasks of filling out charts, administering medication, and responding to the varied needs of their many patients. Death was just part of their daily lives.

Bernardo appeared across the waiting room. His eyes were swollen, and he looked as though he hadn't slept in weeks. He stumbled toward them, as if in a fog. "Esperanza wants to see you," he whispered.

"Go on now," Anna said to Lucita, giving her one more tight hug.

"No, you," he said, meeting Anna's eyes.

She stared up at him in bewilderment. Why did Esperanza want to see her? It didn't make sense.

Clark touched her arm. "Go ahead. It'll be all right." He then motioned for Lucita to climb onto his lap.

Anna rose to her feet, her mind spinning. Simon squeezed her hand gently before he let go. Walking down the hallway, she tried to remain composed, but her legs felt as if they were made of Jell-O. With every shallow breath, the tightening of her chest increased until it felt like it was in a vice. She didn't have any desire to face death. Sadness shrouded her heart as she again thought of her father, who was taken from their family far too soon. And Claire, who never even had a chance to experience life. Death was so cruel. Anna wanted to run away. Yet, she knew this was her last chance to see Esperanza alive. Setting her jaw, she clenched her fists and pushed open the door.

Esperanza's petite body lay motionless on the hospital bed. A monitor beeped methodically in the background. Reluctantly, Anna inched her way across the room and reached for Esperanza's hand, careful not to disturb the IV taped to the back of it. Her fingers were cold as ice. The oxygen tube breathed artificial air into a body gaunt with sickness. Stomach queasy and a lump in her throat, she felt Esperanza grasp her hand. Something hard pressed against her palm. She looked down and her heart skipped a beat. There, in Esperanza's hands, were Lucita's prayer beads.

"Thank you for coming," Esperanza said through labored breathing.

"We came as soon as we heard. I'm sorry we weren't here earlier."

"You're here now," she said weakly, though her smile was strong.

Anna nodded wordlessly, her own anguish almost more than she could bear. Esperanza squeezed her hand again. "I know how much Lucita adores you. Thank you for all you have done for her. You've been such a strong presence, while I ... I feel as though I'm fading away."

Anna swallowed hard, struggling to hold back tears, not wanting this to be true. She didn't want to see Lucita suffer.

"My daughter will need someone to watch out for her once I'm gone. Bernardo means well, but he's going to be dealing with his own sorrow. He's a wonderful man, but coping with grief is ... not his biggest strength. Will you look after my family?"

Anna peered into Esperanza's sunken eyes. This wife and mother loved her family so deeply. She could never refuse such a request.

"Yes, I promise." Anna's stomach twisted. Was she really the best person to look after Esperanza's family? Her doubts lingered until she suddenly realized it didn't matter. All that mattered was that she loved Lucita, and they would make it through this together.

Esperanza exhaled, like air being released from a tire. "Thank you."

Anna smiled faintly. She did not want to let her down; she knew what she had to do.

Esperanza began to gasp for air. She frantically gripped Anna's hand. "Please," she wheezed, "send my family in."

Her eyes filling with tears, Anna gazed one last time upon Esperanza's kind face. She turned and pushed open the door, motioning for Bernardo and Lucita to return. Once they did, Anna lingered near the door, her hands shaking. She knew none of their lives would ever be the same.

Lucita climbed on the bed and sat beside her mother. Bernardo placed his arm around her and then reached for his wife's frail hand.

"I love you both so much," Esperanza began, her breathing irregular. "Please take care of each other and know that I'll always be in your hearts, watching over you."

Tears spilled down Lucita's cheeks. "I love you, Mama. I'll never forget you." She leaned against her mother's chest, giving her one last hug.

Bernardo kissed Esperanza's forehead. "You've always been an amazing woman, the love of my life." His voice faltered. "Thank you for loving me through everything. I'll miss you so much. Good-bye." He folded his arms around Lucita, sobbing.

Anna leaned against the wall as Esperanza's eyes closed and she breathed her last. She was gone. Where her spirit traveled, Anna couldn't say for sure. Even though all religions believed death was a natural part of life, somehow Anna still felt cheated by it. Those she had lost remained in her heart, but sometimes that wasn't enough.

"Love and light, Mama. That's what I wish for you," Lucita said sweetly, holding her mother's hand. "That's what I'll always wish for you."

Anna made her way over to Lucita and enveloped her in a hug. Her small body heaved with every sob.

Clark entered the room, his face somber. Walking over to Bernardo, he embraced him. "I'm so sorry," he said, his voice thick.

Bernardo's eyes, swollen from crying, seemed empty and hollow. It was as if Esperanza's passing had not only taken her spirit from this world, but his, as well.

# 42

The sun cascaded through the treetops, illuminating the cremation urn like the golden leaves of autumn. It was prominently displayed on a small table in a sea of blooming flowers at the edge of Esperanza's perennial garden. The urn was a cylindrical wooden bird house. Esperanza had chosen it herself. Once the scattering ceremony was complete, she wanted the memorial birdhouse to be hung in a tree in her garden in celebration of her life. She also wanted the birdhouse to be a daily reminder to her family that life goes on.

Lucita's string of prayer beads rested on the urn's round, wooden top. Anna stared at the beads, remembering the day she and Lucita had made them. They'd been such an important part of her own spiritual journey, representing her connection with things both in and beyond this world.

She stood among the people gathered outside Bernardo's home and despite the sorrow, she wouldn't be anywhere else. With a deep breath, she walked across the grass and up the porch steps. The dual frame that she and Clark had given Bernardo for Christmas was sitting on a square table. She hoped that Esperanza's memory would always remain as alive as it was today.

She glanced at the other photos on display: Esperanza sunbathing on the beach; dancing on her wedding day; and gardening outside with her precious baby girl. A beautiful portrait of Esperanza sat in the center next to a glass lily Bernardo had made in her memory. The clear stem swirled around a delicate pink flower. A green dragonfly rested upon it. Staring at the exquisite insect, Anna knew that Esperanza had lived her life to the fullest. And, like the dragonfly, she enjoyed every moment.

Meanwhile, Lucita stood beside the magnificent bouquets. Inhaling their bold and fragrant scents, Anna approached her. "How are you holding up, Sweetie?"

"I'm okay. I just wish Mama were here." Her voice was barely above a whisper.

"She is, Lucita. She's here right now." She placed her hand over Lucita's heart.

Lucita nodded. "I know, but I miss her hugs."

Anna wrapped her arms around Lucita. "I know that I'm not your mama, but if you ever need a hug, you just let me know, okay?"

"Okay," Lucita said with a weak smile.

Anna looked up to see Simon walking across the yard. He embraced John, saying something in his ear before they pulled apart.

"It's time," Clark said from behind them, touching Anna's shoulder.

They followed the winding brick path that led to the abundant blooms of the garden. The wind rippled Anna's hair, its cool touch like a soothing hand. Lucita ran her fingers along the large hosta leaves that lined the path, her voice unusually silent. A trickling waterfall from the nearby pond offered a gentle melody.

Bernardo stood at the edge of the garden, his face solemn as stone. He clasped Lucita's hand in his, and they sat down in the front row.

Simon joined Anna and looped his arm around her waist. "You doing okay?" he whispered.

She nodded as they walked toward the front. Sitting beside Lucita, Anna drew in a slow breath, holding the air in her chest a few seconds longer than usual. *I can do this*, she thought. *I can stay strong.*

Clark stood behind a small podium next to the handcrafted urn, facing the group of people who had come to this sacred space. He cleared his throat. "Today we are here to celebrate the life of Esperanza Martinez, an incredible woman who brought such joy to the lives of others," he said, his voice steady and calm. "Her uplifting spirit, luck at fishing, gentle nature and, of course, her love for her family and friends will never be far from our hearts."

Anna squeezed Lucita's hand. Saying good-bye to a parent would be one of the hardest things Lucita would ever have to do.

"Esperanza was a woman who knew what it meant to live out her passion and be grateful for whatever time she had here on this earth. She was an amazing friend who helped me change my life." Clark took a deep breath, looking at each person. "Although she left us far too soon, she's someone I will never forget. Standing among these plants she loved and witnessing the early blossoms of spring, I know her memory lives on in this place."

Clark reached over and grasped the string of beads, caressing them with his fingers. "These prayer beads and all their imperfections symbolize a life that was often filled with challenges. Yet, Esperanza knew that's what living is all about. Lucita shared these beads with her mother and all of the love that went into making them. They were a family who supported one another. Bernardo and his wife loved each other deeply."

Bernardo let out a muffled sob and buried his head in his hands.

"Although Esperanza's body is laid to rest, I know her spirit lives on. Her presence is here even now." Clark smiled and glanced over at Bernardo and Lucita. "I know Esperanza will always be watching over you."

As Simon gently placed his arm around Anna's shoulder, she heard a soft rustling sound. She turned her head slightly to see a majestic doe standing about twenty feet away in the open field. The animal stared intently at Anna, twitching one of its oblong ears. Anna remained perfectly still and held her breath, hoping the animal would remain close. Its deep brown eyes seemed to bore right into her soul. After a few minutes, it released its gaze and scampered through the open meadow into the safety of the towering trees.

Clark carefully lifted up the cremation urn and removed its cover. "As Bernardo and Lucita sprinkle Esperanza's ashes in this garden, let it remind us of how her energy and devotion surrounded everything she loved."

Clark gave the urn to Bernardo and hand-in-hand, he and Lucita walked slowly toward a green azalea bush that stood in the center of the garden. Azaleas were Esperanza's favorite flower. Bernardo lowered the wooden urn close to the earth and, together, he and Lucita poured the ashes around the base of the bush. When they finished, Lucita had a lone tear streaming down her cheek. Bernardo placed his hand on her shoulder as they stared down at the scattered ashes of their beloved wife and mother.

"If you would like," Clark continued, "please grab a small rake from the pile near the edge of the garden as we prepare to commit Esperanza's body back to the earth."

Simon and Anna grabbed their rakes and walked over to Lucita. Others joined them and formed an outer ring around Esperanza's ashes. Although sadness filled Anna's heart, it felt as though Esperanza's spirit really was with them and that it would always be in this place.

"Now, together we rake Esperanza's ashes into the soil. We know that her remains lie among these flowers and plants, which now share her soul. They will grow from season to season in her memory."

Gently, Lucita raked the soil and watched the earth surround her mother's ashes. As she finished, she stood beside Anna.

"Thank you all for coming to celebrate Esperanza's life today," Clark said. "When you are ready, please join us on the porch for refreshments."

Simon squeezed Anna's hand. "I have to help John set out the food. That's not exactly his specialty. I'll be right back."

Anna smiled and turned toward Lucita.

"There was a deer in the field just now. Did you see it?" Anna nodded.

"I know it's Mama watching over me. Now I have a protector in heaven and three here on earth—Papa, Clark, and you." She looked up at Anna, smiling for the first time that day.

"And we'll always be here," Anna said, hugging her shoulders. Then from her pocket, she pulled out a tiny package wrapped in glittering pink paper and handed it to Lucita.

"What's this?" Lucita asked, looking at Anna curiously.

"Something special for you. There's a note."

My Dearest Lucita,

You are an extraordinary girl who brings such joy to so many people. I have been blessed to be your mama. As you read this letter, my time upon this earth has passed. Yet, my love for you remains strong, and my spirit lives on within you. Place this ladybug near your heart and feel my presence with you every day of your life. For whenever you need me, I will be here.

Love Always,

Mama

Lucita's eyes were moist with tears as she gazed up at Anna. "How did you get this?"

"Before your mama died, she asked me to give this gift to you when the time was right."

Lucita carefully removed the paper and held a small gray box in her hand. Lifting the top, she let out a gasp. "It's a ladybug necklace!"

"It's lovely," Anna said. She removed the silver chain from the box. Placing it carefully around Lucita's neck, she secured the clasp.

Lucita examined the ladybug's intricate design. The head and wings were made of smooth silver while the body was comprised of jeweled garnet.

"May this ladybug remind you of how very much you are loved," Anna said. "Your mama and papa are with you no matter what happens. It's their light and love that will always keep you safe."

"That's right," Bernardo said, walking over to them. He bent and looked into Lucita's eyes before tenderly placing the prayer beads into her hand. "I know your mama would want you to have these back. I hope, like the necklace, they always remind you that she lives on in your heart."

Lucita stared down at the stones as a tear tracked down her cheek. "Thank you, Papa. They will."

Then Bernardo stood up and faced Anna. "Thank you for all you have done for my family," he said.

Anna placed her hand on his arm. "I'll always be here. No matter what."

He nodded and smiled. Hope filled her heart.

Bernardo took Lucita's hand and walked toward the porch. Anna watched them for a moment before she began collecting the rakes.

"That was a touching service," Jillian said, approaching her from the back of the seating area. Anna hadn't seen her arrive.

"It was. The service for her at the church was nice, but Bernardo wanted her scattering ceremony to be more personal and intimate. I will always remember her."

"Even though I didn't know her well, I could tell she was special," Jillian said quietly.

"She was," Simon said as he walked up behind Anna. He placed his hand on the small of her back. "We'll all miss her very much."

Jillian nodded. "I see Clark over there." She pointed toward the porch steps. "I'll see you both a little later."

"Are you holding up okay?" Simon whispered in Anna's ear.

"I am. It's been hard on all of us, though."

"Death always is." He enclosed her in his arms and she placed her head against his chest. His heart beat steadily like the rhythm of the waves.

"Thanks for being here," Anna said. "I know it means a lot to Bernardo and Lucita."

"Of course. They're a special family, and I know how much Lucita means to you." He smoothed her hair with his fingers.

"She's going to need us all now." Her voice wavered as she thought of the hole that now existed in Lucita's heart.

"And we'll be here," he declared. "In the good times and the bad."

Anna nodded and closed her eyes, thankful he was near.

# 43

Two weeks had passed since the scattering ceremony, and Anna was pouring a cup of hot chocolate for Lucita.

"What are we going to do today?" Lucita asked. She dipped her lips into the foamy marshmallows floating on the top of her mug.

"Well, my little marshmallow girl, we're going to paint some pictures, and I thought maybe we'd bake some cookies for Mr. Clark and your papa."

Anna walked over to the art station next to the back door and began searching for paintbrushes.

"Maybe cookies will help Papa cheer up," Lucita whispered.

Anna looked at her thoughtfully. "Is he still spending a lot of time in his workshop?"

She nodded. "I hear him crying sometimes at night. I don't think he really wants to spend time with me, though ..."

Anna set the brushes down on the counter. "I know it's hard to understand, but maybe your papa just needs some time alone right now." Anna completely understood the way grief could make people withdraw from everyone they cared about.

"I know, but I miss him."

"I have an idea," Anna said. "Whenever you feel sad or need to talk, why don't you come find me? I'll always listen and try to help."

Lucita hugged Anna's waist. "You sound like Mama. That's what she used to say."

Anna watched Lucita finish her cup of cocoa. She was glad to help this little girl however she could. She wanted to help her understand that one day her broken heart would heal.

They spent the afternoon baking peanut butter cookies and painting pictures of flowers and ladybugs. Lucita even added a colorful rainbow to her blooming garden of tulips. As Lucita finished washing her paintbrushes at the sink, Clark arrived at the back door. Lucita rushed over to greet him.

"Mr. Clark! I'm glad you're here!" She gave him a big hug. "Would you like a cookie?"

"I'd love one!" he answered, biting into the one she offered.

Lucita held out another and laughed as he gobbled it up.

Anna leaned against the counter. "Hey, how many are you going to have?" she teased.

"It's only my second one," Clark said with his mouth full.

"Yeah, but at this pace, you're going to eat them all in two minutes!"

"They're irresistible. What can I say?"

Anna and Lucita sat at the counter eating cookies and drinking milk with Clark. When they finished, he had a frothy milk mustache that made Lucita giggle.

Jumping off her stool, she grabbed Clark's hand and led him over to the table to show off her artwork. She explained every picture in detail, including the names of the flowers and the ladybugs. Then she selected a picture of a tall sunflower for him to take home and place on his refrigerator.

Anna wrapped up a plate of cookies for Lucita to take home to her papa.

"Are you ready to go?" Anna asked, looking over at Lucita.

"I guess so," she said quietly.

"Do you want us to come with you?" Anna offered as Lucita zipped up her sweatshirt. "It's getting dark out there."

Lucita nodded. Then a wide grin spread across her face. "That way Clark can hold the cookies while we dance."

"Wait a minute," Clark said. "What if I want to dance?"

"You better not," Lucita advised. "I wouldn't want you falling down and hurting yourself."

"I promise to be careful," he declared.

"Okay," Lucita relented. "But can you carry the plate and dance?"

"I sure can," he said. Then he leaped out the door and spun in a circle, nearly dropping the cookies onto the porch.

Lucita gasped.

Quickly regaining his balance, Clark smiled timidly. "Maybe I'll skip dancing this time."

"Good idea," Anna said with a grin. She was thankful for Clark's sense of humor. He always had a way of making Lucita smile.

There were no lights on in the barn as Anna and Lucita danced up the front steps, out of breath. Streaks of orange glowed on the horizon as the sky gradually deepened to stunning shades of indigo and violet. The sweet smell of honeysuckle and evergreen lingered in the air.

"That was fun!" Lucita exclaimed. "I liked having a cookie fairy along."

"You're just lucky this fairy didn't eat them all before we got here," Clark said, holding the plate up high.

"No chance of that. We kept a very close eye on you." Lucita laughed.

"I wonder if your papa's inside," Anna said, glancing through the kitchen window. If Bernardo hadn't been working all day, what had he been doing?

"Maybe."

But as they walked through the front door, Anna drew a sharp breath.

There, slumped on the sofa, was Bernardo, staring at them. His eyes were bloodshot, and his jet-black hair jutted out in every direction like the twigs of a bird's nest.

"There you are, Lucita. It's kind of late, don't ya think?" His words jumbled together, and when he attempted to stand, he wavered until he finally fell backward against the cushions.

"Don't worry about Papa," Lucita said matter-of-factly. "He'll be fine by morning. He's just sad." She placed her sweatshirt on the hook beside the door.

Clark looked down at her with concern. "How often have you seen him this way?"

She shrugged. "I don't know. Sometimes." She looked over at Bernardo pensively.

"Why didn't you say anything?" Anna asked, touching Lucita's shoulder.

Bernardo interrupted the conversation. "She doesn't need to say anything about it," he insisted. "I'm fine." He leaned forward, his body swaying from side to side.

Anna ignored him and dropped to her knees in front of Lucita. "Don't ever be afraid to tell us, okay?" she said steadily. "We're here for you."

"I know," Lucita said, pressing her lips together.

"Why don't you go upstairs for a little while?" Clark suggested. He set the plate of cookies on the table. "We need to talk to your papa."

The room fell silent as Lucita went upstairs, the whir of the ceiling fan the only sound.

"That's your wedding album, isn't it?" Clark asked, glancing down at the book lying open on the coffee table.

Bernardo nodded. "I was looking through it and decided to have a drink in Esperanza's memory."

Clark reached down and grabbed the bottle of Jack Daniels off the floor. He poured the last few ounces down the sink. "I think you've had enough for now."

"I could've stopped, you know. I just didn't want to ..."

"I know," Clark whispered.

"It was only a little," Bernardo asserted.

"You had more than a little," Clark corrected him.

Anna glanced down at the album. It was open to a picture of Esperanza and Bernardo holding hands on their wedding day on a beautiful beach. Their faces radiant, they looked like two of the happiest people on earth. Yet, with his haggard face and vacant expression, Bernardo looked nothing like the man in the photo. His eyes were as empty as the bottle of whiskey Clark had just poured down the sink.

Bernardo turned toward the window. "She was a good person," he lamented.

Clark nodded.

"Why did she leave me?" he asked as his voice cracked. "I can't raise Lucita without her."

"Yes, you can," Clark said, gripping his hand. "Anna and I will help you."

*Yes, we will*, Anna thought. *He needs us now more than ever.*

"You can't help me," Bernardo said faintly. "I have to live every day alone. Do you know what that feels like?"

"Actually, I do," Clark said, sitting beside him.

Bernardo was quiet for a moment. "Drinking helps me forget the pain of losing her. It helps me forget everything."

"What about Lucita?" Anna interjected. "You have to be sober to care for her. It's not right for her to see you like this." Stepping toward him, Anna grimaced at the stench of alcohol on his breath.

"What do you know about it?" he snapped, staring up at her. "I can control my drinking. It's no big deal!"

Clark knelt down next to Bernardo. "I know you want to control the whiskey," he said softly. "But after what happened tonight, do you really think you can?"

"Maybe the truth is I don't want to be sober," he announced. "I'm the one who's broken around here. Everyone else seems to go through life and handle their problems. That's why I need the whiskey. It helps me handle my problems better."

"Everyone's broken in their own way." Clark replied. "But we have to do the best with what we're given. You've been given Lucita, and she's an amazing little girl. Don't give up on her. She needs you."

"You make it sound so easy," Bernardo muttered, his body slumping back against the sofa.

"It's not easy, but you're not alone." Clark patted his shoulder. "You have to stay sober." He lifted Bernardo's legs onto the cushion.

Bernardo opened his mouth to respond, but then his eyes closed and his head fell back on a pillow.

"He's hurting so much," Anna said, staring down at him.

"It's hard. There are so many memories for him here," Clark whispered.

Anna knew how haunted she had become by memories of her father and her child. She empathized with Bernardo's grief. She had survived her own heartache by burying herself in work, so part of her understood his inclination to drink. It was the only way he could escape from the pain all around him, the pain that crushed his very soul. She only hoped they could help him see that there were other ways to deal with loss, healthier ways.

"We'll support him as much as we can," she said, peering at the wedding picture one last time before closing the album.

Clark took a blanket from the closet and placed it over Bernardo. His steady snoring filled the room. "I'll sleep here tonight to make sure Lucita's okay," Clark said. "Why don't you go home and get some rest?"

"Okay. I'll bring some breakfast over in the morning." She stepped out into the night, engulfed by the darkness. It was daunting. Just as grief was. Anna understood that Bernardo needed time and space, but she couldn't let him give up so easily. His family was worth fighting for.

# 44

Anna closed her laptop after another day of writing. She had finally revised the part about Claire without completely breaking down in tears. Exhausted, she stared at the luminescent moon outside her window before changing into her pajamas and sliding into bed. She knew the connection with those she loved could never be broken, even in death. They would always remain in her heart. And maybe that really was enough. Feeling a sense of calm wash over her, Anna closed her eyes and began to dream.

She stood alone near the kitchen window. A dense fog shrouded the gardens in mystery. As Anna watched shadows emerge, one of them appeared to be moving. Watching closely, she realized it was the silhouette of a woman. She turned toward Anna and then dissolved back into the mist, leaving no trace of her existence. Anna scanned the mystifying vapor, desperate to know where the woman had gone, to follow her.

Anna stepped tentatively into the mist, quickly becoming immersed in the moist air. She tasted the salty spray on her lips. Soon, she stood beside Athena's fountain. Anna peered up at the statue, bolstered by the strength evident in her expression and touched by the subtle sadness in her eyes. During times of great adversity, sorrow was a constant companion. The past two years of her life had proven that. Yet, what helped her endure was her resolve to tread her own path.

Making her way through the rest of the sleeping gardens, Anna finally stood next to the large oak tree. The birdcages could be seen within its twisted branches. The vast plain beyond the open meadow was obscured. The mist began to slowly lift. Listening to the wind whisper through the trees, Anna remembered what Lucita had told her about this place. She said it was where Lydia had found solace when her heart was troubled. That was comforting to Anna during her meditations because it somehow felt like Lydia was close by.

In the distance, the familiar silhouette of the woman materialized once again. As she drew nearer, her figure came into focus. Blue robes cloaked her body and white curls framed her face.

"Hello, my child," the woman said. Her pale skin glowed and her crinkly cheeks were the color of roses. "I've spent a great deal of time here in this meadow. It soothes me, as I'm sure it does you."

Anna stared at the woman for a long time. "Do I know you?" she asked. "You look so familiar to me."

The woman's blue eyes sparkled. "You know of me," she said. "We have many friends in common. I am Lydia."

Anna held her breath. This was Lydia? It was an honor to meet her. But why had she come? There had to be a purpose for her visit. Anna's stomach fluttered. "Why are you here?"

Lydia reached for Anna's hand, her voice soft-spoken. "I came to see you."

"Me?" Anna's heart pounded. *Why me?*

"You often walk near your tree when you are troubled. Today, you worry about Lucita and her papa. You want to help Bernardo but don't know how."

Anna nodded, feeling the warmth of Lydia's fingers against her own. "He's as lost as I was when my daughter died. I want him to understand that he doesn't have to push everyone away. We're here to help."

"When that same advice was given to you, did you listen to it?" Lydia looked gently into Anna's eyes. The wind tousled her white curls like buoys on the waves.

Anna shook her head.

"Why do you think Bernardo will be any different?"

"He won't," Anna said with a sigh.

"So, can you accept wherever he is in the grief process? Trust that he will find his way, as you did?" Her voice was kind.

"I want to lessen his pain," Anna reasoned, glancing up at the branches of her tree.

Lydia squeezed her hand. "You do not have the power to do that. He has to experience this pain for himself."

Anna met her gaze. "I have to be patient," she whispered.

"Yes," Lydia affirmed. "Now, I best be on my way. Remember, to help Bernardo, you have to accept him exactly as he is."

"That's the only way," Anna said, as if understanding those words for the first time.

Lydia smiled. "My friends are in good hands."

Anna awoke the following morning still entranced by her dream. It had seemed so real. But was that really Lydia? She then realized it didn't matter. The message was clear. She had to give Bernardo time to heal. She had to do the very thing for him that she had needed when Claire died. She only hoped it would work.

CB

The warmer days of spring arrived and Anna's routine included regular visits to her tree.

One morning, Simon found her walking there. He approached her with a steaming cup of coffee. She smiled at his visit, and his thoughtfulness.

"Thank you! How sweet," she said, kissing his stubbly cheek.

He handed her the coffee and laid his hand on her back. "It's good to see you," he whispered in her ear. His hot breath sent tingles down her spine.

She leaned into his touch as they stared across the meadow in silence. Since Esperanza's death, Anna had been consumed with Lucita's welfare and her writing. She hadn't permitted herself to even think about how much she missed being with Simon. Yet, this moment helped her realize that perhaps it was time she focused her energies on him.

"Are you doing okay?" he asked with concern.

She nodded.

"I know you've been worried about Bernardo. How's he doing?"

"He's still struggling." She sighed. "Clark stops by there every day, but alcohol is something Bernardo has always used to numb his pain. Old habits are hard to break. I think it takes every ounce of his willpower to stay sober. And some days that willpower is nonexistent."

"I'm sorry," Simon said, squeezing her arm. "I know you want to support him and help him understand the importance of moving forward with his life."

"That's what's so hard," she said, staring at the long slender grasses bending in the breeze. "He has to want to move forward. I can't force him."

"Spoken like someone who knows," Simon said tenderly.

"It's something you never forget." She took a sip of her coffee.

"Have you made much progress on your writing?"

"Not really. I try to focus, but my mind keeps getting clouded up with everything. I can't help but worry about Lucita. Even meditating is hard right now." She glanced at her meditation spot near the tree's exposed roots.

"You and Clark are keeping a close eye on her," he assured her. "She's going to make it through this."

"I know. I only wish Bernardo could somehow get past his pain. He's a good man who is still trying to find his way ... just like the rest of us. Clark's been talking with him, and it seems the two of them have begun to grow close once again."

"That's a good thing," Simon said, wrapping his arms around her. She closed her eyes, letting his warmth envelop her.

Facing him, she placed her arms around his waist. "I'm sorry that I've been so preoccupied lately. More than anything, I want to honor the promise I made to Esperanza. I want to keep her family together no matter what."

He stroked her back. "You don't have to explain anything to me. I know you have a lot going on right now. I accept that. But I'm happy to help however I can, okay?" He brushed her hair away from her face and smiled.

She gazed into his eyes, her heart swelling. "You may be the most wonderful man on this earth."

"You better not let Clark hear you say that," he whispered.

She laughed, and it felt good.

"Well, I guess it will have to be our little secret then," she said, grinning.

Simon caressed her cheek with his fingers. She closed her eyes, relishing his touch. Then he leaned closer and kissed her, slow at first, but quickly building in urgency, heat, and the unspoken desire between them. The kiss left Anna breathless.

When at last they broke apart, Simon confessed, "I've missed you so much."

"I know we haven't been intimate since our first night together, and for that I need to apologize." She paused and gazed up at him. "Would you like to go back inside the house with me?"

"I would."

"Well, let's go then. The faster we get there, the faster we can get started." Beaming, she abruptly turned around and dashed up the path toward the house excited at the thought of being with Simon again.

Simon raced after her. He caught up to her at the fountain, scooping her up in his arms, and carrying her into the house like a bride on her wedding day.

Upstairs, Simon placed her gently on the bed. She laid her head back on the pillow as he lowered himself beside her. Wrapping her arms around his neck, she kissed him hungrily. His hands roamed up her stomach, across her breasts, and along the lace strap of her bra, searching for its clasp.

Her breaths quickening, Anna buried her hands in his hair, her tongue exploring the moist hollows of his mouth. She raised her arms as Simon pulled off her sweater and tossed it aside. Opening the clasp of her bra, Simon stroked his thumb over the swell of her breast, pulling her nipple into his mouth as her bra fell away. A sizzle shot through her chest and deep into her abdomen.

The touch of his bare skin against hers was like wildfire as his hands explored every inch of her. She raked her nails across his back. His breathing intensified, his mouth suckling her. Anna moaned. Every nerve tingled with delight and anticipation. Heat built in her belly, stirring her, igniting her. She wiggled beneath him, unable to get close enough, wanting him on her and inside her. She called out in ecstasy as their bodies intertwined and merged. Desire consumed them. Time lost meaning. She wasn't sure where she ended and he began. Afterwards, sated and exhausted, she sank into his arms. Simon understood her so well and she had no intention of shutting him out of her life.

# 45

**A**nna was pulling fresh bread from the oven the following Saturday when Simon entered the kitchen.

"Hey there," he said, giving her a kiss on the cheek. "How'd the writing go today?"

"I got in a groove and it went better than it's gone in a while," she said, taking off her apron.

"You were able to focus more?" He leaned against the counter.

She nodded. "I think supporting Lucita through her grief has given me a fresh perspective about the loss of someone you love, whether it's a parent or a child."

Simon touched her arm. "Lucita's lucky to have you. You're an incredible role model for her. And you're lucky to have her too. She's like the daughter you never had the chance to know."

Anna nodded. In a way, Lucita had filled the void that Claire left in her heart. Even though she wasn't her daughter, she loved Lucita so much.

"How do you think tonight will go with Bernardo?" He cut a piece of steaming bread and buttered it before taking a bite.

"I'm not sure. He's so resistant to anyone helping him." She pulled down a wooden bread basket from the cupboard. "I'm surprised he even agreed to let us bring dinner over for his birthday. Clark must have worked his magic again. Let's hope it lasts."

"Everything smells delicious. What did you make?" He shoved the last bit of bread in his mouth.

"You mean, besides the homemade bread you just sampled?" she teased, wrapping the fresh bread in a towel and placing it in the basket.

"I wanted to make sure it tasted all right," he said with a grin.

"Well, did it?" She arched an eyebrow.

"Yes, it did. You can serve it to others and know with complete confidence that it will meet their approval." He reached toward the basket as if trying for another piece.

Anna playfully slapped his hand away. "Thanks for helping me out with that," she mocked. "As for the main dish, I made lasagna, and Clark's bringing a salad and the cake." She placed the bread basket on top of the lasagna that was already on the bottom of the canvas bag. Slipping the handles over her shoulder, she walked toward the back door.

"Could I sample a little lasagna on the way there?" he asked, stepping outside into the warm evening air.

"No, I think you should at least try to control yourself until then."

"That's difficult with you around, you know." He touched her arm.

Smiling, she reached for his hand. She could say the same thing about him.

Strokes of lavender and magenta painted the horizon. White smoke curled from the Martinez's chimney and soft lights glowed from the windows.

"Come in!" Lucita exclaimed, opening the door.

"How are you?" Anna gave her a tight squeeze.

"Great. Especially since you made dinner! Lasagna's my favorite."

"I know. But you're lucky Simon didn't eat it all first." Anna looked over at him and grinned.

"He wouldn't do that and wreck our dinner, right, Mr. Simon?" She gave him her cute puppy dog face.

"Never," he said with a wink. "Hey, can you show me those pictures you made?" He pointed toward the living room wall where she had hung her artwork. "You're quite the little artist."

"Sure," she said, grabbing his hand. "Let's go."

Anna smiled when she saw the table was neatly set for five. Clark had been there already and had placed some freshly cut daisies in the middle of the table as a centerpiece. However, as Anna walked across the room, dirt crunched beneath her shoes. Then she caught a glimpse of dishes piled high in the sink and her smile faded.

"I'm glad you two made it," Clark said, approaching her from the kitchen. He wiped his wet hands on the towel that hung over his shoulder. "Especially since you have the main dish."

"We wouldn't have missed it," Anna said before lowering her voice. "The house is a mess. Didn't Bernardo remember we were coming?"

"You should've seen it ten minutes ago. Be glad Lucita and I cleaned up a little."

Anna turned around to see Bernardo amble into the kitchen. His shirt was crumpled and stained. His gaunt face darkened with the early stages of a beard. He obviously hadn't showered in days.

"Thanks for coming," he said brusquely. "I could've made something though. You didn't need to bring all this food on my account."

"I wanted to. It's your birthday. I thought you could use a nice, home-cooked meal." Anna gestured toward his skinny frame. "Perhaps it's time for us to put a little meat back on those bones."

Bernardo grunted. "I needed to lose some weight anyway."

"How about we get this food on the table?" Simon suggested. "I'm starving."

He finished slicing the bread while Lucita helped Clark toss the salad and Anna cut the lasagna. After they finished eating, Lucita excused herself to play upstairs. Once she was out of the room, Anna looked over at Bernardo. "How are you really doing?"

"How do you think I'm doing?" he snapped. "My wife is dead and my daughter would rather spend time with you than me. Everyone wants me to stop drinking, and I still can't find work. My days are long and lonely. It's the worst time of my life."

"You've been making progress, though," Clark said, trying to be optimistic. "The employment office in town has your information, and you met with a career counselor yesterday."

"It still hasn't brought me work."

"No, but it will," Clark affirmed.

Anna sighed. "Remember that it's all for Lucita. She's the one who needs you the most."

"I know that! Everyone doesn't need to keep reminding me." His voice had a razor sharp edge to it.

"We just want to help," Clark said, setting his napkin on the table.

"Well, none of you know what it's like to have your wife die. As much as you've been through, you haven't had to survive that."

Anna could see how much Bernardo was still struggling. "I know it's difficult, but you have to try and get through every day. That's all you can do. You just need to keep trying."

"What do you know about it? This isn't about you, Anna. You've walked into our lives and tried to fix things, but guess what? You can't! This isn't something that Anna Waters can waltz in and make right. Why don't you go do that somewhere else? I'm tired of you meddling in my life, and I want it to end!"

Anna felt as though the wind had been knocked out of her. How could he be that angry at her? What had she done? She was speechless.

"That's enough," Simon asserted in a calm voice. "Anna has only tried to help you and your family ever since her arrival here. You have no right to talk to her that way."

"I have no right?" Bernardo said. "*You* have a lot of nerve to come into my home and speak to me that way. Get out and don't come back!"

Clark rose from his chair. "I think perhaps it's time for us to go. Good night."

Simon, Anna, and Clark made their way to the door. But before they left, Anna stopped and turned toward Bernardo. Meeting his scornful gaze, she said softly, "When I lost a child, I pushed everyone in my life away. I didn't want to feel. But feelings are what help us experience life, even when we are wounded to the core. Remember, although Esperanza's gone, you have a life here that you need to experience with a daughter who loves you more than you can imagine."

When Bernardo made no response, she stepped into the night.

They walked along the path until they reached Clark's house. Clark paused in front of the monkey puzzle tree that stood at the edge of his garden. "Sometimes we all need a second chance," he said, rubbing the tree's spiny leaves between his fingers. "When my last monkey puzzle tree died unexpectedly, I doubted whether another one could grow here. But with a little encouragement," he looked over at Anna, "I decided to give it a try. I tended to the tree and nurtured it. Now, it's thriving. I just needed to believe it could grow into what it was made to be." He smiled. "Perhaps that's true of Bernardo as well." Then without another word, he went inside.

Simon walked Anna home. Neither of them spoke until they reached her front porch. Anna couldn't get Clark's words out of her mind.

"Bernardo will come around," Simon said, leaning against the railing. "You have to believe that."

"I hope so," Anna said, clasping her hands.

"You don't sound convinced."

"There's so much hurt there," she admitted. "It's like he can't see through it."

"He will," Simon said, stepping toward her. "He'll find his way."

"You sound so sure." Doubts lingered in her mind.

"I've been doing some reading that's helped me see things a little differently these days." He reached for her hand.

"What's that?" She gazed up at him.

"The Tao book," Simon said with a smile.

"Really?"

"It has some good insights. Like how our mind only becomes clear when it's still." He brushed her hair behind her ear.

Anna nodded. "And how we should listen with our spirit rather than our mind. That's something being here has taught me."

"I also like the idea of following my personal journey and helping others along the way."

"That's my problem," Anna admitted with a sigh. "I want to help Bernardo, but he won't let me."

"Sometimes being there is help enough." He

squeezed her hand. "You have compassion and kindness. Right now that's all Bernardo needs. He's a spiritual man. He always has been. But experience can only come through living. Whether through suffering or joy, he has to live his life being true to who he really is."

Anna blinked. "Where'd that come from? It's pretty spiritual, you know. Has the book really changed you that much?"

He shook his head. "No, but I do like how the Tao encourages you to explore and live through your own experiences. I believe they are the best teachers. At least they have been for me. Nothing except my experiences with you and Lucita would have encouraged me to actually consider that spirituality may have something to offer. I'm still a skeptic, but I can see how looking within has helped you come to know yourself in entirely new ways."

Anna wrapped her arms around his waist. "For someone who isn't spiritual, you really seem to get it." His openness to things made her care for him all the more.

"Perhaps you have influenced me more than you thought?" He stroked her cheek.

"Perhaps." Her spirit warmed at the thought.

Suddenly, Anna noticed a bright light coming toward them from across the field. Squinting, she tried to make out what it was.

"What's wrong?" Simon asked, following her gaze.

"I don't know." Her muscles tensed as she walked around back and saw Clark running toward them with a flashlight.

"It's Lucita," Clark shouted. "She ran away."

Anna's stomach dropped. "When? We were just there."

"Bernardo said he went up to her bedroom after we left," Clark explained. "She was gone."

"Oh, no! Lucita doesn't like being alone in the dark.

Why would she leave now?" She nervously ran her fingers through her hair.

"I don't know." He held out his hands. "I came over here as soon as I heard. I'm going to search around my house. Why don't you two look here?"

"Where's Bernardo?" Simon asked, chewing his fingernail.

"He's searching every inch of his property. He's scared to death we won't find her."

"We will," Anna declared. "We have to." Her fingers shook as she ran inside and grabbed two flashlights from the kitchen drawer. Where could Lucita be?

"We'll find her," Simon declared as she came back outside. "Trust in that. She's a strong kid and knows this land like the back of her hand."

Anna nodded, his words providing a small sense of comfort. He touched her arm. "Where do you want me to look?"

"Why don't you check by the statue of Buddha and Athena's fountain? There's someplace else I want to search," she called as she broke into a run.

Nearly out of breath, Anna stopped when she came to the edge of Pepper's Pond. Lucita had to be there. This was where her family had spent some of their happiest times together, as well as the place Bernardo had named after her.

Frantically searching with the light, she at last shined it upon the bank where Lucita had caught her fish with Anna last spring. There, sitting on the ground with Lola snuggled in her arms, was Lucita.

Relief flooded through Anna as she embraced her, tears running down both their cheeks. "Oh, Sweetie! I'm so glad you're okay. We were so worried about you!"

"I'm sorry," Lucita sobbed.

"What happened? Why did you run away?"

"I heard Papa shouting at dinner tonight, saying you

were meddling in our lives. It's like he doesn't even want you here anymore."

"That's not true, Lucita," Anna countered. "He's just struggling without your mama. He loved her so much."

"I know, but it's too hard for Papa to take care of me," she said, leaning her head against Anna's chest. "I know he loves me, but I see how much he hurts. You told me he sometimes needs to be alone. I thought if I left, he would get better faster."

Anna stroked Lucita's hair with her hand. "When I said that, I didn't mean you had to run away. It's just sometimes he needs time alone to think. But he would never want you to leave. He loves you too much."

"I just want him to get better. He's sad all the time. I want him to be happy again."

"I know," Anna said. They sat in silence for a few minutes. Finally, Anna said, "I bet what would make your papa really happy is if you came back home."

"You think so?" Lucita asked, looking up at her.

"Yes, I do."

Anna stood and pulled Lucita to her feet. They held hands and walked toward Lucita's house. Anna held her close. Clark and Simon quickly ran up to them on the path.

Clark wrapped his arms around Lucita. "Thank God you're safe."

Simon ruffled her hair. "It's great to see you. Were you off adventuring again?" Simon asked with a wink.

"Something like that," she said with a smile.

"How did you know where to find her?" Simon whispered as he put his arm around Anna's shoulder.

"Pepper's Pond was the first place Lucita took me when I arrived here. I knew it was special to her."

"I needed a quiet place to think," Lucita said. "Pepper's Pond is where Papa and I have spent some of our best times together. I knew I'd be safe there."

Bernardo ran toward them, his arms wide. "Pepper, you're safe! I was so scared! Please don't ever do that again!"

"I'm sorry, Papa!" Lucita cried.

"It's okay," he said, dropping to his knees and throwing his arms around her. "I'm sorry too. I haven't been the father you needed. I haven't been there for you. I've been selfish. Will you forgive me?"

"It's already done," she said sweetly.

Bernardo hugged her for a long time. When at last he looked up, he said, "Clark, can you find me one of those AA meetings you've been talking about? I think it's time I give that a try."

"I'd be glad to," Clark said, patting his shoulder.

"Papa, you called me Pepper," Lucita said, her eyes moist with tears.

"You will always be my little Pepper." Bernardo squeezed her hand. "We're a family and I will never forget that. I love you."

Lucita ran her fingers across her ladybug necklace. "You and Mama really are watching over me. Did you know there was a deer at the pond tonight? She stood near me and helped me not be scared. And if you look up at the heavens," she pointed upward, "you can see the eagle. Mama's the brightest star in the whole sky."

"She sure is," Bernardo said, picking up Lucita in his arms. "And I know she's watching over us because she brought you back to me tonight. This is where you'll always belong."

Anna's heart warmed as she looked up. There, next to the eagle was Orion. He was gradually fading to the west, as he would soon disappear from the sky until next winter. Yet, she knew his guidance would always be there. Lucita was with her papa, and they were a family once more. Lucita was home.

# 46

"I'm so glad you could make it," Anna said, giving Jillian a hug. "I think you're going to enjoy the Soul Sister Circle. It's been a great experience for me."

"I know it has," Jillian said as they entered the studio.

The flickering candles and soft music relaxed Anna immediately.

"It's very calming here," Jillian said, settling herself on a pillow among the circle of women already gathered there.

"It will help you focus on your inner thoughts," Anna whispered, sitting beside her and placing a blue bolster behind her back.

"Just what I need," Jillian said, taking a deep breath and rolling her shoulders back.

"I know," Anna said with a smile. "It's what we both need."

An hour later, they walked out of the studio with a renewed spring in their steps. Twilight had settled upon the city.

"That was amazing," Jillian said. "I wasn't sure I would like it, but everyone was so honest and open. It's unlike anything I've ever experienced before. I especially liked what Emily said about spring being an opportunity to start fresh again in our lives. I'm inspired to paint more—it's when I connect the most with myself."

"That's great," Anna said. She knew it would help her heal.

They arrived at the coffee shop. Anna held the door for Jillian and followed her inside.

Sitting down at a booth with their drinks, Jillian cleared her throat. "Did I tell you Bernardo came to my café the other day? He asked me if I'd be willing to sell his hand-blown glass."

"Wow!" Anna said, leaning forward in her seat. "I think his work is really beautiful. What did you say?"

"I told him I'd be happy to do it." She shrugged. "I still remember the flower he made for Esperanza's scattering ceremony. It was exquisite." She flipped her hair over her shoulder and took a slow sip of her latte.

Anna smiled. "He really is trying to get his life back together."

"Are things going well with him and Lucita?" Jillian traced the top of her ceramic mug with her manicured nails.

"These days, they're nearly inseparable. She loves hanging out in his workshop, and they take daily walks through the woods. I've never seen her so happy." Anna stared at the stunning watercolor of a beach landscape that hung on the wall beside them. Its shimmering ocean waves crested along a sandy shore, reminding Anna of her dance in the rain with Lucita. Perhaps, when Bernardo was ready, he would return with Lucita to Sullivan's Island and the beach their family loved so much.

"How's his drinking?" Jillian asked, her tone steady.

"He's going to AA with Clark and has stopped cold turkey. I haven't seen him drink anything." She paused and took a sip of her mocha. "He even got a job. It turns out Charlie, who fixed my tire when I first got down here, needed a mechanic. He also lost his wife to cancer. He's taking Bernardo to a grief support group now."

"He's made so much progress," Jillian said. "I hardly recognized him when he came in here."

"When Lucita ran away, it scared Bernardo straight. That night, he swore on Esperanza's ashes that if he found her, he would clean up his life and never lose her again. He followed through on his word."

Anna closed her eyes for a minute. Hope really could emerge from tragedy. It just took a while for some people, like herself, to discover it.

❦

Hands on hips, Anna stood in Lucita's backyard and surveyed the landscape. Large pots of flowering petunias and amaryllises were scattered along the back porch. Colorful lilies and hollyhocks flourished among the ornamental grasses that bordered the side of the house. The smell of freshly mowed grass lingered in the air, and the sun's rays warmed her bare arms. She had become a regular visitor to their house, and on this picture-perfect May morning, it felt good to see Lucita and her papa so close again.

Lucita ambled over to Anna after she finished watering the potted plants on the porch. "It's fun to have Papa back and see him smile. Isn't he handsome?"

"Your mama must've thought he was quite the catch," Anna said with a grin.

Lucita suddenly grew quiet. "You know I still miss Mama a whole lot."

"I know," Anna said, brushing Lucita's long hair away from her face. "She was an incredible person."

Lucita nodded and Anna followed her gaze to Esperanza's birdhouse swinging from the branches of a blossoming magnolia tree. The house was barely visible as the wood blended in with the branches, and creamy white flowers concealed its opening. A family of wrens chattered near its entrance. They had made it their home. Azalea bushes bloomed in brilliant shades of pink and purple beside the fragrant tree. Esperanza's garden was a canvas of color, her nurturing spirit still present.

Lucita touched her ladybug necklace and smiled. "What are we going to do today?"

"I thought we could plant a wildflower garden in memory of your mama. It would be a safe haven for butterflies and ladybugs. What do you think?"

Lucita wrapped her arms around Anna's waist. "That's a fantastic idea! Thank you for loving my family so much!" She ran over to the garden shed and swung open the door. She grabbed two small spades, her garden gloves, and a bag of wildflower seeds sitting on the wooden counter. When she emerged from the white shed, her arms were full all the way up to her chin.

"I guess you're ready to work," Anna teased as Lucita joined her beside the flower bed.

Lucita nodded her head up and down with enthusiasm.

"What are you up to?" Bernardo asked, strolling toward them. He'd become more social lately, welcoming Anna's and Clark's frequent visits.

"Papa! We're planting a garden for Mama. Do you want to help?"

"Of course, I do. Why don't you hand me that hoe and we can get started?"

Lucita dug up the dirt and talked excitedly with her papa. Anna stood a few feet away, watching them. Bernardo and Lucita had experienced such loss, but they had found a way to move forward together. They had truly found strength in each other.

After a few minutes, Lucita looked up. "Aren't you going to help us, Miss Anna?"

"I sure am," she said, pulling a pair of gardening gloves out of her pocket. Stepping toward them, she saw a brown deer emerge from behind a tree and move along the edge of the garden. Bernardo and Lucita were too busy planting to notice it. The deer stared straight at her. Anna smiled. She had kept her promise to Esperanza, and nothing would keep this family apart again.

❦

Anna sat in a wicker chair on her back porch writing. Chickadees and warblers chirped noisily as they flitted among the tree branches. A warm wind blew across the fields carrying fragrant scents of citrus and spice that awakened her senses. The trickling water from Athena's fountain comforted her.

She'd been writing most of the afternoon. She placed her notebook and pen on the table beside her when Clark arrived.

"That's quite a garden you planted at Bernardo's," he said, easing into the wicker chair beside her on the porch.

"Lucita and Bernardo worked very hard on it," Anna said, glancing across the meadow at the flowers dancing like fireflies in the wind.

"Lucita told me the garden was your idea."

"It was," she admitted. "I enjoyed helping them. It was fun to do something together."

Clark nodded. "I can't believe it's been over a year since you came here. Where did that time go?"

"I don't know," Anna said. So much had changed in the past year. Not just for her, but for everyone around her.

"I want to thank you for all you've done," Clark said.

"What do you mean?" She met his gaze.

"I mean, appearances can be deceiving." He put his hands behind his head and leaned back. "When you first arrived here, I believed Lydia wanted me to offer guidance to you, but now I realize it was really the other way around. You showed me the value of openness and honesty in every aspect of my life. You also helped me reach out to Bernardo and Jillian even though they had caused me pain. I owe my renewed friendships with them to you."

"You taught me too," Anna said. "You helped me understand the need to listen to my spirit and not doubt myself so much. I see my worth and that I'm enough just as I am. That's something I will carry with me always."

Clark smiled. "Did you know when Esperanza first met you, she believed you would bring us all together again? That's why she chose you to watch over everyone. Your kindness and determination strengthened the bonds of friendship between us that had once been strained."

He fingered his brownstone necklace and his blue eyes looked at her thoughtfully. "I can never thank you enough for all you've meant to me in the short time I've known you. Lucita is surrounded by people who love her, and we are now a family reunited once again. We've shared an incredible loss, but have learned to accept one another wherever we are on our respective journeys. For me, that's the true meaning of family."

"Yes, it is," Anna whispered. Joy welled up within her. She had made so many wonderful friends that meant so much to her. She had a family here as well as the family she loved back home.

"You've also grown a lot during your time here," Clark went on. "Your journey has taught you to trust and love yourself without question. As your writing leads you down a new path, I know it will be a gift to all who read it. You live your father's words, 'Never stop believing.'"

"Thanks," Anna said, feeling her heart swell.

Clark folded his hands in his lap. "How are things going with Simon?"

"Really well." She smiled at the thought of him. "We have a lot of fun kayaking and spending time outdoors. He makes me laugh and although we have different views on spirituality, it makes for interesting discussions. But what I love most is his honesty. I know he will give it to me straight. I think that's part of the reason things have worked out so well between us."

"Honesty is a good thing. Especially when you're content with who you are."

Anna looked down at her notebook, knowing how true that was. She returned her gaze to Clark. "You know, I was thinking about the dream that led me down here the other day. The one with the tree and the woman. Do you remember me telling you about it?"

He nodded.

"I think the woman in my dream was Lydia."

"That could be," Clark said, stroking his goatee. "Her presence definitely guided you during your journey. But so did the statue of the dark-skinned Madonna in your room. You've become empowered during your time here, which has given you the opportunity to find your own worth within."

She smiled. "And to think it all started with a dream."

"Dreams are like the stars," Clark said, gazing up at the clear blue sky. "They can tell us a great deal if we choose to listen to them."

"A year ago, I knew my dream was leading me somewhere. I just didn't realize how much my life would change when I followed it."

"Being open to things has its advantages." Clark

reached for her hand. "Especially when you stay true to yourself and fulfill your passion. Fear cripples us, but hope gives us strength. Only through allowing ourselves to feel all of life's emotions do we truly live. And that's exactly what you've chosen to do." He squeezed her hand and then pulled out his pocket watch. "You know it's true; friends do make the greatest teachers."

Anna hugged him. He was such a blessing in her life.

When she pulled back he asked, "Are you wearing a new bracelet?"

"Yes," Anna said. She looked down at the silver bangle with the charms from Claire's bracelet: an angel, heart, rose, butterfly, and the letter C. "I had it made in memory of Claire."

"What does the inscription say?" he asked kindly.

She held the bracelet up, reading it. "'Let the light of those we've lost continue to guide us.'"

"I like that," Clark said, touching her arm.

Anna nodded, fingering the charms. "That way, her light will never really go out." Comforted by that thought, Anna knew Claire's spirit would always be with her.

That feeling stayed with Anna all day. And when she walked into the living room that evening, the phone rang. It was her mother.

"How's the writing coming?" her mother inquired.

"I'm almost finished with my first draft," Anna said, sitting down on the sofa. "It took a while, though—much longer than I thought it would."

"You've been through a lot. It should be an inspiring read."

"I hope so. That's the whole point. I want to help people understand that they can get through their suffering, no matter how painful it is. We all have an inner voice that can serve as our guide if we choose to listen to it."

"You'll make a difference in a lot of people's lives. Of that I'm certain," her mother said.

"Thanks," Anna said, appreciating her mother's words. One year ago, she would have gotten a very different response from her. But Anna was also a different person than she was back then. Perhaps her mother had changed some too.

Her mother sighed. "Listen, I know I haven't always been supportive of your decision to stay in South Carolina."

"Yeah."

"I kept telling myself you would eventually change your mind and come back home."

Anna looked out the window at the darkness, wondering where this was going.

"Since Dad passed away, you've always tried to take care of me," Anna said. "I understand that, but I need to take care of myself. I've discovered my passion, and it's opened a whole new world for me. I want to see where this journey takes me. Can you understand that?"

"I can," her mom whispered. "That's what I'm trying to tell you. I'm sorry about everything. I was blinded by my own wish to have you close by. I thought you loved us less because you chose to be far away, but I know now that isn't true."

"It isn't," Anna agreed. "South Carolina is where my soul needs to be. I can't explain it any more than that. It's not that I love you less. I just have to be where my spirit belongs."

Her mother remained quiet for a few seconds. "If this is what you need, then I fully support your decision. I really am glad things have worked out so well for you there," her mother admitted. "But I do miss you."

"I miss you too. But living a thousand miles apart doesn't mean we can't still be a family. Simon and I are really looking forward to our visit next month. It will be nice to see everyone, and Simon's excited to explore Boston. It's a place he's never been."

"I can't wait to meet him," her mother said. "Julia says he's a good match for you."

"He is," Anna said, her heart fluttering. "He really is."

"I've been told South Carolina is beautiful in the fall," her mother went on. "Maybe I'll have to come see it for myself. It was a place your father and I always wanted to visit." Her voice trailed off.

"You're welcome here any time," Anna said.

"Thanks. I know we'll try to see each other as much as we can." Her mother paused. "It seems like you're happy, and that's what matters to me."

"I'm content," Anna countered, "and that's what matters to me."

"It sounds like you've found yourself."

"I have." She fingered the opal necklace around her neck. "Finally, I have."

Anna hung up and thought about her oak tree. She reflected on the freedom she felt in its presence compared to the bonds of her former life. The world had once caged her in, but now she was free. It was time for her to spread her wings and soar like never before.

Snuggled under her covers that night, Anna breathed deeply and fell asleep. Once again, her dreams returned. She found herself in a flowering meadow watching a familiar silhouette walking toward her in a flowing blue robe. Lydia's cheeks were still as red as roses.

Standing beside her, Anna smiled. "Are you coming back to live here for good?"

Lydia shook her head and reached for Anna's hand. "There's no need." Her blue eyes shone like a full moon on a clear winter's night.

"What do you mean?" Anna asked, the wind rippling through her hair.

"Although this house started out as a refuge for you, it has now become your home. May you spend many happy years here watching over those you love. I may return one day for a visit, but for now it's time for me to say good-bye."

As Lydia raised her hand in farewell and disappeared into the trees one last time, Anna awoke, knowing she was finally at peace.

# Epilogue

*Two years later*

Anna was sitting at her desk, lost in thought. The soothing sound of raindrops splattered on the soft, green leaves and cascades of water streamed down the windowpane, mesmerizing her.

"So, how does it end?" Simon asked, entering the front bedroom she had converted into her study. With its abundant natural light and rows of bookshelves, it was a comforting place.

"With contentment and rebirth." She gazed up at him, smiling.

He set down a steaming mug of fresh Viennese coffee next to the printed manuscript on her desk. His skin was bronzed and his wavy brown locks hung just below his chin. Casually attired in cargo shorts and a T-shirt, he stroked his trimmed goatee and looked at her tenderly. "Truly inspirational then," he said.

"Empowering, I hope." She tucked a strand of hair behind her ear. At least it was for her.

Suddenly, a faint cry could be heard across the hall.

Simon leaned down and whispered, "There's our little guy up from his nap. Go ahead and finish up. I'll get him."

"No, that's okay. He's probably hungry anyway." She pushed back her chair and stood up. "Maybe a little quiet time with him will do me some good."

She walked into the ruby-red nursery decorated with cute, cuddly ladybugs. This room had always had such a happy feel about it. Lucita had helped Anna paint the walls and pick out the bedding. She even put the mobile together all by herself.

"Hello there, Sweetie," Anna cooed. "Are you waiting for me?"

The baby kicked his chubby arms and legs wildly in the air when he saw his mommy's face. Anna gently picked him up and sat down in the rocking chair, stroking his thick black hair. "What a blessing you are to us, Samuel Joseph. May you always know the story of your grandfather and how much he meant to me."

Gazing out the window, Anna's eyes settled upon the towering oak tree. The rain provided nourishment to its tangled roots that spread down deep into the earth. Nature always trusted that things were as they should be. But looking back, Anna realized that was true for her as well. She was finally fulfilling her dream of publishing her memoir. Things were exactly as they should be. Gratitude overwhelmed her. She cradled her son in her lap and closed her eyes as he nursed.

When his tummy was full, Anna carried Samuel down to the kitchen and settled back into her writing chair. Smiling, she read:

*The crowded streets near Boston's Faneuil Hall smelled of fresh bagels and buttered lobster as Anna rushed down the cobblestone sidewalk. She stumbled slightly in her heels, reading her latest e-mail message. A light drizzle had begun to fall. ...*

# About the Author

A Minnesota native, Heidi Martin has been an educator for the past fourteen years. She began writing as a hobby and was inspired to create this novel after embarking on a journey that took her far away from her family and friends. The story poured out of her, and when it was finally finished, she knew it was meant to be shared.

Heidi has also written a children's book, *Treasure Hunt*. She lives in Massachusetts with her husband and two children.

# The Refuge
## Heidi Martin

Website: heidimartinbooks.com

Facebook: heidimartinbooks

Publisher: SDP Publishing

*Also available in ebook format*

**Available at all major bookstores.**

CPSIA information can be obtained
at www.ICGtesting.com
Printed in the USA
JSRBC010002260420
5250JS00004B/13